Readers love the B
by Do

The Zozobra Incident

"There are many likable secondary characters who play significant roles in the story. Combine that with the setting, beautifully detailed writing and a solid mystery makes this novel a must read for any mystery lover."

—Gay Book Reviews

The Bisti Business

"All the essential elements that made the first story so engrossing are there, with a fresh new mystery and more interesting characters."

—Michael Joseph Book Reviews

The City of Rocks

"Hands down, this is my favorite mystery series in a long time. Five stars!"

—The Novel Approach

The Lovely Pines

"There were no questions left unanswered, and by the end, I was hungry to read more of the BJ Vinson Mysteries."

—Love Bytes

Abaddon's Locusts

"*Abaddon's Locusts* is another smartly written installment in the BJ Vinson Mysteries. From the start the tension is thick and keeps the reader on edge…."

—QueeRomance Ink

By DON TRAVIS

BJ VINSON MYSTERIES
The Zozobra Incident
The Bisti Business
The City of Rocks
The Lovely Pines
Abaddon's Locusts
The Voxlightner Scandal

Published by DSP PUBLICATIONS
www.dsppublications.com

THE VOXLIGHTNER SCANDAL

DON TRAVIS

DSP PUBLICATIONS

Published by
DSP Publications

5032 Capital Circle SW, Suite 2, PMB# 279, Tallahassee, FL 32305-7886 USA
www.dsppublications.com

The Voxlightner Scandal

Cover Art

Trade Paperback ISBN: 978-1-64108-208-2
Digital ISBN: 978-1-64080-926-0
Library of Congress Control Number: 2019946375
Trade Paperback published November 2019
v. 1.0

Printed in the United States of America

This paper meets the requirements of
ANSI/NISO Z39.48-1992 (Permanence of Paper).

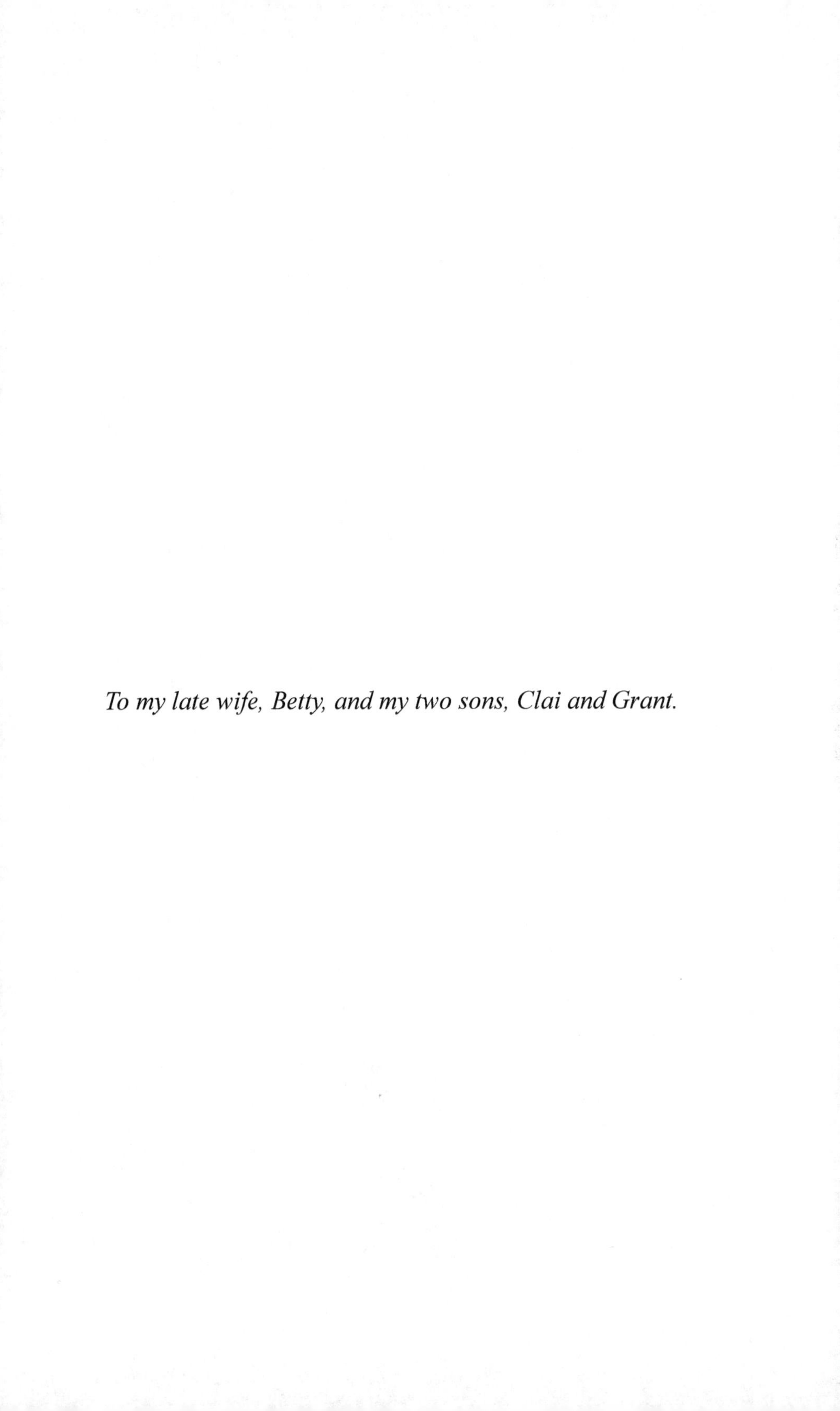

To my late wife, Betty, and my two sons, Clai and Grant.

Acknowledgments

MANY THANKS to members of my Wordwrights Writing Class.

THE VOXLIGHTNER SCANDAL

DON TRAVIS

Prologue

Albuquerque, New Mexico, July 20, 2011

AT EASE in his comfortable North Valley home, Pierce brushed his chin with a palm, raising the irritating rasp of a five-o'clock shadow. The house lay silent, disturbed only by his knocking around in the den and the ticktock of the ornate wind-up clock resting on the mantelpiece. Overhead lights off, a reading lamp cast a soft pool of light, rescuing the room from darkness. He longed for the mellow smell of pipe tobacco, but he'd given up the vice last winter after a suspected TIA, a transient ischemic something or other.

Ensconced in his favorite recliner, he picked up a book from the coffee table and inspected it closely. His latest novel. His third. Just delivered from the publisher this morning. In a rare moment of brutal honesty, he silently admitted the most impressive thing on the cover was his name: John Pierce Belhaven. A good cognomen for an author, it rolled off the tongue and lent gravitas to the banal title *Macabre Desserts.* Although too egotistical to confess being a hack, in moments such as this he silently acknowledged he was no James Lee Burke. Whenever he attempted the Louisiana writer's soaring, poetic passages, they ended up as muddy puddles of worthless ink. What was Elmore Leonard's rule number ten? Leave out the parts nobody wants to read.

His next book would be the bleeding edge… as the younger set would say. And they would be right. His best writing to date. Possibly his signature work. A mystery like the others, the plot taking shape in his brain solved a *real* puzzle. One that had plagued Albuquerque for years. A scandal involving the theft of millions and the death of a respected attorney. A mystery only he could solve because he had a leg up on the competition. Years ago in his capacity as a utility company executive, he'd uncovered a crucial clue but hadn't understood its significance until he researched this new book. He drew a deep breath as if pulling on a forbidden meerschaum. This new work would carry him from humdrum to bestseller. And his interview with Wilma Hardesty on KALB-TV—

aired that very afternoon—put the world on notice he was reopening the moribund Voxlightner case with a hard-hitting exposé leading directly to the killer. All it would take was a little more investigating. Connect a few more dots, and he would be able to cut the Gordian knot.

He reached for a tumbler resting on the lamp table beside his chair and inhaled the rich aroma of Ballechin single malt before savoring its smooth, nutty, slightly honeyed taste. This new book he was laboring over would set them on their ears down at SouthWest Writers, make them sit up and take notice. He would rigorously guard against going pedantic, one of his weaknesses. Solid prose and startling action. That was the approach for this budding masterpiece. He quelled an urge to rush to his office on the other side of the house to riffle through the growing file of research on the case.

A noise from the garage brought him out of his chair. He glanced at the clock. *Ten thirty-four.* Who could that be at this time of night? Melanie? He shook his head. His daughter was home in Grants with her odious husband. Nor would his estranged son Harrison deign to show up at his door, probably not even to pick up his inheritance, should Pierce condescend to leave him one.

He placed his new book on the coffee table and walked to the interior garage door. As he arrived the gas-powered lawn mower roared to life.

What the hell? John Pierce Belhaven twisted the knob and stepped from his kitchen into hell.

Chapter 1

IF THIS was the year of the Arab Spring, this morning's *Albuquerque Journal* neglected to mention it. The international lead story—above the fold—reported the bombing of the government quarter in Oslo and the subsequent murder by gunfire of sixty-nine youth activists of the Labour Party by a native Norwegian terrorist.

The below-the-fold story told of the death of local author John Pierce Belhaven in a garage fire mere blocks from my home. What snagged my attention was that the terrorist attack in Norway took place today, well today Norwegian time. The local tragedy occurred two nights ago local time. Our paper reported foreign events faster than local ones.

Paul strode into the kitchen where I sat at the table, munching an english muffin slathered with cream cheese and dusted with ground black pepper. He brought with him the aroma of his shower. He was using a new aftershave lotion.... Axe, possibly.

He halted at the sight of me. "Whoa, Vince, I was gonna fix omelets."

The rest of the world called me BJ. This young man, my companion and the love of my life, preferred Vince, a pet name derived from my family moniker of Vinson.

"My stomach wouldn't wait. By the way I know why we heard all those sirens Wednesday night. Garage fire down the street."

"Where?"

I checked the news article. "Forty-eight eighteen."

"Belhaven's place?"

"I'll admit you're more neighborly than I am, but how do you know who lives four blocks down the street?"

A minute later he plopped a bowl of instant oatmeal on the table, apparently abandoning the idea of an omelet. "I know him from SouthWest Writers."

Paul joined the professional writing association a year ago when he got his master's in journalism from the University of New Mexico and decided a membership would provide him some valuable contacts. He was probably right, although I never considered journalism as *writing* until he pointed out that's exactly what it was.

"Can I see the article when you're finished?" he asked.

After I commandeered the sports section and handed over the rest, his voice startled me out of a story about the Lobo baseball team.

"This can't be right."

"Uh." I refused to be distracted.

"Vince." He shoved the newspaper in front of me. "I didn't know Belhaven well, but I know one thing for sure. He wouldn't repair his lawn mower. He'd have the kid who mowed his lawn do it or else buy a new mower." He paused. "The rest sounds right. Belhaven would probably spill gas all over himself and somehow manage to light it up. But I'm telling you… he'd never even try it."

"A klutz, huh?"

Paul nodded. "You could say that."

"I'll tell you what *I* can't believe. This happened two days ago, and Mrs. Wardlow hasn't broadcast the gory details all over the neighborhood."

Gertrude Wardlow, the septuagenarian widow living across the street, was a retired DEA agent and the grande dame of our local neighborhood watch. But I had no gripes coming. She'd saved my bacon a couple of times when suspects tried to bring grievances to my home. More importantly she'd warned me Paul was in trouble when a gang kidnapped him a few years back.

"Can I assume you smell a story?" I asked.

"I smell a rat. But you're right, I'm going to look into it. Who do you know in the fire department?"

I gave Paul the name of the AFD Arson Squad commander I'd worked with a couple of times. "And you can call Gene Enriquez if you want to know if there's a police case working."

"*You* call Lieutenant Enriquez, okay? He'll talk to you. You're the confidential investigator, not me."

"Don't sell yourself short. Way I figure it, an investigating journalist is simply a confidential investigator without a license."

Gene, my old riding partner at APD, oversaw homicide. I needed to touch base with him anyway. The powers that be kept threatening to promote him, but he didn't want to become an administrator. Such a move would put him out of the "action," he claimed. The last time I talked to him, he was seriously considering retirement.

I PARKED my white '98 Impala in my reserved spot in the lot at Fifth and Tijeras on Monday morning and took the back stairway to my third-floor office. As usual, I paused a moment to look down on the open atrium hollowing out the core of the office building before pushing through the door labeled Vinson and Weeks, Confidential Investigations. I'd taken the time to stop by the North Valley Country Club for pool therapy before driving downtown to the office. In May of '04—while I was still an APD detective—I exchanged gunfire with a suspected murderer during an arrest attempt. I got him in the head; he nailed me in the right thigh. Ever since that event, I hit the water now and then to keep the leg from stiffening. Swimming was also how I kept my thirty-nine-year-old carcass reasonably fit. I'd first met Paul poolside while doing my therapy. He'd worked as a lifeguard to put himself through college.

Hazel Harris Weeks, the office manager and a key cog in our organization, sat at her desk performing some of her magic on the internet when I came in. A whiz at locating people electronically, she was my late mom's best friend and now my business partner's wife.

She glanced up. "Gene called. Mayor's office and an assistant DA phoned. Slips are on your desk."

"What does the mayor want?"

"Didn't deign to impart that information. ADA wants to arrange for you to testify in the Haggens embezzlement case."

"Charlie?" I asked.

"Police station picking up a couple of jackets." She meant her husband was at APD Records picking up info on either clients or adversaries.

I sighed and walked into my private office. I could get a lot more done if I didn't have to drop everything and testify in court. That had been my lament from the time I was a Marine MP, lo those many years ago. Some things never change.

I knew what the mayor wanted. There was a vacancy on the civilian police oversight board, and he was considering appointing me. Ambivalent about the situation, I was in no hurry to talk to him. To sit in judgment of people I'd served with—even though that was six years in the rearview mirror—didn't seem appropriate. On the other hand, as an ex-cop, I understood the life they lived minute by minute every day. Something else I needed to check with Gene.

Ignoring the mayor's call, I scheduled my testimony on the embezzlement case with the ADA before dialing Gene's private number. Our phone conversations, although increasingly rare, followed a pattern. Brusque greetings and catching up on domestic affairs before getting down to business. Given Gene's family of five children, most afflicted with the dreaded teenage condition, he talked a lot more than I did. Today was no different. After he filled me in on Glenda and the brood, I brought him up to date with news of Paul and me. Once everything was covered, I asked if there was a police investigation of the Belhaven death.

"You mean the writer toasted in his garage? Why? Should there be?"

"You know the answer to that better than I do, but Paul's convinced something's funny. Claims Belhaven wouldn't have attempted to repair a lawn mower or anything else. He wasn't a hands-on type of guy."

"We've had that feedback too."

"So you're looking into the death?"

"Like usual, we're satisfying ourselves everything's on the up and up… unless the medical investigator declares it an accidental death."

"Paul wants to write a story on it."

"Have him touch base with a detective named Roy Guerra. He's handling it for us."

I NO sooner left a message on Paul's voicemail providing him Detective Guerra's name and contact information than Hazel waylaid me with a background check on a Dallas man being considered for an executive position by a local mortgage firm. That would take the rest of the day and half of my tomorrow, but this was the bread and butter of our business. Novels and films romanticizing the lives of PIs—as they called us—were so far off base as to be laughable. Still, the vocation pleased me. I nursed no inclination to bail on the agency and live off the Microsoft-spawned trust fund my schoolteacher parents thoughtfully left me.

Midafternoon I heard Paul's familiar voice in the outer office. Hazel's delighted rejoinder hinted I might be relieved of my current task, at least momentarily. My office manager-cum-surrogate mother—although totally perplexed by my gay life—nonetheless loved Paul as much as she did me. After a hug and a once-over from Hazel, he came through the doorway to invade my private space, and a welcome incursion it was. I never tired of looking on his handsome features.

"Hi. Am I interrupting anything?"

"Nothing uninterruptable," I quipped. "Come on in."

"I talked to Detective Guerra. We're meeting here later, if that's okay. Thanks for getting the contact for me."

"Pleased to do it. What did he say?"

"He has reservations about Belhaven's death, and I added to them."

"Any theories?"

"Couple. I found out Pierce was interviewed on TV the afternoon he died. The interviewer quizzed him about his new book, and his answers might have cost him his life."

"Why do you say that?" I asked as we moved to the conference table in the corner of my office.

"He writes—or wrote—mysteries. Fiction. But according to the interview, his next book was going to be based on an actual event. Do you remember the Voxlightner blowup a few years ago?"

I nodded. "A big scandal. I was still at APD, so it was probably late 2003 or early '04."

Paul flipped out a notebook and clicked his ballpoint pen. "What do you remember about it?"

"Gene and I weren't assigned the case, so I just remember bits and pieces. One of the local lights, a guy named Barron Voxlightner, and a fellow named Stabler found acres and acres of mine tailings in Arizona that tested positive for commercial grade silver and gold. All they needed to do was extract the precious metals and sell them."

"Sounds like a sure thing," he said.

"That's what everybody thought. The whole town wanted a piece of the action. The money poured in. People went crazy."

Paul checked his notes. "I take it they formed a company called Voxlightner Precious Metals Recovery to do the project."

"Right. They took VPMR—as it became known—public and raised fifty million."

"That's a lot of dough."

"Absolutely. And yet the bottom fell out within six months. It turned out the tests were rigged. The tailings were worthless. But before the hammer fell, Voxlightner and Stabler vanished, and the lawyer exposing the fraud was murdered. The thing was never solved."

Paul's face assumed a thoughtful look. "When I was a kid, I thought anyone called Voxlightner was royalty."

"The patriarch of the family, a man named Marshall Voxlightner, was a bigger-than-life legend. An oilman from Hobbs, he moved to Albuquerque and built a big place in the Ridgecrest neighborhood after he retired."

"Yeah, they call it the Castle. I remember reading the guy set up a charitable trust after he retired. Named it after himself and his wife. The Marshall and Dorothy Wellbourne Voxlightner Charitable Foundation."

"They're both dead now," I said.

Paul had done some research. "He is, but she's still kicking. Lives at Voxlightner Castle. Reclusive, they say."

"You know the family history better than I do. Did they have other children?"

He consulted his notes. "Just a daughter named Lucinda. She married a Virginia real estate developer and lives back east."

"So there aren't too many Voxlightners running around New Mexico," I said.

"Unless you include Pierce Belhaven. His mother was a Voxlightner… as was his wife, a distant cousin. She died in 2006 of lung cancer."

Hazel stuck her head in the door, her flinty gray eyes softening as they settled on my companion. "There's a Detective Roy Guerra out here asking for Paul."

Paul looked at me. "We can use the conference room if you're busy."

"You've got me curious. Show him in, Hazel."

A stereotypical South Valley boy strutted through the doorway. Five nine, around one seventy-five, black eyes, black hair. I knew without being told he was bright, brash, and a womanizer to his core. I pegged him at about thirty, a year older than when I made detective.

He clasped my hand without waiting for an introduction. "Hi ya, Mr. Vinson. Heard lots about you from the lieutenant. You've got a rep around the station."

I couldn't help responding to his grin. "Probably a rep for getting my ass shot off."

"But you got him," he said.

I assumed he referred to my murder suspect shootout. "But it shouldn't have happened."

The impish grin grew. "If it hadn't, I wonder who'd be running homicide now, you or Lieutenant Enriquez?"

I came right back at him. "The lieutenant. He's a better cop."

"How so?"

"For one thing, he didn't let himself get shot."

Roy laughed. "I guess he didn't." He turned to Paul and offered a hand. "Hi, guy. I take it you're Paul. Always good to have a face to go with a telephone voice. We gonna hash this over with Mr. Vinson, huh? That's aces, man. Get another viewpoint."

"BJ," I said. "Call me BJ."

"Okay, I'm Roy."

He took a seat with us at the small table in my private office and went over what he knew of the death of Pierce Belhaven. The author was found dead in his charred garage when a neighbor saw flames and called the fire department. It appeared Belhaven had been repairing his gasoline-powered lawn mower. Somehow he'd gotten himself covered in gasoline, which inexplicably caught fire and roasted him. The mower was close to the pilot light of the water heater in the garage. When Roy finished I asked if he bought the accidental death theory.

"I'm acluistic at this point, but I have my doubts. From all I can find out, the old boy wouldn't have picked up a wrench. Hell, he wouldn't even have picked up the gas can. And why do it at ten thirty at night?"

"Ten thirty's a pretty specific time fix," I said.

"That's about the time the neighbor reported it. And the fire hadn't really got started good."

"Just enough to fricassee Pierce," Paul added.

"Anyone else in the house?" I asked.

"No one," Roy answered. "But a crapload of people have keys and the code to the alarm system. Harrison—the son—was estranged, but Melanie—the daughter—was on speaking terms with him. She's married and lives in Grants."

"An estranged son, and he still has keys? How estranged?"

Paul answered. "Pierce wouldn't talk about it much, but the way I got it was they fell out when Pierce put a stop to his marrying a girl back in high school. His son was of age, but the girl wasn't. The girl got so despondent her folks moved away."

"How old is Harrison?"

Roy waggled a hand back and forth. "Thirty-seven, thirty-eight."

"That's a long time to hold a grudge," I said.

Roy lifted his shoulders in a lazy shrug. "Some folks hang on to their grudges better'n they do their pocketbooks. Harrison got caught in the Voxlightner scandal. Wiped him out, I understand."

"How was he involved?" I asked.

"Wasn't an insider," Roy said. "But he was close enough to get on the list of initial investors. Put everything he owned in the company."

"That scam ruined some pretty prominent people," I said.

"Maybe it was more than busting up a romance. Harrison mighta blamed his father for an investment gone bad," Roy suggested.

Paul stepped up to answer. "Could be. Pierce told me he made sure his son was able to get in on the initial offering. Mending fences, you know. Harrison took a bigger bite than he should have, and it backfired. Big-time."

I settled more comfortably in my chair. "The fact we're talking about an old scandal instead of Pierce Belhaven's murder must be because you believe there's a connection. But tell me something, Roy. Why are you willing to discuss an ongoing police investigation with us?"

"The lieutenant says you're solid. So why not bring in a couple more viewpoints? You're an experienced investigator, and Paul's a dedicated snoop. Plus he's promised not to publish anything without my okay first."

I shook my head. "That doesn't wash. You have a whole department backing you up on this."

The detective flashed a smile. He knew how to use his facial muscles. "Okay, I'll level. I just made detective a few months ago, and this case could be a hot potato. Noted author pokes a stick in a beehive and winds up murdered. It's a natural, and I'm hell-bent on breaking it."

"How about your partner?"

"I don't have one right now. They'll team me with someone sooner or later, but I'd like to add a feather to my coup stick before that happens."

His remark made me reconsider my South Valley categorization. Maybe he had a little native blood running around in his veins too.

"Tell me about Belhaven's family," I said. "I remember reading he was a widower. Did he live alone?"

Roy answered that one. "Lived alone but had arm candy… you know, a lover. Sometimes live-in. Sometimes not."

"Who is it?"

"Sarah Thackerson."

"What's her story?" I asked.

Roy raised his chin and studied the ceiling as he recited his files from memory. "Hails from Bisbee, Arizona. Supposedly there visiting her family the night Belhaven bought it. She's around thirty but still taking courses at UNM. School's what brought her up here, apparently. She does… uh, did secretarial and research work for Belhaven. That's how they met about six years ago. She answered an ad and landed the job."

"What makes you think she was his sweetheart?"

"He made it clear," Paul said. "Even brought her to some SWW meetings. Stuck to him like Velcro."

"You said she's thirty. How old was he?"

"Sixty," Roy said. "A May-December thing. We aren't done looking into his finances, but it's pretty clear he was her sole means of support."

"Anybody else in the household?"

"Not the immediate household, but there's a yard boy, I guess you'd call him," Roy said. "Spencer Spears takes care of the grounds. The Belhaven place occupies two lots, so there's a lot of greenery to be tended."

"He'd be the one to repair a mower," Paul put in. "Not Pierce."

"Tell me about him."

Roy rubbed his head with the knuckles of his right hand. "Not much to tell. He goes to school part-time. Central New Mexico. Slow-walking a degree in landscaping, I gather. Twenty-seven, single, but they say he's got women hanging all over him." His mouth turned down in a frown. "He's got an assitude."

"Which CNM campus?"

Roy thumbed through his notes. "Montoya Campus on Morris NE."

"What's his background? Does he have a sheet?"

"He's a local boy. Only sheet's a juvie. Sealed. But old-timers remember it as a fistfight between him and another guy. Probably got dressed down by a judge and let go."

"Where was he the night of Belhaven's death?"

"Jiving at a sports bar. Got there around eight. The thing broke up at closing."

"Witnesses?"

Roy nodded.

I thought for a minute, all the while watching Paul's eager face. This case was important to him, which made my decision easy. "Roy, do you mind if Paul and I look into this Belhaven death? We'll keep you posted on anything we find."

Roy beamed. "Go for it. I'll share what I can."

"Thanks."

Hazel wasn't going to like me taking one more case that didn't pay its own way. In fact when I told her to open a file, her first question was "Who's the client?"

Chapter 2

I MANAGED to pry Gene away from APD headquarters to have lunch the next day at the Courthouse Café. As usual he was rushed until I prevailed upon him to sit back and take a deep breath.

"Okay. Now what?" he demanded.

"Now eat a lunch without gulping it down and take time to smell the roses."

"Grease," he grumped. "All I smell in here is grease."

I knew exactly what was riding his back. "They still pressing you to move up?"

He nodded and snorted simultaneously. "Yeah. I'm not gonna accept it."

"Are you thinking of yourself, or are you thinking of Glenda and the kids?"

He bristled. "I make a decent living. Take care of them okay."

"Face it, Gene, you're already an administrator. When was the last time you went out and worked a case?"

"That case we worked together last year. What did you call it?"

"Abaddon's Locusts." I eyed my former APD partner. "You're avoiding the issue. What are your options? You turn down a promotion, you slam a lid on your career. You've got in your twenty, so you can put in your papers. Or you can accept what they're offering and continue to build on what you have."

He scratched his chin before dry washing his face. "What the hell would I do if I retired? Go crazy, that's what I'd do. Six months tops."

"Charlie and I talked it over. You can join us. Vinson, Weeks, and Enriquez. How does that sound?"

"Not bad."

"It's there if you want it, but personally, I think you're too much of a cop to be happy outside the department."

"I hear you. So Paul met with Roy Guerra on the Belhaven thing."

"Yep. Have you called it yet?"

"Homicide. Autopsy showed he was hit in the head with a blunt object before he caught fire. No smoke in his lungs. He was dead before he lit up."

"Will you have any heartburn if Paul and I work with Guerra?"

"Naw. He's new to his shield and can use the help."

"Do I read anything into the fact he doesn't have a partner?"

"Roy's a quart in a pint pot. He's going to turn out to be a good detective. We'll get him a seasoned partner as soon as I find a good match."

"He and Paul both believe Belhaven's killing ties into his promise to reveal the killer in the Voxlightner debacle."

"What's your take?" he asked.

"Things point in that direction, but I try to keep an open mind. Refresh my memory. Wasn't Everett Kent murdered while looking into the scandal because his law partner Zachary Greystone was involved in incorporating the venture?"

"Not only did Greystone handle the paperwork incorporating the company, he was promoting it big-time," Gene said. "Had a hand in setting up the list of initial investors."

"How was Kent killed?" I asked.

"Shot to death in his office on the fourth floor of the Central New Mexico Bank Building. Working late alone in the office."

"Must have been someone he trusted if he admitted his killer after hours. When was this?"

Gene stretched to ease his back. "End of February or beginning of March 2004."

"Not long before Voxlightner and Stabler took a powder," I noted.

While munching on tacos, we reconstructed as much of the old scandal as we could recall. In the remembering, it was dry, boring stuff, but when bits and pieces had screamed headlines in successive editions of the *Albuquerque Journal* like some Hollywood serial, the scandalous affair gripped all of New Mexico and half of Arizona in its thrall.

The whole thing began when a Nevada mining engineer named Dr. Walther Stabler claimed copper tailings across the Arizona border in the Morenci district contained gold. Marshall Voxlightner's son Barron hauled a ton of dirt to the New Mexico Institute of Mining & Technology for a series of fire assays. The tests consistently showed commercial amounts of gold and silver. Especially appealing was the fact the material did not have to be extracted from the ground because the ore was premined copper tailings.

The mine owners realized the dumps possibly contained commercially valuable trace minerals, but they also faced local pressure to get rid of some five million tons—and growing—of ugly piles of dirt. Therefore they were willing to sell the material for $1.00 a ton, the cost of removal and transportation to be borne by the purchaser.

After a month of positive assays—some of which were performed on samples selected by prospective investors at random from the seemingly unending piles of dirt—Marshall Voxlightner, the retired oilman with a solid reputation—put in $250,000 seed money and agreed to lend his family name to the project. His son promptly incorporated the Voxlightner Precious Metals Recovery Corporation and put his team together. He and his group matched the old man's $250,000, and the venture was off and running.

"How far did they get with the actual project?" I asked.

"After the initial offering sold out, they bought all five million tons of copper tailings," Gene said. "At the same time, a couple of guys—Greystone and Pillsner, if I remember right—were working on permits for the mill to be located down in the Socorro area."

"Pillsner? I forgot Wick was involved." Hardwick Pillsner, a local businessman, made his living—and a pile of money—as a promoter. He'd facilitated the buying and selling of various local businesses. Putting together the Voxlightner operation would have been right up his alley. "Was he an officer?" I asked.

"He's the one who introduced Stabler to Voxlightner. Helped put it all together. But he wasn't even a board member. He had a policy against taking a hand in operating anything he helped form. He just took a stock position for his efforts in this one, I understand," Gene said.

"So Wick lost potential, not money."

"He'd disagree. He considers time as money."

"Can't argue with the logic," I said. "My time is all I have to sell."

As Gene looked at me through tired brown eyes, it occurred to me why we worked so well together. What he couldn't remember, I could. And our memories stretched back a long way. "What happened to the tailings after the company folded?"

He assumed a thoughtful look. "As I recall, the Greystone firm attempted to get the company's money back and were met with a suit to remove the dumps as agreed under the sales contract. Greystone eventually settled for getting back something like a quarter for every dollar."

"So the investors recovered a million and a quarter of their money. Funny. I don't recall shareholders getting anything back."

"The recovery was used to pay off other obligations of the corporation under bankruptcy proceedings. Investors got nothing." Gene glanced my way. "Did you lose a bundle?"

"A bundle to me at the time. I was an APD cop, remember?"

"With a few mil in the bank."

"I never touched any of the trust money. The VPMR investment just ruined me personally for a couple of years."

Over the dregs of our meal we continued to reconstruct the scandal… the crime, really. In early 2004 VPMR's problems came to light when board members expressed concern over the rapid rate of heavy expenditures. Money was flowing like oil from one of Marshall Voxlightner's gushers, and red flags began to wave. The trucking company moving ore from Arizona halted work because of nonpayment. The School of Mines lab wasn't paid for the last batch of assays. Wick Pillsner complained of unpaid rent for the building he rented the corporation on East Lomas.

Everett Kent dealt the nastiest blow when he filched some of the copper tailing material and took it to an independent lab for assay. Traces of gold and silver and even platinum showed up, but not in commercial quantities. He then filed suit in district court—as a stockholder—for a complete accounting by an independent arbitrator. Within a week, he was shot in the back of the head in his office.

But the damage was done. An investigation was underway and couldn't be stopped. Then Barron Voxlightner and Dr. Walther Stabler vanished without a trace. They were last seen huddling together over a conference table in corporate headquarters on a Monday night in March 2004. The next day the *Journal*'s headline screamed something over $40,000,000 of the company funds were missing. Some was traced to the payment of phony accounts, some to bank transfers overseas and a series of cash withdrawals. In retrospect suspicious activity reports should have been filed by the bank, but the principals backing the company were highly respected men with proven business acumen. No such reports were filed.

The FBI moved quickly after the disappearances, arresting company COO John Hightower, and casting suspicion over the other officers and members of the company's board of directors. Eventually Hightower was revealed as a dupe and never prosecuted. His responsibilities were for operations not finances. Doubtless he was lax in the performance of his duties but not criminally so. His reputation in shreds, he moved out of state, no doubt carefully watched by the feds wherever he went.

After the disappearances, authorities concentrated on the search for Voxlightner and Stabler. The locals pursued the murderer of Everett Kent with about as much success as with the rest of the mess. Despite a massive manhunt for the missing men, the investigation went nowhere. The courts took over the dissolution of the bankrupt corporation, and eventually things died out. To the best of our recollection, the whole thing from start to finish lasted just over six months—from early September 2003 to mid-March 2004. Just like that, some $50,000,000 had been sucked out of the fragile economy of New Mexico.

SHORTLY AFTER I returned to the office, Paul popped in wearing what my sainted mother would have called a bright undershirt. Red, sleeveless, and held in place by two narrow straps over the shoulders, it was cut low enough so Pedro peeked out at the world. Man, I loved that tattooed dragon on Paul's left pec.

"Roy and I are going to Belhaven's house for a look-around. You wanna come?"

I'm certain my eyebrows showed surprise. "When arson is involved, either AFD or the insurance company seals the site until the investigation's complete."

"They did, but they released it… according to Roy anyway."

"Anyone staying there now?"

"Pierce's daughter drove over from Grants and plans on staying there temporarily. Why?"

"How's Roy going to explain our presence?"

Paul brightened. "We're APD consultants."

"So I can bill the department?"

"I wouldn't carry it that far."

I grabbed my digital recorder and fixed it to my belt before joining him. We walked down the back stairwell and exited the building to recover my Impala for the ride. From long habit the car practically drove itself to Post Oak Drive NW but wanted to proceed home instead of parking in front of 4818. Roy was already there, waiting in his departmental Ford. And he'd been right. The house was now occupied.

The woman who answered the door introduced herself as Melanie Belhaven Harper. She was pretty enough in the face but a bit dumpy, with the hausfrau look about her. She welcomed us graciously and invited us inside.

"Your people"—she indicated Roy—"have already been through everything, but you're welcome to search all you want. My brother and I were going over my father's will in his office, but I suspect you'll want to look in there. We'll move to the dining room table."

"Thank you, ma'am," Roy said, "but would you mind if we take a look at the will?"

"I don't see why not. It'll all be a matter of public record soon."

"Did your husband come with you?" I asked.

"He's in the middle of overseeing renovations to the El Malpais Visitor Center, so I suggested he remain behind. He's with the Bureau of Land Management," she added. "He and my father were not close."

As soon as Harrison Belhaven rose from the desk in his father's office, I realized I'd met him a couple of times in social settings but knew him as Harris. I pegged him as a year or so younger than my thirty-nine years and put his sister at a couple of years younger. There was nothing elegant about the man. His most distinguishing characteristic was a palpable anger riding his wiry frame. It settled in his brown eyes, rendering him dangerously sensual.

"BJ," he said. "What are you doing here?"

"He's consulting with us on your father's death," Roy said.

I indicated my companion. "This is Paul Barton, who works with me."

After everyone shook hands, Harris swept up the documents he'd been studying and prepared to vacate the office.

"Just a minute," his sister said. "They'd like to look at the will. And I see no harm in that."

Harris looked momentarily undecided. "Yeah, sure."

Melanie handed over the will. "We'll be in the den when you're finished."

"Hmm, no lawyer mediating the settlement of Pierce's estate," Paul noted when they were gone.

"There's probably one named as trustee. But this looks like an amicable disposition of assets."

"Not what I heard," he said. "I figured Pierce cut Harrison out of the will."

"Let's see for ourselves."

John Pierce Belhaven had not cut off his son despite the rift between them. His will was simple. He bequeathed the princely sum of $250,000 each to Sarah Thackerson and Spencer Spears. After a few other minor bequests, the remainder of the estate was split equally between his son and daughter, Harrison Belhaven and Melanie Harper.

"Remind me. Who are Thackerson and Spears?" I asked.

"His girlfriend," Paul said.

"And his boyfriend," Roy added.

"Whoa. A bimbo and a bimbob? How old was this guy when he died?"

"Sixty," the detective answered.

"And he had a girlfriend *and* a boyfriend? I'd like to have met the guy."

Paul grinned. "You wouldn't have learned a thing. I knew about the girlfriend but didn't know Spence did anything but trim the bushes and mow the lawn. Actually Pierce was sorta wimpy."

"Still waters run deep," Roy observed.

"You sure about the boyfriend part?" Paul asked.

Roy shrugged. "The kid admitted it to me. And Belhaven's last will and testament backs him up."

"I'd say so. He bequeathed his two love objects a sum certain and split the remainder between his progeny. So Thackerson and Spears get theirs, and the other two get whatever's left… if anything."

Roy rubbed an eye. "Like I said, I haven't seen the financials yet, but my guess is his heirs'll do all right. Belhaven was supposed to be loaded up with Voxlightner family money. And his wife had more of it than he did. The two kids are already blessed with trusts from her death."

Roy delivered the will to the Belhaven offspring while Paul and I continued to nose around in the office. When the detective returned from the den, Paul pitched in to help with the search. He took on the filing cabinet while Roy worked on the desk. I poked around in Belhaven's appointment book. I often found such books a productive place to start. After we finished we all took chairs facing one another.

"No computer. I assume it's already down at forensics," I said.

"Yeah, for what it's worth. Somebody smashed the hard drive."

"Paul, was Belhaven a cyber man or a pen-and-ink guy?"

"From what I saw at SWW meetings, he did both. I heard him making notes to himself on his iPhone and saw him writing things on a pad."

I turned to Roy. "The phone?"

"Also down at the lab."

"Do you see his notebook anywhere?" I asked Paul.

"Nope. And I was keeping an eye out for it."

"So the killer removed everything relating to the book Belhaven was working on."

"And I understand it was a whopper of a file. Pierce was big on research." Paul looked thoughtful for a moment. "But I think Sarah did most of it for him."

"His girlfriend?" I asked.

He nodded. "She was also his typist and researcher."

I looked at Roy. "You've interviewed her?"

"Sure. Needed to find out where she was and everything, but…."

"But you didn't ask her about any research on the new book."

"Guess not."

"We'll have to plug that hole. Roy, see if she'll meet us here tomorrow morning."

"Here?"

"So familiar things will be handy while she's remembering. Now let's go see the crime scene."

Like many cops and ex-cops, I have a near-mystical belief in walking the scene of the actual crime, usually more than once. We trooped to the garage. The origin point of the fire was near the water heater. A scorched lawn mower occupied the center of the violent scene. There wasn't much physical damage to the rest of the garage, probably because an alert neighbor returning home spotted the glow of the fire. An AFD unit from merely blocks away doused the flames in short order. The garage rafters were lightly charred but remained essentially intact. Had the conflagration pierced the fire-resistant tile over the garage, the flames would have spread quickly through the ceilings and consumed the house. But quick action prevented that.

What the crime scene screamed at me was *murder*. Someone rendered Pierce Belhaven dead from a blow to the head and cleaned out his research on the new book before dousing him with gasoline, throwing matches on him, and escaping through the side door.

Belhaven's next-door neighbor invited us in and seemed to relish telling of seeing a curious orange glow reflect off the fence and investigating to find a fire in his neighbor's garage. He immediately called in an alarm and then beat on the front door trying to rouse someone. Of course, no one remained in the house to be roused. Belhaven lay dead at the center of the mini-inferno. As was becoming the pattern, Roy left most of the questioning to me. I took it that both he and Paul were going to school on my technique.

We called it quits for the day after concluding the interview, but I insisted the appointment book I'd reviewed in Belhaven's office needed to be entered into evidence.

When we arrived home, I put my finger in the top of Paul's tank top and pulled it down, exposing the tiny black dragon occupying his left pec. "The little guy looks restless."

"Oh yeah. But right now he's hungry. After a feeding he'll be raring to go."

Once fed, Pedro prowled for an hour, steaming up our bedroom so much I was afraid one of *our* neighbors would call the fire department.

Chapter 3

THE NEXT morning we returned to the Belhaven house to meet Sarah Thackerson. Sarah looked like what she was, an older-than-average college student who also did secretarial and research work. What she did not look like was the main squeeze of an aging author. At five four she had curves where they were supposed to be and was cute but too mousy. I suspected this was by design. By primping a little, she could probably be quite fetching. Why hide her candle under a basket? To camouflage her real relationship with Belhaven, perhaps.

She regarded Roy, Paul, and me through wary brown eyes while seated at her own desk in the Belhaven home office. "Yes, I did research on the new book," she answered Roy's initial question. "Quite a lot of it actually."

I eased into my interrogation with something simple. "Had Mr. Belhaven selected a title for the work?"

"He'd settled on Voxlightner Metals as a working title. The title he'd publish under hadn't been determined, and it probably wouldn't have 'Voxlightner' in it. He was a member of the family, you know."

"How so?"

"Pierce's mother was one of old Mr. Marshall Voxlightner's sisters."

"So he was a nephew of the oilman."

She nodded. "Mr. Belhaven's deceased wife, Esther, was a Voxlightner as well. Although I understand it was a different branch. Esther had money in her own right and left it in trust for Harrison and Melanie."

Curious. Sarah volunteering such information almost seemed like trivializing her own $250,000 inheritance. I picked up on it.

"I understand you benefit from Mr. Belhaven's will. You and a groundskeeper named Spencer Spears."

She flushed slightly and studied the spot where her wrecked computer had once stood. "That's true. Pierce…. Mr. Belhaven believed in rewarding loyalty. I saw him through two of the first three books he wrote." She glanced up at me defiantly. "And they were better books for it too. I-I did research on those and made a few suggestions…." She ran out of steam—and defiance.

"Do you know what sparked Mr. Belhaven's interest in writing about a family scandal?" I asked.

"He wanted to correct the perception the Voxlightners were responsible for what happened."

"He didn't believe his cousin Barron perpetrated fraud upon the investors?" I asked.

"Definitely not."

"How did he explain Barron's disappearance?"

"He didn't, but he was working on a theory."

I leaned forward to see if invading her space bothered her. It didn't. "Which was?"

"Someone else was the culprit. He was certain Dr. Stabler was involved."

"That's the engineer who disappeared along with Barron?" Paul prompted.

"Yes. But Pierce maintained they didn't disappear together. He always thought his cousin was disposed of some way."

I noticed she gave up the pretense of calling her employer Mr. Belhaven. "Disposed of? You mean killed?"

Sarah nodded without comment.

"Barron had no family of his own?" I pressed.

"He was married briefly when he was younger but divorced. No children."

"You've told me what motivated Belhaven's interest in the book, but you haven't indicated what caused him to pick it up at this precise time."

"He wasn't very forthcoming. I know it was something he'd chanced upon while he was a New Mexico Power and Light Company executive."

"He was retired, wasn't he?"

"Yes. Just recently. But it was something he remembered that had relevance for him when he started looking into the scandal."

"What was it?" I asked.

She frowned, uncertainty stamping her features. "He never told me. He said it was the key to everything, and to share it would be dangerous."

Roy straightened in his chair. "Any idea what it was? Any clue? Any thoughts?"

She shook her head, dislodging some of her tightly pinned hair and making her more attractive. "Not really. I got the feeling it had something to do with some meter readings he saw some time ago."

"Meter readings?" Roy asked. "You mean like electrical meter readings? How could readings be relevant?"

She shrugged. "I have no idea."

Something tugged at my memory. "Roy, I need another look at Belhaven's appointment book."

"No problem. The crime scene lab should be finished with it by now. I'll drop it by your office. You onto something?"

"I remember seeing a notation but can't quite get a fix on it."

For the next hour, Sarah Thackerson searched her memory and shared what research on Belhaven's new book she could recall. It fleshed out some of the bits and pieces, including the fact Belhaven had discovered Dr. Stabler was involved in a scam years before the Voxlightner thing. Following the collapse of VPMR, half a dozen civil suits were filed, but the two targets of these procedures were missing and widely believed to have absconded with most of the company's funds. At least two other deaths had been attributed to the brouhaha besides Everett Kent's, one from a heart attack and the second from suicide. Both were stockholders heavily invested in the corporation.

According to Sarah, she was on her way back from a visit to her family in Bisbee, Arizona on the day Belhaven died. She'd started later than anticipated and stopped in Las Cruces for the night, arriving in Albuquerque around noon on Thursday morning. She drove straight to her apartment in the Northeast Heights, where she learned of her boss's death from a voicemail message left by Spencer Spears. I didn't ask why he didn't reach her by cell. Roy had indicated earlier they weren't on good terms.

Not much of this was new. Roy had already confirmed her visit to her parents' home and an overnight stay in Cruces. The drive to Bisbee was something over 400 miles, so this sounded reasonable.

We were more or less finished questioning Sarah when a sound caught my ear. A lawn mower purred, pulling my glance to the window. Beyond the glass panes, a broad backyard looked better than it should have. New Mexico's vaunted monsoon season hadn't kicked in yet and, in any case, was predicted to be a bust this season. That was not good news for the driest year on record to date.

Belhaven's secretary and researcher returned to her work as the three of us went outside to confront a hard-bodied young man with a small birthmark. Already handsome, the strawberry imperfection on his left cheek rendered him sensual as well. Here was the lawn boy, except Spencer Spears was no boy. He was a man in his midtwenties… and knew it. Masculine grace rippled across his shoulders as he cut the motor, ran a hand through thick hair as dark as roasted coffee beans, and regarded us warily.

"Spencer Spears?" I asked.

He nodded. "That's me."

"Yard and garden look great."

"You the water police?" He referred to water restrictions imposed by the city fathers for the duration of the drought. I shook my head and smiled at his joke. He continued. "I got pretty good at irrigating. Figured out the best time for it and exactly how long to leave the sprinklers on without violating the mayor's ration."

I introduced us and fixed on the lawn mower. "The mower looks new. Where'd you get it?"

"Bought it at Lowe's this morning. I usually cut the lawn on Thursdays, but Pierce's…. Mr. Belhaven's services are tomorrow. So I came in today."

"Admirable. But who's going to reimburse you for the lawn mower and pay you for your time?"

"If Harris or Melanie don't, then I'll eat it. But the place has to be kept up in case they want to sell it." He frowned to himself and seemed to be reasoning things out in his own mind. "Melanie probably won't move in. She and her husband live in Grants. But Harris might if he can get over being pissed at his dad."

"Why was he on the outs with his father?"

"You'll have to ask him. All I can tell you is I never saw Harris at the house until today. Not even for Mr. B.'s sixtieth birthday party a couple of months ago."

Roy Guerra spoke up. "Was he hostile to his dad?"

Spencer screwed up his left eye in a thoughtful way. "Oh, I see. Hostile, as in setting the old man on fire, you mean. Nothing like that. He just gave his dad a good letting alone."

"How long has the rift been going on?" Paul wanted to know.

"All I can tell you is I've worked here for five years, so it's older than that. Like I said, I never saw Harris in this house until his father's accident."

I ignored the reference to an accident. "What are your responsibilities here?"

He looked around the large backyard. "Everything outside the house is mine. I landscape, mow, mulch, fertilize, and trim. I also repair things inside the house. Electrical, mechanical, masonry, that kind of thing. I'm pretty handy."

"Do you live on the premises?" Roy asked.

Spencer shook his head, setting dark curls to dancing. “Nope. Have my own pad. But there’s a room in a little building out back where I sometimes rest my head when something keeps me here late. My place is down by CNM. Just off Morris on Lagrima.”

“Is this your sole place of employment?” I asked.

“Mostly. I go to school there. Central New Mexico, that is. I’ve got the GI Bill, but Mr. B.’s gig—plus a few other customers—keep me solvent.”

“What branch were you in?”

“Army. Rangers,” Spence said.

“How long did you serve?”

“Enlisted right out of high school and saw service in Iraq and Afghanistan. Decided that was enough. Time to start working on my education.” A smile played at the corners of his broad mouth. “The kind I could talk about.”

Maybe a blunt question might shake him. “Where were you on the night Pierce Belhaven died?”

“Wednesday’s a school day. Like I said I usually work on Thursdays. Thursdays and Mondays unless Mr. B. called me in for some special job.”

“Happen often?” Roy asked.

“Enough. This neighborhood was built in the fifties and sixties, so the houses take some TLC. Anyway on *that* Wednesday, I had two classes, went to my place and did homework, wrote a theme… at least got it started. I went malling for a while until beer o’clock, then met some guys at the Hogshead Tavern up on Montgomery.”

“I’m not up on the local slang,” I said. “What time is beer o’clock?”

“Got there about eight. We closed the place down at two.”

“Witnesses, I assume,” Roy said.

“Yeah,” Spencer answered. “Sometimes two, sometimes three. They came and went.”

“But you stayed.”

“Same table all night… except for pit stops. The Hog has the best craft beer in the state.”

“What was your and Belhaven’s relationship,” I asked.

He didn’t even blink. “Employee… employer. Friends. Sometimes even companions when he let his hair down and acted human instead of like a Voxlightner. They’re in a world of their own, you know.”

Recognizing a ploy, I pressed on. “Define companions.”

"Buddies. We'd hoist a glass or two. I'd sit and listen to him go maudlin when he overdid it. Put him to bed once in a while. Next day we were employee-employer again."

"So he left you two hundred fifty grand for putting him to bed a couple of times?"

Spencer regarded me through milk-chocolate eyes. "Okay. Far be it for me to sully a dead man's reputation, but he asked a little more from time to time."

"Define *more*."

He looked down his frame and spread his hands. "All of me sometimes."

"Just to be clear, are you saying you were his lover?" Roy asked, his voice rising.

Spencer's charming grin appeared again. "Don't have an aneurism, man. No big deal. I already told you about it. But just on Thursdays and Mondays."

"For five years?" I asked.

Spencer nodded. "Yeah. He picked me up in a bar—the Hogshead, as a matter of fact—and we fit so well together he wanted to meet again. We did, and it became a permanent thing. Why not? His wife was dead by then, his son wouldn't talk to him, and his daughter lived in Grants with a husband Pierce couldn't stand. The guy was entitled to some companionship, wasn't he?"

I could see Roy was bursting to introduce Sarah Thackerson into the conversation. I preferred he didn't at this point, but he was in charge.

"What about Ms. Thackerson?" he asked, his cheeks somewhat flushed.

"What about her? Oh. I see what you mean. She was his *beard*, I think the term is."

"Are you saying she didn't go to bed with him?"

"Sure she did. But I was the one who meant something to Pierce. She was merely his thing on the side." He frowned. "Of course, he left her $250,000 too, so…."

We waited, but he didn't pursue the matter further, although I could see from his eyes he was reevaluating the situation. After a brief grimace he smiled. "If he was playing around with Sarah, that's all it was, playing around. *Ours* was the relationship that counted. Might sound strange to some ears, but Pierce loved me."

"And you? Did you love him?" I asked.

"I was fond of him, and he knew it. I never tried to smoke him, and he appreciated that. Think he liked having a straight guy respond to him.

Lots of gays do, I guess." Spencer frowned. "Didn't have any idea he was about to get the cosmic dope slap. Bummer."

Paul must have heard my mental caution because he kept his mouth shut, although I saw his lips twitch.

"Anyway," Spencer went on, "we had a good relationship. It satisfied both our needs."

Paul broke his silence. "His emotional and your financial, I gather."

Spencer smiled pleasantly at him. "Aren't most unions based on economics? Husband works and feeds the kids, wife takes care of husband and family."

Paul's look turned dark, so I stepped in to avoid a confrontation. "That might be the way it worked in the last century, but not so much anymore. It's more of a partnership."

Spencer spread his hands. "That's what I'm saying. Our partnership took care of everybody's needs. The fact he loved me and I was fond of him was a plus, right?"

Paul and I left Roy to collect Spencer's alibi witnesses and returned to the office.

"Something about that guy," Paul said on the drive back. "He's a hip-shooter."

"To the contrary. I have the feeling he told us exactly what he wanted and not one iota more."

"He didn't seem guarded to me."

"More than you think. He's pretty good at dropping pearls among his hipster talk."

Paul fell silent, and I was left to wonder at the fact we found Spencer's casual attitude toward his lover so objectionable, while Pierce Belhaven probably understood and even relished it.

I'd noticed glances Spencer threw Paul's way. They weren't motivated by avarice—not monetary avarice at any rate. Even so, I had no doubt Spencer bedded the ladies at every opportunity. As I parked in my spot in the lot on Fifth, I reached the conclusion Spencer Spears was a pansexual—someone who was gender blind. Someone capable of forming a romantic attachment to anyone who appealed to him regardless of gender or mannerisms or physical attributes. Was there anything wrong with that? Not that I could see… so long as neither party hid his motives, as seemed to be the case with Spencer Spears and John Pierce Belhaven.

Chapter 4

WHEN PAUL and I went to the office the next morning after an early therapy swim at the country club, a surprise awaited us. Hazel waved a phone slip in my face the moment I came through the outer door.

"You have a call you need to return right away."

I accepted the pink slip with a name and number printed in Hazel's careful handwriting. "Lucinda Caulkins.... Caulkins," I mumbled.

"She's old Marshall Voxlightner's daughter," Hazel said. "Caulkins is her married name."

"Ah." No wonder my office manager was so animated. She either anticipated a client to pay for the work we were already doing or someone demanding that we cease doing it. Either way an advantage for the firm's bottom line from her perspective. "Okay. I'll give her a ring."

Paul joined me as I placed the call and activated the speaker phone when someone answered the ring. I identified myself and was asked to hold.

Within a minute a calm, well-modulated voice came on the line. "My name is Lucinda Caulkins, Mr. Vinson. Thank you for returning my call. I wonder if it would be convenient for you to drop by and speak with my mother? She has a matter she would like to discuss." The hint of a slow drawl reminded me she had lived for the last several years with a real estate developer husband in Virginia.

"Certainly. When would be convenient?"

"Would two suit your schedule?"

"See you at two." At Paul's frantic pantomime I hastily added, "Would it be permissible to bring an associate?"

"Of course."

A UNIFORMED maid answered the door, but a slender woman with frosted brown hair stood behind her in the foyer. She stepped forward and offered a hand as the maid discreetly slipped away. Her simple but elegant outfit wasn't off the rack.

As we exchanged greetings, I identified Paul as my associate. Lucinda Caulkins greeted him as politely as she had me before leading the way to a large, comfortable room. I would have called it a living room, but in this setting, it was more properly a drawing room. The outside of this stone-and-brick edifice might truly resemble a medieval castle, yet the interior was modern, with big airy rooms… although the effect was spoiled somewhat by furniture that might easily have come out of the Victorian age.

A small, thin woman I'd completely overlooked when we entered the room rose from the depths of a tufted wing chair with the aid of an ebony cane. Despite being emaciated she moved with alacrity. Her smile was welcoming, not formal.

"Mother," Lucinda said, moving to the older woman's side, "may I present Mr. B. J. Vinson and his associate, Paul Barton. They've come at our invitation. My mother, Mrs. Dorothy Wellbourne Voxlightner."

"Of course. Welcome to Voxlightner Castle." The frail hand she offered still had strength in it. I estimated she must be in her mideighties. Her voice reminded me of her daughter's without the slight, acquired southern drawl. I'd heard stories about this woman all my life, and here she stood, without hubris, not a prima donna or misanthrope, but warm and charming.

She startled us with a tinkling laugh. "I used to be so self-conscious over such a pretentious description of our home, but Marshall was adamant about it. Over the years it's become easier."

"It *is* a castle, ma'am," Paul put in, a smile dimpling his cheeks.

"I like this one," the older woman said, taking his hand to shake and pat at the same time. "You must call me Dorothy."

"Wouldn't dream of it," he said, bringing her hand to his lips.

She drew him to a big camelback sofa and pulled him down beside her. "I didn't know they made them like this any longer." She addressed Paul. "Tea? Coffee? You don't look old enough for highballs."

"Thank you, ma'am, I'll pass."

After I also declined refreshment, Lucinda put things back on track. "Mr. Vinson, I understand you're working with the police on Pierce's murder, is that correct?"

"Both Paul and I are consulting with Detective Roy Guerra, the officer in charge of the investigation."

"Then we have a proposition for you." Lucinda glanced at her mother and received a small nod before proceeding. "As you may be aware, my brother, Barron, disappeared on Monday, March 15, 2004 and has not been seen or heard from since. We believe it is time to have him declared dead. We would like your help."

I wasn't able to hide my astonishment. At a minimum my eyebrows must have reacted. "I am surprised you haven't taken that step before now. New Mexico law requires only a waiting period of five years. Five years elapsed in 2009."

"My father wasn't willing to live the scandal all over again. And any such petition was certain to raise it. Then, of course, that was the year my father died, and probating his estate occupied our attention. Since then we've honored his wishes."

"Likely out of inertia," Mrs. Voxlightner put in.

Distaste edged Lucinda's voice when she spoke after a slight pause. "When Pierce told us he was going to recreate all the details with his new book, we objected. But he claimed he was going to expose the perpetrators and exonerate the family."

"Did he identify these perpetrators?"

She shook her head. "No. He rudely refused to reveal anything. Said it was too dangerous. And given what happened to him, perhaps he was right."

"You believe someone involved in the scandal killed Pierce Belhaven?"

Lucinda leveled a cool stare at me. "What other explanation could there be?"

I turned to Mrs. Voxlightner. "Are there children other than Mrs. Caulkins and Barron?"

She shook her head. "Barron was our only son."

"All right. I understand the situation now, but you don't need my services. As I understand the Uniform Probate Code, you are not required to conduct a search for your son. If he has not been seen nor heard from this past five years, that is sufficient. Your attorney can file a petition for a declaration of death."

The tiny elegant woman sitting beside Paul on the sofa cleared her throat and claimed the room's attention as she reached for a leather-clad folio on the coffee table. "I fear we're not making ourselves clear. Because Pierce was so certain he could uncover the swindlers who looted the precious metals company, we want you to investigate his death and bring his murderer to justice. If in the process you determine exactly what happened to Barron, that would be a plus for us."

She opened the folio and held out a photo in her graceful fingers. "This is the way the world last saw my son. It's the final image of him I have as well. This is not acceptable to me."

I took the FBI wanted poster of a wild-eyed image of Barron Voxlightner staring back at me. The legend read: Wanted for Murder and Grand Theft.

"This is not the way I want to remember my son. Nor do I want others thinking that of him. Locate Barron if you can. If not please see if you can determine what happened to him. When you are finished, we will have my son declared dead… if it's appropriate."

The room was still while I nibbled on my lower lip. "Mrs. Voxlightner, the police and a couple of insurance companies investigated that situation years ago. They had no luck, so it's doubtful I can do better."

The lady smiled at me. "But don't you see? Pierce swore he uncovered something he believed would lead him to the answer to the mystery. Since you're investigating his death, you just need to find what that was. While he did not share his information with us, I do know it was something he came across while he was with the New Mexico Power and Light Company."

"You are aware his files were stolen and his computers destroyed, aren't you?"

"Come now, Mr. Vinson, we have faith in you. I've made some inquiries and am satisfied you can uncover something for us. If nothing else, make certain Barron has truly vanished without leaving a trace. Please provide us with whatever contract you require, and we will give you an appropriate retainer."

"On one condition, Mrs. Voxlightner."

"And what, pray tell, is that?"

"You'll call me BJ instead of Mr. Vinson."

"Agreed. And I am Dorothy."

HAZEL WAS pleased as Punch with the news *someone* was going to foot the bill for what she knew I would do come what may. She insisted on delivering the contract and collecting the retainer personally. I think she was motivated by a desire to see the interior of Voxlightner Castle, a privilege not accorded to many. Meanwhile, I went through the formality of notifying Gene of my engagement on a case that might brush up against an official police investigation. Paul would do the same with Det. Roy Guerra. While we were already involved—more or less by invitation—the fact we had a paying client might at some point put our motives at odds. Unlikely, but possible.

As agreed earlier, Roy delivered Pierce Belhaven's appointment book. Books, actually, since APD collected several dating back as far as 2003, which would assure us of covering the scandal from beginning to end. Voxlightner Precious Metals Recovery had been incorporated on September 1 of that year, but Barron personally financed a series of fire assay tests in the months immediately prior. The venture ended on March 15, 2004 with the disappearance of Barron Voxlightner and Dr. Walther Stabler. The scam took less than a year to pry almost $50,000,000 out of investors.

THE CHARLIE Weeks part of Vinson and Weeks, Confidential Investigations, was involved in another assignment, so Paul volunteered to help me go through Belhaven's appointment books. We settled down at the table in the corner of my office, where we started with the newest and worked backward. APD found no diary, but Pierce had made comments in his appointment books, virtually rendering them into a journal.

I quickly found the note that had insinuated itself into my memory. On Monday, January 10, of this year Belhaven circled a comment in red ink: *Meter readings are key! That's what he meant.* Okay, what meter readings? And who is the "he" Belhaven reference? I alerted Paul to watch for any notation referencing meter readings.

When one does not know what one is looking for when reviewing nine years of another man's hen scratchings, the process grows tedious and boring rather quickly. At times my eyes glazed over, causing me to go back and review a page or two all over again. A chink in Paul's investigative armor appeared when he all too readily bailed on me when Roy Guerra called and invited us to accompany him on an interview with the AFD arson supervisor. I recognized Paul'd had his fill of donkey work for the day—his disco leg had jiggled for the last half hour—and agreed he should go with Roy while I kept at the drudge work. Despite the feeling I was searching for a raindrop in a drought, there was *something* here, and I was determined to find it.

Pierce Belhaven wrote in a precise hand except when he was tired. The morning notations were clear, but as the day wore on, his writing became more difficult to read. He apparently possessed an acerbic mind. After some of his appointments, he categorized a certain individual or individuals with either gushing or caustic comments. He also changed his mind about some of his associates, as one time they would be a "fine fellow" and at others a "stodgy clod."

I found one entry referencing Paul and some issue at SouthWest Writers. I smiled at his characterization: *A toothsome handful!* If the old boy only knew.

By the time Paul returned with Roy, I was down to the last couple of books without finding much of interest. The unread books covered the years 2003 and 2004, the period when the scandal occurred. Nonetheless I was wiped out and gratefully put aside the examination of the appointment-cum-diary books to hear the results of their interview with Lanny Johnson, the AFD lieutenant in charge of arson.

"Didn't learn much," Roy said as he claimed a chair in front of my desk. "The fire was deliberately set using book matches tossed on Belhaven's gasoline-soaked clothing."

"Matches? Plural?"

"Yep. Ignited a whole book of them and tossed them on the body. Gasoline caught and toasted Belhaven but didn't do much damage to the garage."

"How much gasoline was used?" I asked.

"Enough to cover the body," Paul said.

"Anything else on or around the body?"

"Just the remnants of a burned-up rag. You know, like mechanics use to wipe their hands on. Wasn't much of it left."

I rubbed my tired eyes and sat back in my chair.

Paul read me pretty well. "What are you thinking, Vince?"

Roy scowled. "What's with this *Vince* business? I thought everybody called you BJ."

"There are always contrarians," I replied, unwilling to explain it was a pet name. "Why the arson charade?"

"Trying to make Belhaven's death look like an accident," the detective responded.

"Obviously. But why? Roy, did Belhaven have life insurance?"

He nodded. "Multiple policies, I understand."

"Who are the beneficiaries?"

"The son and daughter. Two-point-five mil each."

"Which probably contain double-indemnity clauses in case of accidental death. This is just speculation of course. Have to see the actual policies to know my premise holds water."

"I get it," Paul said. "The arson was to make it look like an accident."

"How old were the policies, Roy?"

"Haven't viewed them yet, but I understand they have gray hair."

"Have you found the murder weapon?"

"Nothing in the garage looks plausible. Office of the Medical Investigator says it was probably metal, although the condition of the corpse makes that iffy."

"Something like a wrench?" Paul asked.

"Yeah. Or an aluminum bat. And we didn't find either one of those. Found some tools in a shed at the back, but none of them tested positive."

"Was the skin broken on his head? Enough so there was blood?"

"Couldn't say for sure… you know, because of the fire. No obvious evidence of it."

After another fifteen minutes of hashing and rehashing the situation, Roy took his leave while Paul and I tackled the appointment books again. Paul picked up the blue-clad volume for 2003. Within five minutes he let out an "Aha!"

"What?" I asked.

"You said Pierce mentioned readings? I got meter readings."

He shoved his book over to me. Under August 2003 Belhaven had made a terse comment: *May-1800 kWhs; June-1825 kWhs; July-1829 kWhs. What the hell is up?*

I took kWhs to be kilowatt hours. There was no name or meter number or address, but the numbers had been significant enough to catch Belhaven's attention. Why? Had his responsibilities involved monitoring accounts to watch for unusual readings? Did he keep an eye on friends or family? Was this part of his job, or was he simply a snoop?

I got up from the table and went to my computer where I pulled up the New Mexico Power and Light bills for my home. After reviewing a number of monthly invoices for the past year, I reached the following conclusions: my average usage was around 700 kWhs and according to the utility company, the average household usage was around 650 kWhs. Belhaven spotted someone using around three times the voltage for a period of three months. Given the readings were spotlighted in his journal, he clearly believed the level of usage was unusual, and he knew the individual the meter belonged to. The penned comment "What the hell is up?" led me to that conclusion.

I picked up the phone, dialed, and argued my way through a secretary to speak to an old golfing buddy of mine. He agreed to a meet.

AT FOUR that afternoon Paul, Roy, and I walked into the plush office of Watson Moore, executive vice president of NMPL, which is how the public knew the New Mexico Power and Light Company. Back when we'd hit the links together, we'd called him Watt, a nickname we felt appropriate to his vocation. The moniker stuck.

After a little light joking about various muffed shots on the fairways we both remembered—albeit differently—we got down to business. He heard us out before leaning back in his black leather executive chair.

"Back in those days we kept an eye out for extremely unusual usage for a couple of reasons. Could signal a malfunctioning meter and alert us before we billed someone for a sum they wouldn't be able to pay. And frankly—and as an ex-cop you know this well, BJ—it helped us respond to official requests to spot illegal activity, such as indoor marijuana cultivation and the like. And that was a part of Pierce's job. Those readings would have been called to his attention."

Roy spoke up. "Can you identify the meter for us?"

Watt nodded in his low-key way. "We should be able to find them, but it will take some time. Who do I call with the information?"

"Call me," I said, casting an eye at Roy.

He raised an eyebrow but nodded. "Yeah. Call BJ. He'll pass it on to us."

After noting down the information Belhaven highlighted for us, Watt ushered us out with a parting comment about a shot I'd sent into the duck pond on the Paradise Hills Golf Club the last time we played.

As we stepped into the elevator, Roy turned to me with a grin. "Great work. Just a matter of time before we know the perp."

"What perp?" I asked. "What do three successive monthly electrical meter readings tell us?"

Paul stepped into that one quickly. "Where to start our search for answers."

Chapter 5

I DIDN'T wait for Watt to get back to us. Friday morning Paul and I looked up Richard Quintana, the CPA more or less forced into retirement by the looting of VPMR. I'd known Ricardo—as his intimates called him—casually for several years. He once flirted with gay life before deciding it wasn't for him and marrying a nice young woman.

Ricardo made a face like a bulldog chewing a wasp when he saw me standing on his doorstep, but he opened the door and stepped back to admit us. He groused all the way back to his study.

"You're here to stir up all that mess again, aren't you? Needless to say, I'm not interested in contributing." From the profusion of ledgers scattered around his home office, the CPA had not gone out of business, merely retained a few choice customers and worked solo out of his home.

I put a cheerful note in my voice as Paul and I settled in chairs before his cluttered desk. "Sure you are. You'd like to see the perpetrators run to ground like everyone else."

"Thought that was already done."

"You mean Voxlightner and Stabler?" Paul said. "What if there were more people involved?"

"Look, sonny, the time for blamestorming's come and gone. The feds turned me upside down and inside out before putting me out of business and declaring me innocent."

"Let's not get ahead of ourselves, Ricardo. Nobody's declared innocent yet. The powers that be said there was no evidence you were involved. By the way, meet my associate, Paul Barton."

They nodded at one another; neither offered to shake hands.

"We just want to get a better idea of the lay of the land. Do you mind if I record this, so I won't have to take notes?" After he nodded consent, I did the prelims—identifying the time, place, and individuals involved—before striking up a conversation.

"Those were pretty good days… back then, I mean."

"Twenty-oh-three started out all right. Course it didn't take long to fall apart. When was it we invaded Iraq? Sometime in March, as I recall.

My personal world was okay until the day Barron Voxlightner and Wick Pillsner introduced some of us to a fellow by the name of Dr. Walther Stabler." Ricardo played around with the last name, making it clear he held nothing but disgust for the man. "That was a bad hair day, I can tell you."

"When was this?" I asked.

"June 24, 2003. It's stamped in my memory for the rest of my life. They invited me and Zach Greystone and Newt Williamson to lunch, and we walked in like eager puppies wagging our tails."

"An accountant, a lawyer, and a banker," I said. "They went straight for the jugular, didn't they? What was the purpose of the lunch?"

"About what you'd expect. Introduce us to that scam artist Stabler, talk up the project. But they didn't come empty-handed. Barron financed some fire assays on material taken from the Green Mesa tailings."

From prior research I knew fire assays were tests conducted by labs using fusion to determine the amount of metals in a sample. In other words tests to determine the potential value of ore.

"Green Mesa?" I asked.

"Yeah. Tailings from the Green Mesa Copper Mine over in the Morenci District of eastern Arizona were gonna make us all rich. That shoulda told us something. The place wasn't green, and it wasn't on a mesa. Just five million tons of dirt out of a hole in the ground."

"Easy to see that now," I said. "But back then everyone was hopeful. Tell me, do you think Barron and Stabler absconded with the company's money?"

"And left the rest of us holding the baby. They're the ones who disappeared. Nobody woulda thought it of Barron in a million years. Almost killed the old man, I can tell you."

We spent another hour with Ricardo and fleshed out the picture a little. Barron financed a series of fire assays out of his own pocket, using the facilities of the highly regarded New Mexico Institute of Mining and Technology in Socorro, which we locals still called the School of Mines. The assay reports Barron and Stabler passed around at the initial luncheon detailed commercial grades of gold and silver, with trace amounts of platinum. Heady stuff to dreamers.

Further assays confirmed values of seventy dollars, almost twice what was commercially viable. Wick Pillsner, a pro at that sort of thing, put together a slick business plan. And when old Mr. Voxlightner put in money and lent his name, the race was on to get on the initial investors' list.

Ricardo fished around in his desk, pulled out a smooth, gray-streaked lump of metal, and handed it to me. "This is what was produced by the initial assay test. They call it a prill… or bullet or button."

The lump lay heavy in my palm. *Lead or gold?* Ricardo read my mind.

"It's gold all right. Maybe a little lead and some silver and a few other things. But it's got enough gold and silver to grab a fellow's interest. I keep it around to remind me not to let dreams overrule reason."

I tossed it to Paul, who examined the button critically before commenting. "I can't believe a hunk of metal like this is enough to generate a public offering of fifty million."

"Young man, that little hunk of metal and a lot more like it were mental laxatives to the gullible, including me. Hell, I'll bet you put some money in the venture, BJ."

"What little my cop's salary allowed."

"Yeah, right. I knew your old man, remember?"

"How far did they get with the actual project?" Paul asked.

"They bought the tailings over in Arizona. Worked out a contract with ASARCO down in El Paso for the smelting. Had a mill site picked out in Socorro."

I threw a thumb at the prill Paul held. "Let me understand something. They conducted *two* assay tests?"

"After they made this little button, they lumped a bunch of them together and ran them through another procedure to produce doré. That's what they call the stuff they send to the smelter to be made into bars or ingots."

"I understand such tests are time-consuming."

"And expensive," Ricardo said.

"Did they do the two steps in tandem?"

"They made the prill one day, allowed it to cool overnight, and did the second step the next morning."

"Who took possession of the prill in the interim?"

"Stayed with the School of Mines. Dr. Damon Herrera locked it away where it couldn't be touched."

"When everyone went back the next morning for the next test, were you allowed to physically examine the prill?"

"Sure. Held it in my hands. Turned it over. Bit it. Smelled it."

"And you're confident it was the same button produced the day before?"

Ricardo nodded and accepted the prill from Paul. “The first day it was still glowing hot, so nobody could handle it. But it looked the same.”

I tapped the button of metal now lying on his desk. “If I understand you, the School of Mines conducted the fire assay tests, not Dr. Stabler.”

“That’s right. But he dictated what they used for the carbon source in the furnaces. Coal dust, ground charcoal, and whatever. Oh… and powdered lead oxide.”

“What kind of furnaces.”

“Big suckers.”

“Coal fired?”

He shook his head. “Electric.”

Chapter 6

A RESPONSE from Watt Moore at New Mexico Power and Light was crucial now that I knew the fire assays were conducted in electric furnaces. Even so I couldn't rush things. He'd call as soon as he located the information.

In the meantime I dithered over who to contact next. Hardwick Pillsner seemed to be the logical target. Wick had made a career of being a glad-hander. He'd been a football star, first at Albuquerque High and then for the UNM Lobos. Combining his local fame with a natural gift of gab, after graduation he struck out on his own, putting together business deals. At first he had no business sense, but Wick knew how to earn as he learned. He soon understood not only the jargon of the business community, but also the elements of a good deal. He married his high school sweetheart and built a family and a reputation. Older than I was, he remained too much of a jock to suit me. I'd grown out of that phase, but he never did. Nonetheless I enjoyed a decent relationship with him based on my Young America Football League years when he coached the Scorpions, my YAFL team. When I phoned he readily agreed to an appointment.

Monday morning Paul and I drove to Wick's one-story, slump-block office building at 3300 Lomas NE. The receptionist looked as if she fit Wick's mold… curvy, bouncy, cute. She seated us in a loungelike waiting area, and after volunteering that Mr. Pillsner would be off a long-distance call momentarily, she offered refreshments. We both accepted water. I glanced around the spacious room as we waited.

A soft, peach-colored material I couldn't identify covered the overstuffed Chesterfield on which Paul and I rested. Two tufted barrel chairs sat opposite us across a low, circular piecrust stand used in lieu of a modern coffee table. Across the room stood an étagère holding pictures and mementos of Wick's athletic career. A hidden fan wafted the faint scent of lilacs through the room. He'd spent some money on his reception area.

"Did I tell you I filed my first story on the Voxlightner thing the other day?" Paul asked as we waited.

"Who with?"

"*Journal*," he said. "Going down again this afternoon to talk to them about it." There was an edge to his voice.

"Again? Thought you did everything over the internet."

"Usually. But the editor asked for a couple of changes, and I wanted to meet him. Seems like a nice guy… good staff. I'm hotfooting it down to the paper as soon as we're finished."

Wick Pillsner, with his hulking, athletic build and pug face, didn't look like a paper pusher. He dominated any room he graced with his presence, including his own reception area. I could tell Paul was intimidated by the human dynamo who bustled in and swept us up in his enthusiasm. Never taciturn, Wick was always excited by something or someone. Before we were even seated, he was off and running about his latest project… a solar-powered energy panel. Eventually he ran down and leaned back in his plush executive chair, tapping a crystal letter opener against the palm of his left hand.

"I hear you're looking into the old precious metals scam, BJ." His voice resonated with the suppressed energy of an evangelistic preacher.

"That I am. *We* are, actually. And we've come to pick the brains of the guy who's a walking encyclopedia on the affair."

"The fellow who suffered the most, I'd say. Sometimes I think I should have run for the hills like Barron and Walther. Except I didn't have the millions they made off the theft to sustain me. That scandal left me an extreme case of red ass, I can tell you."

"You put a lot into it?" I asked.

"I put everything in it—my money, my time, my reputation. I didn't work on another project for damned near a year. And don't forget, my time *is* my money."

Paul waved around the richly furnished office. "Seems like you landed on your feet."

Wick rewarded him with a wan smile. "I can't begin to tell you how much harder it was than it should have been. My reputation is what brings me customers. And it took quite a whupping back in '03 and '04." He shuddered. "It was worse than starting all over." He laid aside the letter opener and straightened in his chair. "How can I help?"

Wick had been involved earlier and deeper than I'd imagined. In December of 2002, a business associate in Nevada introduced Wick to Dr. Walther Stabler and his plan to recover millions of dollars from copper-ore tailings. Wick professed to be interested when Stabler offered to fund a fire assay out of his own pocket on some sample ore. Wick was impressed but claimed to be wary. Once they worked out the elements of a deal, Stabler drove him to the Morenci dump. Wick took a dozen samples from various places and hired the New Mexico School of Mines to assay them. When each and every test proved to be commercial, Wick was convinced and stopped spending his own money.

He took the deal directly to Marshall Wilson Voxlightner, the richest, most conservative natural resources man he knew. The old man was only mildly interested, but his son was fascinated. Barron and some of his cronies put up $250,000 to start the necessary preliminary work on the project. As it began to look like a true commercial venture, his father matched the initial amount, which provided the seed money for proving up the venture and getting a business and investment plan going.

"Weren't you paid for your time?" I asked.

"Made a deal. I'd be paid in stock. Gave it all my time and got paid nothing. It was going to be my ticket to a beautiful retirement."

Wick contributed little more to our store of knowledge except he'd seen both Barron and Dr. Stabler the day they disappeared.

"That would have been in March of '04?" I asked.

"The fifteenth to be exact. I'd kept my two-room office downtown at the Central New Mexico Bank Building and leased this entire building to them. The company was circling the drain, so I stopped by for a face-off with Barron. I couldn't afford to have my name associated with a disaster." He gave a mirthless laugh. "Fat chance. I was already up to my eyeballs. Anyway I bearded Voxlightner and Stabler in their own den. They were going over bank accounts and invoices in Barron's office when I barged in. Barron admitted right on the spot he'd located a dozen phony accounts paid out of company funds. I lowered the boom. Told them I was calling in the FBI."

"Did you?" I asked.

"Hell yes. But that night the two of them disappeared."

"What time did you see them?"

"I left about one thirty in the afternoon. They were still going over the books. I spent the rest of the day fielding bitch calls. Voxlightner hit me right in the belly of my business, I can tell you."

The memories were apparently difficult to take because his features turned thunderous. "Called this FBI guy I know from Kiwanis but didn't really tell him anything he didn't already know. Went home about eight that night, and when I drove past this very building, I saw the lights on. No cars in the lot, but I checked anyway. As the landlord, I had keys. Nobody here. Papers scattered everywhere in Barron's office, Stabler's, and even Hightower's."

Paul spoke up. "Hightower?"

"John Hightower, the mining exec they hired to run the project."

"He was left to face the music," I said.

"Him… and me too. Spent hours… days… weeks talking to the feds, the bank examiners, and I don't know who else."

"No evidence of foul play in the office?" Paul asked.

"Nothing except everything was left out on desks, file drawers open. That kinda thing. No overturned chairs or blood on the floor. Nothing so gory. They got in their cars and hauled ass for somewhere unknown. Stands to reason they had a bolt hole prepared."

"So you think Barron and Stabler engineered the whole thing?"

"Who else? Hard to swallow. I'd known Barron since we were both kids. Stabler, I didn't know at all."

"Do you think the whole thing was a scam, or did someone get greedy and loot it before the company proved itself?" Paul asked.

Wick shrugged, his bulldog face flushed. "We'll never know. The mill never went into production. I know Everett Kent claimed he did assays showing the ore was worthless. How do you do dozens of assays showing gold and silver when there isn't any? But then, I'm not a mining man."

"Did you think about raising some more money and going through with the project?" Paul asked.

"Are you kidding? I'd have been run out of town."

I turned practical. "Who would have to cooperate in order to loot the corporate bank account?"

Wick shrugged. "Barron and Stabler, I guess. Don't really know."

AS WE returned to my downtown office Paul looked thoughtful. "Kinda cavalier, wasn't he?"

"Meaning…?"

"Sorta nonchalant about something so significant to him."

"Wick's never been one to sail close to the wind," I said. "If he went all out for VPMR, he must have believed in it."

"Sounded to me like he was trying to delete himself."

"Pardon?"

Paul fluttered a hand. "You know, fade into the shadows. If I got this straight, he's the one who put this over the top. At least with the investing public."

"True. And like he said, he paid a price for it."

When we arrived at the office, I was pleased to learn Hazel had succeeded in pulling together the investigative reports from the FBI, Treasury, Security and Exchange, and the local police. A staggering amount of paper-shuffling stared us in the face. Paul headed for the *Albuquerque Journal* on North Jefferson to discuss the story he'd filed as I settled down with the FBI report.

At the end of the day, we met and filled one another in on what we'd learned. Distilled down to the essence, while VPMR was heavy on technical know-how, there wasn't anyone paying much attention to the minutiae of administration. We'd learned a simple signature stamp gained entry into the firm's bank accounts. As often as not the stamp rested in someone's unlocked desk drawer.

Even so, the investigating authorities failed to come up with solid evidence of who was behind the looting of Voxlightner Precious Metals Recovery Corporation. They took the obvious—and easy—way out, concluding Barron Voxlightner and Walther Stabler were the perpetrators. They conducted a nationwide search for the two without finding either of the men. They simply vanished from the corporate headquarters of the company on Lomas Northeast on March 15, 2004. Not even their vehicles were located.

Tired of dealing with the problem, I sat back and regarded Paul. This man, whom I loved above all else, was throwing unconscious signals that puzzled me. He'd returned from the newspaper claiming his article was accepted with minimal edits, yet his attitude was different. I'd worried drudgery work would discourage Paul, and perhaps that was happening. I mentally shook my head. No. He'd sopped up everything we'd learned with a growing excitement.

That night despite Pedro's and my interest, we didn't manage to get anything started. While I lay on my side of the bed in disappointment, Paul snapped his fingers. "Just think. Somebody walked off with fifty mil. Just like that!"

"Not the entire fifty," I said. "They spent a few millions securing the tailing pile, leasing the mill, and the like."

"Okay," he acknowledged. "So it was only forty. That's a hell of a paycheck, even split two ways."

Chapter 7

THE NEXT morning as the sun went about its job of heating up the atmosphere—the calendar had turned to August yesterday—Paul and I went to Belhaven's place and found it a beehive of activity. The burned remains of a lawn mower and a few scorched panels from the attached garage lay on the driveway alongside a warped water heater. Carpenters bustled around repairing whatever the flames touched inside the garage. Spencer Spears stood in the middle of the activity without seeming to contribute to the effort. Observing and learning, I took it.

Aside from that, the whole Belhaven clan was gathering, most likely for the reading of the will, although its contents were pretty well known. Harris Belhaven and his sister, Melanie Harper, greeted us at the door. Upon entering we were introduced to Melanie's husband, Cagney, who shook hands with each of us with the short instruction to "call me Cag." Without much digging we confirmed he worked for the Bureau of Land Management at the El Malpais Visitor Center at Exit 85 off I-40 in Grants. We also picked up that he and his late father-in-law weren't on the best of terms. If I had to guess, I'd say it was because of Cagney's untamed woolly beard and mustache. Like what was left of his curly brown hair, they were prematurely graying. I put him at around my age.

No one voiced objections to our snooping in Pierce's office, so we went back to find Sarah Thackerson running her nimble fingers over the keyboard of a new Dell desktop computer. She greeted us somberly and felt moved to explain she was helping the family tie up a few of Mr. Belhaven's loose ends.

After politely acknowledging her presence, Paul and I once again tore apart Belhaven's inner sanctum. No piece of paper was too miniscule to escape scrutiny. Belhaven had a collection of old-fashioned tapes and cassettes, as well as some disks. When we went through all of them, at least superficially, the two halves of the dead man were clearly revealed. Many of the items were porn films, some heterosexual; others, gay. I vaguely wondered if somewhere there weren't films depicting a ménage à trois? Nonetheless the items confirmed—at least to me—that Belhaven was engaged in sexual relationships with both his secretary and his yard boy. A potentially messy arrangement.

After spending most of the day at the Belhaven house, it wasn't worth driving downtown to the office. I called Hazel for an update… which contributed nothing new to my store of knowledge. Thereafter Paul and I picked up an early dinner from a local restaurant and headed home. Paul was quiet during our meal. Jumpy. Drudge work does that to a man sometimes.

This time there was a payoff. Tonight Paul apparently wasn't so deeply entangled in the Voxlightner scandal and turned his attention to where Pedro and I both wanted.

DET. ROY Guerra paid me a visit at the office the next morning. Paul had gone to the county clerk's and assessor's offices to check public records for anything of interest. I handed over the report on the Voxlightner case I'd dictated to Hazel earlier. He scanned it.

"Interesting. But it doesn't tell us much we didn't already know."

"True. Nonetheless you've got to start somewhere."

"I've learned a little," Roy said. "It didn't take much effort to loot the company. Everyone concentrated on the fire assays, thinking if there was skullduggery, it would be there. The company's financial and administrative practices and controls were virtually nonexistent. It wouldn't be hard to slip in false invoices among the blizzard of expenses the firm was incurring. Things were moving so fast, management was scrambling to keep up with events."

"Nobody was looking out for the company's dead presidents," I suggested.

"Huh?" He looked at me blankly for a moment. "Oh. I see. You're hip to some old-timey jive. Money, you mean. At first the front office was doing what it was supposed to do. Paying for legitimate expenses. A gal by the name of Thelma Rider acted as office manager until she quit… before the scandal broke, I might add. From what I can gather, she was a good secretary but in over her head managing the entire office. She was just papering over cracks, especially when things were smoking."

I smiled at his payback for my slang. "Moving so fast, you mean. Do you have an address for her?"

"According to someone who worked with her, she lived somewhere in the Northeast Heights. One of the streets named after states. You know, like Colorado or Florida. The feds interviewed Rider," Roy went on. "Didn't seem to be interested in her."

"I understand APD handled the investigation of Everett Kent's murder."

"The lawyer who got whacked in his own office? Yeah. It went nowhere."

I demurred. "It went somewhere, all right. It ran right into the Voxlightner scandal and got twisted up in the mess. Easy to say Barron and Stabler were responsible, since they were tarred with all the other brushes."

Paul joined us at that point and dumped a pile of papers on the table. "Hi, Roy."

"Hey, man. Looks like you've been busy."

"Spent a fortune on photocopying and wore out my welcome in the clerk's and assessor's offices. From what I can see, it's about as useless as a teapot made out of chocolate. Maybe you guys can find something."

"What're you looking for?" Roy asked.

"Anything of public record on the major players," I answered. "And it looks like there's plenty."

Paul waved a hand over the pile. "Most of it's suits filed after the scandal blew up. Pissing in the wind for the most part. Someone even tried to sue old Marshall Voxlightner, and all he did was get taken like everyone else. I made duplicates for you, Roy."

"Thanks," the detective said. "I checked the courts like I promised. Came across a jacket or two, but most of the people involved were as clean as can be."

"Any arrests or complaints at all?" I asked.

"John Hightower had a jacket because he was suspected of being involved in the theft. Wick has a juvie record, but I didn't break into it to see what the problem was."

"Nothing since he was emancipated?" I asked.

"Nope. Kept his nose clean once he turned eighteen."

"But he was sued a lot after the company fell apart," Paul said.

"Successfully?" I asked.

"Nope. He was Teflon. Claimed he was taken like everyone else. Lost his shirt."

"So nobody tapped his pocketbook in court?"

Paul shook his handsome head. "Like I said. Teflon."

Roy pulled out notes from his attaché case. He was the only detective I'd ever seen lugging one around. "There was one person in the company with a record. The Thelma Rider I told you about."

"Who's she?" Paul asked.

"The so-called office manager. She had a record back in Chillicothe, Texas."

"For what?"

"Prostitution and petty theft. Overnight stuff. No real jail time. Chillicothe sent me a copy of the file."

"I'd like to talk to her."

"Start with the Chillicothe PD," Roy suggested.

When I opened the woman's file, a mousy, unattractive woman looked out of a police-blotter photo. To be fair most people were not particularly attractive in such circumstances.

Paul frowned. "Wonder where they found her? Wonder *who* found her?"

"Dunno," I said. "But maybe John Hightower can tell us."

"Where is he?" Paul asked.

"He left town as soon as the feds allowed him to go. But Hazel will find him for us." I turned to Roy. "Ricardo Quintana, the accountant for VPMR, told Paul and me that Stabler was involved in a scam before. Did you find a jacket on him?"

Roy shook his head. "Found some old newspaper articles about a Nevada scam. Lots smaller than VPMR. Peanuts really. Accusations got tossed around, but nothing came of it. So no jacket on Stabler."

HAZEL INDEED ran John Hightower to ground. He lived in the Tempe, Arizona, area, a bitter, premature old man at the age of fifty-three. Or that's the way he sounded on the telephone. Reluctant to relive those bad old days, he acted as if each question was a potential trap to drag him back into the nightmare. It took virtually an hour on the speakerphone for Paul and me to confirm most of what we already knew from talking to others. His sole contribution was that Barron hired Thelma Rider, the office manager. The way he remembered the incident, she was recommended to Barron by someone, but Hightower didn't know who.

I next contacted the Special Agent in Charge of the FBI task force that originally investigated the crimes, who proved to be an amiable stone waller. He confirmed many of the facts we'd gleaned from our investigation so far, tried to pick my brain, and contributed nothing new. His attitude made it clear he considered the case solved with the disappearance of

Voxlightner and Stabler. Roy later made available the information shared by the FBI with APD, and it amounted to bug dust.

Friday afternoon after touching base with all the numerous jurisdictions that participated in the investigation of VPMR, I holed up in my office. Before tackling the investigation, I thought about Paul for a moment. Had his attitude changed, or was it just my imagination? Last night had been terrific, as wonderful as ever. Even so things were different between us.

I got up and moved to the small mirror I used to make sure my tie was straight or my hair combed. A moderately good-looking man with apple-green eyes, what my mom called mocha hair—I considered it a peculiar color of brown—worn moderately long, and a sandalwood complexion stared back at me. I exercised and kept trim, but it was impossible for me to look through a younger man's eyes and measure attractiveness. I fingered the small lentigo on my right cheek and considered forcing the issue with him. No, let Paul be Paul. When he was ready, he'd bring it out in the open… whatever *it* was.

That out of the way, I sat back down, picked up my miniature Toledo blade letter opener, and began tapping the tip on my desk blotter. My typical mode of ruminating. My investigation—actually, Paul's and mine—had not turned up anything of consequence. The only thing new was the note in Belhaven's appointment book noting three separate electrical meter readings. I glanced at the calendar. We'd talked to Watson Moore at New Mexico Power and Light eight days ago, and he hadn't gotten back with us yet. I stifled the urge to dial his number. He was a reliable guy. As soon as he found the information, he'd call. Unless he'd taken a vacation or fallen ill or…. *Rein in your imagination, Vinson.* Watt was a responsible man. Give him time.

Despite Paul's and Roy's tunnel-visioned concentration on the events of 2003 and 2004 as the genesis of Belhaven's killing, I needed to keep an open mind. Even so I'd gone along with the decision to look at VPMR because of Mrs. Voxlightner's—Dorothy's—charge. I felt sort of like the old Roman god of household doorways who looked in both directions simultaneously, at the beginning and at the end. Janus was his name.

I dropped my letter opener and reached for the growing file on the case. After riffling through the papers—it's a good thing Hazel organized my files—I came up with the name of the defunct company's office manager. According to my notes, Thelma Rider returned to Chillicothe, Texas sometime before the scandal really broke. I tried the number Hazel located for her and found it disconnected. I raised a sergeant in the

Chillicothe Police Department who told me she died in an automobile accident in December 2010, about eight months ago.

"Anything suspicious about it?" I asked.

"Left a bar at midnight and took on an oak tree about fifteen minutes later."

The sergeant apparently knew Thelma—as he called her—and confirmed my impression of a rather quiet, timid woman. After she returned to the Texas town of her birth in late 2003, she lived on the family farm with her parents until they died. She continued living on the farm, although it went fallow after the parents passed on. She didn't work, but everyone in town knew Thelma had been the office manager of a big company out in New Mexico and figured she'd put away some money. Her dead father was known as a tight-fisted old cuss, so the townsfolk figured there was enough mattress money to sustain "the girl" in her sedate lifestyle. Her only extravagance seemed to be a weekly trip to a local bar, which everyone figured proved her undoing.

"Can you tell me the date and time of her death?" I asked the sergeant.

"Hold on. Have to pull the file."

A few minutes later he was back on the line. "Saturday, December 11. It probably happened after midnight, but the report reads Saturday. Nobody found her until later Sunday morning. Folks spotted the wreck on the way to church."

"She died immediately?"

"On the spot. Broke her neck. Wasn't a bad accident. Just enough to do the job."

"Autopsy?"

"Nothing suspicious, so there wasn't one."

"Will you send me whatever you can for the record?"

"What did you say you was investigating?"

"A murder up here tying back into the company she worked for."

"Guess she didn't have nothing to do with that," the officer said with an apparent attempt at humor.

"No but what happened up here might have something to do with her."

"What does that mean?"

"I'd take another look at the accident," I said before closing the call.

WATT MOORE rescued my day by phoning around four. After discussing the looming financial disaster facing the nation, he apologized for the delay in getting back to me. But he delivered gold—metaphorically speaking. "Sorry it took so long, BJ, but it required a good deal of effort to wade through everything and find what caught Belhaven's eye. The figures you gave me match readings for three months in 2003 at a residence at 2551 Georgia Street NE."

"Whose residence was it?"

"The account holder was a woman by the name of Sadie Burke. Spelled B-u-r-k-e."

"You know anything about her?"

"Nothing except…. Well, I'll be damned. She listed herself as a secretary at the old Voxlightner Precious Metals Recovery Corp. Looks like Pierce might have come up with a clue, after all."

"I'd say so. Do you know who owns the house on Georgia?"

"Sorry, can't help you."

"Don't worry, you already have. I can take it from here. Thanks, Watt."

By the time we closed the office an hour later, Hazel had not only located the current owner of the property on Georgia, but we also knew he had nothing to do with the scandal. He was a professor at UNM who'd moved to Albuquerque from Texas last year. Hazel learned the owner of the home from early 2003 through mid-2010 was an outfit called LMZ, a local real estate investment company. A REIT.

I dictated notes for the file while Hazel went about looking for Sadie Burke. Shortly before I snapped off my office light and prepared to go home, she stuck her head in the door.

"No luck finding Sadie Burke. The closest I can come is a fictional character in a book. I'll take another pass at it tomorrow."

"Thanks."

Chapter 8

PAUL AND I managed to get in a round of golf early Saturday morning at the North Valley Country Club, and it seemed like old times. The cloud I'd sensed between us dissipated in the hot sun. The club was blessed with a number of trees to provide shade, most of which I'd kissed with at least one white-dimpled ball.

We returned home after the round to the tragic news twenty-two Navy SEALs died in Afghanistan that day when their Chinook was shot out of the sky by insurgents. Some of them were part of SEAL Team Six that took down Osama bin Laden the previous May. Lord rest their souls.

On Sunday we dressed in our best casual clothes and attended services at the nondenominational Temple of Our Lord on High. We'd discovered the church last year when its minister, Bishop Justin Gregory, helped a friend caught up in the sex trafficking trade. The good bishop guided a great young man named Jazz Penrod through the difficult withdrawal from the crack cocaine his kidnappers hooked him on. Since that time I'd regularly supported the congregation with my tithes and occasionally my presence. Today my imagination ran away with me again. Paul seemed to sit a little farther from me in the pew than he usually did. He had never been able to totally expunge an unjustified jealousy toward the fetching Jazz.

BLACK MONDAY hit the stock market on August 8, 2011. The Dow Jones tumbled over 700 points after Standard and Poor's downgraded the United States' credit rating from AAA to AA+ because of reluctance of Congress to address the nation's credit limit problem. The action was the first time our rating took such a hit. Predictably the markets tumbled, exceeding the loss of the previous Friday. I had a little trouble dragging my mind back to matters at hand.

Roy Guerra wanted us to drive down to Socorro to interview Dr. Damon Herrera, the man who oversaw the fire assays for VPMR, but when Paul agreed to accompany him, I opted to pursue the Georgia Street lead.

I ran by the office to clear my desk—Hazel always had something for me to sign—before heading to LMZ on San Pedro NE. The manager of the

REIT was a man named Theodore Donaldson, a retired real estate broker, who got bored playing bridge and stepped in to manage an office for a group of investors who knew nothing about real estate. He claimed it was like herding cats but reckoned the mental agility required to deal with the group kept him from going stale. He had been a golfing partner of my dad's in years past. In my book he was one of the good guys on this earth.

"BJ," he boomed when I walked through the door.

"Ted, you old dog. Are you still kicking?"

"Kicking *and* biting."

After ten minutes of reliving golf shots—and my folks—we got down to business. "Ted, how far do your records go back? And how good are they?"

"Back to when we started twelve years ago, and better than most. Why?"

After I explained what I needed, he turned to a computer terminal on his desk and started his search, leaving me to examine my surroundings. The LMZ office was small, probably just Ted's cubbyhole and what looked to be a conference room behind a glass wall at the end of the room. The presence of only two file cabinets told me his records were automated, but a line of heavy black binders on a shelf to the right of his desk looked as if they held official documents. I wondered if there was one for each piece of property held by the trust.

Soon enough he found a file he wanted, grunted to himself, and retrieved one of the black binders. A few minutes later he adjusted his glasses and glanced at me.

"The trust bought the property, a two-bedroom stucco, in August of 1999. Good producer. Kept it rented until we sold it to a UNM prof in August of last year. Got a good price. Now let's see, you were interested in the first half of 2003."

"I understand you leased it to a woman named Sadie Burke during that period."

My statement brought a frown and a reexamination of something on the computer file. "The property was rented to some fellow named William Stark from March thru August 2003 on a six-month lease. *He* sublet it to the Burke woman."

"How long was the sublease?"

"May and June."

"Wonder why she didn't lease it herself?" I asked.

"Could be a number of reasons. This Stark fellow might have gone out of town for a spell but was coming back. She might not have needed a place long enough to sign a lease, and it was cheaper to sign a sublease with Stark. Month-to-month rentals are higher than leases, you know."

"Could they have lived there together?"

Ted scratched his chin over that one. "Coulda, but it would be a mighty strange arrangement, a fellow and his girl signing leases back and forth."

"What can you tell me about Stark?" I asked.

Ted fiddled with his glasses again and poked a few buttons on the machine. "Not much on the application. Seems he was a construction worker. There you go. That's probably the answer right there. Went out of town on a job and found a way to cover his rent while he was gone."

"Do you remember him?" I asked.

"That was before I came to work here. I'm an investor but didn't have anything to do with running the office until later." He punched another button. "Looks like another fellow subleased it from Stark after the Burke woman moved out. A fellow named Adam Stanton rented it for July and August 2003. Not much on him."

I collected what information I could on Stark and Stanton, including social security numbers and references. On the way back to the office, I puzzled over why the names Stark and Stanton sounded vaguely familiar. Neither name had shown up in the Voxlightner file before.

I handed over the information to Hazel when I got back to the office. She hadn't heard anything from Paul. But before I even got Stark's and Stanton's references called, she stuck her head in my door.

"Something's fishy. The social security numbers don't match."

"Which number?"

"Neither one of them."

The references turned out to be phony as well.

A little bell went off in my head. I googled both names and instantly understood why they seemed familiar. William Stark—or more likely Willie Stark—and Adam Stanton were characters in Robert Penn Warren's Pulitzer Prize winning novel, *All the King's Men*, based loosely on the life and death of the Kingfish, Governor Huey P. Long of Louisiana. Someone owned both a sense of history and humor.

I CONTACTED my old riding partner at APD and asked Gene to see if he could get the Chillicothe authorities to look into Thelma Rider's bank account. I was willing to bet they'd find regular payments from some source. She, or someone she knew, used her residence to fire assay some material. And somehow whatever they produced influenced the results of the School of Mines assays of the VPMR samples. So far as I was concerned, this answered Paul's question of whether or not the company would have survived on its own. If I was right and the test results were skewed by introducing outside material, the answer was no. Looting the company had been the goal all along.

This reasoning pointed a finger directly at Dr. Walther Stabler, but did it necessarily mean Barron Voxlightner was one of the conspirators? It's possible that wasn't the case at all. If so, then logic argued Barron was really dead, not just legally dead.

My poking around in the trash pile of history told me the prime mover behind VPMR was Wick Pillsner, not Barron Voxlightner. He brought Stabler to Albuquerque, put him together with Barron and his investors, and induced old man Voxlightner to invest, thereby lending his considerable reputation to the venture.

Yet it was hard to see how Wick had prospered from the scam. He traded his sweat for stock, a considerable amount, but it turned to ashes like everyone else's. His reputation took a hit. Even so he stayed where he was and worked for years to overcome the humiliation and rebuild his business. Today he was a successful entrepreneur and well-respected among Albuquerqueans. How did he survive such a blow to his business solar plexus? *By stealing the money, killing Voxlightner and Stabler, and pinning it on them?*

I called Gene back and talked him into taking a look into Wick's bank accounts as well. Why did I call him for these sorts of things? So he and Detective Guerra could put their heads together and figure out probable cause, tying it into the APD investigation of the murder of John Pierce Belhaven.

Because the jump in electrical usage in the spring of 2003 at 2551 Georgia NE was Pierce Belhaven's lynchpin to solving the old scam, I decided to visit the address. A middle-aged woman losing the battle to keep her hair blonde, answered my ring and listened to my spiel but said she'd feel more comfortable acceding to my request if her husband were home. I agreed to come back around six and took my leave. Already halfway there I aimed the nose of the Impala for home and arrived in time to see Detective Guerra's departmental Ford pull away from the curb.

My one true love got pumped when I told him what I'd learned about the Georgia Street address. He needed the uptick because he considered his trip to Socorro a bust. Dr. Herrera was as reluctant to talk about old times as most of the people we'd encountered, but he was adamant nobody could have fiddled with the tests. He'd taken the time and effort to pull up the test results for VPMR and make copies. Herrera also reviewed the security procedures practiced at the time, and Paul agreed they seemed adequate.

Once Paul rushed through the telling, he turned back to the results of my day. "So how do we run down Willie Stark and his henchman, Adam Stanton?"

"As I recall the book, Stanton was Stark's nemesis, not his henchman. I believe Dr. Stanton assassinated the governor in the halls of the capitol for disgracing the doctor's sister."

"And it was based on a real dude?" Paul asked.

"The author took his inspiration from the life of Huey P. Long, a real-life governor of Louisiana in the 1930s. Long was quite a character, just like Warren's Willie Stark. Long served out his term as governor even after he was elected to the US Senate."

"Vince," Paul said, "your penchant for history is showing. But Louisiana?"

"If Long hadn't been assassinated in 1935, he might have given Franklin Roosevelt a run for his money in the '36 presidential election."

"So how do we figure out who *our* Stark and Stanton really are?"

"Follow the money. Somebody real, not characters in a book, paid rent on the house on Georgia." I smashed a fist against my chair arm. "Son of a bitch!"

"What is it?" Paul asked, his eyes as round as washers.

"Sadie Burke."

"The woman who sublet on Georgia Street?"

"I should have remembered when Hazel told me all she could find was a fictional Sadie Burke."

"Don't tell me. She's out of *All the King's Men* too."

"Exactly. Now I'm curious. Do you remember Wick Pillsner telling us the night Voxlightner and Stabler disappeared, he stopped by the office and found that Barron had discovered some phony accounts?"

"Several, he said."

"I want to take a look at those records. Maybe some other Robert Penn Warren characters show up."

PROFESSOR DIGGS, the present owner of the home on Georgia Street, generously allowed Paul and me to go through his home later in the day.

Once he understood why we were interested, he became curious over the details of a scam that took place in his home before he arrived in Albuquerque.

"That might explain the 220-volt wiring in the garage," he said, leading us into the attached area. Sure enough there were several 220-volt outlets. "And maybe you can tell me what this gizmo is," he added as he pulled down a receding ladder concealed in the ceiling. He took a few steps up, grasped something in the storage area, and handed it down to Paul.

I didn't know what the rusted, rectangular piece of metal was, but it looked as if it had been exposed to considerable heat. It resembled an outsized grate to an electric grill. After examining the item for a few minutes, I used my handkerchief to lift the thing and prop it against the wall. The professor agreed not to touch it again until Detective Guerra could pick it up. Diggs admitted he and his wife both handled the piece of metal and agreed to fingerprinting for elimination purposes. Paul would need to do the same.

Declining a cup of coffee or tea from the now-friendly homeowners, we returned home. That Paul was pleased with what we'd accomplished today became clear when he allowed Pedro to prowl. Even so, something seemed different.

"Paul…?"

"I'm worn out, Vince. Can we talk tomorrow?"

Chapter 9

BUT WE didn't talk the next morning. Paul left early for another conference with the *Journal* editor, and Gene got permission for Roy Guerra and me to visit the local FBI headquarters to go over the VPMR accounting ledgers still in their custody. These had been referenced in the FBI reports I'd already seen, but I wanted a chance to review the financial transactions myself. We ended up examining a stack of records in a stark, uncomfortable little room I figured was used to grill suspects.

Neither Roy nor I were accountants, but after tracing a couple of invoices through the books, I understood the system Richard Quintana had set up for the company was pretty traditional. It had some fail-safe and backup procedures, but what humans can invent, humans can circumvent. The first thing I noticed was that many of the invoices were presented by "Sadie Burke" and given the final okay by Thelma Rider. Burke habitually used blue ink; Rider, green. I took a closer look at the handwriting. Was it the same? Close, but I couldn't be certain. I surreptitiously slipped an invoice for servicing the company's water cooler into my pocket. Gloria McInnes down at K-Y Labs could do a handwriting analysis for me. As a double-check, I filched three more minor invoices for comparison purposes.

Armed with a list of characters from *All the King's Men* Hazel had prepared, I soon found some of the phony invoices. A $10,000 invoice to Sugar Boy Equipment Rentals was undoubtedly named after the faithful, stuttering Willie Stark bodyguard identified only as Sugar Boy. The A. Stanton Equipment Company was probably named after Anne Stanton, Stark's sometime mistress and sister of his killer. The Stanton invoice for $125,000 was countersigned by Jack Hightower, the general manager. This gave me pause for a moment until I thought of my own office procedure. I okayed anything Hazel put before me. A man busy organizing the transportation of five million tons of tailings, locating and building a processing plant, and overseeing a horde of other chores likely relied on his office manager in a similar manner. Irwin Services and Littlepaugh Industrial Chemicals were suspect as well, since they were also characters out of Warren's book.

THE NEXT morning Gene phoned to say the APD lab confirmed the rusted piece of metal found in the attic on Georgia Street was from an electric furnace, probably accidentally left behind when the device was dismantled and removed from the premises. Aside from the professor's and Paul's, two other sets of fingerprints were identifiable, and a third was smudged so badly it was of no value. The identifiable prints were Dr. Walther Stabler's and Thelma Rider's. So far as I was concerned, we'd located the residence of Thelma and identified her as the mythic Sadie Burke. This raised the question of why Hightower or anyone else working in the office at VPMR failed to notice an employee who logged in invoices was never around.

I placed a call to Richard Quintana and found the answer. "Never met the lady. Sent her lots of stuff and received some. She worked from her home. I was their CPA, not their bookkeeper, but I was on-site more than for most of my clients. VPMR wasn't very well organized."

"So I gathered. Let me guess, Burke lived at 2551 Georgia Street."

"Fits with what I remember, all right. But she didn't stay long. Moved somewhere, I believe."

I took a shot in the dark. "I understand Thelma Rider lived at the Georgia Street address too."

"Don't really know the answer but seems like I recall someone saying they bunked together."

"Would the date Burke left be about the same time Thelma Rider resigned from the company?"

"I believe Thelma stayed on a month or so longer than Sadie. Is this significant?" A wisp of hope tinged his voice.

"Possibly. Just trying to run down the facts."

After hanging up, I sat for a moment wondering how soon Gloria at K-Y Labs would get back to me. There was little question in my mind the two women were one, but she could ice the cake by verifying the two signatures were made by the same hand.

In response to a phone call, Zachary Greystone invited me over to his law office at Greystone and Hastings LLC. As it wasn't a long walk to the law firm, I exited my building by the Fifth Street door, crossed the street, and walked east on Tijeras to the First Plaza Galleria on Third. Greystone had cued his receptionist, so she ushered me into his office without delay. He rose from his black leather, high-back executive chair to shake my hand.

"Been expecting you, BJ." He indicated an overstuffed chair in the corner of his spacious office and joined me on a small settee positioned at right angles to my chair. A svelte blonde entered with a tray holding a coffee carafe and a teapot. I chose tea, which she poured before fixing her boss a well-creamed coffee.

"I heard you're stirring up all the old Voxlightner mess," Zach said after he nodded his thanks and the secretary withdrew.

"Mrs. Voxlightner asked me to take a look."

"Heard Belhaven thought he turned up a vital clue that would reveal all."

"So I understand," I said.

"Have you found it?"

"His notes were stolen, and his computers destroyed the night he was killed. So we have little to go on."

"The fact he was murdered in his own home must mean he was onto something. Hope you can find it. What can I do for you?"

For the next thirty minutes, Zach reviewed what he knew about the scam, spending too much time—as did most of them—on his personal loss and humiliation. After his lawyer's mind was convinced Barron and Walther were onto something valuable, he actively promoted the public offering.

Zach confirmed the accuracy of most of what I knew but contributed little else. He knew Barron hired Thelma Rider after someone—he thought Wick or Hightower—recommended her. He recalled she left the company in January 2004 to return home to care for a terminally ill parent. Of Sadie Burke, he knew nothing at all.

Upon exiting the building, I got through to Newton Williamson at the Northeast Heights National Bank, which, contrary to its name, sat on the downtown corner of Second and Central NE, a short distance from where I was. He told me to come on over.

After we were seated in his office, Newt groused a little more than most about recalling unpleasant history. He was entitled. He had been the bank vice president in charge of the VPMR account. An account from which a large amount of money scooted out the back door, so to speak. I had no doubt there were plenty of red flags along the way, but somehow they'd not been called to his attention quickly enough. His contribution to my store of knowledge was three large wire transfers to foreign bank accounts. There had been a fourth, but by then, Newt was aware something was going on and managed to stop it, preventing the loss of an additional $5,000,000. I suspected his obvious reluctance to relive the situation grew from his belief he should have been on the ball and blown the whistle on the company's shenanigans. As was true of everyone else I'd spoken to, he still found it hard to believe Barron Voxlightner was a part of the scheme. Nonetheless he accepted the general verdict that his friend was guilty.

On my return to the office I was tempted to cross Tijeras and stroll the civic plaza with its lattice-covered walkways and gushing fountain. I resisted and arrived back at my desk in time to take Gloria McInnes's call. The signatures of Sadie Burke and Thelma Rider were made by the same hand.

"She was good, BJ. Almost a professional, you could say. But everyone here agrees the signatures were executed by the same person."

I thanked Gloria and hung up. A little more progress. But where was it leading? Too soon to say.

Chapter 10

THAT EVENING—AFTER Paul let Pedro roam and play to the point of exhaustion—we lay side by side in bed as our breathing slowed. Everything seemed so normal I was loath to explore our feelings at the moment.

Paul spoke into the darkness. "I checked the intruder lights this afternoon. They're in good order."

"Good to know. What prompted you to check them?"

"Just seemed like a good idea. When Pierce started poking into things, somebody offed him, so…."

"True. But there are two of us, and we're in better physical shape than Belhaven. Not so old."

"If you're saying there's no danger, that's a whole 'nother thing."

I thought before I responded. In the faint glow of the bathroom nightlight, I contemplated Paul's pleasing profile as he lay on his back and almost choked at the thought something might go wrong between us. "You're right to be cautious. And it's careless of me not to feel threatened." I paused again. "But you know, I don't. Not once have I felt in danger."

"They say that's when you're most vulnerable."

"True. Thanks for reminding me."

The room got quiet again, although I knew he wasn't asleep. Then he confirmed it. "Do you think I should get a carry permit?"

"If you'll feel safer with a weapon, why not?" I asked.

"Guess I could."

I didn't know the decision Paul reached because he dropped off. Comfortable in the warmth of his presence, I should have followed him quickly, but he'd made me consider I was putting him in jeopardy again by involving him in my case. Not so. This was his case as much as mine. He'd determined to investigate his friend's death as a journalist; taking me along with him was coincidental. He was in it, danger or no.

And then there was that unknown thing hovering between us. I've said many times a good investigator needs at least a small dose of paranoia, and that might be all it was. But I didn't think so. Paul wasn't a touchy, feely sort of guy, but at home he found occasion to touch me.

A hand on mine, an arm draped over my shoulder, that sort of thing. But this was absent now. I wasn't sure when some gulf, imaginary or real, opened, but it was slowly penetrating my consciousness.

I WAS more interested in pursuing the new lead than I was in rummaging around in more of the old stuff, so I prevailed upon Ted Donaldson to drag out the real estate investment trust's old records and discovered "Willie Stark," "Adam Stanton," and "Sadie Burke" paid rent with money orders. Stores selling the orders—and certainly the post office—required proper ID from purchasers of such instruments, so that argued they went to the trouble and expense of creating fake identification papers. Not too hard a chore in this day of electronic machines. And the payoff was certainly worth the expense.

Surveillance photos? Undoubtedly there had been some, but who would keep them for eight years? Worth a try, but probably a dead end like everything else so far.

One thing puzzled me. Why had "Adam Stanton" sublet the property after the so-called Sadie Burke left? If the conspirators finished creating the substitute prills for the tests, why did they need another sublessee? Time to sit back and sort out a few things.

Thelma Rider was obviously Sadie Burke. Her role in everything was rapidly becoming clear. She was needed to introduce and approve phony invoices when the gang—and I now considered it a gang—was nibbling around the edges of the Voxlightner company. She also provided the place where the substitute prills were created. Why not lease the place in her own name? Two reasons. She needed an address for the nonexistent employee, Burke, and she didn't want her name on anything to do with an address where exorbitant electrical usage might someday be of significance in a criminal case. But nothing in her background argued she possessed the technical know-how to fire assay ore.

Dr. Walther Stabler was either William Stark or Adam Stanton. The temptation was to say he was Stark, the original lessee of the house. But I sensed a subliminal presence. A bigger, more organized phantom brain moving all the players like a chessmaster. Stabler was key, but the shadowy image I perceived was local. He knew who to touch, who to avoid, and how to approach people. This description fit Barron Voxlightner to a T, but it also neatly matched the mover and shaker Hardwick Pillsner. Barron fled—or at least disappeared—while Wick stayed to face the music. Did that mean anything?

But why the two subleases. Burke's made sense. Why the one in the name of Stanton? Thelma Rider's sudden departure caught the others by surprise, that's why. *The mastermind behind the plot wanted distance between himself and the activities at Georgia Street.* And he wasn't finished at the stucco house on Georgia. Why? More assays to make certain they had enough? Time to dismantle and get rid of the equipment necessary to conduct the fire assays? Had the intense heat damaged the garage, requiring repair and cover-up work? All of this rang true to me.

Then something hit me… right between the eyes, so to speak. If Barron was the mastermind behind the scam, he intended to disappear and live out his life in some foreign paradise. Why put the extra layer between himself and the other schemers? I began to think like almost everyone else I'd talked to about the scandal. Barron Voxlightner was not that kind of man.

I made a few photocopies, thanked Ted for his help, and headed back to the office where I dictated a memo of my findings before picking up the telephone and dialing the Chillicothe, Texas, Police Department.

I ended up speaking to Philip Anderson, the same sergeant I'd spoken to a few days earlier. He heard me out and asked a dozen questions that told me he owned a brain, despite his whiskey voice. He then summed up the situation.

"You've found evidence Thelma was mixed up in the brouhaha over there in Albuquerque even though the feds told me she was clear of it. And now you want me to reopen her accident case because you believe her coconspirators out there killed her to shut her up?"

"That's it in a nutshell."

"Why would they wait this long? She didn't plow into the oak until last December. That's what? Five or six years after your case blew up. Why kill her then? She kept her mouth shut."

"What's the most likely reason, Sergeant?"

"Money," he said after a pause. "She was trying to tap someone for a bigger piece."

"That's the most likely motive. Will you take a deeper look into the woman? Bank accounts, phone records, anything that might help us?"

"Yeah. Seems like it's worth a shot. She doesn't have any relatives still living, so getting her exhumed shouldn't be much of a problem."

After the call I felt I owed my client an update. Dorothy Voxlightner listened to my careful explanation to the end without comment. "I'll send this to you in writing, Dorothy, but I felt it was time to touch base with you."

"Thank you. Although you didn't say it aloud, I sense you question Barron's position in all this mess."

"I have some doubts about his involvement, ma'am. They're mostly cerebral without much to back them up."

"I hear you have good instincts. But that's depressing as well as reassuring, isn't it?"

"Yes, ma'am. If we're both right and Barron wasn't involved in the rip-off, then…."

"Then he's dead," she finished for me. A deep sigh followed. "I would prefer to have my son alive and innocent. I fear this is not possible, so I will settle for the other conclusion." With that she murmured her thanks and hung up the telephone.

Chapter 11

REFERRING TO notes I'd made about money orders used to pay rent at LMZ, I plodded through five useless calls to Walmart and Smith's Food and Drug in search of more information, namely a video of the purchaser. Mostly, I got horselaughs. Who keeps videos for eight years? The last call—the one I almost didn't make because I was losing what little hope I had—restored my faith in plodding.

"I got a whole bin full of tapes, mister," a bored voice at a minimart inside a corner gas station said. "Some of them might go back that far. Welcome to come root around if you want."

"Be right over," I said. "Who do I ask for?"

"Bud. I'm the only guy here today."

I reviewed my belief that every confidential investigator must have the patience of Job plus Job's grandfather as I tore out of my office's parking lot and headed for Bud's Minimart and Gas. The only rain we'd been blessed with thus far during our monsoon season merely dampened the streets without the need for windshield wipers. A high established itself above the state and stayed there, which precluded the flow of moisture from either the Gulf of Mexico or the Gulf of California… until today. I drove through a downpour to the gas station on San Pedro NE.

Bud proved to be Bud Abbott—not the old comedian we watched on late-night reruns of reruns—but the owner of the mart. He was heavy, florid, and slow-moving. But his head was screwed on right. He asked who I was and why I wanted the tapes before conducting me back to the stockroom area, where he opened a bin and waved to a jumbled pile of tapes.

"Dunno if it's got what you want. Whenever I need a new tape, I grab one and tape over what's already on it."

"How long do you keep those new tapes handy?"

"Keep three months' worth behind the counter, then they get dumped into the bin. Or if I get lazy, I just tape over those. Word of warning. I used to date-label them in ink but haven't for the last few years."

"So if there's something from back in '03, it's probably got a label?" I asked.

He wiggled a hand back and forth. "Chances are pretty good."

"Whether or not you labeled the plastic cover, the tapes themselves are date and time stamped, right?"

"You got it. Anyway have at it."

Have at it, I did. I emptied the bin hoping to get to the older tapes, but Bud had obviously rooted around in the container a couple of times himself, so there was no logical order. I ended up making two stacks: those with a label, and those without. After an hour of searching, I came up with a tape for July 2003. According to my notes, Adam Stanton paid his sublease to LMZ on the third of July with a money order from Bud's Minimart and Gas. With Bud's help I viewed the tape and found an image of Dr. Walther Stabler purchasing a money order on the first of July. Bingo! Stabler was Stanton. But who was Stark? My earlier search of LMZ's files told me Stark never purchased a money order at Bud's Minimart to pay his rent, so my task here was done.

I'd pinned down two of the three lessees of the Georgia address, but the third—the most important—still eluded me.

When I left the station, the rain clouds had cleared away, and a bright sun was hard at work drying out the wet concrete and asphalt.

PAUL HAD spent the day with Roy Guerra, and I gathered from the review of their activities, the two of them devoted more time to educating Paul in police procedures than in pursuing the case itself. Even so, this would prove to be invaluable to my companion in the future.

The next day, a Saturday, Paul and I drove to the Smith's Food and Drug on North Fourth, which I'd managed to pin down as the place Stark purchased his money order for the first month's rent on the Georgia Street address. A polite inquiry at the customer service desk almost got us laughed out of the place, but I persisted and learned the former assistant manager, a man named Abner Brown, often worked the service desk back in 2003.

Unfortunately—for me at least—Brown had transferred to the store on Freedom Boulevard in Provo, Utah. The helpful clerk even looked up the telephone number for me. Alas, Mr. Brown left Smith's Food and Drug last year to take employment with a competitor in Las Vegas. No. They didn't know how or where to reach him. I confirmed the man's name as Abner R. Brown and turned once again to the clerk.

"Sorry," the kid facing us from behind the counter said. "We don't keep tapes that long, but we'll have a record of the purchase. They're all on the computer, so I might be able to find the one you're looking for."

I took in the young man staring back at us and knew at once he'd like nothing better than to play with his company's computer. "Be obliged if you'll give it a shot. We're looking for a money order purchased in late April or early May, sold to a William Stark."

"How much was it for?"

"Seven hundred and fifty dollars."

"Don't happen to have the MO number do you?"

I took a look at my photocopy and cited a number for him.

He futzed and mumbled and uttered an expletive or two but eventually gave us a thumb's up. "Got it. Everything matches, and…." He let that hang there for a moment as he poked a few more buttons. "Yup, Abner Brown was the guy who sold it to him."

Paul and I thanked the young man and headed for the Impala. "We'll let Hazel run down Abner Brown for us," I said as we sped up North Fourth on the way home.

"Why bother? How in the hell could a man remember one in a zillion money orders he's sold since May 2003? That's what… eight years ago?"

"And change," I acknowledged. "But it's a lead, so you run it down no matter how improbable."

Paul wanted to work off some nervous energy, so we changed clothes and headed for the tennis complex at the North Valley Country Club. One court was vacant, and he spent an hour and a half humiliating me. My boy was charged up. Was it something personal or just his competitive nature?

HAZEL LOCATED Abner Brown by noon Monday. He now worked as the manager of the Albertson's Mission Center store in Las Vegas, Nevada. She confirmed he was on shift today and gave me the telephone number of the store. I always place my own calls. It smacks of arrogance to me for Hazel to get an individual on the other end and then ask him to waste his time waiting for me to come on the line. I dialed and punched the conference call button, allowing Paul to listen in.

We waited while the automated operator ran through a list of options available to any caller until finally, a human voice answered and asked us to hang on again. After five minutes Brown answered his end of the call. From his voice I pictured a short, brusque man. I didn't wait for him to express his impatience. "Mr. Brown, this is B. J. Vinson in Albuquerque. I'm a confidential investigator. We've had a murder up here, and I'm chasing down leads."

"Oh. Who got murdered?"

"Local author named John Pierce Belhaven."

"The mystery writer? I've read a couple of his books. Who killed him?"

"That's what we're trying to find out. Now I'm going to ask you to do the impossible. I want you to think back to May 1, 2003 and tell me who bought money order number 881166515 from the Smith's store on North Fourth here in Albuquerque."

"Hell, Smith's can look that up for you."

"They already have. But I happen to know the fellow they claim bought it, didn't. I was hoping you might pull a hat trick out for us and tell me who he really was."

"Who does Smith's say it was?"

"A man named William Stark."

The line went dead for a moment. "Who did you say you were?"

"A licensed confidential investigator named B. J. Vinson."

"You the cop that got shot? Probably about that same time."

"A year later. May the tenth of '04, as a matter of fact. You have a good memory."

"Now I'm going to surprise the crap out of you. I do remember selling that money order."

I felt my eyebrows twitch. "You do? Why?"

"It's kinda odd. You know we sell orders with just the dollar amount on them. The buyer fills out the payee and his own name. But we do require ID and enter the name of the purchaser in a log. And that day—"

"May 1, 2003."

"Could be. Sounds right. Anyway I sold this money order to a fellow I recognized. But the name he gave me wasn't the name I knew him by. When I called him on it, he said he was buying it for this guy Stark and insisted I put Stark's name down in the log."

"Did you do it?" Paul asked.

"Yep. But I made a note of the real purchaser too."

"Who was the real customer?" I asked.

"Hardwick Pillsner."

"Are you positive, Mr. Brown?"

"Absolutely. Seen his face plastered over the newspaper a hundred times. Especially after what happened in the Voxlightner thing."

"Why didn't you inform the authorities at the time?"

He let out a breath, rattling the phone. "Didn't connect them, I guess. And nobody ever came around asking questions."

"You're positive enough to testify to this in court? And by the way I have a recording of our conversation."

"Well, sure, if my testimony's needed. My civic duty, right?"

"Absolutely," I said before thanking him and closing the call.

Bingo! Wick Pillsner is William Stark.

A familiar tingle swept through me, confirming we'd had a major breakthrough in the case.

WE'D IDENTIFIED the three players in Pierce Belhaven's much-vaunted clue about electrical meter readings. Now what to do with the information? I certainly wasn't going to rush over to Wick's office and confront him with what I'd learned. Paul and I walked the short distance to the police station after I alerted Gene we were coming. Roy Guerra sat waiting for us outside his lieutenant's office.

The two cops heard us out before listening to the recording I'd made of our conversation with Brown.

Gene leaned back in his chair and rubbed his nose. "Hard to see how Wick profited."

"Profited?" Paul asked. "There was forty million or so missing before that rip-off was over."

"Did Wick's lifestyle change?" Gene asked. "Any indication he got filthy rich all of a sudden?"

"Well…." Paul had no answer.

"He survived a hard blow to his business," I said. "That was a while back, but I don't recall him starving and walking around in rags. He had income from somewhere."

Gene was still hesitant. "The feds took a hard look at him, including his finances. They didn't find anything."

"If it were me, I'd wait until the spotlight was turned off before I started spending stolen money. Wick's still relatively young. Fifty to fifty-five, I'd guess."

Roy consulted his pocket notebook. “Fifty-five. How long would you wait to claim some of the ill-gotten gains?”

I thumped the calendar on Gene’s desk. “Seven years seems like a reasonable time. Leaves him plenty of years to enjoy retirement, go on vacations, buy tropical islands, and do all the good stuff.”

“If that was the plan,” Gene said, “Belhaven put a size twelve boot right in the middle of it by stirring up the scandal again. And it can’t have escaped Wick you’re questioning everyone all over again, including him.”

A uniform knocked on Gene’s door and handed a slip of paper to Roy.

The detective sat straight up in his chair. “Son of a bitch! Dr. Herrera’s dead!”

“Who?” Gene asked.

“Damon Herrera, the guy down at the School of Mines who conducted the Voxlightner fire assays. Killed in a mugging on the street in Socorro last night.”

A chill ran down my spine. Someone was closing doors behind himself. I’d seen it as a Marine MP, as an APD detective, and as a confidential investigator. My glance swept Paul. Why the hell had I taken him with me to interview Pillsner?

“Should we warn Brown in Las Vegas?” I asked.

“Damn, do you think Wick will even remember Brown?”

“You willing to risk his life on Wick’s memory of events eight years ago?”

Gene reached for the phone. “I’ll call Las Vegas PD.”

Chapter 12

TIME BLURRED with activity. Despite the breakthrough we'd accomplished in identifying the three Georgia Street conspirators, we were now more or less dependent upon other jurisdictions to do the on-site interviewing.

Sergeant Anderson in Chillicothe convinced his superiors to take another look at Thelma Rider's fatal accident and concluded something wasn't right about it. A fresh look at tire markings at the crash site indicated her car had come to a complete halt before accelerating into the tree that supposedly killed her. A review of her bank account revealed a monthly deposit of $5,000 from an offshore bank, yet her balance grew only moderately because of withdrawals. She was a quiet loner; her one night a week at a local bar being her sole extravagance. What did she do with her money?

It turned out she did have family, after all. A nephew inherited her house and personal property. The young man hadn't changed anything in the dwelling except to replace an uncomfortable mattress and store the heavy, lumpy, queen-sized pad in the shed out back of the house. He was as astounded as everyone else when Anderson cut open the mattress cover and found it stuffed with hundred-dollar bills. Thelma evidently wanted her security close at hand. According to Anderson, $1,000,000 in $100 bills weighed around twenty-two pounds.

Anderson looked for a recent connection with Wick Pillsner and came up with nothing. Phone records showed no call to or from Wick, and Anderson identified all the numbers stored in her phone as local. The postal service couldn't provide evidence of mail contact. Her computer revealed no email to or from Wick or anyone else in New Mexico. She could have deleted such messages, but her provider, Gmail, after a tussle over confidentiality, confirmed no messages to or from New Mexico since she left Albuquerque sometime in June or July 2003. She was involved in the Voxlightner scandal all right but seemed to be a dead end so far as linking to the other conspirators.

My business partner, Charlie Weeks, learned Pillsner and his wife visited her family in Dallas a good part of last December, including the weekend of the eleventh when Rider was killed. Wick took short flights from Dallas during that time, but none showed flight plans for the Texas panhandle.

The Socorro PD quickly reached the conclusion Dr. Damon Herrera's death wasn't what it seemed at first, but there was little to support their suspicions. The good doctor had gone to a local market for groceries and was attacked upon the return to his car. His watch, ring, cell phone, and wallet were all missing—appropriate to a street mugging. He had been killed by a blow to the head, delivered by something like a wrench. When Gene asked Socorro PD to check, they found $1,000,000 equally divided among three of the prof's mattresses. His wife and children professed not to know they had been sleeping on riches. Once again, there was no evidence of contact with Wick.

That proved nothing. Socorro was only an hour's drive south of Albuquerque, so it wouldn't have been difficult to slip down there and back, but there was no way to determine Wick's whereabouts at any given time without alerting him to our interest. Gene wasn't willing to tip our hand at this point, although I argued Wick was already on the alert if he was cleaning up after himself.

Upon reflection it seemed to me that Rider's murder—if it was murder—was off-kilter. We weren't poking around in the Voxlightner thing back in December, although Belhaven probably was. The entry in his journal detailing three months of unusual electrical readings on Georgia Street was made sometime in September or October 2003, if I remembered right. When had he recognized the significance of them? What prompted his recollection of the readings? With nothing left of his notes, there was no way to know. Or was there?

I dialed the Belhaven house, and the woman I wanted to speak to picked up the phone. "Hoped you'd still be working there," I said to Sarah Thackerson.

"Won't be for much longer," she said. "About to get all Pierce's affairs wrapped up and delivered to the attorney."

"I know we discussed this before, but I'd like you to think about it again. Do you know what caused Belhaven to recall those old meter readings and understand their significance?"

An exasperated sigh came over the line. "I've already told you I can't. I've thought about it a great deal lately, and I can't come up with anything."

"Do you remember where you were and what you were doing when he mentioned it to you?"

Sarah took her time and talked herself through the last few weeks. Her mumbling sharpened into speech. "We were here in the office. He'd asked me to do a lot of research on fire assaying, you know, the equipment and the process. I recall he said something." The line was silent for another moment. "He said, 'It's electric? How about that, it's electric! That's what he meant.' And that was all. I asked him about it, but he said he'd put two and two together and came up with four. He talked like that sometimes."

"Thank you. That helps a lot." As an afterthought I asked if Spencer Spears was still around.

"Oh yes, the family needs to keep the grounds up until they decide whether or not to sell."

I hung up, pleased with the call. I now knew what triggered Belhaven's memory. He'd learned the equipment required for a fire assay was electrical. And it surprised him, as it had me.

Then reality grabbed me by the collar again. Okay, so Belhaven figured out the reason for the excessive residential electrical usage. But how had he determined who the real lessees of the residence were? Bud Nelson at Bud's Minimart and Gas on San Pedro hadn't mentioned anyone else looking for the same thing I was. Nor had Brown, the former service counter attendant at Smith's Food and Drug. No, Belhaven made the identification another way. Perhaps through the power and light company where he worked. Had he taken the next step? The one I was searching for?

About that time Paul and Det. Roy Guerra bustled into my office. They'd been to Socorro to consult with SPD on Herrera's death.

"Wow, Vince, do you know what a million bucks in $100 bills looks like?"

"Like power, I'd guess."

"And how!"

"Learn anything new?"

"Not much. Just eliminating things, mostly. If the Rider woman hadn't been killed last December, I'd write this off as a mugging gone wrong," Roy said. "Because of the money we found, and the fact two people died less than a year apart, I'm convinced they were partners in crime, but damned if I know what sparked their killing. Hell, the killer didn't even try to recover the money. And the money's what ties them together."

"Hit and run," I said. "The killer didn't want to spend one second more with his victims than he needed to. Kill them and get out. That's what he did. If it's what we think it is, the killer's got his own millions stowed away."

"Wonder if Wick Pillsner would let us take a look at his mattress?" Paul joked.

"Why stuff money in a mattress? It doesn't do anyone any good there," Roy put in. "And while a million bucks is a lot, it doesn't seem like much considering what was looted from VPMR.

"It isn't. My guess is this was just security money. Most of VPMR's funds went overseas, so Rider and Herrera both probably had more to come. I'm convinced they reached an agreement not to touch a dime of the overseas loot until enough time passed to take the heat off," I said.

"That must be it," Paul said.

"Belhaven punching the beehive panicked someone. Presumably Wick. He had to make sure the others didn't act precipitously. He was trying to stop Rider and Herrera from surfacing the money. They must have worked out a plan to make sudden wealth appear to be legitimate. An inheritance, a business investment. Something." I sat back in my chair and sighed in exasperation. "All of that argues the conspirators were in contact with one another. But we can't find any evidence. In Rider's case, she lived the existence of a hermit."

Roy spoke up. "Couldn't find any evidence of Herrera being in regular contact with Pillsner… and not at all with Rider."

"What did you find linking Herrera with Wick?" I asked.

"An invitation to Wick's Christmas party last year. Look hard enough, and we'll probably find he was invited every year. Him and about a hundred others. By the way, Socorro let us look around in Herrera's computers."

I glanced at Paul. "Yeah," he said. "I roamed around his work computer and his personal laptop. Nothing. And I checked his trash bin too. He probably deleted messages from there."

"True, but his provider could likely reconstruct the traffic, if not the messages."

"That's assuming they'll cooperate. They're pretty secretive."

"All the internet providers fight subpoenas like they're strychnine," Roy said.

"Still," Paul said, "if the bad guys kept in contact, it's likely through computers. We just need to figure out how, and I've got an idea or two."

THE NEXT morning before I left for the office, Paul downloaded something called TeamViewer to my home computer. Once that was done, he asked me to activate the program and give him control of my computer. By providing a code and password furnished by the program, I complied.

Soon the background on my screen went black, and Paul moved my cursor back and forth willy-nilly from his own laptop. Spooky. He opened a file I used to save personal messages we exchanged. I watched in amazement as he typed a message to me on my own computer. I followed the instructions he gave me to take control of his machine and typed in the words *This is it.* He moved to my side from his desk with his laptop in hand. There on his screen was the message I'd just typed.

"This is how they did it?" I asked.

"That way or through Dropbox. They can exchange messages without actually sending anything."

"So nothing goes over the internet?"

"It's over the internet, okay, but it leaves no footprint. Nobody can see it except those involved."

"How long has this been around?"

"Since around 2005, I think, but I'd have to check."

"Okay, but how does one party know another wants to connect?"

Paul wrinkled his nose. "The one wanting to make contact has to tell the other party to open TeamViewer. Phone or email, most likely."

"That shoots down your idea. There's no record of contact."

"But what if they set up a schedule of times to be available. Like the first Wednesday of every month at 4:15 p.m."

"That might work," I said. "But this covers years, so it might even be quarterly or semiannually. A prearranged schedule makes more sense." I paused. "But what about the password. Does it stay the same or change?" I asked.

His face fell. "It's different every time."

"So again, there has to be contact."

"Yeah," he acknowledged, "but maybe they carried unregistered phones to pass info around."

"Then why would they need TeamViewer? They could just talk to one another." I thought for a moment. "That doesn't mean the idea's all wet. Passing a code back and forth would be harder to find than long conversations. Hold on. Let's check their cells."

I grabbed my phone to call Chillicothe PD while Paul got on the trail of Roy Guerra. Anderson still had Rider's desktop and soon found TeamViewer had been downloaded.

"Great. Now take a look at her cell phone," I said.

"Didn't find one," he came back at me. "She had a landline at the house, but I didn't find a cell."

"Thanks."

Roy called back a few minutes later and said Socorro PD found TeamViewer on Herrera's machine. Bingo! We'd learned how the bad guys—as Paul called them—passed messages back and forth… even if I hadn't yet figured out how they'd exchanged passwords. Burner cell phones we hadn't yet located probably held the answer to that.

Chapter 13

AFTER WE went to bed, I was trying to get a reluctant Pedro to come out and play when Paul suddenly sat up. "What was that?"

"I didn't hear anything." I liked the way one of the dragon's inked claws clutched Paul's left nipple.

He swept back the covers and stepped into a pair of Levi's. I was slower, so he reached the front hallway before I got out of the bedroom.

"Fire!" he yelled. "Front porch."

He went for the fire extinguisher, but I ran for the flower beds along the driveway. This wasn't the first time my house was firebombed.

He slowed the flames, and my flower bed dirt finished the job. We must have been a little noisy during our labors because lights up and down Post Oak Drive flared as the neighborhood came out to see what the detective fellow at 5229 was up to now. By the glow of the porch light, we stared at the remains of a Molotov cocktail as a siren screamed in the distance. One of the neighbors had called 911.

"Good thing it didn't go through the window," Paul said. "Woulda been lots worse."

"Take a look at the screens. I replaced the regular mesh with something more substantial years ago."

"Hey, this is like when Puerco and his Santos Morenos tried the same thing during the Zozobra caper." Paul and I had only recently met at that time and were cautiously feeling our way toward a relationship.

"Exactly."

"Belhaven died because someone set his house on fire," he reminded me.

"Belhaven died because someone hit him in the head before setting him aflame in his garage. I don't think the perpetrator believed this would kill us. But it would cause us some distress and possibly injure one or the other of us."

"Harassment?"

"Warning."

A fire truck and an EMT team arrived to find there wasn't much to do other than write a report. A police unit arrived on their heels, and I asked them to let Lt. Gene Enriquez know everything was all right. Too late. His brown Ford eased to the curb within minutes, Roy's blue one right on its tail.

"You guys okay?" Gene called as he walked up.

"Fine. I take it you heard the police call and recognized the address."

"You got it. Looks like you're gonna need a new paint job."

"And some bricks sandblasted."

"Way I figure it, you pay someone to firebomb your porch every five years or so as an excuse to redo the outside."

Roy didn't understand the inside joke. "See who did it?"

"Nope, we were in bed."

"You called it in?" Gene asked.

"One of the neighbors must have."

"They mighta seen something more than flames." He turned away to instruct the patrolmen to call in help to canvass the area.

My across-the-street-neighbor—the area's one-woman neighborhood watch—appeared in her nightgown covered by a heavy robe. "Are either of you injured?" Gertrude Wardlow asked.

"Just fine. Did you see anything?"

"Heavens no. I was asleep until the sirens woke me. But I'll bet someone did, and I'll find out who."

I didn't call her off. She'd do a better job than the cops.

Gene finished dispatching his troops and greeted her courteously. He had a lot of respect for her years in the DEA.

A few minutes later as we stood in my front yard discussing things, a patrolwoman walked up to Gene. "Neighbor across the street and two houses down heard a car at 11:00 p.m., about the right time. When it pealed out, he looked through the window. But all he saw was a dark shape. SUV, he thought. Couldn't identify it again. Aside from that, nothing."

"Wick Pillsner?" Paul asked. "We're beginning to close in on him, and he knows it."

"How does he know?" I asked.

Gene answered, "How does he *not* know? Wick's connected in this town. You've been asking questions, so he's bound to have heard about it. A dime to a donut, he knows you're running down three electrical meter readings and trying to tie them to whoever rented the house on Georgia Street. That's too close. Raises too many questions."

"Maybe."

I declined the police minder Gene wanted to leave outside my door. Even given the events of the night, I didn't feel unduly threatened. Something wasn't right. Tossing a Molotov cocktail onto a fellow's porch was a pretty inefficient way of getting rid of a target. Delivering a message? Now that was another thing altogether. *Leave me alone or I'll come at you for real!*

No one could convince me this was Wick Pillsner's method of doing business. I'd watched him when he coached me as a kid. He went right for his opponent's jugular. Take care of him. Get him out of the game.

And I'd known of a few business deals he'd been involved in. Ride right over the opposition. Hit them where they were vulnerable before they even knew they were vulnerable. No warning. No waving a fellow off. Simply take care of him before he became a problem.

My mental exercises convinced me of one thing. Wick Pillsner did not firebomb my house this evening, but I *was* closing in on him, so I'd better watch my back. And Paul's back, as well. That left me with another puzzler.

Who firebombed my home… and why?

THE NEXT morning Hazel went into her mothering mode when she learned of the fire. I think she was more concerned over Paul's carcass than mine. Ah well, he was a loveable cuss.

Once we got past that little piece of drama, Charlie, Hazel, and I gathered around the big table in our conference room. Paul and Detective Guerra sat in on our session. After Paul finished explaining the TeamViewer theory, Roy came up with the same question I asked Paul last night. "Why do they need this TeamViewer thing? If they had unregistered cell phones, why not just talk?"

Charlie nodded to emphasize Roy's questions.

"Because the mastermind behind all this is a very cautious man," I said. "In all likelihood he simply texted a date and time for contact, nothing more. At the appointed time, each party activated TeamViewer, and the party on the receiving end entered his code, texted the caller his password, and they were in contact."

"I still don't understand," Roy said. "Talk, deliver your message, and hang up. How is that any riskier than this other thing?"

"Let's say someone found one of the unregistered phones. The authorities could use them to establish contact between point *A* and point *B*, that is, say, Albuquerque and Chillicothe, but not to determine who the individuals were. And if they texted everything, there would be no voices on record anywhere, simply a text of times and dates and what was probably passwords. But passwords to what? Not many people would connect that to a TeamViewer. It would be a mystery within an enigma thing. Smart as hell, in my opinion."

Roy scratched his head. "But like you said, a text would be evidence of contact."

"My guess is when—or if—we ever find one of those cells, you'll see it was purchased in California or Wisconsin or Tennessee or somewhere, so it carried a prefix not associated with any of the conspirators. You might be able to prove a text pinged off an Albuquerque tower, but that would be all."

Paul asked Roy to drag his laptop from his attaché case, downloaded the TeamViewer software on it, and demonstrated what we were talking about.

"Be damned!" was all Roy said. Apparently convinced, he moved on to other matters. "What do we do about Wick Molotoving your house?"

I kept my doubts to myself. "We'll never hang the firebombing around his neck… or anyone else's. A car in the night."

"You're probably right," he acknowledged.

Charlie rubbed a hand over his balding scalp and adjusted his glasses. "Don't see why Wick would do such a thing. What did it gain him? He knows BJ's not going to let go of anything. Damned dumb reaction from a damned smart man."

"That's got me puzzled too," I said.

Hazel spoke up. "He had something in mind, you can bet on it. BJ, you better ask Gene to put a patrol car in front of your house… at least at night."

"He's already offered, but it's a poor use of manpower. If Wick wants to deliver a message, he'll find a way to deliver it."

"That's all it was?" Hazel asked, her voice rising on the last word. "A warning?"

I managed to get us off the subject by pointing out the attempted firebombing ended up in this morning's *Albuquerque Journal*. In light of that we decided it was time for another report to Dorothy Voxlightner, our client.

I decided to deliver it in person while Roy and Paul drove down to Socorro to take another look for a stray cell phone. As soon as Hazel transcribed my dictated report, I asked her to arrange a meeting for two that afternoon.

DOROTHY VOXLIGHTNER answered the door herself and invited me into the drawing room, where a silver carafe of coffee and a porcelain pot of tea waited. I chose tea. As soon as we were settled, she scanned the report, placed it on the coffee table, and looked me in the eye.

"What is the report not saying?"

The report I'd handed her did not contain the name Hardwick Pillsner. That was the only fact I'd omitted. Why? To give her cover in case she and Wick came face-to-face. But in the clear light of day, I changed my mind. She was entitled to know.

"It fails to say Hardwick Pillsner is the man who originally rented the Georgia Street address."

"Why omit it?"

"Did you read the *Journal* this morning?"

"I did. I saw the article on the attempted arson at your home. That was Wick?"

I shrugged. "I can't ignore the possibility it might have been. I hope the fact you engaged me to look into Belhaven's murder isn't common knowledge. I take it neither you nor your daughter is accustomed to discussing private affairs openly."

"You are correct."

"Good. Keep it that way."

"This makes sense to me," she said after taking a sip of coffee. "Wick—using my son's contacts—put together the metals company. I gather from your report you assume the assays were phony."

"Is there any other explanation for conducting assays at Georgia Street? Wick… or more likely, Dr. Stabler… got his hands on some high-quality ore. They probably mixed in some of the Morenci ore to keep the reports from being too rosy."

"So it was a scam from the beginning?"

"Judging from the independent assays Everett Kent had done prior to his murder, I'd say so."

"Does this exonerate Barron?" she asked in a small voice.

"No, ma'am. This just points us to an unexpected player, the brains behind the scheme. It doesn't prove anyone's innocence."

"How do we do that?"

"You allow me to continue. We're not near the bottom of the barrel yet."

"By all means keep on digging."

"*That*, Dorothy, I fully intend to do."

She was struck by another thought, or perhaps it was there all the time, waiting to be given voice. "Does this mean Wick killed my son?"

"The temptation to say yes is strong, but we're lacking proof. I'm sorry to say, it does mean Barron is probably dead. But as agreed, we're not through digging yet."

"Assuming you are right, is it likely Wick also killed Pierce?"

"We need to clear up the precious metals recovery scheme first. That will possibly lead us to Belhaven's killer."

THE NEXT day I attended a business meeting at Wick's office building on Lomas. I wasn't totally an interloper. A week ago a friend of mine asked if I was interested in a new venture Wick was putting together called the Rio Puerco Land Development Project. I'd not given him an answer, but I had written down the time and date of the meeting. The whole town knew my late father left me a sizable trust, so I was always getting tips for "great deals."

Wick seemed surprised to see me but didn't question why I was there. He knew my history, and a buck is a buck no matter where it comes from. The pitch for a residential real estate venture on the Westside was of interest because of the availability of a sizable tract of land purchased from heirs to an old Spanish land grant. The mayor's office was represented, signaling his support, as was the chairman of the Bernalillo County commission.

At the conclusion of the meeting, I kept my seat, speaking briefly with some acquaintances until the room gradually emptied and Wick gravitated to me.

"Surprised to see you, BJ. I hear it's hard to get you to part with any of your inheritance."

I stood in order to be on a level with him… minus a couple of inches. "My father was a wise man. He invested his funds well, and I've made very few changes in lo these many years." I realized with a start my parents died in a car wreck on Friday, January 31, 2003, more or less at the beginning of the Voxlightner scam. No wonder some of it was so hazy in my mind. I'd been wrapped up in grief and settling my parents' affairs while holding down a job as a cop at the time. "Still, there are some discretionary funds, so I occasionally make investments."

"You'll never make a better long-term investment than the $10,000 minimum it takes to get in on this one."

"It sounds interesting."

"Good. Take a brochure and make the right decision."

Then he made it easy for me. He brought up the Voxlightner thing—indirectly—instead of me having to introduce the subject.

"I hear you're investigating Pierce Belhaven's murder. Making any progress?"

"You know anyone who'd want him dead?" I asked.

"Pierce? Nah. He was harmless."

"Someone didn't think so."

He squinted as he looked at me. "He and his son were crossways."

"Do you really think Harrison would kill his dad?"

"Is it true he left his secretary and his yard boy a quarter of a mil each?"

I ignored his question and introduced a new element. "He also announced on TV he was reopening the Voxlightner Metals incident."

Wick let that lay for a second. "Nobody's anxious to relive that painful stuff all over again. Like I told you the other day. I got hurt, but I want to let sleeping dogs lie. Doesn't benefit anyone to stir up that mess again."

"True for most of us, I suppose." I let a little pause develop. "Especially anybody with dirt on his hands who wasn't caught up the first time around."

"Barron's and Walther's disappearance wrapped the mystery. Bastards are probably living it up somewhere spending our money." He slapped the back of the chair beside him. "I've got to get moving. Have an appointment. You think about the Rio Puerco investment, okay?"

"I'll give it due deliberation."

I watched his retreating back as he left the room. He didn't seem tense.

BEFORE I escaped my office—hopefully for the entire weekend—the mayor's office called to press for an answer as to whether I would serve on the civilian police oversight board. I declined. My concern was I was too close to the police department, and my decisions would constantly be second-guessed by the press and others because of my relationship with Gene. I recommended another highly respected confidential investigator in town who had once been a cop but whose ties were more cleanly broken.

As I headed down the back stairway for the parking lot, feeling liberated by my decision, Gene called my cell and proposed a drink. I agreed and asked where.

"How about 5229 Post Oak Drive?" he asked. "You still have bourbon, don't you?"

"Sure. Be home in twenty or so."

"Be there in half an hour. Will Paul be home?"

"Probably. He pretty much works out of the house except when he's somewhere with me or with Roy."

"How're they working together?"

"Good. Think they've decided they trust one another."

"Okay. See you soon. But I want some alone time."

I puzzled over the request. Gene occasionally came over for a drink, but he seldom invited me to my own home for libations.

Paul's Charger was gone from the driveway, so he was out somewhere, and I couldn't help but wonder where. I managed to get into more comfortable clothes before Gene rang the doorbell.

We took seats in the den where the wet bar was handy. His tumbler held bourbon rocks; mine, Scotch neat. He got right to what was on his mind.

"I've decided not to put in my papers."

"Does this mean you're going to accept the promotion?"

"Not sure about that yet, but I can't retire. The department's in bad shape, BJ. Ever since we got hit by pay cuts to balance the city's budget last year, we've lost a lot of officers. Morale's lousy—not just because of the pay thing, but because the public's raising hell over the police union's financial hijinks and wrongful deaths claims and whistleblower harassment."

"People are jumping ship?"

He rubbed the cool glass across his brow. "Not so much that as attrition and people leaving for better pay."

"How high are the personnel losses?"

"Ten percent. Heading for twenty, most likely. I'm pretty sure there'll be a Department of Justice investigation sooner or later. Hell, some of the rank and file are asking for one."

"Civil or criminal?"

"At this point who knows? There were nine fatal shootings by cops in 2010, and four so far this year."

"Some of them were on your watch. And you hate to bail when things are tough for your brother officers."

"That and the fact I might need to protect my own ass before this is all over. Being given homicide after taking down the sex trafficking ring last year was a curse dressed up as a blessing. Bolton was up to his elbow in alligators even without the sex trafficking thing." Lt. Chester Bolton was Gene's predecessor at homicide.

"What's the promotion they're talking about?" I asked.

"Two possibilities. Northeast Area command and Criminal Investigations Division."

"Hell, either one of those is commander rank. And CID simply bumps you straight up the line. You'd not only have homicide but sex crimes, organized crime, robbery, the whole shooting match."

"Yeah. That's the most logical move. But then I get the full brunt of the DOJ investigation, if there is one."

"Is your rabbi going to survive?" Gene's mentor in the department was the current police chief.

"Touch and go. This thing might eventually take him with it."

"Sorry to hear that. How does Glenda feel about your decision?"

"She won't say so out loud, but I think she'd rather I take my 90 percent retirement pay and run."

"Any way I can help, buddy, let me know. By the way, I turned the mayor down on the oversight board appointment."

"Good. Other than all that shit, how are things going?"

I filled him in on the Voxlightner case as it presently stood.

"Good progress, man. Looks like Hardwick Pillsner might have got his wick caught in the doorjamb."

"That's the way it's pointing, but I don't have the evidence to bring a case."

"Not yet. Damn, I miss that part of the job. You know, getting out there and chasing the perp to ground."

I looked at my old partner—my best friend in the world—and thought about discussing Paul. I valued Gene's levelheaded common sense. But somehow it seemed wrong to bring up my relationship problems. So I held my tongue.

Gene left before Paul returned home from checking Dr. Herrera's computers again. Paul found a document on the good doctor's personal laptop labeled Current Events with nothing in it. Paul explained that Herrera deleted everything in the file, making it the likely document he used to pass messages back and forth. I left a call for Sgt. Anderson in Chillicothe to look for an identical blank document on Rider's machine.

"Isn't there some way to recover deleted files?" I asked.

"Yep," Paul acknowledged, "but it takes more expertise than Socorro PD has. They signed out the laptop to Roy so APD can have a go at it. I'm hungry. You want me to fix something or go out?"

"The Cooperage sounds good to me."

Paul hesitated before agreeing. Don't tell me something wasn't wrong. He loved their roast beef.

Chapter 14

THE NEXT morning—what I had hoped would be a lazy August Saturday—Mrs. Wardlow rang my doorbell around 10:00 a.m.

"I need a moment of your time, BJ. I learned a smidgeon about your firebomber."

I invited the widow inside, where she declined refreshments as we settled in the den. Paul came in from the kitchen and gave her a peck on her powdered cheek.

"Mr. Elderberry"—the neighbor three doors to our left—"said he was having trouble sleeping Wednesday night and went out to sit on his porch. He has those big wicker wingchairs out there, you know. He was debating on lighting up a cigarette. His wife forbids him to smoke in the house, you see. Anyway he noticed a car approaching from the east. I say noticed, but he actually heard it. The motor, that is. The lights were off as it drove by. It stopped in front of your house, and someone opened the door, lit a torch, and threw it on your porch."

"Did he see who it was?" Paul asked.

"Couldn't tell at that distance. He's getting on, you know. The arsonist must have turned off the interior lights because it was dark until the torch flared. When the man got back in, he stepped on the brakes, and the rear lights flared enough for Mr. Elderberry to see it was a New Mexico license plate. Couldn't read it, I'm afraid."

"What kind of car was it?"

"Bulky. Like an SUV."

"Man or woman driving it?" I asked.

"Couldn't tell. Too dark. He referred to the driver as *he*, but upon questioning, Mr. Elderberry couldn't be sure he was right."

"Why didn't he report this to the police last night?"

"Poor dear didn't want to be involved. But he was the one who called the fire department Wednesday night." She covered a smile with her hand. "He didn't know he'd end up on the dispatcher's screen, anyway."

"Anything else?"

"Afraid not."

I gave her a nod. "Thank you, Mrs. W. I knew you'd find something."

She smiled, rearranging her wrinkles pleasingly. "SUV. That doesn't match the make of Mr. Pillsner's vehicle, does it? I suspect he drives a Mercedes or something similar."

Sly old gal. She'd sought to lessen the impact she knew I was looking at Wick by tacking a question onto her stunner.

"Silver Cadillac CTS. And I warned Paul not to talk to you."

"Don't blame him. He's no match for someone with my experience. I'm afraid I can't overcome my DEA training."

I glanced at Paul's flaming cheeks, but he had sense enough to change the subject. "That doesn't mean Pillsner couldn't have rented or borrowed or even stolen another car to do his dirty work."

"True."

"But it makes one think, doesn't it?" Mrs. W. said.

"Once again… true."

PAUL BOXED my ears on the golf course Sunday. After the game we enjoyed a quiet day. More relaxed than it had been in a while. I'd like to say I got some rest, but Paul's victory on the links fired up Pedro's libido, and I almost cried "uncle" on that front too. If I couldn't claim to be rested Monday morning, at least I was sated.

As soon as I arrived at the office, I put Hazel to work searching the motor vehicle files for vehicles owned by the characters populating our little drama. I was taken aback by the number of SUVs she returned with. In this day of gas prices north of $3.00 a gallon, who could afford to operate one of those boats? Every Belhaven in New Mexico owned one, as did Sarah Thackerson. Spencer Spears drove a muscle car.

I considered phoning Spence to repair the fire damage to my porch but ended up calling the handyman who usually kept my abode in good working order; I tried to put the incident out of my mind and concentrate on what was at the root of the problem, the Voxlightner Metals recovery scam.

Hazel located and engaged a Las Vegas investigator to interview Abner Brown and verify his recollection of Wick Pillsner as the individual who purchased the cashier's check for the payment of the first month's rent on 2551 Georgia Street. She also asked him to caution Brown that *someone* seemed to be cleaning up after himself on the Voxlightner scandal.

I asked my partner, Charlie, to ride herd on Lt. Lanny Johnson's AFD arson investigation on both the Belhaven residence and my own. After that I talked Paul into going to the *Albuquerque Journal* on Jefferson Street NE to prowl the newspaper's morgue in search of photographs and articles about Hardwick Pillsner. Once everyone was dispatched in pursuit of his or her own task, I picked up the phone and dialed Gene. Once I brought him up to date, I asked the question I'd called to ask.

"Do we have enough probable cause to get subpoenas for Wick's office and home?"

Before answering he asked me to walk him through Abner Brown's declaration Wick was the purchaser of the *William Stark* money order to pay the lease on the Georgia Street address.

"Brown knew Wick?" he asked.

"Knew him by reputation, seeing him around town, and in newscasts. That sort of thing. Remember, Wick was a jock with a rep back in his younger days."

Doubt was evident in his voice. "If I was the judge, I'd ask this Brown fellow how he remembered a single money order he sold eight years ago."

"He has the answer. Believing Wick Pillsner to be the purchaser, even though he had ID with Stark's name on it, prompted Brown to note in the register Wick paid for the money order."

"Refresh me. Money orders aren't filled out, are they? You buy an MO for, say, $100, and that's all the money order confirms. The purchaser fills out the rest, right?"

"Correct. However, the seller keeps a log of who bought the MO and asks for proper ID."

"And this was done?"

"Smith's Food and Drug says so."

"Okay. Tell you what. You get me this Abner Brown's affidavit plus the Smith's Food and Drug log showing the notation, plus a photocopy of the completed money order, and I'll see what I can do."

"Deal. I hope the supermarket keeps copies of money orders that long. But we know they do have logs from back in 2003. Do you have any suggestions in the meantime? I hate to twiddle my thumbs while I wait for the Brown statement and the store's information."

"You interview everyone?"

"So far as I know."

"I'm sure you caught all the principals, but how about some on the edges? Like the KALB-TV host Wilma Hardesty."

Gene had been doing some digging of his own, or else he was reading Roy Guerra's reports. "Paul did that."

"The accountant and the two attorneys?"

I frowned. "*Two* attorneys? I talked to Zach Greystone, but Everett Kent's dead."

"How about Hilda Hastings?"

"Zach's partner?"

"Yep. The Hastings in Greystone and Hastings LLC."

"How was she involved?"

"Started investigating after Kent was killed in their office," Gene said. "She might have some info."

I hung up the phone and asked Hazel to contact Ted Donaldson at LMZ to ask him to reach out to the REIT's bank for a copy of the Stark money order. That would be faster than going through Smith's Food and Drugs. They were taking their time coming up with the money order register.

ALTHOUGH THESE August days were some of the hottest in recent history, the temperature on Tuesday the thirtieth wasn't one of them. The thermometer wasn't expected to get over 95 or 96 degrees. The day was overcast, which meant the vaunted—but not infallible—New Mexico monsoon season was trying to do its job. So far the humidity only served to render our oft-repeated mantra—yes, but it's a dry heat—false. But this great state, which I loved dearly, had one advantage over many other dry, dusty places: our summer nights were cool and comfortable, almost without fail.

I entered the Greystone and Hastings law firm precisely at 1:55 p.m. to meet my two o'clock appointment. A smiling receptionist with silver tips to her hair took my name and let Hilda Hastings know I was here. I deliberated over how to treat her as I waited. To my mind she wasn't a candidate for being in on the scam—although Zach Greystone needed a look-see. She'd only become involved after her partner, Everett Kent, was murdered. Even so my professional paranoia demanded caution.

I knew Hilda casually through mutual acquaintances at family picnics and various other social venues. She was small but big-boned, which rendered her shape… *shapeless* was the only word I could come up with.

She entered the receptionist's area offering a handshake and a welcoming smile on her pleasant features. "Hello, BJ. I haven't seen you since the country club party last Christmas."

"Where I seem to recall we shared a polka."

"A waltz," she corrected. "My old bones won't put up with a polka."

We moved into her office, where the atmosphere became more businesslike.

"I hear you're looking into the Voxlightner thing."

"You hear right, Hilda. What can you tell me about it? How did you get mixed up in it?"

"Everett Kent was a friend of mine, as well as a colleague."

"Any clue to who killed him?"

She spread her hands in frustration. "He was killed in an office just down the hallway. He often worked late after his wife passed on, but he always kept the outside door locked when he did so. He admitted his own killer to the offices."

"Remind me how he was involved."

"You know about our senior partner, Zachary Greystone, being a big promoter of the whole deal. Once he was convinced the assays were accurate, he was sold, as were Wick Pillsner and Barron Voxlightner and some other movers and shakers. When things went wrong, Everett wanted to know why. He went to Arizona, got a pickup bed full of the tailings, and took the material to an independent lab for a series of analyses. Paid for the tests out of his own pocket. All of them showed traces of precious minerals, but not in commercial quantities. He raised such a stink that Barron Voxlightner and Walther Stabler up and disappeared. But not before…."

"Not before taking care of Everett Kent." I completed her sentence for her.

She lifted her gaze and met my eyes. "I stepped in where Everett left off."

"Didn't you fear for your own safety?"

"Barron and Walther had already disappeared. There wasn't much to fear."

I met her green-eyed stare. "Everett Kent wasn't killed because of his assay tests, Hilda. He was killed for something else he knew."

She jumped as if poked. "What? What did he know?"

"I'm not sure. But I found a reference to three meter readings in spring 2003 in Belhaven's appointment book. And he made a cryptic note saying *so that's what he meant.* I suspect the 'he' referenced was Everett Kent. I assume you've been through his files."

"Not much of them left. Whoever shot him in the back of the head made off with most of them. We talked about his findings not long before his murder, but he gave me no clue. Although…."

I waited her out.

"When we were talking about the fire assays he'd paid for, he was surprised by the way they were done."

"He was surprised at least one of the furnaces was electric."

Her eyes widened. "Which means the meter readings have significance."

"Do you know if he asked Pierce Belhaven to do any research for him at the utility company? Like look up some meter readings?"

"He and Pierce were friends. Friendly acquaintances is probably more accurate, so it's possible he approached Pierce." Hilda frowned. "This means…."

I left her alone this time, preferring she make the connections on her own.

"BJ, Kent was killed sometime on the night of March 10, 2004. That was a Wednesday. Barron and Stabler disappeared the following Monday evening." Her gaze hardened as I watched her start thinking like a lawyer. "And Pierce Belhaven was killed three weeks ago."

"After he announced on TV he'd found a clue to unravel the Voxlightner Metals scam."

Her breath caught in her throat. "Everett's clue."

"We don't know that for sure."

"Have the police made any progress in solving Pierce's killing?"

"Not much," I said. "How about Kent's murder? How far did they get?"

"Murder by person or persons unknown. After all the folderol, that's all it means."

I pressed her. "No clues at all?"

"None. The police took this office apart, but it's a place of business. There were scads of fingerprints, stray hair. All kinds of forensic evidence leading nowhere."

"No gun or shell casings?"

"No, although they said it was a small caliber. A popgun." She stood and poked the desk calendar with a finger. "Are… are we suggesting they were killed by the same man? But Barron Voxlightner and Walther Stabler have been gone for seven years."

"There are a couple of things you might not know. Thelma Rider, who was a clerk in VPMR, was killed in Chillicothe, Texas, last December. And Dr. Damon Herrera, who conducted the assays for the group, was killed two weeks ago in Socorro."

"I read about Herrera. A mugging, I believe."

"That's what it was made to look like. But I have my doubts."

"Are you saying someone else was in on the scam?" She paused for a moment. "Or have Barron or Stabler come back?"

"I seriously doubt that, Hilda."

WHAT A difference a few days makes. September opened with a projected 72-degree high, as measured at the Albuquerque Sunport. Any Albuquerquean will tell you the rest of the city is totally different from our airport. I was pretty sure it would hit ninety or better downtown, which sits in the belly of the Rio Grande Valley. On Friday a parcel arrived UPS from Las Vegas.

The private investigator I'd hired did a good job. He'd questioned Abner Brown thoroughly and repeatedly, asking the same question in half a dozen different ways. Upon reading through his notarized statements, there was no question in my mind Brown knew Wick Pillsner, at least by sight, and recognized him as the purchaser of the money order in question.

That same day an attested photocopy of the money order log for March 31, 2003 arrived from Smith's Food and Drug headquarters in Salt Lake City in response to Hazel's request. The log showed a $750 money order, number 881166515, sold to William Stark with a notation by the clerk that the purchasing party was believed to be Hardwick Pillsner, an individual known by reputation to the clerk.

I put those, as well as the copy of the actual money order Hazel ran down for me, in my attaché and hied myself over to APD headquarters, documents in hand.

WICK PILLSNER remained a genial glad-hander Monday morning, even after we handed him a subpoena for the search of his offices on Lomas NE. Gene took this as an opportunity to get out of APD headquarters and served the document himself. He allowed me to accompany his team. Paul was with Roy and another crew serving a similar subpoena on Wick's home on Rio Grande Boulevard NW.

Wick glanced up from reading the document. "Have at it. I'm an open book. Some of the business files require confidentiality, but I'm sure you'll accord them proper treatment. But the subpoena specifies I hand over any and all documents relating to an address on Georgia Street. *That* demand I can't accommodate. I have no connection with such an address and don't recall one in the past. I suspect you'll soon be able to tell me if my memory's faulty or not."

With that he told his receptionist to cooperate completely and returned to his own office to get on the phone. *To his lawyer?* Maybe. But the snatches of conversation I heard coming out of there sounded more like the Rio Puerco Land Development Project, the investment I'd been invited to participate in.

When Gene's team became too intrusive, Wick moved into the conference room, where he continued to make calls. If any of them were to his lawyer, the man should be fired because he never showed up.

While Gene and his people were mostly concerned with the past—as in the Voxlightner blowup—I was interested in the present. If I was right, Wick and his cohorts—namely Thelma Rider and Damon Herrera—had plans to legitimize their ill-gotten gains, and a big-time development on the Westside of Albuquerque might present such an opportunity.

I settled in Wick's executive chair and proceeded to study the voluminous file on the development project. Gene stopped by to grouse.

"We're here to collect the files and haul them back with us, not to pour over them now."

I lifted the folder to show him the name on it. "Wick might be able to defend against taking this one. It's a new housing development scheme."

"Why are you interested? Gonna invest a million or two?"

"This seems like a perfect opportunity to legitimize stolen money to me."

That got his attention. "How? There'd have to be a legitimate source for every dollar invested."

"True. But he's had seven years to set up those sources."

Half an hour later, after photocopying a few pages from the file, I sat with Gene as he spoke to Wick at the conference table.

"Here's a detailed list of the files we took, Wick. Look them over at your leisure and have your attorney contact us if you see anything amiss."

Wick glanced through the list. "I might need a few things you're taking in order to proceed to closing. Any problem in photocopying them for me?"

Gene agreed, and while he was out finding someone to accommodate the request, I spoke with Wick.

"You seem to be pretty copacetic with the subpoenas."

"Why not. It isn't my first dance, you know. Back when the feds were looking into the Voxlightner mess, they all but shut me down. At least Gene lets me retain enough documents to close on a couple of deals." He stirred in his seat. "What's this Georgia Street thing all about?"

I considered my answer. To clue him might serve to put some pressure on, always a good thing when you're trying to pin something on a target. But it tips your hand as well. Perhaps a partial answer would serve the former without completely accomplishing the latter.

"The police have located some old electrical meter readings on a house at 2551 Georgia Street."

"What's unusual about that? I have meter readings on my house. So do you?" He seemed only mildly interested in the subject.

"Triple and quadruple the kilowatt hours normally metered to the residence. This lasted for three months."

"When was this?"

No reason not to answer. He already knew the months involved. "Billing for May, June, and July 2003."

He frowned in thought. "Before all the Voxlightner mess started."

"Yeah. About the time somebody would be phonying up fire assays."

"Hell, that's easy enough. Go find the man who owned the house at the time."

"A real estate investment trust. Leased for six months, including the relevant period."

"A REIT? Which one?"

"LMZ"

"Who'd they lease it to?"

"A man named William Stark."

He looked as though the name didn't register. "Never heard of him. Go find this Stark fellow and haul him in. Maybe he still has some of our money left."

I kept my voice steady. "I suspect that's exactly what we'll do before this is all over."

Then I saw it. The exact moment Wick remembered buying the money order at Smith's Food and Drug. His eyes flickered once. Exactly once. Nothing more. "Good. Go get him, BJ."

GENE AND I sat in his office at APD while clerks carefully checked individual files delivered against the list taken from Wick's office. Once that was reconciled, the financial experts would have a go at some and detectives at others.

"Gene, I saw the instant he recalled Brown selling him the money order and the to-do over the name of the purchaser."

"Chances are he doesn't even remember who the clerk was. Besides we already alerted the Las Vegas PD."

"Reinforce it. Let them know the suspect remembers the incident now."

Once that was done, I hit Gene with something else. "Can we get a wiretap on Wick's phones?"

"I dunno. Why?"

"If he's going to go for Brown in Las Vegas, he can't do it himself. He knows we'll be keeping an eye on him. He'll have to reach out."

"Hell, BJ, if he reaches out, he'll reach out the same way he did with Rider and Herrera. That team-finder thing."

"TeamViewer."

"Yeah. That."

"Only if there's someone else involved in the Voxlightner mess we don't know about."

BROOKINGS INGLES'S office was a block from APD on Fifth and Roma NW, so I made an unscheduled call. Rumor held that Brookie, as he was known to his intimates, was the longtime lawyer for Albuquerque's organized crime bosses. Undoubtedly Albuquerque had crime, but I'm yet to be convinced it was organized. Nonetheless Brookie had defended some very shady characters in his years as a defense attorney.

His secretary wasn't put off by the fact I had no appointment, leaving me to believe this happened regularly. I waited while he completed a phone call, but in mere minutes Brookie arrived to shake my hand. He was about an inch shorter than my six feet and weighed in at around 190. Every time I saw the man, I had the same thought. Suave. Gene described him as *oily*, but I thought of him as *suave*.

"BJ, what can I do for you?"

"I want to pick your brains for a minute or two."

I didn't perceive of Brookie as gay, and I had pretty good gaydar. But he was soft around the edges in a way some people thought of homosexuals. Wasn't always true, of course, but perception is everything, as they say. He waved me to a seat and reached for a cigar humidor. I declined the offer of a stogie, so he settled into his chair and went about the ritual of clipping and firing up one.

"Is this the billing kind of picking or the nonbilling kind?" he asked through a cloud of blue smoke.

"The nonbilling kind. Simple question. If one of your better-connected clients needed a task of a somewhat dubious nature accomplished in Salt Lake City or Denver or Las Vegas, would he contact an individual in his own locality or reach out to a native of those cities?"

Brookie scratched an ear. "Leave my clients out of it. If someone in Albuquerque wanted help, say of a wet nature, for instance, he'd likely go to a reliable local source and contract his work. That way there's a guy standing between the fellow in Albuquerque and the fellow in whatever city it is who'll get paid for his work." He waved the cigar, causing its tip to redden momentarily. "Course if he had somebody he really trusted, he could send him to, say, Salt Lake, but he'd be a fish out of water. Wouldn't know the local culture, so to speak."

I rose and shook his hand. "Thanks. Bill me if you want."

"Naw. I didn't tell you anything you didn't already know."

"But you confirmed my thinking."

"The grapevine says you're working on the old Voxlightner thing."

"You know anything about it?"

"Didn't invest, didn't follow it, and didn't defend or sue anyone over it."

ONCE BACK in the office I took out the sheets I'd photocopied from Wick's Rio Puerco Land Development Project and spread them on the small table in the corner. The proposed budget reflected a requirement of $45,000,000 for the first phase of the project. This acquired the land for all three phases but only built out 200 homes, two shopping centers, and three parks. Although I am no expert, the design, layout, and planning for the project seemed thorough and professional. My guess was Wick needed around $10,000,000 in order to get the deal off the ground. Three banks apparently pledged construction loans and support in providing mortgages for purchasers. Wick had evidently been working on this for some time as permits for sewage, water, and electricity were either in place or pending. He'd invested some of his own money in the project, I judged.

After digesting this information, I turned to what really interested me: Wick's list of subscriptions. A total of around fifty names with dollar amounts opposite each made up the list. After it was typed, it had been worked over liberally in Wick's handwriting. The big dollar subscribers led off the list:

Hardwick Pillsner Investments (Albuquerque) $2,500,000

Siedel Trust (Dallas, TX) 1,000,000

Forge Family Trust (Phoenix, AZ) 1,000,000

Voxlightner Family Trust (Albuquerque) 500,000

Sarah Thackerson 100,000

Spencer Spears 100,000

The top six names accounted for about half of what Wick needed. The next forty-five or so added not more than a million dollars at a quick glance. To further complicate things, Wick had lined out the second name, Seidel Trust, and its million bucks. I chuckled to see a handwritten note that *B. J. Vinson is interested. He should be worth $1,000,000.* Dream on, Wick.

Given the way my thoughts were turning, it didn't take much imagination to conjecture the Seidel Trust out of Dallas represented Thelma Rider's reinvestment of part of the Voxlightner booty. The million in her mattress was only a part of what she'd stolen, and she likely held the slender end of the stick.

The Forge Family Trust in Phoenix was probably Herrera. I knew enough Spanish to know *herrero* meant blacksmith in English.

The Voxlightner Family Trust pledge surprised me due to the way the VPMR thing went south. Of course when Dorothy gave the pledge, she wasn't aware of my suspicions of Wick. In that light, the investment made sense. Wick's strong point was putting together real estate developments. However given what I'd shared with her the other day, Wick could likely strike Dorothy off the list too.

Thackerson's and Spears's names gave me pause. A hundred grand was forty percent of their inheritance. Had they known Wick? An interesting question. Damn! Exactly when was this list made? Look as I would, I found no date on the sheet.

I sat back in my chair, wished for a bottle of cool water I was too lazy to fetch, and thought about things. There were two names missing from the list: Barron Voxlightner and Dr. Walther Stabler or any pseudonym representing them. Was the omission of Barron almost as good as a death certificate? Did that apply to Stabler as well? More than likely the good doctor planned his escape route long before things went sour. He simply vanished, taking his share of the spoils and breaking all ties with his fellow conspirators.

The Herrera connection was relatively easy, but why did I think the Seidel Trust was Rider? Because it was Texas-based, and Wick scrubbed it. Didn't make sense to invest for someone you'd already killed. Undoubtedly there was a Seidel in Thelma's background.

The three of them—Wick, Herrera, and Rider—had over seven years to create fictional people or trusts or corporations and slowly build up bank balances. I shook my head at the patience of the group. I'd heard of gangs doing something similar, though usually someone got greedy and moved too quickly. But maybe Thelma Rider ran out of patience and started pushing Wick to launder her money, and that's why she died last December on a road outside of Chillicothe, Texas. Wasn't the million-dollar mattress enough for her?

I looked at the papers spread on my conference table and nodded. A good day's work well done.

Chapter 15

THE NEXT morning I settled down with Paul at the kitchen table to go over the newspaper clippings he'd spent yesterday gathering and photocopying at the *Journal.* He'd run up quite a tab on his Visa card. Not surprising. I'd asked for everything he could find featuring Wick Pillsner, and he'd brought *everything.*

I was more interested in discussing our relationship, but things had returned to normal—sort of—so I kept to the case.

While Paul concentrated on articles having to do with the Voxlightner scandal, I scanned the others looking for something inadvertently disclosed, something to point me in another direction… in other words, something atypical in Wick's life.

The only thing I learned I didn't already know was Wick was a mountain man. He eschewed lakes and rivers and the sea for peaks and cold rushing mountain streams. A couple of photos before an imposing mountain cabin in the Jemez Mountains north and west of Albuquerque showed he was a hunter, albeit with a camera, not a rifle. He'd snared several record trophies with his lens.

Finding nothing else of interest, I turned to the articles covering the old precious metals scam. Wick's fingerprints were all over the Voxlightner fiasco, but I knew that already. He helped conceive the idea, promoted it, and stood before the world when it turned to ashes, facing the consequences and sharing in the loss. Had I not known of the damning Georgia Street connection, he would have grown in my estimation.

"Nothing here," Paul said as he threw aside a clipping after about three hours of searching.

"Maybe not. But it needed to be done. And these articles give us a clearer picture of the whole Voxlightner affair. Reaffirm some things."

"But there's nothing here to incriminate Wick Pillsner."

"I don't know about you, but I have a fuller understanding of the man now."

"I guess so. But it's so damned frustrating. I'm sure he was in on the scheme, but there's nothing to…."

"Nothing to nail him? Don't you think the feds would have found anything if it was obvious?"

Paul rubbed his forehead. "Nuts. Like you said, the search had to be done. What now?"

I showed him copies of the Rio Puerco Land Development Project and pointed out my suppositions about who the heavy investors really were before turning to what puzzled me.

"There's no date on this list. But something about it bothers me."

"Besides being lined out and the hen scratching in the margins, what?"

"If I'm right about the two trusts being the erstwhile office manager, Thelma Rider, and the School of Mines' Dr. Herrera, respectively, then why didn't he scratch the Forge trust? Herrera's dead too."

"Maybe he hadn't gotten around to it yet. That list was created on a computer. Wick was probably always updating it. You can delete and insert things anytime you want. And he put the investors down according to the size of the investment."

"Then why didn't he delete both of the trusts?" I persisted. "He's known for a while they were no longer available."

"Maybe he thought he could take over Thelma's trust and found out he couldn't."

"So he scratched it from the list. But the Forge Family Trust isn't marked off," I pointed out.

"Maybe Wick was still working on taking that one over and hadn't scratched it out yet."

"Possible. But why are Sarah Thackerson and Spencer Spears on the list of potential investors. Thelma was killed last December—"

"And he scratched her out."

"But Pierce Belhaven didn't die until July 20. How would Thackerson and Spears know they had $250,000 coming from his will in time to make the investment?"

"Maybe Pierce was fronting them the money."

"Then why isn't he on the list?"

"Not his type of investment?"

"If that's true he wouldn't lend them 40 percent of their inheritance for something he didn't believe in himself. Besides, he was investigating the old scandal and wouldn't go out on a limb for them with Wick's project. Belhaven was bound to have suspected Wick by then."

I surveyed the papers strewn out before us. "Paul, here's what I'd like you to do."

I gave him five specific names from Wick's list of investors and asked him to interview each to find out what he could about how and when they were solicited. Sarah and Spencer were at the top of his list. Paul was scheduled to meet with Roy Guerra this afternoon, but he promised to start checking first thing in the morning.

GENE CALLED me at home that evening.

"Somebody took a run at Brown in Las Vegas," he said.

"Took a run at?"

"Two hoods cornered him in an alley near where he works."

"A mugging?"

"Don't think so. He got stabbed, but the policeman that LVPD put on him arrived in the alley in time to prevent anything worse from happening."

"How bad was it?" I asked.

"Shoulder wound. He'll live… thanks to the officer's intervention."

"Did the cop catch the attackers?"

"No. They headed in different directions when he arrived, but he ID'd one of them. Known bad guy. Not a street bum."

"Connected?" I asked.

"I'd say so. Belongs to one of the families in Vegas."

"Maybe Wick Pillsner just made a bad mistake."

"Hell, BJ, both of those thugs are in Maryland or Miami or Mexico by now. And nobody's gonna admit to anything."

I sighed. "You're probably right. I wonder if it's time to make the Georgia Street connection public information. If the world understands Brown's statement is known to the police, maybe it'll provide him some protection."

"Not a bad idea. Might also shake Wick up a little."

"Paul can write an article for the *Journal* about an attempted hit in Las Vegas with an Albuquerque connection."

"Do it."

PAUL WAS delighted with the idea and sat down at his computer immediately. In a few minutes he brought me the first draft of his article. After accommodating some of the suggestions I made, he wrote a piece leading with the headline "Near Fatal Attack on Las Vegas, Nevada Man with Albuquerque Connections." The body of the article went on to say

Abner R. Brown, formerly of Albuquerque, was stabbed in an alley near the Mission Center Albertsons where he was the manager. Brown had recently been questioned regarding a money order he sold that connects to the Voxlightner precious metals scam of 2003 and 2004.

There were another hundred or so words to the column, but those few said everything I wanted. Paul emailed a copy to Gene so he could alert the LVPD when the *Journal* checked the facts of the story. Thereafter Paul sent the article to his contact at the newspaper.

"That oughta earn me some change," he said with satisfaction. Then he frowned. "I-I'll follow up on it tomorrow morning."

It hadn't occurred to me Paul would be paid for his efforts, but that is the way it is in the journalistic world.

THE MORNING was already hot, but I opened the windows to savor the aroma of roses my mother had planted all around the perimeter of the house. The sensation was pleasant yet off-putting. I missed my folks like crazy in moments like this.

Paul was already up and running by the time I headed to the office. Hazel took my copy of Wick's subscription list and set about trying to track down the two trusts I suspected represented Rider and Herrera.

This left me free to phone some of the people I hadn't assigned to Paul. He intended to make his contacts in person. I was satisfied with a telephone interview with three friends of mine far down the list in the $10,000 level. The result was mixed. Two had regular interaction with Wick and were invited to invest while either on the golf course or at a civic meeting. The third heard about the investment opportunity from a friend and contacted Wick to pledge his money. Nothing out of the ordinary about any of them.

Charlie came in from interviewing a prospective hire on another case, gave his recorder to Hazel for transcription, and joined me in my office.

"You asked me to look into the two cases of arson. AFD hasn't gotten far. Gasoline was the accelerant in both cases, Belhaven's garage and your house. Lieutenant Johnson found nothing to pursue in the garage fire, but he pinned down the vehicle used in your firebombing to a blue 2010 Toyota RAV4."

"That's pretty specific."

"They found it abandoned not a mile from your house. Stolen the same afternoon from a retiree who lives in the neighborhood."

"Any forensic evidence?" I asked.

"No fingerprints. A few stray hairs, but the owner lends it to his nephews from time to time, so who knows where that will lead?"

"Any damage to the vehicle?"

Charlie's glasses reflected light as he shook his head. "Reeked with gasoline, but otherwise, no."

"So dead end."

"Likely. The vehicle was abandoned in the alley behind a strip mall, and nobody reports seeing anything suspicious."

"Cameras?" I asked.

"Not in the alley, but in the parking lot. Lieutenant Johnson's getting me a copy of the tapes. Maybe we can spot a suspicious driver picking up a car in the lot."

"Don't hold your breath. He'd have to be a known arsonist or someone involved in the case to be classified as suspicious. Besides, would you park your getaway car in a mall where you know it'll be surveilled, or on a quiet side street?"

"Where the neighbors will know immediately it doesn't belong," he finished my thought for me.

"True. Six of one, half dozen of the other."

"They already talked to both the mall tenants and the neighborhood. Nothing so far."

"Okay. The video's worth a shot, I guess."

"You want to bring me up to date?" Charlie asked.

I gave him a brief post. When I stopped talking, Charlie looked thoughtful for a moment. "This attempt on Brown in Vegas might be enough to get a wiretap on Wick's phones. Do you want me to approach Lieutenant Enriquez?"

Funny thing about Charlie. In social situations addressing my old riding partner as "Gene" was no problem, but when it came to police business, Gene became "the lieutenant." So was Charlie built; so would he remain.

"Please do."

Hazel stuck her head in the door. "BJ! Pick up line one. Something's happened to Paul."

I lunged for the phone. "Hello!"

"Dammit, Vince, he ruined my Charger!"

"Who ruined it, and are you all right?"

"Busted wing, maybe. But my car's totaled. Ow!"

"Where are you?"

"Intersection of Copper and San Mateo. Some joker T-boned me. EMTs are here."

I heard another voice in the background.

"Okay, okay! They tell me I gotta hang up so they can look at my shoulder."

"I'll pick you up—"

"Gotta get an X-ray.... UNM Emergency."

Normally Paul called me on my cell, but he'd punched the office number on his phone. That told me he was shaken, but *how badly was he hurt*?

IT REQUIRED all my powers of persuasion to get Hazel to stay behind and man the telephones, but I escaped the office and climbed into my Impala alone. I tore out of the parking lot in the grip of a panic I'd not known before and raced east on Lomas Boulevard to the hospital in the University of New Mexico area.

I arrived in time to watch Paul shrug off the EMTs who wanted to take him inside in a wheelchair. But he was no match for the steely-eyed blonde nurse who ordered him into the chair and wheeled him inside. He was able to tell me he was okay before they whisked him through a pair of double doors barred to me.

Taking a seat in the waiting area, I silently joined half a hundred others to nurse my grief and fears and anxieties. Only a couple of giggling children and three noisy teenagers in the far corner managed to live their lives as they normally did. The rest of us batted glum back and forth across the room.

When I called Hazel to tell her what little I knew, she peppered me with half a dozen unanswerable questions before I convinced her I knew nothing at this point except he was mobile and moving under his own power.

I closed the call and resumed staring at a worn spot on the tile floor and remembering things: pulling a suffocating gag out of Paul's mouth after rescuing him from a kidnapping designed to put pressure on me, harboring doubts about his motives when others suggested he was playing me for a sucker, and my utter joy when they were proved wrong. I recalled pleasant morning breakfasts, romantic dinners, competition on the golf course and in the swimming pool. And Pedro. Wonderful nights of watching Pedro prowl as his owner made mad, passionate love to me. Paul. My rock. My Adonis. Despite myself my mind slipped to the unknown something I sensed between us.

Filled to the gullet with waiting, I approached the desk and asked about his condition.

"Are you a family member?"

I saw red as I stared at her, but my rage disappeared as quickly as it flared. She was merely following orders. It wasn't her fault society didn't recognize our relationship. "His uncle. B. J. Vinson."

She disappeared for a moment and then returned to tell me his dislocated shoulder was being treated as we spoke. She directed me through swinging doors to a small waiting room in the treatment area. As I settled in for another wait, the sound of his baritone voicing expletives from behind a nearby curtained alcove heartened me more than I could describe.

A few minutes later he appeared, bare-chested with his left shoulder swaddled in elastic bandages, his arm pinned to his side.

"Vince!" he exclaimed. "What did they do with my Charger?"

"Forget the car. What about you?"

"Dislocated shoulder."

"Didn't know they bound a dislocated shoulder. Thought they put it back in place and sent you home."

He cooperated as a nurse put his right arm through the sleeve of his shirt and drew the garment over his disabled shoulder.

"Hello, Mr. Vinson." A doctor I knew slightly appeared and answered my question. "Immobilizing and sheathing's standard treatment these days. The X-ray showed no break, but I want him to wear the shoulder support for a week and then see his own doctor for follow-up."

"Vince," Paul interrupted impatiently. "The car. My laptop and all my notes are in the Charger. We gotta get them."

"Okay, settle down. I'll take care of it. But right now we're going to get you home."

Hazel alerted Gene to the collision, and he reached me by cell while I was settling Paul, a bit woozy from painkillers, on the sofa in the den.

"How is he?"

"Dislocated shoulder. He'll be okay. What happened?" I asked.

"Patrolman who answered the call said Paul was headed south on San Mateo by the Walgreens on Copper. Dodge Caravan came out of Copper and hit him amidships. T-boned him. Paul's lucky he wasn't hurt worse."

"The other driver?"

"Gone. Disappeared. The van was stolen this morning. It wasn't an accident. My guess is the Caravan followed him until the driver knew where Paul was headed and got around him to set up the ambush."

"Damn! The Charger?"

"Hauled off to the yard," Gene said. "It's total scrap."

"Paul's computer and notebooks were in the car. Probably his backpack too."

"The bad guy didn't get away with them. Patrolman on the scene has all Paul's personal effects. He's delivering them to me. What was Paul doing?"

"Face-to-face interviews with five of the investors in Wick's Westside scheme."

"Somebody didn't like that. This was your second warning, BJ."

"And there won't be a third one."

Gene cleared his throat. "Charlie got hold of me about a wiretap this morning. My people are doing the paperwork. Takes a ton of it, you know. I'll keep you posted."

I THOUGHT I was a bad patient, but Paul had me beat by a mile. Even though I could tell he was shaken up inside more than he let on, he wouldn't stay in bed or on the couch. He'd lie down until he thought of something he needed to do and hop up to go do it. He actually wanted to go shopping for a replacement for the Charger, but I put a stop to it.

"Vince, I'm afoot. I've got no wheels."

"You're not going anywhere in the next day or so. You don't need wheels."

He turned grumpy but gave up on the idea of visiting a car dealer. Even so he went to the room we use as an office and called his insurance agent. Thankful he was venting his frustration on someone other than me, I heated a bowl of his excellent green chili chicken stew and took it to him. By that time he was car-shopping online.

A few minutes later, I heard a holler from the home office. "Look, Vince! Here's one just like mine. This is the one I want. You hear me? We need to get down to the Dodge place before it's gone."

"No way. Have you even talked to your bank about the wreck?"

"Oh yeah. The bank. No, but I talked to the insurance company. Will they pay the bank or me?"

"They'll pay the bank. The bank will give you the excess over the loan payoff."

"So I'll have to finance the new car just like from scratch?"

"That's the way it works."

"Okay. Better call the banker."

"Eat the stew before it gets cold," I admonished as I left the room.

Chapter 16

I STAYED home the next morning with my restless patient. Gene called to say he had Paul's personal effects from the wrecked Charger and took the opportunity to bring me up to date on the accident investigation. The patrolman and a supervising sergeant questioned everyone at the accident scene, but Albuquerque was like everywhere else. Accidents, fistfights, and arguments collect a crowd. Although most of the spectators arrived after the collision took place, the officers found two individuals who heard the crash and responded to offer help. Both of the good Samaritans concentrated more on getting Paul out of his wrecked car than on the second vehicle, other than to notice there was no driver in the Caravan.

One of the Walgreens employees claimed he saw a man walking with a limp down the sidewalk to the west, but the clerk was more interested in the accident itself. Upon questioning he recalled a man—no bigger or smaller than most men—with a baseball cap, bill pulled low over his face, hobbling down the street. Young? Old? Young, he thought but wasn't sure. He hadn't paid that much attention.

After hearing what Gene had to say, I agreed it was a staged crash, intended to either injure or kill Paul. Wick Pillsner was a six two, two hundred pound, fifty-five-year-old man built like the jock he once was, so if he was behind the incident, he must be hiring local muscle to do his dirty work. A sudden rage blurred my vision and set my heart to pounding. If the bastard wanted to send a message, he should have delivered it to me. He wasn't going to get away with it. He'd just made the biggest mistake of his life. Before he attacked Paul, this was an assignment like a hundred others. Now it was personal.

I calmed my racing pulse and settled my jangled nerves as Gene brought me up to date on the wiretap we'd discussed. He was having trouble finding a judge to issue a warrant but got permission for a pen register and tap and trace. He could see any number dialed from the phone and any number that called the phone, but he couldn't listen in on conversations. Not ideal but better than nothing.

Upon closing Gene's call, I sat in the den and thought things through. The driver of the Caravan was—as Paul called it—*without wheels* after the wreck. Anyone who deliberately crashed his vehicle needed a second party nearby to pick him up. Or he'd take a bus. Central, a block to the south, was a major bus artery. This didn't wash. He had no assurance he wouldn't be at least *slightly* injured in the crash. He could have called a taxi, but that was impractical for the same reason. I put aside completely the idea he would walk wherever he was heading. Even if he wasn't injured, he was bound to be shaken after such a crash. Staging a T-bone took skill if someone intended to walk away under his own power. I examined each option and settled on the idea a confederate picked him up.

Gene's pen register and tap and trace might be more valuable than I'd first considered it. The wind quickly spilled from that sail when I realized Wick probably used an unregistered cell phone to set up the attempt.

Later in the evening, after figuring the painkillers and a little distance from the event might make Paul less excitable, I questioned him about the crash. He gave me a tired grin.

"You figure I've settled down enough now?"

"Something like that. I don't think you realize how badly you were shaken."

"Probably not. You know, it's the old 'take a bullet for the team and plunge right back into the fray' syndrome."

"Walk me through the incident."

"Hasn't Gene already done—"

"From the cop's point of view. I want yours. For example, did you notice anyone following you?"

He paused to think before answering. "Nope. I was just going along minding my own business."

"Did you notice the Caravan pass you?"

"Yeah. Think so. I was in the right-hand lane anticipating turning west on Central. Several cars passed on the inside. Van might have been one of them… from a few blocks back."

"Did you see the driver?"

He shook his head before wincing and touching his bum shoulder.

"Your neck sore?" I asked.

"Everything's sore. Didn't notice any of the drivers."

"How about when he came out of Copper to slam you?"

About the car crash, Paul knew less than I did. He'd caught a mere glimpse of the Caravan as it barreled out of Copper to plow into the passenger's side of Paul's Charger. Paul was thrown right, restrained by the seat belt, and then slammed against the driver's side door. He claimed he hadn't lost consciousness but was disoriented by the crash. If the van had T-boned the Charger from the other side, Paul might not have survived. Fortunately the other driver didn't want to chance traffic blocking his attack. A shiver ran down my back at the thought of what might have been.

"You had five names on your list to check. How far did you get?" I asked.

"Just two. I was headed for the third name when the accident… uh, the attack happened. I hit Sarah Thackerson and Spencer Spears first, since they're just four blocks down the street."

"Both of them still working at the Belhaven house?" I asked.

"Yep. They claimed they recently decided to invest in Wick's project. They already knew about their inheritance and overheard Harrison and Melanie talking about the Rio Puerco project one day. That is, Sarah did. She did some looking into the prospects and decided it was a good place to put part of her money. She claims Spencer went along for the ride. There's some bad blood between those two. But I guess he didn't object to ping-ponging off her tip in order to make a buck."

"Makes you wonder why she told him." I thought over my question and then answered it. "Maybe she didn't. Maybe he overheard her or saw her notes or something. Or maybe she tried to bury the hatchet."

Paul gave a wry smile. "Between Belhaven's girlfriend and his boyfriend? Who'd have thunk it? The way they bitch-talk one another, makes you wonder. Way I figure it, each thought he or she was worth more to Pierce than the other. Think Sarah was more pissed than Spencer was. Just about everyone knew about her relationship with Pierce. His came as sort of a surprise."

"Are you satisfied there *was* a relationship?"

He glanced over at me. "A $250,000 one, at least."

"Both of them admit they knew they'd inherit, but they'd have to move fast to take a hundred-grand leap on the Rio Puerco thing."

What tipped Wick off that Paul was on the move and prompted him to set someone on my lover's trail? Paul left Sarah and Spencer no more than half an hour earlier. Had one of them contacted Wick? If so, why?

That one wasn't too hard. If I were contemplating putting $100,000 into a project and someone came around asking awkward questions, I'd want to know what was going on. One or both of them might have called the guy who was proposing to take their money. Still… half an hour was not much time to organize a shadow.

The other thing niggling around in my mind was the subscription list I'd copied from Wick's files. If Sarah and Spencer didn't commit to invest until after Belhaven's death, the list had been updated recently. If that were so, *why wasn't the Seidel Trust deleted* instead of just being crossed out? Maybe I was wrong; it didn't represent Thelma Rider.

No. I was willing to bet a beer I was right about the trusts. They were Rider and Herrera coming along for the ride to launder some of their stolen money. So Paul's comment must be on track. Wick thought he could manipulate himself into Thelma Rider's trust but failed. He was still working to salvage the Forge trust. Only thing that made sense.

A WEEK later Paul was fit to be tied as I drove him to his doctor's office where he was relieved of the restricting bandage and cautioned to treat his wounded wing gingerly. Fed up with the invalid stuff, he claimed he had things to do, like finding the guy who'd destroyed his cherished Charger. Once out of the doctor's office, I drove him to the Dodge dealership on East Lomas where he negotiated for a black Charger almost identical to the one totaled in the wreck but a couple of years newer, a 2009. He handled the transaction like a pro.

APD HAD made no progress on locating the individual who stole the Caravan and plowed into Paul's car. Not surprising. For years Albuquerque occupied the top spot on the list of metropolitan areas experiencing high rates of car thefts. I made no effort to solve it because I was convinced I already had the fellow who ordered the attack in my sights. And he would pay. My problem at the moment was that Paul, who assessed the situation the same way I did, was more inclined toward direct retaliation.

The morning after Paul got his wheels again, I sat in my Fifth and Tijeras Street office and watched through the north-facing window as New Mexico's monsoon performed one last act before dying by drenching downtown. This year's La Niña squeezed us dry the first part of the year with something under an inch of rainfall. The second half was proving a bit better but nothing to brag about.

Turning back to my desk to consider the Voxlightner problem, my next task was to take a harder look at the disappearance of Barron Voxlightner and Dr. Walther Stabler. Hazel found no trace of the men in several searches around the globe via the internet. She was one of the best, and few men can simply vanish from one place and live for years in another without leaving some sort of trail. It can be done, of course. Spooks do it all the time, but they have a network protecting them. Barron and Walther didn't have that advantage.

This led me back to Dorothy Voxlightner's conclusion that Barron was really dead. Okay, let's accept that for the moment. It was difficult to hide a body so it wouldn't be found. Albuquerque's west mesa is a popular disposal ground, but inevitably someone stumbles across a corpse. In 2009—merely two short years ago—a woman walking her dog came across some bones, uncovering what was now known as Albuquerque's West Mesa murders. The official conclusion was the eleven women and one child buried there were the victims of an as-yet-unknown serial killer.

As a result of all this cogitating, I dug into the old FBI and police files from the 2004 investigation… and discovered a discrepancy. The FBI files claimed both Barron's and Walther's vehicles were gone from VPMR's rented offices at 3300 Lomas the evening of March 15, 2004. That building was now Wick Pillsner's office. However the *police* report indicated Walther Stabler's Crown Victoria was still there until the morning of Tuesday the sixteenth. Even so the investigating detectives could locate no one who saw it being driven away that morning.

If the police investigation was to be believed, Barron and Walther did not disappear simultaneously. Barron departed first. Interesting. Stabler, without question, was one of the original conspirators. Barron was mostly tainted simply by his disappearance. This led me to speculate how things would go down if Wick and Walther decided to get rid of Barron. How would they dispose of the body? Simple. Put it in Barron's own vehicle and drive it to a dump site. But this would have left them with a vehicle to dispose of. Easy enough to leave it on a dimly lighted street with the keys in the ignition. It would disappear all right, but would it do so quickly enough? Too big a risk. Besides, according to APD the second vehicle, Stabler's car, sat in the lot on Lomas all night long.

And if Walther Stabler elected to disappear after he and Wick had killed Barron, he wouldn't do it in his own vehicle. He'd beg, buy, or steal another to reach a metropolitan area big enough for him to disappear. So they needed to get rid of *two* vehicles.

This led me down another path. Given Wick's penchant for closing doors behind him, why would he leave Stabler alive to potentially testify against him one day? So maybe there were *two* bodies, as well as two cars.

Why was I convinced Wick was a part of this? Aside from evidence of his collusion in the Georgia Street part of the scam, it probably took two men to pull off the murder of Barron Voxlightner—who'd not been a small man—and the cover-up afterward. Newspaper photos at the time showed Walther Stabler as short and thin.

I glanced at the police report again and picked up the telephone. I knew the investigator who'd written the report. He was still on active duty with the APD but was out on a call. The receptionist promised to have him return my call as soon as possible.

Detective Dale Fuentes sounded just like he did half a dozen years ago when I'd spoken to him last. After bringing one another up to date on our lives, I turned to the investigation.

"Dale, I'm looking at your report on the Voxlightner scam that says you saw Dr. Walther Stabler's Crown Victoria in the company's parking lot as late as Tuesday the sixteenth. You remember that?"

"Do you remember what you had for breakfast a week ago? But I got notes I can dig out and refresh my memory. You want me to do it?"

"You bet. Now… maybe?"

"Nah," the old cop said. "Gotta look them up and study them a bit. Tell me again what you're looking for."

I went over the discrepancy between the FBI and APD files regarding when Stabler's car was last seen. He promised to call back before the day was over.

An hour later Fuentes kept his word. "Got it, BJ. And I'm beginning to remember a few things. Good to know the old noodle's not gone soggy."

"What I need to know is when Stabler's car was last seen."

"Okay." I heard him shuffling through pages and talking to himself. *Nope. Not there. The fifteenth… sixteenth…* "Here it is. A witness saw Stabler's Crown Vic in the lot at zero-three-zero on the sixteenth."

"At half past midnight?" I asked.

"You got it."

"Was it seen in the lot later than that by anyone?"

"I found a note saying I checked the lot around two, and the car was gone."

I suppressed an expletive and thanked him for his help. Christ! I'd almost gone off the track because of a carelessly written report. Fuentes wrote the exact time in his notes, but it showed up in his report as "the morning of the sixteenth." I consulted my notes and confirmed what I remembered. Wick clearly and unequivocally told me he had stopped by the VPMR office around eight o'clock the night Voxlightner and Stabler disappeared. He'd said the lights were on, but *there were no cars in the lot*. "Wick, you're a liar," I muttered aloud.

In a way this made things simpler. It made sense that Wick closed *two* doors behind him. And he probably knew where Stabler's share of the loot was and how to access it. Now to the logistics.

In my mind's eye I saw Wick enter the office where Barron and Walther pored over the company's books. I saw anger build, accusations fly. With Barron's indignation focused on Walther, it would be easy for Wick to walk up behind the unsuspecting man and disable or kill him. Wick would have loaded Barron into Voxlightner's own vehicle, a 2004 Chevrolet Blazer, and started for the dump site. Stabler probably cleaned up the office—if the deed was done there—and followed along behind to bring Wick back to the office. This accounted for his car being seen in the parking lot at a later time.

Hmm. Another problem. Nobody reported seeing Wick's car in the same parking lot. That meant it was stowed somewhere else temporarily. There was a popular eating and drinking place an easy walk away, a likely place. This alone indicated premeditation.

Had Wick permitted Stabler to leave the dump site alive? Everything that happened since suggested not. Stabler disappeared as thoroughly as Barron. I could see Wick killing his unsuspecting coconspirator and driving back to the office in Stabler's car. Except… what did he do with the Crown Vic?

If those men drove two vehicles to some remote site but neither of the cars came back, how did Wick get to his own car? He had to have some method of transportation. Another conspirator? Unlikely. He was slamming doors behind him, not opening new ones. So how did he get back to town? And where *was* the dump site?

PAUL WAS pumped enough from getting a new car to let Pedro come out and play that night. And play he did. He and his master seemingly forgot the doctor's admonition to take it easy for a while and really let loose. At the end of it, I was as sated as any guest at a drunken, libertine feast. I couldn't take a minute more of the man I treasured most in this world yet craved him at the same time.

The next morning Paul seemed recovered while my legs still shook if I put a foot down wrong. We sat in the breakfast nook eating his delicious chili omelets… this time laced with red not green. And if you have to ask red or green *what*, then you aren't a New Mexican.

"Wonder how the insurance investigator's doing?" he asked out of the blue.

"What insurance investigator?"

Paul managed to look sheepish and sexy at the same time. "Uh-oh. Did I forget to mention a Tri State insurance investigator talked to Roy Guerra the other day?"

"You did. Paul, we've got to keep one another up to date on things. And I thought you were making written reports like the rest of us."

His cheeks darkened. "Guess getting banged up and buying a new car got in my way. I'm behind on my reports. But yeah. Last week this Dallas insurance guy came knocking on Roy's door. Checking out Pierce's hefty policies."

"The ones naming Harris and Melanie as beneficiaries?"

"Two and a half mil each for his son and daughter. And two more for Thackerson and Spears—"

"Whoa. Thackerson and Spears get insurance money in addition to their inheritance?" I exclaimed. "How much?"

"A mil each. And with double indemnity…."

"Each gets twice the amount. That's serious money." My turn to be embarrassed. I would eventually have dug deeper into life insurance, but I should have done it sooner. "We knew about the policies benefiting Harris and Melanie. The other two are a surprise. Did the beneficiaries know about the policies?"

"The insurance guy didn't know, so Roy made inquiries. Son and daughter said yes. Girlfriend and boyfriend said no."

"The insurance guy, as you call him, is someone worth getting to know. What's his name?"

Paul shrugged. "Dunno. But I'll find out and set up a meeting, okay?"

"Good. As soon as possible."

I spent my day fruitlessly trying to figure out where Wick Pillsner dumped one or two bodies and got back home. Gene ran the vehicle identification numbers for Barron's Blazer and Walther's Crown Victoria through the national register again. Nothing. That didn't mean a lot. Stolen vehicles often carried phony VINs. Still, neither car surfaced again.

Paul spent his time running down the Tri State insurance investigator and arranging an appointment in my downtown offices the next day at 9:00 a.m.

Paul and I got up earlier than usual that morning because I'd been neglecting to swim lately, and that was the only way I kept my leg from growing stiff. The wound in my right thigh from Thornton Hsu's .38 revolver was never going to forgive me for being careless enough to let the suspected killer get the drop on me.

We arrived at Fifth and Tijeras NW with me walking better but dragging a little from the early morning exercise to find a small black man with a bristle-brush haircut waiting in my inner office. My companion introduced me to Nathan Tibedeau of Tri State Life Insurance.

"Nice to meet you, Mr. Vinson," he acknowledged my greeting in a soft voice.

Nate Tibedeau confirmed the insurance policy essentials as Paul had related them. The policy naming Harrison Belhaven as beneficiary dated from twenty years back and was paid by Esther Caulkins Belhaven until her death in 2006, when John Pierce Belhaven assumed the payments. The one paying Melanie Belhaven Harper was similar except it was taken out sixteen years ago.

The policies favoring Spears and Thackerson dated back only two and three years, respectively. Tibedeau's contribution to the discussion was limited to some procedural details, affirming it was not mandatory a beneficiary be notified of his or her interest in a policy. He also noted life proceeds paid directly to individual beneficiaries are generally exempt from income taxes.

By the end of the meeting, Paul and I had imparted much more information than we received. Even so the session was necessary.

Chapter 17

THE NEXT morning Gene and I met for coffee at a Starbucks in the North Valley where I recited my theory that Wick killed both Barron Voxlightner and Walther Stabler and stashed them and their cars somewhere. He heard me out before commenting.

"Makes for a good story. It makes a lot of sense too, but there isn't a shred of evidence supporting your supposition." He paused for a sip of espresso. "Although it sure would answer a big question. How in the hell do two men disappear without leaving a trace? I know it happens, but not as much as you'd think. Most of those who are never found are just what you're supposing. Dead. And both of these guys had baggage. Baggage called money. In a way money makes disappearing a lot easier, but as much cash as these two moved around, they should have left a trace."

After examining the theory for half an hour, we agreed to check for rental cars or cabs to see if we could pick up a trace of the two. Neither of us was hopeful. Seven years was a long time to keep such records. In turn I agreed Paul and I would use our weekend to check out Wick's cabin in the Jemez Mountains. It was remote enough to warrant a look for a hidey-hole big enough to contain two cars and two skeletons. The feds searched it years ago, but the place was worth another check.

Paul was game since he couldn't swim, play tennis, or golf for a couple more weeks because of his bum shoulder. I dug out directions to the place from the files, changed to cargo shorts for comfortable driving, and we headed for the mountains. Even though we might encounter some rough territory, Paul wanted to try out his Charger, reasoning that because there was no record of Wick owning a four-wheel drive vehicle, Paul's bomb was up to the task.

We took the old road north to Bernalillo, caught US Route 550 at the north end of town, and turned west. It always amazed me this little town had a traffic problem at least as bad as Albuquerque's, a metropolitan area at least twenty times larger. Nonetheless we eventually broke free of civilization and scooted west toward an even smaller place. After crossing a salt encrusted arroyo called the Rio Salado—in which I had never seen water—we entered San Ysidro. As a lifelong history buff, I knew this village of fewer than 500 souls had been established as a farming community in 1699 when a fellow called Juan Trujillo put down his roots and named his home after Saint Isidore the Farmer. Two years ago a movie starring Helen Mirren and Joe Pesci called *Love Ranch* was filmed outside the town.

At the north end of the village, we turned right onto State Road 4 and traveled up a broad valley said to have been inhabited by man for the last 4,500 years. This route eventually led us through Jemez Pueblo where native people gathered following the Pueblo Revolt of 1680. Also known as Popé's Rebellion, the uprising of several indigenous Pueblos drove the Spanish out of New Mexico. Twelve years later the Spaniards returned to reoccupy the territory.

Beyond that lay the red-rock country of Jemez Springs with its two Roman Catholic retreats, the Congregation of the Servants of the Paraclete and the Handmaids of the Precious Blood. In my youth my parents occasionally took family excursions to this country and allowed me to ride the natural falls at Soda Dam into the pooled waters of Jemez Creek. Somewhere past the jutting promontory known as Battleship Rock lay my favorite place on earth: the vast grasslands and volcanic domes of Valles Caldera. Just two months earlier the Las Conchas wildfire—caused by a tree falling on a powerline—devoured 150,000 acres, threatening the Los Alamos Lab, two pueblos in the area, and Valles Grande, itself.

Almost immediately past Battleship, we followed the dictates of our map, turned onto a forest road, and headed into the mountains. Long before we reached the cabin, I was convinced we were whistling Dixie. The drive along the paved highways hadn't taken too long, but this portion along a tortuous unimproved road—although not difficult—was slow going because of its winding course. By the time we reached the cabin, we would have been on the road at least three hours, and reports indicated Wick was in his downtown office early on the morning of March 16, the day after the two men disappeared. Nonetheless we persevered until we broke out into a small clearing and spotted the house—it was more than a cabin—pictured in the files. The place was closed up tight. The Pillsner family wasn't in residence this weekend.

The trees, mostly pines and spruce with a few aspen groves dotting the landscape, grew close together. This part of the Santa Fe National Forest hadn't been thinned or seen a controlled burn in a couple of generations, making it prime for a wildfire.

Two hours of searching anywhere a car could be made to go in this wilderness resulted in nothing. To the best of my knowledge, this wasn't mining country, so there were no shafts or holes in the vicinity. And beneath the thin topsoil, the bedrock was lava, which would require heavy equipment to excavate a crater big enough to hide two cars.

"Well crap!" Paul exclaimed as we made our way back down the mountain. "That was a wasted afternoon."

"Maybe so. But it was something we needed to do. If I'm right, there are two cars and two bodies hidden somewhere. We've just eliminated one of the possibilities."

He waved impatiently at the forest surrounding us. "Yeah. And another million possibilities right outside the car window."

"Don't think so. I believe we've eliminated this entire mountain range. Took us too long to get here. And between here and Albuquerque, there aren't many suitable places."

He snorted. "There are a thousand roads leading off every which direction."

"Too close to civilization. This might look like wide-open country, but have you ever gone anywhere no one else has been before you? I seriously doubt it. Paul, it's not easy to hide two bodies, much less two vehicles."

"The cars are probably down in Mexico."

"Possible. But if they disappeared that quickly, Wick had help in making them vanish. And if he did, he made himself vulnerable when the news of the disappearances broke. He'd be susceptible to blackmail and/or exposure. My take on Hardwick Pillsner is he wouldn't allow that to happen. If I'm right and both Voxlightner and Stabler are dead, he did it himself without the assistance of anyone else."

"Maybe Herrera helped him, and that's why he's dead now."

"Possibly. But why would he kill Stabler and let Herrera live another seven years?"

As we turned out onto the highway, I experienced a twinge of sadness. Another time, Paul would have suggested we stop in the woods and make whoopie.

I SPENT half of Monday rechecking what Gene had tasked Roy to do earlier—call car rental places to see if someone rented a vehicle to Hardwick Pillsner on or about the fifteenth of March back in 2004. Unfortunately I was making my calls right as the New Mexico State Fair kicked off, and most people I spoke to made it clear they'd prefer to be renting cars to out-of-town tourists rather than looking up ancient records. I didn't even have Paul to help me with the chore. He was off with Detective Guerra reinterviewing principals in the old scam.

While I always try to keep an open mind, I became so obsessed with the idea Wick did away with the two VPMR officials that I was in danger of developing tunnel vision. Both Hazel and Charlie cautioned me against falling in love with my own theory. Even so they pitched in to help cover the bases. Midafternoon we gathered at the table in the corner of my office.

"Nothing," I said. "But Wick *had* to have a way to get back from wherever he hid the bodies."

"Maybe his wife helped him." Charlie suggested.

I considered the Wick I'd known for years. I saw his brutality in the way he played his sport, his determination when he coached me and a host of other tweeners in the art of football. This also gave me an insight into the clever way his mind worked and the speed with which he could change directions when the winds blew against him. I easily pictured him undertaking illegal acts, even violent ones, but I could not see him involving his family in any misdeeds.

"That's a possibility," I acknowledged. "But somehow I don't believe he'd involve them. He'd want to keep his image squeaky clean with his family."

Hazel put in her two cents. "Not everybody kept records that far back. Even so I'm willing to bet he didn't rent a car… under his own name, anyway."

I smacked my forehead with enough force to hurt. "Of course he didn't. He used the name he rented the house on Georgia Street under. William Stark."

She stood and stretched her back. "Here we go again."

Hazel found what we were looking for within half an hour with one of the larger locally owned car rental places. William Stark rented an SUV on the night of March 14, 2004. At Stark's request the vehicle was delivered to a cabin in the Sandias and picked up in the parking lot at a bar and lounge near VPMR's 3300 Lomas location on the morning of the sixteenth. A rough map of how to reach the delivery spot was still appended to the order. The bill was settled with a prepaid Visa card in the name of William Stark.

"I'm amazed anyone keeps records that far back," Hazel said, although she'd spent most of the day checking such records.

"Insurance and police," Charlie said. "They keep them for insurance purposes and so cops can trace people's movements. But I'm floored Wick made such a bonehead mistake."

"He needed a way to get back to Albuquerque in a timely manner and figured the cover of William Stark would be enough," I said. "He used the best cover he had. It's mighty hard to move around this world and leave no traces at all."

"Lucky for us."

"Let's not count our chickens before they hatch," I cautioned.

I wasted no time in getting the information to Gene. Within the hour he let us know the Voxlightner family once owned a 10-acre spread on the mountain at what seemed the terminus of the rough map in the car rental agency's files. Marshall Voxlightner, not Barron. When I contacted Dorothy, she confirmed the entire family and a few friends made liberal use of the mountain cabin until she sold the property shortly after the precious metals fiasco broke in 2004.

GENE GOT a search warrant for the former Voxlightner property on Sandia Peak by noon the following day. An appointment with the police chief to discuss his promotion left him unable to serve the paper himself. Det. Roy Guerra welcomed Paul's and my company the next day as we drove up the back of the mountain in his departmental blue Ford.

The present owners were a family named Gillis who waved away the need for a warrant and invited us to search wherever we wanted. They were the second owners following the sale of the tract by the Voxlightners, having been in residence only two years. They had never seen abandoned cars and certainly not stray human bones.

After our exhausting search showed nothing, we came off the mountain frustrated, but I was unwilling to let it go. Wick wouldn't have parked the cars in the woods. He'd have hidden them someway. A Chevrolet Blazer and a Ford Crown Victoria concealed somewhere on the mountain held what was left of Barron and Walther. I *knew* it and was determined to prove it.

The next day I began my search in earnest. A few people I knew held privately owned plots in the Cibola National Forest, and on Sandia Peak in particular. Several phone calls developed some interesting information. The man everyone pointed to as being most knowledgeable about the Sandias was Foxy Slight.

Foxy was not easy to find. Reclusive and described as about halfway hostile—which I read as loopy—he lived in a board cabin in a small canyon a mile or so off the paved Sandia Crest National Scenic Byway, the road running to the top of Sandia Peak. Apparently he could hear a car approaching from half a mile away and was never home when Roy, Paul, and I arrived. After the third try Roy stopped at the nearest neighbor's place to ask about Foxy. The man about laughed us off his place but in the end agreed to get word to Foxy some folks wanted to talk to him about the old Voxlightner place. He suggested we not mention one of us was a badge-wielding lawman.

As we came off the mountain yet again, Roy asked why I was so set on locating a character who went by the name of Foxy. "That name oughta tell us you can't trust his word."

"If we approach him right, I'll wager we can get a load of information from him," I said.

"Vince is a history buff," Paul volunteered. "From all we've heard, it sounds like this Foxy is one too. If so, Vince can communicate with him."

"What are we looking for?" Roy asked.

"Old mines," I said.

"Mines?"

"Mines or mining shafts. I know there are some up there, but I can't find a sign of one on any of the maps."

"Sign?"

"You know," Paul said. "A crossed pick and shovel on the map."

"I didn't know they mined anything up there. I know about the coal at Madrid, but that's a long way from the Voxlightner place," Roy said.

"Uh-oh." Paul made no effort to hide the sigh in his voice. "You just asked the wrong question."

So I delivered my history lesson. "The Spanish mined the Sandias and the Manzanos long before the Anglos got here. And before the Spanish, the local natives likely did as well. The Spanish are said to have operated five gold mines somewhere near Placitas. They used Indian slaves to work until Popé's Rebellion. After the Pueblos threw out the Spanish, the natives are supposed to have filled the mines with dirt."

"Be damned," Roy said.

"There's an old legend the Aztec emperor Montezuma shipped a fortune in gold northward to keep it out of the hands of Cortez's invaders. The stories say it's hidden in the foothills near Placitas."

"Placitas is at the north end of Sandia Peak. That's a pretty good distance from the Voxlightner property."

"True. Don't forget there's the Galena King Mine in the Manzanos where they mined lead and fluorspar for years. One *Albuquerque Journal* report said they hit a vein of gold."

"The Galena's too far south of the Voxlightner place," Roy objected.

"And there's supposed to be nothing in between? There are lots of reports of lost turquoise mines. And then there are the coke ovens about a mile and a half off the Sandia Peak road. That's evidence of mining."

"Okay, okay. I'm convinced. But shouldn't we be asking the people at the School of Mines instead of a fellow named Foxy?"

"Good idea," I said. "You pursue them while I hunt for Foxy."

THE STATE fair had barely concluded when New Mexico's biggest show, the Albuquerque International Balloon Fiesta, kicked off. Both Paul and I had our fill of fighting bumper-to-bumper traffic, wearing layered clothing, and jostling crowds to participate in the Fiesta, but we weren't averse to getting up early and watching the grand ascension on TV on the first Saturday in October. But if you've never been to the festival before, it's well worth the trouble to witness pilots readying their crafts, hear the throaty hiss of burners, be overwhelmed by colors, some of which were never dreamed of by the rainbow, hear exclamations uttered in a myriad of languages, and finally watch as hundreds of balloons launch into the blue Albuquerque sky. The special shapes in particular delighted children. Darth Vader, the Creamland Cow, a water bottle, a lady bug, three different bees, and countless more shared the skies with the Yellow Sub and ordinary-shaped balloons.

Of course this also meant the streets were clogged with traffic, the hotels and motels were full, and people were more concerned with pleasure than with answering a confidential investigator's pushy questions.

WHEN I finally ran Foxy to ground, the name described the man. He owned a sharp nose, which contributed considerably to his nickname. But the appellation defined the man's character as well.

The neighbor had done his task well. After a couple of fruitless trips up Sandia, Paul and I found Foxy Slight at his cabin. A small, sly, and suspicious man, he was reluctant to talk until I told him what I knew of the Sandias. Forming the eastern edge of the Rio Grande Rift Valley, the mountains, actually a single mountain with two crests, the northern known as Sandia Crest and the southern as Sandia Peak, rose a million or so years ago. K-spar crystals in the Sandia granite gave the mountain a distinctive pink color, especially in the autumn light, giving rise to the Spanish name of Sandia, meaning watermelon. Local Pueblos call the mountain Bien Mur—big mountain—or Sleeping Turtle because of its distinctive shape. The Tewas and the Navajo had their own names for the hulking mass of rock.

That was enough to loosen Foxy's tongue. I'd given the geologic history, but he recited the human past, from the critically important gap between the Sandias and the Manzanos, which means apples—or more appropriately apple trees—in Spanish. Tijeras Pass served as a trade route to the Rio Grande valley for millennia. His discourse was interesting to me, but Paul was beginning to fidget beneath our host's outpouring of dialogue. Even so I heard Foxy out until he spoke the magic words.

"Heard tell you was interested in the old Voxlightner place."

"That's right."

"Right nice place when the old man was alive. He come up hardscrabble hisself, so he was sociable with the locals. The old lady was standoffish, but okay. The kids, though. Thought they was made out of diamonds and emeralds. Didn't want nothing to do with the local folk. Brought their own friends."

"You ever run into a man named Hardwick Pillsner?"

"Wick? Sure. He used to come up all the time. He wasn't too uppity to talk to a man. I always liked Wick. And he was sure a corker of a football lineman in his day."

I let him run on for a little, hoping he'd say something that would catch my ear. Eventually, I interrupted to ask about old mines in the area.

"Hell yes. They's abandoned shafts all through this country. Have to be careful where you put your boots. Liable to step into one of them. Some of them's kinda growed over and hard to spot."

"Any big ones in the area?"

"A whopper. A hole as big as a locomotive engine in the side of a canyon wall. Or used to be."

He caught my attention. "When was the last time you were in it?"

"Who said I been in it?"

"Come on. Bet you have a pickax and a miner's helmet in that cabin over there. You've probably tested rock in the tunnel a dozen times."

His smile heightened his resemblance to a varmint. "More like a hunnert, I'd guess. Traces but nothing commercial. Anyways I was off in that direction 'bout three months ago. This is September? No? October. Lordy, where did the year go? It was probably last May sometime."

"Anything different about it over the years?" I asked.

"Why don't you let me in on what you're looking for, and I'll tell you what I can. If you're planning on opening up the mine, save your money."

"No. I'm looking for a 2003 Ford Crown Victoria and a 2004 Chevrolet Blazer. With a body in each of them."

"Lordy! You talking about murder. When?"

"The night of March 15, 2004."

His eyebrows shot up. "That's a long time back. I can tell you for certain there ain't no vehicles in the place. Over the years the shaft's closed up. But back in them days I was a little more hopeful and went inside regular-like. You can't go more'n fifty feet into the adit now, but I'm here to tell you nobody stashed two cars in there. I found them, I'd be riding in style not bumming around in a worn-out pickup."

My heart sank.

"But you know," he said slowly, "I got a more likely place for you. What you're saying might explain something I been puzzling over for years."

"How many years?" Paul asked.

"Since something like five er ten years. Hop in the truck. I wanna show you something."

I would have preferred the comfort of Paul's Charger, but Foxy knew what he was doing. Pretty soon he was climbing over rocks that would have stopped the Dodge cold. I thought I'd break my neck on the ceiling of the cab before we entered a large glade with an area in the middle protected by a rusted fence bearing a No Trespassing sign.

We piled out of the pickup and trailed him to the fence where he ignored the warning and vaulted over it easily. Paul and I followed a bit less deftly. Foxy gestured to a large hole in the ground, circular in nature, with a big chunk torn out of the far wall. The interior was black, so I couldn't tell how deep it was. Foxy picked up a stone and tossed it inside. A few seconds elapsed before we heard it hit bottom.

"This here was a vertical shaft around a hunnert feet deep. Some fellers dug it out in the fifties when they thought they'd found gold. They used to be some gold mines up in the Placitas area, they claim."

"A couple of hundred years ago," I said.

"Anyhow this big mother's been gaping here ever since I was a kid. I got fifty years in the country, you know. Family come here when I was six. There used to be a rickety wood ladder fixed to the side, and you know how kids is. It was a hole to be explored, so I explored it. Been down in it a hunnert times at least. Even repaired the ladder a few times when rungs rotted away."

"When's the last time you were down it."

"Been years now."

"How come?" Paul asked.

"Cause the last time I come here, it was different. See the caved-in place over on the other side. It used to be solid, but something tore out the side. Dumped a few tons of dirt and rock down in the hole. And the ladder weren't there no more. I found a couple of pieces of charred wood up on the ground, but that's all."

"Someone dynamited it," I said.

"I figure."

"Can you remember when it was?"

"Not exactly. But like I said, five-ten years back. After that happened I used to come across pieces of metal around the area once in a while."

"You still have any of it?" I asked.

"Hell no. Metal's money. Hauled it down to Albukerk and sold it to a scrap metal place on Juan Tabo, just off of Central."

"Damn," Paul said.

Foxy gave his crafty smile. "But I kept one piece. A license plate. New Mexico, it was."

"Where is it?" I asked.

"Back at my place. Come on. I'll show you."

Once we arrived back at Foxy's cabin, I understood why he kept the plate. One wall of the shack's front room was covered in vehicle licenses from several states in varying stages of rust. He tapped one of them.

"This here's the one I picked up out at the shaft."

The number, 300-BTE, looked vaguely familiar. I'd seen it in some of the reports on the Voxlightner investigation. I was pretty sure it was the plate off Walther Stabler's Crown Vic.

Bingo! I'd found Wick's body dump.

"Mr. Slight?" Paul began.

"Call me Foxy."

"Foxy, why didn't you report this to the police?"

"How come? A feller finds all kinds a things up here. Can't call the sheriff's office on everything. Before long they'd figure you was crazy."

"But the whole countryside was looking for two men who disappeared."

The little man shrugged. "I didn't know nothing about it."

Foxy demanded $100 for the rusty license plate. Paul and I put our wallets together and managed to come up with the ransom. I wrote out a statement for Foxy's signature while he and Paul went back to the partially collapsed mine shaft so my companion could take pictures.

Chapter 18

PAUL AND I sat in Gene's office while he and Roy examined the rusty license plate, now protected by a clear plastic bag. It was from Stabler's Crown Victoria, all right. I'd checked the records the minute we got back to town yesterday afternoon. And Gene was rechecking them right now.

"Yep. It's the plate from Stabler's car," he acknowledged. "I'll need a statement from you and Paul and this Foxy fella."

I handed over a manila envelope. "Already signed and notarized. Also Foxy Slight's statement and a certified copy of the car rental contract in the name of William Stark."

"How do you figure it went down? Why the dynamite?"

I leaned forward in my chair and tapped Gene's desk. "With his world collapsing around his ears, Barron Voxlightner was at VPMR headquarters that fatal night determined to get to the bottom of what happened."

"And he probably asked Stabler to help him figure it out," Paul said.

"Talk about the fox in the hen house," Roy added.

"Wick stopped by the company's offices. Voxlightner might or might not have found something incriminating, but it didn't really matter. The company was looted by then, and it was time for the perps to get out of town. So Voxlightner needed to disappear as well, to come in for his share of the blame."

"Poor sap," Gene said. "He probably didn't take a dime."

"That's my take too. At any rate Wick and Stabler killed Barron, probably in the VPMR offices on Lomas. They loaded Barron into his car and arranged for Wick to drive him up to the mine shaft."

"And Stabler followed to drive Wick back to town."

"Or so he thought. Wick already had a disposal spot picked out. The mine shaft isn't more than a thirty-minute walk from the Voxlightner cabin where he'd ordered a rental car delivered the night before."

"That proves intent," Gene said. "Think Stabler knew what he intended?"

"We'll never know. My guess is the two of them discussed the situation and came to some sort of agreement."

I paused to reclaim my train of thought. "Wick and Stabler drove in two different vehicles to the shaft and got the Blazer down the hole with Barron's body inside. While Stabler looked over the side to see if the Chevrolet was visible, Wick popped him on the head and shoved him down the shaft. Then Wick maneuvered Stabler's Crown Vic into place and sent it over the side."

"Coulda gone down something like that," Gene said. "But there were two of them to get the Blazer down the shaft. Wick had to get Stabler's car over the side by himself. And that's not easy."

"Remember Wick's an athlete. Even if he carried some years at the time, he was still in good shape. He probably positioned the car at the brink with the motor running, put it in gear, and tossed a rock on the accelerator."

"That's probably the way it happened," he agreed.

"But I think something went wrong," I said.

"How so?"

"I suspect Wick intended to dynamite the opening to the pit once he was done. He brought the explosive for that purpose."

"So?" Roy asked.

"I think the Crown Vic didn't go down right. Maybe got wedged partway down. So Wick dropped a stick down the hole, which is why Foxy picked up scattered metal and a license plate for some time afterward. That's also why the ladder was completely gone with only some charred wood left. The stick probably drove the cars a little deeper. Then Wick dynamited one side of the shaft to send a few tons of earth down on the cars. After that he walked to the Voxlightner place, got in his rental, and came down the mountain. He parked the rental at the bar and lounge where he'd stowed his own Caddy."

"Lotta damned theory based on an old license plate, some charred wood, and chunks of metal." Gene sighed. "But it makes a lotta sense. How in the hell am I going to be able to tie Wick with this mysterious Stark fellow?"

"Simple. We have Brown's testimony that Wick bought a cashier's check at Smith's Food and Drug in the name of William Stark."

"Did Wick pay for it with Stark's Visa card?"

"Nope. Cash."

Gene leaned back in his chair. "Touchy. I gotta think on this some. Not sure I want to brace Wick with what we know without excavating the pit and seeing what's down there." He held up a hand to forestall Paul's objection. "Proof of what's down there, not conjecture."

"Who's going to pay for it?" I asked. "It'll cost a bundle."

"Might take what we have to the FBI and let them spend their money."

"Would they be interested?" Paul asked.

"Only if they're gonna get publicity and credit for solving a case."

DOROTHY VOXLIGHTNER insisted on paying for the excavation needed to expose what lay at the bottom of the abandoned mine shaft in the Sandias. A few days before her crew arrived at the site, Gene put a watch on Hardwick Pillsner. Albuquerque might legally qualify as a city, but it was more like a gossipy, overgrown small town when it came to the way its citizens reacted.

For the two days it took to excavate the shaft, members of the Albuquerque Police Department, the Bernalillo and Sandoval County deputies—since no one was quite sure who had jurisdiction—and someone from the FBI were on-site. The Cibola National Forest ranger was also on hand to see the damage done their 10,678-foot high piece of rock called Sandia Mountain was kept to the minimum.

We came upon the remains of the Crown Victoria first. Damage from the explosion went beyond extensive to catastrophic. I estimated Foxy had probably carted off the entire rear end of the big car to sell as scrap.

When it came time to remove the crumpled Blazer, I called to inform Dorothy Voxlightner. She insisted on being present for the extraction. When my warnings were disregarded, Paul went to Voxlightner Castle and picked her up.

What we assumed to be Barron's body was mostly skeletal and relatively intact. Dr. Stabler had a car dumped on him and was not so lucky. As the crane brought out the Blazer, Dorothy rested against Paul's shoulder. Tender feelings for my lover reached new depths at that moment. I said a quiet prayer of thanks Barron's body wasn't evident. Once the Blazer was on solid ground, we found his grisly remains behind the rear seats of the vehicle. She insisted on taking a look, but almost immediately broke down. Paul escorted her back to the Charger while I hung around the mine shaft with Gene to wrap things up.

The Office of the Medical Investigator conducts all autopsies in the state of New Mexico. Forewarned they had a crew on-site at the time the bodies were recovered. The doctor in charge conducted a brief viewing of the two skeletal corpses before ordering them placed into the ambulance. After Paul took Dorothy back home, Gene, Roy, and I talked with the excavation crew.

"My guess is, the vehicles lodged about three-quarters of the way down the shaft," the red-headed crew chief said. "Somebody dumped something—probably a stick of dynamite—in the hole, and up she went. From the condition of the Crown Vic, I'd say its gas tank went off and ripped up the tail end of the car. Then it went to burning until the whole north side of the wall caved in on them."

"More dynamite?" Gene asked.

"Coulda been. Or maybe it was weakened by the first blast. I can show you the fill we took out first. A test might still be able to find evidence of dynamite. Traces of nitroglycerin, maybe. Seven years ago? Never can tell."

THE HEADLINE—ONE of Paul's stories—in the *Albuquerque Journal* the next morning reported the recovery of two bodies on the east slope of Sandia Mountain believed to be the missing tycoon Barron Voxlightner and Dr. Walther Stabler. The article went on to say both disappeared on the evening of March 15, 2004 and were thought to have fled upon the breaking of the Voxlightner scandal. The discovery was forcing the authorities to rethink their conclusions about the old crime.

I could only wonder at the exquisite torture those words provoked in Dorothy. The discovery might lead to vindication… but at what price? Even if she accepted the probability of her son's death years ago, proof of her conviction must have been difficult to face.

OMI, sensitive to the public interest in the old case, rushed the autopsies and released the results on Monday. DNA evidence proved the bodies were Voxlightner and Stabler. Voxlightner died as a result of a blow to the head by a blunt object. Stabler's cause of death was likely the same, but having a large car dropped on him rendered the verdict less certain.

Because at least one of the murders was likely committed in Albuquerque and Gene already had an ongoing investigation, the other jurisdictions stepped back and allowed him to take the lead.

"How's this going to affect your coming promotion?" I asked.

"Dammit, BJ, this is probably my last field investigation. At least let me enjoy it!"

I CAME to admire Wick—in a weird sort of way—after the discovery of Voxlightner's and Stabler's remains. He must have been aware he was under observation but made no effort to flee. He set off a minor panic once when he flew his private plane to Gallup for a business meeting. Otherwise he remained in town and went about his life as if everything were normal. Maybe it *was* normal to him. He'd lived with the knowledge he'd killed at least two men for over seven years. And that didn't include Everett Kent, the lawyer murdered in his office, or Thelma Rider or Dr. Damon Herrera. Or John Pierce Belhaven, for that matter.

Was Wick technically a serial killer? Is a man who kills serially in order to keep something in his past from unraveling the same as a man who kills multiple victims out of some dark compulsion? Not to my mind. They are different sorts of evil. Of course, no one had so far proved Hardwick Pillsner killed anyone. Not yet, anyway. But I intended to correct such a deficiency.

THE FORENSICS team was still working at the shaft in the Sandias and on the vehicles when Roy, Paul, and I gathered in Gene's office. The subject quickly became whether or not there would be forensic evidence after all this time.

"Sir," Roy addressed his lieutenant, "you know as well as I do fingerprints can last forty or more years."

"Provided they're not exposed to water," Gene said.

"It rains up in the Sandias more than down in Albuquerque," Roy said, "but the terrain's steeper, so runoff's faster. I doubt moisture would penetrate very far."

Gene turned to look at his newly minted detective and raised a thick eyebrow. "Now think about that for a minute. This is a hole we're talking about. Rain falling in it has no runoff capability. So what does it do?"

Roy grimaced. "Soak through to the bottom of the hole."

"And," Paul added, "some of the rain from higher ground pours over the side to add to the moisture content."

"Okay. I see your point."

I let a little silence grow. "It might be fortunate Voxlightner's body was inside the Blazer. The vehicle may have provided some protection from the water. It's possible they may find biological and trace evidence on it."

Gene sighed aloud. "The windows were shattered. No use wasting our time speculating. The forensics boys will find something if it's there."

"One of the team told me they found a length of pipe with an elbow joint at one end," Roy said.

"If I had to guess, it's the murder weapon. Used on both of them," I said. "Unfortunately I'm betting it was found outside the cars."

Roy nodded. "Yeah. It got several good soakings over the years."

Gene picked up a letter opener and poked the blotter on his desk. "We'll see what the lab can tell us."

"What do you do about Wick until then?" Paul asked.

"Nothing. Beyond keeping an eye on him, that is. We don't have anything to hang on him at this point beyond him using the name of William Stark. And even that isn't proven yet." Gene tossed the letter opener aside and leaned back in his chair. "Tell me again who this William Stark fellow is… or was?"

"Have you ever read William Penn Warren's *All the King's Men*?"

"Saw the movie. Good one. Won a bunch of Oscars."

"Broderick Crawford won one for playing…."

He picked it up right on cue. "Willie Stark." Gene sat straight in his chair. "Be damned. Willie Stark. William Stark."

"And Sadie Burke was his devotee and sometimes lover."

"Isn't that the name the Rider woman used to rent the house on Georgia?"

"And we ran into other characters in the book."

"Be damned. Wick peopled his fantasy get-rich-quick-scheme with characters from fiction."

DOROTHY CALLED and asked me to visit her at Voxlightner Castle. Paul had developed a good relationship with what I considered to be a lonely, tragic woman, so he accompanied me. She greeted me with old-world courtesy and Paul with a broad smile. After the obligatory coffee and tea, she was silent for a very long time before finally speaking.

"For me it seems like it's over now, but I know that to be far from the truth. Wick must be made to pay for his crimes. For… for killing Barron." She set an untasted cup of coffee on the table before her. "I thought I would be overjoyed to finally learn what happened to my son, but this isn't true. Not even locating him so he can be buried properly gives me much satisfaction. I simply have a different sort of emptiness."

"In the first place, ma'am," I said, "we don't know for certain Wick is the killer. Everything points in that direction, but unless the forensics team can come up with something from the abandoned mine pit…."

She looked at me with a glint in her eyes and broke the silence I'd allowed to grow. "Is there any question in your mind?"

I hesitated but couldn't lie to her. "I'm confident Hardwick Pillsner killed your son and Walther Stabler, as well as some others. But at this point I can't prove it."

She swiped at her eyes. "I believe you are correct in your assessment. And if you believe he killed Pierce, then you have fulfilled your assignment."

For the life of me, I don't know why I hesitated, but I did. "Reason tells me he did that killing as well."

She studied me mutely. In her day she must have been a formidable woman. Still was. "But you are not certain?"

"I would like to hear what Wick has to say when the time comes. But to show you I'm not padding the bill, I'll go off the clock as of now."

"You'll do no such thing. I want proof Wick killed my son. And I want proof he killed Pierce Belhaven."

I cocked an eyebrow at her. "As perverse as this sounds, we are more likely to find proof of a seven-and-a-half-year-old murder than a three-month-old one."

"Please get this bastard for me, BJ."

"We'll do our best, ma'am," Paul said, earning a mournful smile from the widow Voxlightner.

As we drove away in my Impala, Paul glanced over his shoulder. "She's a nice lady."

I nodded. "But she has claws you haven't seen yet."

He turned back and settled in his seat with a laugh. "I'd bet on it. You seemed kinda hesitant back there when she asked if you believe Wick killed Belhaven. You have doubts?"

"Not doubts exactly. But it has a different feel about it. Wick had close connections with all the other victims. He moved in their circles. So far as I can tell, he and Belhaven weren't connected. I'm sure they knew one another because they both revolved around the Voxlightner family, but Pierce's killing feels different."

"How?"

"Well, for one thing, how did Wick gain entry to Belhaven's house?"

"Rang the bell and got invited in."

"Think about that for a moment. Belhaven uncovered the clue about the Georgia Street address. But Abner Brown, who sold Wick the money order for rent on the place, said no one else contacted him about who actually bought the money order. Even though Belhaven probably didn't *know* Wick was involved, he must have suspected. Would he have let someone he even remotely considered as a killer into his house at night when he was alone?"

Paul considered his answer. "Pierce was a strange guy. Timid at times and aggressive at others. He could have let Wick in the house in the belief he could talk him into confessing. But I've got a better one. What if Wick phoned him, said he'd heard an afternoon TV news program, and offered information to help solve the puzzle?"

"Could be." I clapped him on the nape of the neck. "Good job, guy. You just poked a hole in my theory. Shows the old noodle's working."

Paul basked silently in reflected glory until we arrived home. As usual we went around back to enter the house through the kitchen. Paul once asked me why we took this route, and I told him it saved my creaky old bones from having to maneuver the steps at the front porch. The real reason was the back way was often the nearest. Paul's Charger in front of me on the drive rendered that false. But a pattern is a pattern.

As Paul keyed the back lock, I caught movement in a reflection in a kitchen window. I instantly shoved him to the ground and dropped onto my back, clawing for my pistol as I fell. The boom of a weapon barely preceded the pane of glass shattering where Paul stood a millisecond earlier.

Chapter 19

TWO MORE gunshots reverberated around the yard, but I saw enough to know the gunman was firing wildly now that I had my little .25 caliber Colt Junior in hand. He disappeared around the garage as I got off a shot. I scrambled to my feet and charged for the back gate, ignoring Paul's cries of protest. He didn't know what the shooter carried, but he knew my weapon was a wildly inaccurate and underpowered peashooter.

By the time I reached the alley, the ambusher had disappeared. Which backyard did he cut through? The house to my left had a dog, and it wasn't barking. The shooter had crossed the alley and cut through someone's property to the street behind us. I vaulted a fence and raced through a neighbor's yard. Upon reaching the street I saw no one but heard a retreating car motor. Not a racing one, just a normal purr.

Paul and I split up to knock on every door in the neighborhood. No one I talked to had seen a stranger in the area. Not surprising. At this time of day, around 2:30 p.m., there was little foot traffic.

When Paul and I met at the house after our search, we sat on the front steps and talked things over. He'd had no better luck than I had. I expected Paul to be shaken, but he wasn't. He was mad.

"Second time the bastard's come for me."

"I suspect he was here for both of us this time."

"Somebody doesn't like us working on this case."

"Unless you've been chasing someone's girlfriend… or boyfriend."

He gave me a look. "I haven't. You?"

"Nope. So do you know what that means?"

"What?"

"Somebody just made a mistake."

"Shouldn't we call the police?"

"Don't worry, someone already has."

A few minutes later a patrol car with flashing lights arrived, followed by the brown Ford I was expecting. Gene got out of the Ford looking gruff. Gruff was his cover for caring.

"Who'd you piss off this time?" he called as he approached. The officer who'd just arrived stood aside deferentially.

"Any number of suspects," I said.

"I've told you time and again, you're a pain in the ass. The shooter wasn't Wick Pillsner. According to my man keeping watch on him, he's in his office on East Lomas."

"Somebody he hired," Paul said. "Just like the bozo who T-boned me."

"Likely," Gene said. "You guys all right?"

"Wouldn't be if Vince hadn't seen a reflection in the kitchen window."

"See who it was?"

I shook my head. "Didn't even see the car he drove off in. We canvassed all the neighbors, but your guys can do it again."

"So he parked himself in the alley and waited for you to come home, and nobody noticed?"

The older neighborhoods in Albuquerque had drivable alleyways behind the houses. The newer areas forewent such conveniences as the price of land escalated. Their backyards simply met at a fence line.

"Most people around here are retirees, Gene. Lots of folks napping this time of day. I could sit behind my garage, and nobody would spot me. But no, I think he probably picked us up on the way home, parked his car on the street behind me, and hoofed it to the back of the house."

"What kind of detective are you? You didn't notice a car tailing you?"

"Don't think he was behind me long enough for me to spot him as a threat."

Gene's officers did no better with the neighbors than we had. His team retrieved the spent bullet embedded in our kitchen wall and hauled it to the forensics lab on North Second Street. They'd confirm it was a .38 slug and check to see if it came from a weapon used in a previous crime but would learn little else. The cops didn't locate the other two projectiles, confirming my suspicion the would-be assassin, rattled when he failed to hit either of us, shot wild.

"The shooter was new to this, wasn't he?" Paul asked.

"I'd say so. That tells me something too."

"What?" Gene and Paul asked simultaneously.

"I can't see Wick hiring a rank amateur to try to get at us. And isn't it a little late in the game? We've already found two men he killed. Pierce's killing I understand. Somebody was trying to stop the dam from breaking. But it's broken now, so the attack on Paul and this one on the two of us doesn't make sense."

"It does one thing," Gene said.

"What?" Paul asked.

"Sows doubt," Gene answered. "BJ's making a good point. Maybe sending us running to find answers will raise questions about what we've found."

"Would you repeat that?" Paul said.

"He means send us on a wild goose chase," I explained. "But if you get a good fingerprint or biological information off what came out of the mine shaft, there won't be any doubt."

"Already have. Fingerprints anyway. Badly degraded but usable. And they're Wick's."

"You have his prints on file?" Paul asked.

Gene grinned. "Thank God for the college years. Wick got drunk with a bunch of frat boys, and when a brawl broke out, everyone was hauled to the station. They were released, but we still have his prints."

"Where did you find the print from the dump site?" I asked.

"Prints, actually. One on the Blazer's dashboard. The other one on an inside driver's side door handle on the Crown Victoria. He tried to wipe everything clean but missed those two."

Paul couldn't hide the excitement in his voice. "Then we've got him."

"Maybe a little closer but probably about a year away."

"Huh?"

"Gene means it'll be a long time before this comes to trial, and a defense lawyer's going to try to explain those prints away."

When his team was finished, Gene couldn't resist a little BJ sniping. He held up the evidence bag holding my little Colt. Since I had fired at the assailant, Gene was taking the weapon in. "What were you gonna do if you hit him with this? Put a Band-Aid on him and give him an aspirin? Crap, where's your Ruger?"

"In the trunk of the Impala, where it usually is."

"Next time just spit at him!"

THE FOLLOWING morning Hazel greeted someone entering the outer office. A moment later she stuck her head in the door to my inner sanctum, her owl-eyes expressing surprise.

"Wick Pillsner wants to see you."

I closed the file on the desk before me. "Send him in."

I rose as the balding, hawk-nosed man entered my office, offering a hand in greeting. Accepting it, I regarded the fiftyish jock refusing to give in to flab. The gray in the hair and the wrinkles on the face were there, but so were the muscles in his arms. How much time did this guy spend in the gym? I gestured him to a chair as I pressed a button on my digital recorder, which lay on my desk. He showed how sharp he was by agreeing we probably needed a recording of the visit and asked for a copy.

"BJ," he got down to business. "I understand you're the prime mover behind the renewed investigation of the VPMR disaster. I also understand you believe I was behind the looting of the company."

Albuquerque has always been a gossipy town, but this guy's connections went far beyond simple chin-wagging. Some of his contacts probably reached into APD. "I've not expressed any such conclusion publicly."

"You're too careful for that. But I'm assured that is your conviction."

"And if it is?" I asked. Doubtless he knew exactly what Paul and I had been doing. But that was not why he was here. He'd come to see what I knew about the investigation, pick up information so he could prepare a defense against it.

"Then I'm here to say you're wrong."

"Okay, you've put your denial on record. But you're in the wrong place. Now that Barron Voxlightner's and Walther Stabler's bodies have been located, APD has taken charge. You need to see Lieutenant Gene Enriquez and go on record with him."

"And I will," he said, regarding me coolly through frameless bifocals. "But you're the one who found them. You broke it open, so I wanted to tell you face-to-face… your old coach isn't a killer."

"Low blow, Wick. Leave our past out of it. People do things and need to be held accountable regardless of what or who they've been in the past."

"Fair enough. But I want to look you in the eye and tell you I've made no attempt on you or your associate Paul Barton."

"I hope that's true. But you need to be in Lieutenant Enriquez's office, not mine."

He thanked me for my time and departed, leaving me to puzzle over the visit. He was mining for information, but he could have done this with a phone call. No. He was trying to deliver a message. And the only sensible thing was his denying the attempts on Paul and me had been his doing. Somehow I didn't have a problem accepting that at face value.

That was the moment I decided to change the focus of my investigation. Who made two attempts to harm Paul and me? And why? Could they have been red herrings as Gene suggested? Possibly. But the Voxlightner case was firmly in APD's hands now. Paul and I found Belhaven's reason for reopening the investigation and used it to expose Wick's role in the scandal. We'd found the two missing men. All that remained now was for APD's lab to process the evidence and for the FBI, who'd gotten interested after the hard work was done, to trace the missing money.

If Wick wasn't responsible for the attacks on Paul and me, who was and why? We weren't involved in any cases together other than this Voxlightner thing. There was Belhaven's killing. But they were one and the same case. Or were they? Logic said yes, but logic wasn't logic until all the p's and q's were known.

I thought over Wick's visit again. He didn't exhibit the demeanor of a desperate man. But many perps didn't until they were on the way to prison. No. He was more like a man delivering a message. Charlie would say Wick was merely spreading bug dust to cloud our vision, but I wasn't sure this was his intent.

Was he telling me he hadn't killed John Pierce Belhaven? Gene claimed I sometimes got caught up in weird theories roaming around in my own head. And that was true. But I always maintained a man shouldn't fall in love with a concept to the point where he refused to lift his gaze and look around occasionally.

Dorothy originally tasked me to find Belhaven's killer, although that was really a back door to finding out what happened to her son. Even so, an assignment was an assignment. I'd originally tackled it from the old Voxlightner scandal approach. Now I would try it another way and see if it led me back to Hardwick Pillsner.

PAUL WAS nonplussed when I told him that evening that I was returning to the Belhaven household to ask my questions anew.

"Why? It's clear Wick killed Pierce to keep him from doing what we did… expose him."

"That's not totally clear to me. Possible, yes. Highly probable? Again, yes. But what's the harm in working the case from a new standpoint while APD unearths the evidence to convict him?"

"Harm? I've already written and sold three stories about this case. And I wrapped it up with a neat bow."

I knew what bothered him. He'd allowed me to read the three pieces and responded to all my suggestions except the last one. I told him it was a bit premature to file the third and final pretrial story. But the editor pushed him for copy, and he'd submitted it anyway.

"What's more important? Your journalistic reputation or finding a killer? Besides if we turn up evidence leading elsewhere, that should enhance your standing, not diminish it. You fought the battle to the clear and evident end."

His look told me he didn't buy into my conclusion. I'd anticipated playing with Pedro that evening, but the dragon slept quietly on his master's chest throughout the night.

Breakfast the next morning was a subdued affair, but I could see he was thinking things over, not sulking. Like all of us, he pouted on occasion, but it never lasted long or went too deep. He agreed to accompany me to the Belhaven house after the kitchen was straightened.

Except for a brief good morning chat with Mrs. Wardlow who happened to be sweeping her sidewalk when we emerged from the house, we were silent on the four-block walk. Sarah Thackerson answered the doorbell. Her smile of greeting faltered before claiming her face again.

"Mr. Vinson, Paul. Nice to see you again. Are you still at it? I understood everything was settled."

"It's not wrapped up until a jury says so, and we're a long way from that," I said. "Is anyone else around?"

"Just Spencer. At least I hear his lawn mower, so he must still be here. He comes and goes on a schedule only he knows."

"Neither Harris nor Melanie are here?" I asked, referring to Pierce's son and daughter.

She shook her head. "No, although Harrison will be here later. He decided to move into the house. I guess he's overcome his dislike of his father." She looked stricken to have said such a thing aloud.

"I'd heard they didn't get along," I responded. "Do you mind if we come in for a few minutes? There are some questions we need to ask."

She backed away. "Certainly. Let's go to the office. That's about the only place I go in the house. It's not like when Pierce… uh, Mr. Belhaven was here."

"I understand." Once we were seated opposite her desk, I brought the conversation back to Pierce and Harris. "What was at the bottom of the trouble between father and son?"

"I don't like to gossip. Besides I don't know what caused the rift. Sometimes little things got on Mr. Belhaven's nerves."

"Like?" Paul asked. Perhaps he was coming out of his funk.

"Like it bothered him that Harrison wouldn't settle down and get married."

I wasn't willing to let go of the other angle yet. "Was there anything unusual about Mrs. Belhaven's death?"

Sarah glanced at me, a look of surprise on her face. "As I understand it, she died of lung cancer. She was a heavy smoker."

"When was that?"

"August 2006."

I allowed an obvious frown to claim my features. "I thought you told us earlier you came to work for Belhaven in 2005. Wouldn't you have known what killed her?"

Her left hand flew to her throat and fiddled with her collar. "I was still attending the University of New Mexico pretty much full-time back then. So I simply did my work and went home. I wasn't privy to family affairs at the time."

"I see." Clever response. I switched directions on her. "Has the estate been settled?"

"Oh no. I understand the process will take a year or so. But I've received my bequest, if that's what you're asking."

"That was fast."

Sarah licked her cupid's bow lips. "The lawyer handed out a few preliminary checks at the reading of the will. He's the executor of the estate, you see."

"He's getting the smaller bequests out of the way. Unusual but not unheard of. Did Spencer get his $250,000?"

When she nodded, I continued, "Your insurance as well?"

Sarah didn't try to hide her surprise. "You know about the policy? I guess everything's public when somebody gets murdered. Mr. Tibedeau interviewed me but said it would take a few weeks until the claim was paid. Mr. Tibedeau's the insurance company's investigator."

"We've met," Paul said.

"Did Tibedeau indicate there'd be a problem paying the insurance because Mr. Belhaven's killer isn't known?" Paul continued his questioning.

"But he is known. It's Mr. Pillsner. And I hear you two are the ones who exposed him."

I beat my buddy to the punch. "While Mr. Pillsner is doubtless responsible for a lot of things, killing Pierce Belhaven might not be one of them."

Sarah's brown eyes widened. She put a hand to her cheek. "Oh my goodness! Then who?"

"Maybe someone who profited from Pierce's death," Paul suggested.

I glanced at him. Maybe upstaging him in his developing professional life was harder for him to accept than I thought. We'd have to have a heart-to-heart.

Sarah muddied those waters. "Pierce made a number of bequests in his will. He was a very generous man."

Paul was relentless. "But not everyone has a life policy paying double in case of violent death."

"Are you suggesting *I* killed Pierce? That's ridiculous. I was on my way back from visiting my family in Bisbee. I spent the night Pierce was killed at the Super 8 Motel in Las Cruces. You can check my registration."

"I will," he snapped.

Paul wasn't making questioning Sarah Thackerson any easier. I slapped my knee to command attention. "We already have. And you are absolutely correct. You were registered in room 201 at the Super 8 on West Bataan Memorial. Checked in at 4:30 p.m."

Paul wouldn't leave it alone. "You coulda made it home in another three hours or so."

Hostility coarsened her throaty voice. "I don't travel well. I was tired, so I checked in for a dinner and a good rest. Any crime in that?"

"Sarah," I said, "who do you think killed Belhaven?"

"Mr. Pillsner would be my first choice. He had a reason, didn't he?"

"If you picked a second choice, who would it be?"

"Harrison, I guess. He hated his father."

I asked the question already asked. "Why?"

Her cheeks picked up a soft blush, and I'm certain her ears hidden beneath the lush hair were aflame. "As I told you, I'm not quite certain why." She shook her head. "I understood it might have been because Pierce prevented him from marrying some girl years ago. That was before

I knew any of them, of course." Then she surprised me by volunteering Harris had been having financial difficulties recently. "He's a stockbroker, you know. And from what I've read, the markets took a bad fall."

"Black Monday was August 8. Belhaven was murdered a couple of weeks before that, on the night of July 20."

She bristled. "Yes. But the stock market business has been wishy-washy for most of the year. I know from hearing Pierce talk that Harrison was having money problems."

"I see." I'd get Hazel to have another run at Harrison Belhaven's finances, but I didn't want Sarah Thackerson to think I'd moved him to the top of my suspect list. "How about Melanie Harper?"

"She's standoffish, but she's okay. She loved her father. Pierce could be a bit foolish at times, but she wouldn't do him harm." Sarah's eyes hardened. "That husband of hers, though."

"Cagney Harper? He had a problem with Pierce?"

"More like Pierce had a problem with him. Mr. Belhaven didn't like the man." She paused and tapped her lips with a long finger. "Didn't like Melanie marrying someone below her station."

I hid my surprise. "I understand Harper works for the Bureau of Land Management over in Grants."

"Runs the El Malpais Visitor's Center. But Pierce thought Melanie should've married a doctor or lawyer."

"Something of a snob, was he?" I asked.

She surprised me again by nodding. "About some things. But he was a wonderful man with some flaws. Just like the rest of us."

"How about Spencer Spears?" I asked.

A look of exasperation flitted across her face. She smoothed long brunette locks back from her left cheek. "That one!"

"Why don't you like him?"

Sarah's cheeks rouged up again. "He's an opportunist. Always cozying up to Pierce." As if aware of what she'd implied, she explained herself. "He wheedled money out of Pierce. Spence bought a car and was forever needing money to tinker with it, get insurance coverage. That's all I meant."

I adopted some of Paul's tactics. "You meant exactly what you said. He cozied up to your employer. Your lover. He was your competition, wasn't he?"

I expected a reaction but not the one I got. She stood and threw a pencil on the desk. "I think you should leave now. I'll let Harrison know you called."

"What time will he be home?"

The change in pace flustered Sarah. "I believe the markets close early… you know because of the time difference. He hasn't been living here long enough to establish a pattern, but he's usually home by six. Unless he has a business meeting, that is."

We thanked her for her time and took our leave. Paul was silent for the first two blocks of our walk.

"Sorry. Guess I wasn't too suave back there with my interview technique."

"No harm done. We got what we needed. But you and I need to talk."

He ran a hand through his curly brown hair. He never wore a hat or cap except on the tennis court or golf course. "Nah, I'm over it now. Everything's aces."

I led the way up onto the porch and keyed the lock before stepping aside. "You might be over it, but I'm not."

I fixed us a drink before we settled in the den. I gave him a long stare. He avoided my eyes. "Okay, what gives?" I asked. "Something's bothering you."

"I just got pissed you read my story on this Voxlightner thing and okayed it before I submitted it. Now you're off on a wild goose chase looking for Pierce's killer. My article tells the world Pillsner did it."

"No, you pointed out that clues were pointing to him. And be fair… I looked at your article *before* Wick Pillsner walked into my office."

"I've read the transcript of that meeting. All he did was deny he tried to harm either of us, but he denied he killed Voxlightner and Stabler too. He's a liar. How can you give his words any credence?"

I sighed and studied the tumbler in my hand. "After a while you learn to listen beyond the voice. You listen to the man's tone, his inflections. You read his body language. I could be dead wrong, but I believe him when he said he made no attempt on either of us. That doesn't mean he didn't kill Belhaven, but even if he did, someone else tried to harm us for some reason I can't fathom. Two attacks, Paul. I don't know about you, but I take attempts at bodily harm personally."

He set his empty glass on the coffee table. "I guess, but…."

"But what?"

"But nothing."

"Oh no. You don't get off that easily. What's behind all this, Paul? We're walking on rose petals here. What's eating at you?"

"I'm just getting started, BJ. And I have to be careful about my reputation. I feel like I shot myself in the toe."

BJ. He said BJ, not Vince. Something was going on here. But from the way he was acting, now wasn't the time to probe. I got up. "Okay. Tell me when you're ready."

"Tell you what?"

"Whatever's bothering you."

"I already said—"

"Please, Paul. There's something bothering you, and it's not your professional career."

"All right!" He leaned back in the chair and closed his eyes like a man exhausted by life. "There's somebody down at the *Journal.* I guess I didn't want to disappoint him."

I fell back into my chair. He opened his eyes and looked at me. "This guy?" I asked. "Who is it? The editor you're writing for?"

His cranium wobbled like a bobblehead doll. "No. Not the editor." He closed his mouth, and a silence grew between us, chilling the air and making it hard for me to breathe. "There's this kid. A copy boy, I guess you'd call him. He… he really likes my work. We've mostly talked on the computer, you know, edits and things. So I guess I was pissed because I'd settled things one way, and here you were trying to stir them up in another direction."

"So you have an admirer at the paper."

"Yeah." He cleared his throat. "I guess."

"And how old is this boy?"

"Eighteen… twenty."

I experienced something. Brain fade, maybe. My saliva tasted toxic. "How far has it gone?"

"How—" he choked on his word. "How far? It hasn't gone anywhere. Nothing. Nowhere."

"Paul, be reasonable. If it was nothing or nowhere, we wouldn't be having this conversation. What do you want from me? Permission?"

His eyes flew wide open. "Permission? Permission for what? I don't want to do anything with him." His jaw snapped shut with an audible click. "But sometimes I think about it."

I heard the words as if underwater. Distant. Indistinct. Yet somehow crystal clear. The thirteen-year age difference between us loomed large. "When… when you're with me?"

His visage turned thunderous. "No. Never. I love you, Vince. It's just…. Well, I've never been tempted before, and it scares me."

I released a long breath. "I take some comfort in that."

"What should I do?" he whispered.

His question blew away some of my building confidence. "It's your decision. I have no claim over you beyond making you understand how much I treasure you. As long as that's enough, everything will be fine. When it's not, then…."

He focused on me. Really focused. "I'm not breaking up with you, Vince. I've got five awesome years invested in us, and I'm not ready to give you up."

"Nor am I. You'll have to fight your way through this. I'm here for support… or to talk if you need to. But there's one thing I won't put up with, Paul. You can't let personal problems interfere with your professionalism. Ever."

The frightened, unconvinced look on his handsome face sent my senses reeling.

Chapter 20

NEITHER OF us rested that night. I tossed and turned so much, Paul mumbled something about my restlessness bothering him. He collected his pillow and headed for the couch in the den. As frightened and confused as I was, I took some solace he hadn't gone to the other bedroom. That would have seemed… permanent.

Saturday and Sunday staggered by. I wanted to discuss our situation root and branch, but his panicked look whenever I got close to the subject convinced me we'd never get past the leaves. I barely slept.

Feeling like waterlogged driftwood, I made it into the office by nine on Monday morning. Paul had been gone when I woke from a fitful sleep. I tried with all my strength to keep from wondering where he was but failed.

Hazel, sharp enough to ask what was wrong, accepted my excuse of a lousy night's sleep and dumped things on my desk for me to sign: checks, reports, a final billing. Whatever. I could have been signing a petition for the extermination of homosexuals for all I knew.

Eventually she left me alone to puzzle over what to do next. What I wanted to do was go find Paul, wrap him in my arms, and never let go. What I did was call Harris Belhaven and ask for an appointment. When he found out I wanted to talk about Pierce's death, not reinvesting my father's trust fund with him, he settled for a drink at the Apothecary Lounge on East Central near the main Presbyterian Hospital campus later in the day.

I relented midafternoon and called Paul's cell, but it went to voicemail. I left a message inviting him to join Harris and me but got a text half an hour later saying he had something on and would pass. He'd fill me in tonight. *That* left my imagination running all over the place.

WHEN I met Harris at the Apothecary, he'd lost much of the anger I'd noticed before but none of the sensuality. I wondered what Paul was doing right at the moment, and the proximity of the two thoughts shook me. I almost muffed our greeting.

"Th-thanks for taking the time to see me, Harris."

"No problem. It's after trading hours. Sarah told me you'd been by the house."

A waitress appeared to take our order. Once she left I got the conversation going again. "I gather you've moved into your father's house."

"Halfway. Haven't cleaned out my apartment yet. Probably this weekend."

"Did Sarah say why I called?"

"Something about Dad's death?"

"I'm taking another look at his murder."

"Why? The whole town knows you found Barron and Walther and laid them right across Wick Pillsner's back."

I studied the man across from me. Brown eyes, brown hair, tanned skin. His personality was probably brown as well. I couldn't see him prospering as a stockbroker. Didn't appear competitive enough. Thanks to his father's death, he wouldn't have to worry about finances any longer. I paused as the waitress delivered our drinks. "Wick has things to answer for, but what if your father's death is not one of them?"

Harris blinked, giving him an owlish appearance and rendering him less attractive. "Of course it is. He did it to stop Dad from reopening the old VPMR thing. What else could it be?"

"If that was the goal, it wasn't successful, was it?"

He frowned over his bourbon and water. "There are always unintended consequences. But all right, suppose Wick wasn't responsible. Who could it be? My father was a quiet man. Innocuous. And I understand all the research on his Voxlightner book disappeared."

"Which immediately threw suspicion in a certain direction."

He asked his question again. "What other motive could there be?"

"Money."

His reaction to my answer showed surprise, uncertainty, but I didn't discern fear. Until he tumbled to the fact this made him a prime suspect. Then it flashed briefly across his face before being swamped by outrage.

"Don't look at me! I haven't spoken to my father in five years. Except when I'd run across him at a function or something. Then we mostly glared at one another. Hell, I didn't even know he was going to leave me anything."

"Why?"

"We had a serious falling out years ago."

"I heard he interfered with your marriage plans."

Even in the muted lighting of the bar, I saw amazement in his eyes. "That was twenty years ago."

"Long time to hold a grudge."

"Grudge my ass! My old man saved me from myself back then. I was too young to know what it was all about, and *she* certainly was. That's not why I refused to have anything to do with John Pierce Belhaven."

"What was?"

He paused, his face darkening. "Because while my mother lay dying, my father betrayed her with the slut working in his office."

"With Sarah?"

"That's the one."

"Then why is she still working in your house?"

"Because no one knows more about my father's affairs, meaning finances and obligations, than Sarah Thackerson, that's why. And when those ends are all wrapped up, she's gone and good riddance."

I sat back in my chair and steepled my fingers. Had he protested a little too much? "So you didn't know you would be in your father's will?"

He dismissed my question by waving a hand in the air. "Didn't think of it one way or the other."

"Were you aware he held a life insurance policy with you as the beneficiary?"

"For years. But I didn't know if he kept it current."

"He paid the premiums, not you?"

"Yep. Melanie had one too."

"As did Sarah and Spencer Spears."

His features crumpled into a frown. "Those I didn't know about until after he died."

"Did your sister have the same reaction to Sarah you did?"

"Melanie was over in Grants. She wasn't as exposed to what was going on as I was."

"Are you on good terms with your sister?"

"Mel and Cag are okay."

"Cag?"

"Cagney Harper, her husband. Dad didn't like him, but he's a good guy. The right one for Melanie, I think."

"Harper and your father were estranged too?"

"More like just left one another alone. Said hello at family functions and then retreated to neutral corners."

"What's your take on Spears?"

"Opportunist. If you want my opinion, Pierce and Spence were lovers too."

Interesting. Heretofore it was "Dad," but when tied to Spencer, Belhaven became "Pierce." That told me a lot about how Harrison Belhaven probably felt about gays.

"What makes you think they had a liaison?"

"Just the way they acted. Of course, I wasn't around much. Only when family matters dictated my presence. But I think Spencer Spears would bed anything that walked."

"He ever come on to you?" I asked.

He turned dark again. "I wasn't around much after he arrived on the scene. But one time Dad told the Sarah bitch to call and ask me for something in my files. Had to do with a stock back when I was my dad's broker. When I dropped it off at the house, I met Spears."

"And?" I prompted.

"And he moved on me."

"What did you do about it?"

"Let him know if he tried that again, I'd put him on the ground and call the cops. Supercilious son of a bitch laughed at me." Harris looked me in the eye. "But he never tried anything again."

"Do you mind telling me where you were the night your father was killed?"

"You snooping around for my alibi? I was home. Alone."

"Doing what?"

He hesitated, presumably to let me know he wasn't pleased with the question. "Reading some trade journals and watching TV."

"So you don't have an alibi."

I watched Harrison Belhaven swell up. My dad and I once ran across what he called a hognose snake out on the west mesa. The serpent hissed and puffed himself up to nearly twice his size. That's what Harris reminded me of now. It was obvious he had no response, so I hit him with another one. "I understand this hasn't been a good year for stockbrokers."

Lips compressed, he managed to make his words legible. "I've had better." He straightened in his chair and tossed back the last of his drink. My string had run out. He slammed down the empty glass and leaned forward. "But just like you, my mother left me a trust fund, so I don't have to live off my earnings. If you want anything else, forget about it."

He rose and stalked away, his stiff spine signaling his anger had returned. I clicked off the digital voice recorder on my belt and left money on the table for the tab before following him outside.

Harris's silver Infiniti turned right onto Central and squealed up the street as I came through the door.

I DROVE home from the Apothecary to find an older model VW bug parked in front of the house. The vehicle may have been old, but the bright yellow color looked recently applied. I parked behind Paul's Charger in the driveway and, because it was closer, went in the front door. Paul sat in his recliner in the den with a young man on the sofa opposite him. The stranger was small, no more than five eight, and trim. His curly white-blond hair rendered him cute rather than handsome. He didn't blip high on my gaydar… but he blipped.

Paul rose with a smile. "Hi, Vince. Can I introduce someone to you?"

The young man scrambled off the couch and licked his lips nervously.

"This is Jack Orson from the *Journal.* I don't know exactly what he does down there, but he reads my articles and makes recommendations to my editor. Jackie, this is BJ Vinson. You know, the detective."

Not my lover, my mate, my significant other. Just "the detective." My heart dropped into my stomach. Nonetheless I played nice. "Hi, Jackie. Nice to meet you. Am I interrupting anything?"

Jackie indicated some papers on the coffee table. "No, sir. I just brought some corrections to Paul."

I noted the absence of glasses. "And he didn't even offer you something to drink?" Crap, was the kid even old enough for alcohol?

"No, sir. We went over the suggested edits. One was kind of tricky and needed explanation. So… so I brought them over. Anyway nice to meet you. I better get on the road."

"No need to hurry," I said, taking a bit of sadistic pleasure in the kid's discomfort.

Jackie glanced at his wristwatch. "I've got a ball game in an hour, so need to get moving. Some of us play sandlot baseball every Tuesday." I didn't remind him this was Monday.

Once the door closed behind Jackie, Paul and I stood watching his VW lurch away from the curb.

"I gather I make him nervous." I allowed a sharp bite to edge my voice.

"I didn't know he was coming over, Vince. I swear. He made up an excuse and brought the edits over even though he could have emailed them."

I looked Paul in the eye before turning and walking back to the den. "He's made the first move. Now what?"

Paul caught up and stood in front of me, his eyes blazing. "What do you mean, now what? I have to put a stop to it, that's what."

"He's kind of cute."

Paul's ears turned red. "Screw that noise, B. J. Vinson. I told you we haven't done anything."

"You also told me you were tempted."

He dropped into a chair. "I… was."

I thought about his reaction to Jazz Penrod, a handsome, sexy mixed-blood kid who helped me with a case over in the Four Corners area a few years ago. I sat down beside Paul and put a hand on his shoulder.

"My time for confession." I cleared my throat. "I understand how you feel about Jazz now. No matter that I'm committed to you and Jazz understands and respects the fact, you've identified him as the competition. You know why? Because if the situation were different, Jazz is who you'd like to be with. I don't feel the same about Jackie, but the kid puts it into perspective for me."

Paul was quiet for almost sixty seconds. "Vince, I'm glad this happened. His coming over, I mean. When I saw you side by side, there's no question about what my head told me. I'm yours."

"Paul, I'm not interested in what your head tells you. I want to know what your heart says."

He gave his patent, soul-melting grin. "My heart told my head what to say. My place is here."

He stood suddenly and moved into my arms. Our kiss burned away the jealousy and doubt still lingering somewhere inside me.

Pedro had a ball that evening, and I slept like a log for what was left of the night.

THE NEXT morning I sat at the desk in my office wondering if I would make it through the day. My old bones wouldn't stand many more reconciliations like last night's. Just as I was praying Hazel wouldn't find something for me to do, she stuck her head in the door.

"Gene's on the phone. Needs to talk to you right away."

My hand shook as I reached for the telephone. She noticed but was prudent enough not to mention it. I didn't even get a chance to say hello; Gene yelled for me to get down to Wick's office right away.

I didn't feel up to hurrying, but I must have done a decent job of it because Gene didn't mention my pace. Blue-and-whites, with light bars flashing, filled the parking lot and sat at the curb in front of Wick's building. Trucks from all three local TV stations completely blocked the south side of Lomas.

"What's going on?" I asked as I labored out of the Impala.

"Wick's inside. He's threatening to blow his head off," Gene said.

"What happened?"

"I sent a couple of guys to arrest him. The DA feels we've got a decent case in the Voxlightner and Stabler deaths. He pulled a gun and ordered them out. Because there were civilians in the building, they complied. Then Wick sent everyone else out. His secretary was scared witless, but she managed to make us understand her boss was locked in his office threatening to kill himself."

"What does he want? Suicide by cop?" I asked.

Gene shrugged as a blue Ford pulled up. "Here are Roy and Paul."

"Thanks for including Paul."

"He's done good work in the case. He's entitled."

We all huddled with the sergeant in charge of the team. SWAT hadn't been called out yet.

"Can we talk to him?" I asked.

"Tore out his phone when his wife called," the officer said.

"What about his cell?"

"Seems to be dead. Probably pulled the battery."

"Could he already have shot himself?" Paul asked.

Gene nodded to the building. "Got someone stationed outside his office window. No sound of gunshots."

"How about if we go inside and talk to him through the door?" I asked. "We might be able to talk some sense to him."

"If you've ever been in his building, you know there's no way to stand outside his door without being exposed," the sergeant said. "The wall to his personal office is completely made of partially frosted glass."

"We can get close enough to yell at him," I said.

"Yell what?" the sergeant asked.

"Remind him of his wife and kids. And I think he's got a grandchild or two."

"He won't even talk to his wife."

"No, but that's probably because he's ashamed. He's been a big man in this town for a long time. Now he's accused of murder and theft. Before it's over he'll want to talk to her."

"She's on her way down in a squad car," Gene said.

"In the meantime let's try it," I said.

"I'm willing," Gene agreed.

"No way," said the sergeant.

"Way," I said. "There's a slump-block wall we can stay behind. It's clear across the reception area, but we can make him hear us."

Wick's shout greeted us the moment we stepped through the front door to Pillsner Enterprises. "Stop right there! Don't come any closer. Get out."

"You can't sit in there for the rest of your life," Gene called.

Unfortunate choice of words, because Wick could do exactly that. "Be reasonable, man. We just want to talk things over."

"I oughta invite you in and put a hole in your head, BJ. You're the one who stirred this thing up all over again."

I whispered to Gene. "He's got cameras all over the place. He can probably see what's going on in and outside the building."

"Damned right I can!" he called. "Can hear you too."

"Pierce Belhaven is the one who stirred the pot, Wick. Killing him's what got me involved."

"That's one thing you can't hang on me. I didn't kill the old busybody. I mighta done bad things, but I didn't murder Pierce Belhaven."

"Is this a confession?" Gene called.

"A confession to not killing Belhaven? Yeah."

I pulled my digital recorder off my belt and held it in front of me. "How about the other bad stuff?"

A long silence grew. Gene had his mouth open to speak when Wick replied, "Yeah. A deathbed confession, I guess you can call it."

"Hey, man!" I yelped. "Don't do anything rash. Think of your wife and kids."

"I am thinking of them. I can't put them through a trial. Another scandal."

"When you talk like that, you're not thinking of them," I said. "Can I come closer? Up to the door, maybe?"

Gene grabbed my arm and shook his head.

"Don't worry, Lieutenant. I won't shoot him. He was just doing his job. Yeah, BJ, come on."

Gene refused to let me go unless he accompanied me. He pulled out his sidearm and put himself in front as we walked to Wick's office door.

"The gun's not necessary, Enriquez. I'm going to open the door, so we can see one another."

Gene came to a halt and raised his weapon. "Slowly."

The latch clicked, and the door opened to reveal a disheveled Wick Pillsner standing with both hands open at his sides. "Go ahead. Shoot me. It's the easiest way out."

"Not gonna be any of that. Step on out and we'll talk."

"I can talk fine right here. BJ's got a recorder in his hand, and mine's running in the office. Everything will be on record. Now convince me my family's gonna be better off with me in the big house than in the grave. I can't put them through the agony of a trial. Can you imagine the headlines?"

"You don't have to go to trial," I said. "Talk to the DA and make a deal. A full confession and financial retribution will keep you off death row, and there won't be the spectacle of a trial."

"There's still headlines."

I waved dismissively. "There already are. Killing yourself means you won't have to face them, but your wife and family will. Sounds selfish to me."

Wick took off his glasses and rubbed his eyes. I grabbed Gene's arm to keep him from rushing the man.

"And there's something else," I said.

Wick looked up. His stare did not look so formidable without glasses to lend his eyes strength. "What?"

"The feds are going to come at your bank accounts and investments with a vengeance looking for pilfered money. And you won't be around to fight for the untainted money that's rightfully theirs."

"You're an asshole, BJ, but a smart asshole. You know the right buttons to push." He took a tentative step forward. "Okay, Lieutenant, hook me up. But take me out the back way to avoid the cameras. Please."

Chapter 21

FOLLOWING THE arrest of Wick Pillsner, I avoided news interviews with a terse "no comment" until Dorothy Voxlightner publicly thanked both Paul and me for our help in locating her murdered son. Thereafter I gave as complete an interview as possible on an open case, careful to include Paul's contribution at every opportunity. He reveled in the new-found attention at first, but soon became as sick of it as I was. Even so it gave him a professional boost. Editors, once remote, now proved receptive to stories, not only on the Voxlightner scandal, but also on other matters.

Wick insisted I attend his first interview with the DA, perhaps hoping I would put in a good word for him. If that was his intent, he misjudged me. The man was directly responsible for multiple murders and indirectly responsible for the deaths of two VPMR stockholders. I held no fondness for my childhood football coach.

His interview confirmed most of what we'd already figured out about the case. Stabler's intent from the beginning was to earn a few dollars with his scam. But when he hooked up with Wick, the dream grew bigger until it reached the grandiose scale only someone like Wick could pull off. But the good doctor hadn't reckoned with his partner in crime's cautious and protective nature. Once Stabler witnessed the death of Barron Voxlightner and assisted in the cover-up of the murder, he was no longer safe. In the end the scammer was scammed… out of his life. Barron's death was preordained; Stabler's was simply a matter of eliminating an inconvenience.

The heavy use of electricity at the Georgia Street address was what we figured, three months of producing prills with sufficient gold and silver content from *real* ore Dr. Stabler brought from Nevada to support the scam. Dr. Herrera, who conducted the phony assays at the School of Mines, merely substituted them for the second part of the testing process. Because a red-hot prill doesn't look like a cool one—especially when viewed through avaricious eyes—no one caught on to the switch. The real miracle was that none of the neighbors noticed one house in the neighborhood had been converted into an assay lab in preparation for the scam.

Wick tried to lay attorney Everett Kent's murder on Stabler and claimed no knowledge of Belhaven's death.

I thought this over carefully. Nothing we'd turned up in Stabler's background suggested he was a killer. Wick himself portrayed the man as a small-timer trying to scam a few dollars. But once Wick turned the con into a caper, perhaps Stabler changed as well.

Paul expected things to proceed rapidly after the confession, but the more likely scenario was the feds would keep Wick on ice until after all the money they could find was recovered. But come what may, Hardwick Pillsner would never see the light of freedom again. He sent for me once more as we waited for the FBI to make its final moves. He wanted to hire me to protect his legitimate assets from forfeiture. I declined, pointing out he needed an attorney, not a confidential investigator. Looking back on it, I believe he thought I might help him hide assets to ensure their safety. Did he really think I was still a scraggly kid adoring his football hero of a coach?

IN EARLY November before the cold winds of December moved in, interviews with cops, the district attorney's people, and the press eased up to the point where I could devote meaningful time to the primary task of my contract with Dorothy Voxlightner, the identification of her nephew's killer. I believed Wick's denial of responsibility for Belhaven's death. I also considered him truthful when he claimed Stabler killed Everett Kent. Why? Because it gained Wick nothing to protest his innocence in those two killings. In fact the denial delayed his plea deal with the district attorney's office.

It wasn't clear that Dorothy remained interested in proceeding since the primary goal of her engagement had been fulfilled. She now knew with certainty her son was dead and who killed him.

Even so I was now convinced the armed attack on us in our own backyard and the T-boning of Paul's car were perpetrated by Belhaven's killer. That made it personal. The investigation would go on, paying client or no.

The close of the Voxlightner case plus Paul's and my reconciliation—if that's the proper word for what happened—should have given me a clear head for the investigation, but I was truly shaken by Paul's temptation to stray. Cold chills ran down my back every time I thought about it. Yet I understood. And this shook me almost as badly as the thought of losing Paul. A thirteen-year age difference is not exactly a May-December thing, but neither is it a pairing of peers. The beginning of such a relationship should have been the troublesome part, but as I actually lived it, the future looked more dangerous than the past. Face it, Vinson, *you'll begin to dodder long before he does.*

Hazel put me to work on a couple of cases that had nothing to do with the Belhavens and the Voxlightners, which helped me shake off the mood I was in… thanks to the case and my near miss with Paul. At times it's helpful to have a bossy office manager in your life. Thursday afternoon rolled around before I returned to enumerating the possibilities surrounding Belhaven's murder.

For one, a stranger could have rung the doorbell and talked his way into the house with robbery on his mind. But a stranger robbing Belhaven would have taken something other than the research on his book. Nor would Paul's and my involvement have elicited personal attacks from a stranger.

Someone as yet undetected in the Voxlightner imbroglio might have been motivated to try to stop Pierce from reopening the scandal. Possible but improbable. If this was the case, it was someone Wick wasn't aware of because he'd purged his soul this past week with respect to the wrongdoers. He'd pointed to only three others besides himself: Stabler, Dr. Herrera, and Thelma Rider, who'd weakened before the scam was complete and abandoned New Mexico for her native Texas and presumed safety.

There were other possible suspects, but they remained just that. Possibilities. The banker was semicomplicit because he failed to recognize patterns of behavior that could have tipped the authorities.

The lawyer who enthusiastically promoted VPMR hadn't seemed to benefit either monetarily or by reputation. He took a bath when the stock became worthless.

The accountant was virtually driven out of business and reduced to retaining a few clients to work from his home.

The stockbroker almost lost his business and had a long, hard slog to get back to normal. All the insiders in the scandal lost reputations and money. Still, each of these possibilities would need to be reexamined and considered.

The final option was to search for Belhaven's killer among the members of his own household… family or bimbo or himbob. My inclination was to rush to judgment on the rash and rascally Spencer Spears. Nonetheless the obvious was not always the best place to look. Spencer with the strawberry mark on his cheek would get a close inspection, but so would the others.

READY TO get back in the groove again, I asked Hazel to dig deeper into Harris Belhaven's and Melanie Harper's finances while I interviewed them again. This was a solo task; Paul was working on a paying gig for a sports magazine on the scholarship policies and graduation rates of the Lobos, New Mexico University's football team.

Recalling Harris's stiff-necked retreat from the Apothecary two weeks ago, I elected to talk to his sister first. Sarah Thackerson answered the phone at the Belhaven house, which took me by surprise. Because of Harris's dislike of the woman, I thought she'd be gone. Sarah said Mrs. Harper had returned home.

A phone call to the residence in Grants earned me an invitation to speak with both Melanie and her husband tomorrow afternoon. I hoped Paul would make the drive with me, but he'd already scheduled two interviews at the U, chasing a story about budgeting. Things seemed like they were back on track for the two of us, but an out-of-town trip might have cemented them. Was my insecurity showing?

EARLY THE next morning, I herded the Impala west on I-40 and began the long climb toward the Continental Divide, which lay not far on the other side of Grants, my destination. The fact that the trip was mostly uphill made playing tag with semis a bit irksome.

As a dedicated student of history, I knew Grants began its existence as a railroad camp in the 1880s when three Canadian brothers of that name contracted to build a stretch of rail for the Atlantic and Pacific Railroad. It later became Grants Station, and finally Grants. I don't know when it lost the apostrophe it presumably boasted in earlier years.

Today it was a town of somewhere around 9,000 souls that served as the seat of Cibola County and the gateway to the El Malpais National Monument and the El Malpais National Conservation area. El Malpais translates into the Badlands, a name reinforced by a vast area of black lava spewed from volcanic eruptions. New Mexico was conceived in violent contractions of the earth's crust and born in pyroclastic flows.

Eighty or so miles after leaving Albuquerque, I exited the highway via Ramp 81 and picked up Santa Fe Avenue, the town's main drag. The Harper home, a redbrick pitched roof similar to but a little larger than others in the neighborhood, sat on a broad, manicured lawn on East Sargent Street. Melanie must have been keeping an eye out for me because she exited the front door with a small basket on her arm, locked the house behind her, and crawled in beside me as I watched from the driver's seat.

"Cag's at work. We're meeting him there," she announced without preliminaries.

The attractive, stuccoed El Malpais reception center occupied the high ground at Exit 85 at the west end of town. Melanie sent me scooting for one of the shaded tables in a picnic area while she disappeared inside. A moment later she headed for the table I'd selected, trailed by her tall, hirsute husband. The mustache and patriarchal beard were his most noteworthy attributes, as they were when I first saw him in Albuquerque. His uniform lent him an air of authority missing back then.

I liked Cagney Harper the moment he opened his mouth to say hello and gripped my hand in a firm shake. Belhaven must have been prejudiced against facial hair if he failed to get along with this fellow. We spent a few minutes discussing sites of note in the immediate vicinity: Acoma Sky City, the Ice Cave and Bandera Volcano, El Malpais itself, El Morro National Monument, and a host of others within a couple of hours' drive. I was familiar with most, which put me up a notch or two in his estimation. Before long I was comfortable enough to broach the question of his father-in-law's attitude toward him.

"I wasn't good enough for his daughter."

Melanie hugged his arm. "Little did Dad know."

"He thought Melanie should have married a doctor or a lawyer, not a BLM slug."

"Supervisor slug," she put in.

"That's it?" I asked.

"That's it," he replied. "I didn't have anything against him. What father ever figures his little girl's marrying up to her potential? But he was so obvious about his feelings, it was just easier to skip the family functions."

Neither of the Harpers objected to my prying into their daily lives. I looked for things suspicious and patterns that might clue me to something hidden. What emerged was the picture of a man devoted to his work and his woman, and a woman totally wrapped up in her man and his work. She had been a homebody until recently when she took an afternoon and evening job with a local store. He'd recently started working part-time at a grocery store. Their circle of friends tended to be restricted to neighbors and people Cag worked with.

Both of the Harpers taking on jobs struck me as odd but began to make sense when we discussed their children, a boy and a girl, both college age. Cagney Jr. attended Virginia Military Institute, while Marcie was in her freshman year at the Grants' campus of New Mexico State. It was probably simple-minded prejudice on my part, but I associated military institutes with "salvaging" young men and women who had taken a step or two down the wrong path.

"Why did your son decide on VMI?" I asked.

"We encouraged him," Cag answered.

"Disciplinary problems?"

Melanie spoke up. "My Aunt Lucinda suggested the school might be good for him. And her husband was able to get Cag Jr. enrolled."

My questioning the couple about their son's choice of school was the only time I sensed any dissembling. I didn't push things. Hazel would be able to find out if the boy was ever in legal jeopardy.

I left Grants with an invitation to return and join Cag on the two-and-a-half-mile Gooseberry Springs Trail to the top of Mount Taylor. Standing at around 11,300 feet, the mountain was the southernmost of the Navajo's four sacred mountains. They call the peak *Tsoodzil*, meaning Blue Bead Mountain or Turquoise Mountain.

I CALLED the office on my hands-free phone on the drive back to Albuquerque to ask Hazel for a more thorough search on the Harpers, including their offspring. She'd already found signs of financial distress in the family, despite Cag's decent-paying job as a midlevel manager with BLM and Melanie's trust fund from her mother. She also informed me she learned they'd hired an attorney to expedite the payment of Belhaven's insurance policy.

By the time I arrived back in the office, Hazel had located a juvie record on the Harper son. Strangely, it wasn't sealed. Charlie had friends in police departments all over the state—including the GPD—and learned the two charges were drug related. Possession for personal use. Cag Jr. apparently contracted a heroin habit. This explained why he was a year older than his sister, but both were freshmen in college. The son had been in rehab.

Charlie's cop friend painted a broader picture, which explained why the juvie record was no longer sealed. The kid, a budding and promising athlete, got in over his head and stole from his parents to support his habit. Still unable to pay for his drugs, he'd been pressured into dealing, which was a separate, more serious charge. The boy required trips to three different centers before he was able to claw his way back to sobriety. I asked Charlie to find a licensed investigator in Lexington, Virginia, to check on Cadet Harper.

SATURDAY MORNING I decided to go to the downtown office where I could spread all the case files out on the conference table in order to go over details one more time. I'd no sooner gotten settled than Gene made a rare appearance in the office. I usually went to him or lured him out of APD headquarters with the promise of a meal, but here he was, bigger than life.

"This is a rare honor." I indicated a chair in front of my desk. "What's the occasion?"

"Can't a guy have a chat with his old running buddy?"

"A man can, but he doesn't very often. What's up?"

Gene got up and closed the door even though we were alone in the office. "Morale, that's the problem. Has Guerra said anything to you?"

"Not to me. I don't know about Paul, but I can ask."

"I told you a while back we might be having a Department of Justice investigation. Way things are going, I'd bet on one sometime next year. The department's down 10 to 15 percent. Hard to fill new academy classes."

"Bad publicity or bad pay?" I asked.

"Some of both. City canceled some promised raises, and that hasn't helped. We're competing with pretty big departments for officers. Denver, Phoenix. And they pay better than we do."

I shrugged. "We all suffer through hard times."

"Says the man with a trust fund."

"Trust funds suffer along with everything else when things go bad."

"Twelve million bucks would have to suffer a hell of a lot before you'd even notice," Gene said. "At least police shootings are down."

I asked about the police chief. "What about Huddleston?"

"He's tired of it all. Trying to decide whether to bow out now or to see it through the investigation. He'd like to go now but probably needs to stay and protect his ass."

"That would be my assessment," I said. "How about you. You solid?"

"So far as I know. And my position will be a little bit stronger. My promotion's approved. Becomes official first of the month."

"Great. CID?" I asked, meaning the Criminal Investigations Division.

He nodded.

"That's commander rank. Acting or permanent?" I asked the question because temporary rank was often assigned until a new department head got some time under his belt.

"Permanent, thanks to Huddleston. His parting gift."

"Not a bad one. When's the celebration?"

"Not till after I'm settled in the office. I'll let you know. Anything new on Belhaven?"

I filled him in on the visit to the Harpers in Grants. He promised to do an official records check on each member of the family. I prompted him to do the same thing for Harris.

"I'll ask around the Grants PD about the Harpers," he said as he got up. "I know a couple of guys over there. Maybe they can add something about young Harper's situation."

He got back to me sooner than expected, but it wasn't about the Harpers. He called Monday morning to say that Wick Pillsner had been shanked in the Metropolitan Detention Center.

Chapter 22

I YELLED an explanation to Hazel on the way out the door. According to Gene they'd taken Wick by ambulance to the University of New Mexico Medical facility on Lomas. On the drive up the hill to the university, I pondered what this meant for my investigation of Belhaven's murder. Maybe nothing; maybe everything. I reached Paul on the hands-free to let him know what was going on and cautioned him to watch his back. If an unknown someone was closing doors behind him, he had an awfully long reach to penetrate the detention center. Still… better safe than sorry.

Wick's family stood around the waiting room as I joined Gene and a uniformed officer whom I took to be a detention center cop. Gene cleared my arrival with a "he's okay" endorsement to the sergeant, whose name tag read Ryan. The man continued his explanation of what happened.

"Like I said. Pillsner was in the shower. A detainee entered the area, walked straight over to him, and stabbed him in the back with a homemade shank without saying a word. We hustled Pillsner here to UNM immediately."

"Who was the perp?" Gene asked.

"Lowlife loser. Not too bright. Name's Lanigan. Elmer Lanigan. Three-time loser waiting for trial on felony assault and rape charges."

"Any idea what prompted the attack?" Gene asked.

"Lanigan claimed Pillsner made a move on him. Said he didn't put up with that shit."

"You believe him?" I asked.

The sergeant shrugged. "At this point I got no idea. Coulda been a beef of some kind. But there's no complaints about Pillsner molesting or propositioning other prisoners. Except for Lanigan's."

"He could've been paid to do it," Gene said.

"Anything's possible. Lanigan was locked up before Pillsner arrived and hasn't had any visitors, but another inmate mighta brought word to him. The man's not all there."

"How's Wick?" I asked.

"Still on the operating table," Gene said. "According to the doctor we talked to, he suffered two wounds high on his back delivered with moderate force. Neither are believed to be life-threatening, but they won't know that for sure until they finish with him."

We waited another hour before a medic showed up to deliver the news. He came to us first because his patient was in the custody of the police. Wick would recover. He was to be housed in a secure area of the hospital until he could be returned to the detention center. We could not talk to Wick because he was still under the effects of anesthesia. The surgeon left us to go talk to the injured man's family.

We remained long enough to watch the family's reaction to the doctor's news. Once the surgeon left, Wick's wife, Virginia, gathered her children around her and talked to them quietly. As Gene and I walked through the waiting area to the parking facility, Virginia Pillsner stopped me with a hand on my arm.

"This is your fault, B. J. Vinson. All your fault."

Gene, who was right behind me, stepped between us. "No, ma'am. This is Wick's fault. Nobody else's."

Once outside I assured my old partner I was okay and not suffering from guilt or remorse. His comment was right on the mark. Wick was a murderer and a thief. I simply happened to be the one who found him out.

GENE ALLOWED me to watch the interrogation of Elmer Lanigan with him at APD headquarters. We observed through a two-way mirror as Sergeant Don Carson, who succeeded me as Gene's riding partner after I was shot, faced the accused assailant. As Don went through the preliminaries of Mirandizing and identifying the inmate, I studied the human wreck sitting opposite him. Although the man declined a lawyer, Gene was cautious enough to make sure a public defender sat in on the interview.

"Do you know why you're here, Mr. Lanigan?" Don opened.

"Cause I shanked the queer son of a bitch—"

"Mr. Lanigan," the lawyer interrupted.

"Shut up. Anybody can see I done nothing wrong. Evil's got no right being in the jail house with me and my friends. He wanted to do me, so I done him first."

"What do you mean by *do you*?" Don asked.

"Don't answer—"

"You know, put his hands all over me, and God knows what else."

"Why didn't you just report him?" Don asked.

"He dissed me, man. Nobody disses Elmer Lanigan and gets away with it. But everything's all right. I checked it with God first, and he said to go for it. Put the unnatural fornicator down. So that's what I done."

"The Lord told you to do it?" Don asked.

"Clear as day. Just like he told me about that pervert in Kansas City back in '09."

"Mr. Lanigan!" the public defender exclaimed.

Lanigan came up out of his seat as far as his manacles allowed. "You shut up and get outta here! You don't, I'll figger you're dissing me too."

"He stays, Mr. Lanigan, and for the record, I recommend you listen to what he has to say. But tell me about this man in Kansas City."

Between interruptions by the public defender, Lanigan calmly told of killing a man he'd picked up in a gay bar for the fifty dollars the victim carried. Then he told of another attack in Denver a year ago. With difficulty Don brought him back to Wick.

"When did Mr. Pillsner proposition you, Elmer? Can I call you Elmer?"

"Sure," Lanigan said before screwing his eyes half-shut and glaring at Don. "You do it with respect, you can. But not like that beer guy. He said it with a sneer."

"Beer guy?"

"Yeah. You know, the Pilsner man."

"You mean Detainee Pillsner. When did he disrespect your name?"

"Night before I paid him back."

"What did he do?"

"Asked me if I was any kin to Elmer Fudd. You know the dick with the shotgun always trying to blast the rabbit. But old Bugs Bunny is too sharp for him. Just like this Elmer was too sharp for the beer guy."

Now I knew why Lanigan stabbed Wick, and it had nothing to do with an indecent proposal. Nor was he a hitman controlled by some unknown hand in the Voxlightner scandal. Hardwick Pillsner might have the moxie to run with the movers and shakers of New Mexico, but he wasn't equipped to survive a prison environment.

THE NEXT morning Roy Guerra let Paul and me know John Pierce Belhaven's finances showed considerable funds lodged with Garrick Investments… not his son's brokerage house. Since Jim Garrick was my own stockbroker, I strolled over to visit him. His firm occupied the building on Third and Gold that formerly housed the local Merrill Lynch office, a four-block jaunt from my own locale. Jim greeted me enthusiastically, but not—as it turned out—because he managed my trust. He was pleased over the outcome of the Voxlightner mystery.

"Damned good work, BJ. I never accepted Barron had anything to do with scamming his family and friends."

"A lot of people had trouble with that. Pleased things worked out okay."

"Except for Wick, maybe." He shook his head. "Hard to believe it about him too. But if I'm honest, it's easier to see him in that role than Barron. It'd be like a game to Wick."

"Murder's a pretty grim game."

"I figure he got in too deep and did what he thought he had to do. Wrong as hell, but that'd fit his mind-set, I reckon. Heard about what happened to him. He gonna be all right?"

"He'll survive the attack."

Jim's mouth went south in a frown. "Maybe this one, but if he gets what he deserves, he'll be spending a lot of time in prison. Hope he learns how to behave there."

"Wick's got a lifeline. He knows how to make money. Once he settles down in a permanent cell, he'll get another scam going. That'll either make him a bigwig in the prison or get him killed for real."

"BJ, I hope you'll have the Christian grace to tell him that."

"I think that message is already delivered."

Jim felt comfortable enough with me to discuss some of the details of Belhaven's business without disclosing confidences. He confirmed a lawyer was already probating the estate. Sufficient withdrawals had been made to satisfy Thackerson's and Spears's portion of the inheritance. And as I'd already learned, the estate's administrator had also approved disbursals to both Melanie Harper and Harrison Belhaven. Jim let me know without saying that the amounts were modest pending the settlement of the estate. That was doubtless a lifeline to the Harper side of the equation… and likely provided needed relief for Harris as well.

As he had little else to say on the matter, I left and walked back to my office where I found Roy and Paul waiting for me.

"Find out anything new?" Roy asked after we were seated at my small conference table.

I relayed what little I'd learned and asked about their morning.

"Seems Harper Jr. was in more trouble than we thought," Paul said.

"The lieutenant asked me to do a deeper background check on the kid," Roy explained. "What we already knew was right. He'd been busted for heroin, but what we didn't know was he got in a shootout with his dealer."

"A shootout? With guns? Any bodies in the street?"

"Nobody was that good of a shot. When Cagney Harper Jr. couldn't pay his bill, his supplier turned him into a dealer. The problem was, Harper kept dipping into his merchandise and getting deeper in the hole. Things came to a head when the dealer said he was going to put Harper's sister on the street to cover Junior's debt. The kid freaked and went after the dealer with his dad's handgun. Traded some shots. Nobody got hit, but that brought everything out into the light and probably saved Harper's life. Forced him into recovery."

"And the dealer?"

"Thank God he wasn't connected. Small-time independent supplied by a relative in Mexico. He went down for a long stretch. Harper now has a conviction on his record, but the judge gave him the opportunity to expunge it if he stays out of trouble."

"Sounds pretty normal," I said. "The white kid gets a second chance. The Hispanic dealer gets prison."

"Don't kid yourself," Roy said. "The dealer got plenty of chances to straighten out his life, but the money was too easy. Anyway, this was his third strike."

"How big a financial stress did this put on the Harpers?" I asked.

"Lawyers for criminal trials—especially attempted murder trials—don't come cheap. The Harpers remortgaged their house to the hilt and borrowed more money on top of that. Pretty deep hole, I'd say. Then there's the cost of two kids in college to consider."

"Were the Harpers desperate?"

"Pretty near. Melanie went to work clerking in a store. Cagney Sr. took a second job."

"So Belhaven's death was fortuitous for them."

Roy nodded. "I'd say so."

"Any sign that Belhaven's dislike of Cagney Harper went any deeper than the man wasn't good enough for his daughter?"

Roy laughed. "Maybe the beard, but nothing deeper than that."

"Pierce could be something of a snob," Paul said. "The way Roy describes it makes sense to me."

"Do we know how much Melanie's mother's trust provides her?"

"The mother's trust? Not much. Equivalent of three grand a month after taxes."

"Didn't know you pay taxes on benefits from a trust," Paul said.

"You don't on a revocable trust," I said. "The trust pays those taxes. But the beneficiary pays them in an irrevocable trust."

"Which was this?" he asked.

"Initially it might have been a revocable trust. But upon Mrs. Belhaven's death, it automatically became irrevocable."

Roy didn't appear interested in trust details. "So Belhaven's death solved a few problems for the Harpers."

"It appears so. Do they have alibis for the night he died?" I asked.

"Mrs. Harper worked the night shift at the Handy Kitchen, a kitchenware store. The store closes at nine, and she's out of there no later than nine thirty."

"And Cagney?" Paul asked.

"Worked his second job at a grocery store that night. Also gets off at nine. After that he claims he was home. They alibi one another… for what that's worth." Roy paused. "Mrs. Harper ran into a neighbor lady when she arrived home, and they talked for a few minutes."

"It's a seventy- or eighty-mile run right down I-40," Paul said. "Plenty of time for either one to get to Albuquerque by ten thirty."

Roy nodded and agreed to have the Grants PD help us as much as they could.

SINCE HARRIS Belhaven's last words to me had been "If you want anything else, forget about it," Paul decided to have a go at him by saying he wanted to do an article on John Pierce Belhaven, the writer. To my surprise Harris accepted an invitation to a late lunch at the downtown Flying Star. I headed to APD to see if I could turn up anything on Harris to help Paul with his lunch.

I medically retired from the APD six years ago, so many of the faces I encountered at the headquarters were new, including the cop guarding the desk admitting people to the inner sanctum. But like a lot of the newbies, he recognized me because I was one of the last partners to ride with the new commander of CID. The gatekeeper admitted me without a problem. Roy Guerra was out, but Don Carson was in. We sat down and discussed yesterday's interrogation of Lanigan. He reached the same conclusion Gene and I had. Wick did something to tick off a semisane hood and paid the price.

Don knew nothing about the Harpers but cheerfully pulled up what he could find. As a licensed confidential investigator, I have databases available to me that nearly match the police department's, but because the subjects lived in another town, Don might possibly learn something I wouldn't. All he turned up that I didn't already know, was Cag Harper had a running war with the meter maids in Grants. He'd chalked up close to $150 in unpaid tickets until recently. I surmised he paid them upon receiving partial settlement of his father-in-law's estate.

Harris, Don was a little more familiar with. I learned the Belhaven scion had two ex-wives, both of whom took him to court at least once for violent behavior. The second Mrs. Belhaven still had an order of protection out on him. They apparently argued over the possession of a Han Dynasty vase of questionable character he picked up on an Asian trip, but which she received in the divorce. The anger I perceived in him apparently ran deep, and he was prone to violence. Would Paul be safe asking a bunch of personal questions? I rested a bit easier realizing he would be conducting the interview in a public place. Even so… how much protection was that when facing a violent man? About the only thing I could help to prepare him for his upcoming meeting was a text to be careful.

I left APD, recovered my car from the lot, and headed up Central for the Southeast Heights. Harris's neighbors in the Highland neighborhood where he lived before moving to his father's house might be able to shed a little light on his daily activities.

Slog work like ringing doorbells tends to piss off the subject when he or she finds out about it, but this is an essential part of a confidential investigator's life. I hit a dozen homes up and down the block and on the street behind Harris's former residence. Fully a quarter of them went unanswered, but a few gave me suggestions of other people I could contact. I quickly gained a pretty good idea of the man's social life. He worked, came home, drank, and vented his spleen by arguing with neighbors at the least provocation… and sometimes for none at all. Harris was proving to be a small man in my book. Someone who husbands himself to himself and collects anything and everything. According to gossip the two divorces almost did him in.

His one friend seemed to be a man he worked with at the brokerage house. I knew no one in his employer's firm, a nationally recognized investment broker. This made the next step a bit trickier. Mess with a man's neighborhood; that's one thing. Mess with his livelihood, and that's another.

Nonetheless, I invaded the premises of Stout Investments on West Central Avenue while Paul was treating Harris to lunch mere blocks away. Harris's friend Charles Williamson was in and available. As we sat in his semiprivate cubicle, I wondered at the lack of loyalty Harris claimed from his friends. Williamson freely talked about his workmate's sloppy business habits and his enduring anger tending to rise and fall without any discernable cause. Before long I recognized Williamson retained a semifriendly relationship with Harris by being what he was… a salesman. He treated Harris like a potential client, playing to his strengths and preying on his weaknesses. On one thing Williamson was adamant. Harris was honest when it came to business dealings. In personal relationships? Not so much.

I concluded the meeting before Harris arrived back in the office, carrying with me a much firmer picture of the man. He was overlaid with all the niceties of civilization, but his sense of self-preservation overrode everything else. He was on decent terms with his sister and his great-aunt Dorothy but wouldn't hesitate to use either of them. Was he capable of murder? In my estimation that depended upon one single factor. How desperate was he? No matter how many friends and acquaintances he could claim, Harris Belhaven was a lonely man.

I was curious about how Paul would read him. Would he fall for the solicitous stockbroker or see through him? I didn't have long to wait. Paul sailed through my door and plopped into a chair.

"Man, that guy's about as deep as a dishpan."

"You caught that, huh?"

"Hard not to. He's all out for number one. Don't think he can even count to two."

Paul went on to explain how Harris painted his relationship with his father as "cool," not "fractured." My mate let him play that card for half an hour before he trumped Harris, asking about things others had already clued us into, such as his pettiness, the tendency to lose his temper, and his so-so record at work. Harris danced a little before he lost his temper and started describing everyone in colorful terms. Wait until he learned I'd talked to Williamson.

Paul did learn one new fact. The life policies on Pierce Belhaven had not yet paid. Not too surprising. The insurance company knew the police considered the insured's death as a homicide, and with no one yet named as the killer, they'd delay payment for as long as possible. We knew at least one of the beneficiaries had already engaged an attorney to press for payment.

My payback came as I was preparing to leave for the day. Hazel put through a call from Harris Belhaven.

"Vinson, you fucking queer, how dare you question my coworkers. I'll—"

"Doing my job, Belhaven. Just doing my job."

I hung up the phone and joined Paul in the front office where he was saying goodbye to Hazel. He held his tongue until we were preparing to get into our separate cars in the parking lot.

"Pissed, was he?"

"He didn't like queers asking about his business."

Paul laughed. "Then tell him to stop being queer about his business."

Chapter 23

I DETOURED four blocks to the Belhaven house to see if I could catch Spence Spears there before heading down to his apartment in the CNM area. He'd told me Mondays and Thursdays were his days reserved for the Belhaven house. This was Tuesday, but who knew which way the wind blew now that Pierce was dead?

If my notes were right, the sky-blue Plymouth Barracuda with white racing stripes sitting at the curb in front of the house belonged to the said Mr. Spears. This raised an issue about Harris. He professed to distrust and dislike the yard boy, yet the guy was still working at the house. And the last time I checked, Harris felt the same about Sarah, who'd caused a permanent breach with his father. That sent my paranoia soaring. Was all as it seemed with Sarah and Pierce's son? With Spence and Harris Belhaven for that matter?

Judging that Harris had already left for work, I allowed the sound of a lawn mower to lure me around to the house's huge backyard. Spence was a good landscaper. His plants looked healthy and vibrant, even this late in the year. He'd planted enough chrysanthemum and oriental lily and Japanese anemone to keep color in the yard and provide a subtle perfume less heady than his spring plants.

Spence was at the far end of the lawn with his back to me, but when I approached, I failed to take him by surprise, probably owing to the lesser buzz of an electric mower. Interesting choice. Pierce Belhaven gets fried by the old gas-powered mower, so the family switches to electric.

Spears flipped the Off switch and turned to confront me. "Hello, Mr. Vinson. Been expecting you."

"Why?"

"You're investigating Pierce's death, aren't you?"

"Most people figure I caught him when Wick Pillsner confessed."

"Don't know much about that. Just what I see on TV. But Harris's nose is all out of joint and Sarah's walking on eggshells. I figure you got them spooked."

"You think either of them did it?"

"Or both of them maybe." He laughed. "Naw. Harris is too wimpy and Sarah's too…." He thought that one over a moment. "Well, let's just say she's no Olive Oyl."

"Meaning?"

"Not aggressive like Popeye's gal."

I hit him with something to shake him. "Detective Guerra tells me there's a hole in your alibi."

No physical reaction at all. "He does, does he?"

Roy hadn't said a word, but I'm not obligated to stick to the truth when interviewing suspects. "Somebody or the other says you disappeared for a while. The bar's not far from the North Valley. You could have slipped out, killed Pierce, and made it back for the next round of drinks."

"Who says that?"

Still no rise from him. "I don't know, but Guerra does. I'm sure he'll check things with you again."

"Hope so. I don't want something like that hanging over my head. I'm righteous, man." He laughed aloud. "Better a drunk than a murderer, right?"

He stood still long enough to give me the names and phone numbers of his drinking buddies the night Belhaven died. He was well prepared—or else they were best buds.

"The Hogshead's on Montgomery near I-40. How long does it take you to get from there to here?" I asked.

He gave me a look saying he knew I'd already timed it. "Ten minutes if I rush it."

"I did it in eight."

He shrugged and flipped on the mower's motor, raising his voice over its subdued purr. "I drive the speed limit."

MY NEXT chore was to chase down Spence's drinking buddies. Two of them, kids named Neal and Chuck, were what you'd expect college undergrads to be. While showing the world they were wise to its ways, their vulnerabilities were on clear display. Both swore Spence was at the tavern all evening, but it was hard to tie down their own movements. Apparently one left for a short period, trying to hook up with a girl. The other came and went to hit the head, make a phone call, talk to friends, hit on a girl.

Rocky Lodeen, the fourth man at Spence's party on the night Belhaven died, was older than the other two and—like Spence—a vet. I gathered they both served in Afghanistan, although in different units patrolling different locales. When I ran him down at the coffee shop at CNM's Montoya campus, Rocky pinged slightly on my gaydar as rough trade, someone who'd use another man for his own needs and then abandon him. His hard veneer was real and not assumed. I suspected he'd volunteered for the Army to escape what he viewed as worse conditions back home. After I introduced myself and separated him from the other students he was rapping with, he was willing to talk, waving a muscular arm sporting a snarling black panther wrapped sinuously around it to make an occasional point. When he thrust the arm forward, the tattoo appeared to launch an attack. How different from Paul's placid Pedro.

He took a sip of the coffee I'd bought and addressed my question. "Yeah, man, I was right there soaking up some suds when Spence showed."

"What time was that?"

"Who knows? That was four months ago. I usually hit the Hogshead after my shift."

"Where do you work?"

"Northeast Heights Auto Body Shop out on San Mateo."

"What time do you get off work?"

"That was a Wednesday, right?" I nodded. "Six. By the time I clean up it's seven. Hit the place half-eight or a little later."

I noted Rocky's European way of saying seven thirty. Did they use that in the Middle East too? "Didn't you take time to eat?"

"Usually grab something at the Hog."

"Okay, you were there before Spencer. You have any idea when that was?"

"Maybe half an hour after I got there. I was just finishing up a corned beef on rye."

"How is it you don't remember when you arrived that night, but you're clear about eating a sandwich and when Spencer got there? Seems like a clear recollection to me."

"Thought we cleared that up. And I always eat a corned beef there. They put together a damned good sandwich. You ever eat there?"

I pressed on. "At first you seemed uncertain about your movements, but now you recall details on when your friend arrived?"

"You questioning my word?"

"Trying to understand your word, Rocky. There's a big difference. I'm hunting someone who killed a man. That's serious business."

"On this side of the pond, maybe. Wasn't so much over there. Kill them before they kill you."

"Pierce Belhaven wasn't a threat to anyone."

He gave a faint smile. "You sure? He's dead, ain't he?"

I stared into his hooded gray eyes. "It's true that Belhaven alive was a threat to some people. But dead, he was an opportunity."

He held my gaze a moment before he broke contact. "If you say so."

"I do. Now assuming Spencer got there around eight, did he leave at any time?"

"Not that I remember. Sat and drank and talked about women and baseball."

Rocky eyed me across the table with a half smile across his face. If someone were inclined toward the coarser trade, he would have been devastating. This guy didn't go looking for hookups. He simply waited until they came to him. Men, women, it probably didn't matter. Spencer, maybe? Spencer… definitely. They likely tore up the bedroom when they went at it.

"You wanna know why I remember that night?" he asked.

"Why?"

"Because of that South Valley cop. Guerra, I think his name was. He put me through the ringer on this shit once already."

"I'd be disappointed if he hadn't."

I kept Rocky sitting in the coffee shop for another half hour while I pushed him for detail. I could see from his eyes he knew I was trying to trip him up, but he stuck to his story. He'd been at the Hogshead all night until they broke up at closing.

I returned to the office after leaving CNM to clear my desk of whatever Hazel had loaded it up with, nursing the feeling Rocky Lodeen had been sparring with me. Charlie agreed to do a background check on Rocky while I finished the day on the telephone with various people in his buddy Spencer Spears's world: his landlord, his employer, and a counselor at CNM. He and his strawberry birthmark had charmed them all.

That night, I couldn't help but compare Pedro to the black panther living on Rocky Lodeen's brawny arm. I far preferred the amiable dragon to the threatening cat. I glanced at the man sleeping beside me. Paul's articles on the Voxlightner scandal were earning him attention and assignments. This was both good and bad. It meant he was building a reputation in his field, but it also meant he had less time to spend with me on the hunt for Belhaven's killer. The tension that had existed between us was gone now—or lay hidden to rear its head again later. But that's a danger in any relationship, right?

THE NEXT day Charlie rapped on my office door and meandered over to the table in the corner of my office. I joined him there. His blazer held the sweet smell of pipe tobacco.

"Find anything on Rocky?" I asked.

"Sergeant Lodeen's a complex man," he said. "Infantry platoon noncom by the time he reached Afghanistan in 2009 as a part of the surge. Records show he was a good soldier. Demonstrated bravery and decent leadership skills. Even so, he got a general discharge early this year."

My interest surged. "For what?"

"Too quick on the trigger. His unit got ambushed once while on patrol. Lost some buddies. Seems he was largely responsible for repelling the attack. Saved some lives. But after that he'd shoot first and take a look afterward to see who he shot. Sometimes it was friendlies."

The hair of my neck rose. "Now his remark about killing across the pond makes sense. He killed and got away with it. Anything else?"

"He came here after his release from the Army."

"Why here? Why not back to California?"

Charlie shrugged. "Don't have an answer… yet. He works as a body man in an auto repair shop. Minor jacket. Recreational drugs, once. Drunk and disorderly, twice. One DWI."

"Finances?"

"There aren't any to speak of. Lives on his paycheck. Rents a one-bedroom apartment. Spends his money on booze."

"Women?"

"They spend their money on him. Never been married. Dates occasionally but doesn't seem to have anyone in his life right now."

"That matches what I've learned."

"Do we put a watch on him?"

"Not sure what a tail would find out. We already know he's close to Spence, so nothing to gain there."

"Spencer have a jacket?" Charlie asked.

"His background's about like Lodeen's. Enlisted in the Army and served his full enlistment. Served in Afghanistan without a problem. Came back to Albuquerque after he mustered out and kept his nose clean except for a couple of dustups in bars. Never been married. Girlfriends in and out of his life. Belhaven—as a lover—was simply a matter of economics to Spence. May have been getting it on with Lodeen as well."

"Based on…?"

"My gut feeling," I said. "Plus some signals he was sending."

"So what do we do next?"

"Use Guerra to shake them up," I said. "But first I want to know what the investigator we hired to check on Cag Jr. at the Virginia Military Institute has to say."

Charlie got him on the speaker phone, and the man confirmed Cadet Cagney Harper Jr. was present on VMI's campus during the entire week of July 17 through 23. On Wednesday of the week of Belhaven's death, Cag was standing guard duty as a form of punishment. The kid was having a rough time coping with the academy's strict discipline.

ROY GUERRA was happy to help out. He wasn't doing any better than we were at closing the case, and while he no longer stayed close to learn my technique, he was still cooperative. On Monday morning he called Harris, the Harpers, Sarah, and Spencer down to APD for questioning. I prevailed upon him to send for Rocky Lodeen and have him report in a little later than the others.

Roy enlisted the aid of another new detective, Glenann Hastings, with whom I worked the Abaddon's Locusts case last year. She was smart and pretty and fit into about any stratum of society you could name. Roy would do well to snag Glenann as his partner. Detective Sergeant Don Carson also assisted.

Paul considered this an event worthy of pulling him off another assignment—for which he was fighting a deadline. He joined me in a room that didn't exist when I was a detective with the force, a space full of electronic equipment allowing viewers to monitor recorded interviews going on in multiple locations. Roy put Melanie Harper in one room while Glenann questioned Cag Sr. in another. Don Carson, the most experienced of the detectives, tackled Harris Belhaven in yet another. From what I could see, Harris's anger was back, riding his shoulders like a cowboy hugging a bronc. Sarah and Spence sat in the waiting room as far apart as possible. Lodeen hadn't yet arrived.

Gene joined us in the communications room—if that was what it was called—to monitor the interviews. Things went about as expected. Melanie seemed confused, Cag bemused, and Harris enraged. Nonetheless, details of the interviewees' financial stress slowly emerged. Melanie and Cag were literally saved from bankruptcy by Pierce's death. It rescued Harris from a terrible year for investments. He apparently needed the partial settlement from Pierce's estate as much as his sister and her husband.

I chanced to glance at the waiting room monitor to see how Sarah and Spence were doing in their respective corners in time to see Rocky Lodeen escorted into the room. He stood in the doorway for a second, glancing around. When his eyes settled on Sarah, he walked over to her. She looked up and greeted him with a smile. There was no audio, but the brief conversation seemed amiable. Then she nodded in Spence's direction, and Rocky ambled across the room to his buddy, giving him a fist bump, which passed for a handshake among a certain group. When he settled in a seat beside Spence, I turned my attention back to Don Carson's interview with Harris, who wore a thunderous look. Paul moved to my side and watched the monitor with me.

"HOW MANY times do I have to tell you? I did not kill Pierce Belhaven. Hell, he was my *father*, for crying out loud. And don't throw me the 'fractured relationship' card, either. We were *dispassionate* but not *fractured*."

Don gave him a long look. "View this from my side of the table, Mr. Belhaven. You had a poor, probably resentful relationship with your father, your ex-wives were draining your trust income, you had a disastrous year at your job, and you have no alibi."

"How did I get in the house?" he demanded.

"With the key you never returned."

Harris's face turned red. "And the security code on the home alarm?"

"It's never been changed."

"I didn't know that."

"Your father's death rescued you from bankruptcy. And when the life policy pays—if it does—"

"Bankruptcy? That's a stretch. And what do you mean, *if it does*?"

"The insurance company's not going to pay a policy to your father's killer. They're going to withhold payment until the murderer is identified. Regardless of what your lawyer says," Don added.

"Is that true?" Paul whispered in my ear.

"They'll delay as long as possible, but the lawyers Harris and Melanie hired will eventually force them to pay."

I watched the monitor as Harris reached the conclusion he should have some time ago.

"Speaking of lawyers," he said, spitting the words out, "I think it's time I called him in here."

"Your choice. But if you're sincere in your denial of having anything to do with your father's death, the lawyer will put a muzzle on you and prevent you from helping to find his killer."

Don terminated the interview when Harris insisted.

MELANIE WAS more mortified than offended at being questioned about her father's death. She seemed totally at sea about details. By referring to her pocket calendar, she came up with the fact she'd worked a two-to-nine shift that Wednesday afternoon. She was home with her husband after that.

She only became animated when Roy touched on her son. Then she went defensive, even though we knew Cag Jr. had been on campus in Lexington the entire week. Perhaps understandably he remained a sensitive subject for her. She haltingly confirmed her son's troubles, including his arrests. I felt sorry for her. It was as if every question about Cag Jr. was a lash of a cat-o'-nine-tails.

CONVERSELY, CAG Harper Sr. appeared to relish talking about his son's legal difficulties as a matter of pride at how the boy faced up to his problems and did something about them. He was more reticent about discussing the financial difficulties Cag Jr. brought on his family. Glenann worked a bit harder at Cag Sr.'s rub with his father-in-law and where he'd been that night. He stuck to his guns. He'd worked at his second job that night but had been home when his wife came in after her shift. They ate a late dinner, cleaned up the kitchen, and then spent the rest of the evening watching television.

SARAH REMAINED distant when questioned by Glenann, but doggedly insisted she loved Pierce Belhaven and could never do anything to harm him. She appeared to shiver as she answered the question. Sincere or contrived? Hard to know. I found it difficult to believe this thirty-year-old brunette loved the sixty-year-old writer in a romantic way but could understand a fondness permitting intimacy. Plus he was her sole means of support.

Sarah maintained at least an outward calm even when Glenann bit down hard and pushed her on how much she benefited from her lover's death. Not once did Sarah even mention the word *lawyer*.

Her overnight stay in Las Cruces the night of Belhaven's death was convincing, and the maids at the motel had confirmed they remembered her because she'd taken the time to chat with them while asking for recommendations on places to eat. To the best of their recollection, the bed had been slept in and the room exhibited signs of habitation. But as Paul once said, it was only a three-hour drive from there to Albuquerque.

SPENCE'S STUDIED charm didn't work on Don Carson. I watched the kid send subtle messages. Doubtless the room was full of pheromones by the time the interview ended, but the little doo-dads didn't speak to one another. I don't believe Don caught on that Spence was engaged in some nonverbal flirting.

Don spent most of his time detailing Spence's movements on the day of Belhaven's death. The young man fingered the birthmark on his cheek and recited a tale of drinking at the Hog, as Spence called the tavern. Don reviewed Spence's finances, which looked to be stressed but not strained. The purchase of his 2010 Barracuda would have been beyond his capability had not Belhaven cosigned the bank's loan. That said, Spence met each payment on time. Nothing appeared amiss in his bank account, but he seemed to have money to occasionally take women on dates to restaurants. His principal outlay seemed to be for drinking at the Hogshead and elsewhere. Doubtless Belhaven donated money over and above Spence's earned wages for over and above services performed. Of course, all of this changed when Spence received his bequest from Belhaven's estate. At no time during the interview did he ask for an attorney.

THIS WAS Roy's second go-round with Rocky Lodeen, and he went at the young man a bit aggressively, which might have been the right approach.

"You claim you and Spencer Spears were at the Hogshead the night of July 20 until midnight or later?"

"No, I said until closing. At least that's what I marked down in my social calendar."

"Listen, smartass, this may be a game to you, but it's murder to the state. You get a civil tongue in your head."

"Yes, *sir*." It came off as just short of snarky.

Roy led Lodeen through the same story the young man gave me earlier. He was at the Hogshead when Spence arrived eight or after, and they remained until closing. Lodeen also gave the detective the names of the other two who made up the party.

"The other two—" Roy paused to check his notes. "—Neal Chutney and Charles Mumfrey claim they weren't there the entire evening. They came and went, leaving the two of you alone."

"So?"

"So what if you and Spencer Spears rode over to Post Oak Drive and confronted Belhaven."

"Why would we do that?"

"Who knows? To extort some money from him to finance the evening, maybe. And as soon as Belhaven saw the two of you together, he knew you were more than just friends and got jealous. Put up a fuss. Threatened to cut Spencer off. This would have seriously impacted your income. A fuss turned into a fight, which turned into murder. Maybe you were defending yourselves and Belhaven was accidentally killed. That might earn you some consideration with the judge."

Lodeen laughed aloud. "Tube didn't say nothing about a fight."

"We don't tell television reporters everything. What about it? You help us out?"

"Dream on, guy. I didn't lay a hand on the old man."

"But you admit going there that night."

"Don't admit nothing. I was at the Hog all evening. Ask the people at the tavern. They'll tell you."

"I did. They tell me there was a lot of coming and going at the table. I think Spencer was tired of servicing the old boy and talked you into helping him put an end to it. You killed Belhaven while Spencer trashed the office."

"You're nuts. But tell me why he'd do that. To the office, I mean?"

"To make everyone think exactly what they did. Belhaven's murder was to stop his investigation of an old crime."

Rocky sighed and tapped his fingers on the metal table. "I didn't do nothing, and you can't prove I did."

"Not yet," Roy said with an appropriate amount of menace in his voice. "But I'm working on it."

Chapter 24

SOMETHING ABOUT Rocky Lodeen piqued my interest, so the next day I asked Hazel to start a deeper background check on the man. In return she put me to work on a case a Boston confidential investigator contracted our help for. A young woman, an heiress in fact, was believed to have run off with a boyfriend to the fabled city of Taos.

I say fabled because it was both a town in northern New Mexico rich in art history and a nearby iconic Native American pueblo awash in indigenous culture. It didn't take long to find the pair registered at the Sagebrush Inn as Mr. and Mrs. Jonathan Smith. Smith turned out to be the boyfriend's legal name, and they'd been married in Las Vegas, Nevada two days prior. As the woman was of legal age, there was nothing to do but report the situation to the Boston PI and wonder why he needed us to do a simple survey of motels and hotels. Even so, Hazel was pleased we'd earned some billable hours, and if she was happy, I was happy. Sometimes it was hard to figure out who was boss at Vinson and Weeks, Confidential Investigations.

On Wednesday Hazel put the results of her investigation of Lodeen on my desk, and it proved interesting and disturbing at the same time. Rockwell B. Lodeen was born in a small Southern California town and raised in the Los Angeles area. A high school graduate, he'd entered the school of hard knocks for his advanced education. He spent a few years in the movie industry as a gofer, meaning he was an errand boy running and fetching for just about anyone on the set. He graduated to production assistant, which likely meant he did the exact same thing but for fewer people. But then I'm not in the movie business and have an imprecise grasp of such things.

Then he became a stuntman, one thing I *did* understand. He took falls and other life-or-limb-threatening jobs in order to preserve the health and looks of more valuable talent. To my mind, that included car crashes. Paul's "accident" at San Mateo and Copper early last September sprang to mind. A T-bone would be one of the basic moves in a stunt driver's repertoire. Lodeen left the movie business rather abruptly and entered the Army. A little more digging revealed why. He'd almost killed a man in a drunken brawl and got a break on the charges by enlisting. It didn't take long for him to mess up that gig by killing Afghans indiscriminately. If that didn't prove escalation of his violent tendencies, I don't know what would.

With this information in hand, I became more interested in Rocky's finances beyond what Charlie had turned up. Hazel located a checking account in a local bank where he deposited his paychecks—which were on the low end of the professional scale for a vehicle body repairman—and a savings account now drained to almost zero. She found no car loan for a 2009 black Cougar, the vehicle he drove away from the interview at the police department two days ago. Activity in the checking account was limited to a few cash withdrawals and a monthly check for his rent on a place on Pitt NE not far from CNM's Montoya campus and quite near Spencer Spears's apartment.

I poked into the MVD database and located a registration for Rocky's Cougar. Once I located the name of the dealer, I phoned and ran into a brick wall. The dealership wouldn't part with the information, not to a "PI," as they saw fit to label me. I hung up and ran Roy Guerra to ground. If they wouldn't talk to a licensed confidential investigator, maybe they'd respond to an APD detective. Roy agreed to give it a try and phoned me back within thirty minutes.

"Paid cash for the car on October 4."

"Cash?"

"Combination of cash and a cashier's check."

"Give me the details of the cashier's check."

Roy told me the check was purchased from Rocky Lodeen's bank. How? Presumably using cash, but Hazel could check on this for me later. The balance of the car's purchase price was paid in cash, likely money from the depleted savings account. Why not include it all in one check? The most likely explanation was Rocky's inexperience with such transactions. The dealer also said Rocky test drove the car twice a couple of weeks before the purchase.

"Do you understand the significance of this?" I asked Roy.

"He got his hands on a lot of money."

"On the day following the payout of Belhaven's bequest to Sarah Thackerson and Spencer Spears."

"Coulda been one buddy loaning another buddy some Washingtons after hitting the jackpot."

"Could have been. But it could also mean Rocky Lodeen was hired to do the hit on Belhaven."

"I gotta go talk to that man," Roy said.

"Hold on. Let's plan our approach. Don't want to tip our hand too early. Let's gather some more information. You see if you can find a jacket on him anywhere other than what we've already located. Check all the jurisdictions where you know he lived, no matter how short the duration. I want to talk to Sarah Thackerson again."

"Not Spears?"

"Not yet. I want to hear what she says about Rocky."

I TRACKED Sarah Thackerson down at her apartment. Apparently she had now severed her relationship with the Belhaven family… or vice versa. She answered the door in smart casual clothes and with her hair flowing loose, a far more attractive look for her. She frowned and removed her black-framed reading glasses when she recognized me.

"Mr. Vinson. I didn't expect you."

"Sorry to drop in unannounced, but I have some more questions. Have you finished your work at the Belhaven house?"

"Yes. Harris could hardly wait to get me out the door. I think he resented having to rely on me to clean up some details."

"Like?"

"Like Pierce's royalties. They had to be switched over to the estate, which took paperwork. But everything's finished now."

We stood for an awkward moment in silence before she opened the door wider and stood aside. Her apartment looked like the student's abode that it was. Compact, but she'd made it comfortable. What I assumed was homework took up most of the small kitchen table.

"Surprised you haven't moved to larger quarters," I said, "given your recent inheritance."

"That inheritance is going to see me through my degree. I'm not going to look for another job."

I settled across the table from her, careful of bumping knees. "What can you tell me about Rocky Lodeen?"

"Spencer's friend? Not much."

"Did he hang around the Belhaven home?"

"Pierce didn't approve of us bringing friends around."

"Does that mean he was never there?"

"Sometimes, like when Spence needed help with heavy lifting or something. I don't know if he paid Rocky or just called on his friendship."

"Do you know how they met?"

"In class, I gather." She shrugged. "Come to think of it, I don't know if Rocky *goes* to class. More likely they met in a bar. Spencer always talks about the Hogshead, so that's probably it."

"You're not familiar with the place?"

She hesitated. "I've been there once. A friend from school and I ate there. It's too much of a good-old-boy place for my taste."

"I noticed Rocky came over and spoke to you when he entered the APD waiting area the other day."

"I know him to say hello to. That's all."

"I got the impression it was friendlier than that."

Sarah sniffed. "He'd like it to be."

"He's decent enough looking."

She leveled a brown-eyed stare at me. "Come now, Mr. Vinson. Don't tell me you judge a book by its cover."

Despite myself, I grinned. "Not personally, but there are those who do."

"I'm not one of them."

Sarah put up with me for another half hour as I shot questions about Rocky and Spence at her. She appeared quite detached from either of the men. Her interest level registered low. I got the distinct impression she felt Spence took advantage of Pierce Belhaven. Based on my last conversation with Spence, he felt the same way about her. In Sarah's opinion Spence and Rocky bonded over automobiles, beer, sports, and women. She speculated they had no interests beyond those four things, although she grudgingly admitted Spence was building himself a reputation in the landscaping field. She denied knowing anything about the source of financing for Rocky's Cougar. A bank loan, she assumed.

"Any word on Belhaven's life policy?" I asked as I prepared to close things down.

"I hired a lawyer to help move things along. I think they'd delay paying a penny until the murder was solved, but my lawyer says they can't do that unless they have some proof the beneficiary had something to do with the death of the insured."

This last sounded rehearsed, so I assumed she was parroting her lawyer.

As I left the Riverview Apartments—a good ten miles from any river I knew of—I realized her apartment house was around the corner from Spencer Spears's. Convenient, although if Sarah was to be believed, she had no interest in Spence… or Rocky. The fact she and Spence were satisfying the carnal appetites of the same older man erected a wall tinged with animosity between them.

I raised Spencer Spears on his cell phone. He was at a new customer's place on the Westside of town but agreed to meet me around five for a drink at the Hogshead.

I arrived at the tavern early by design. I wanted to get the lay of the land to determine how easy or difficult it would be for Spence to leave without being noticed by his companions. The place was relatively large but made cozy by dim lighting, a low ceiling, weathered brown nailhead plank walls, and partitions made to look reclaimed. The butt end of one of the 64-gallon barrels giving the tavern its name was affixed to the wall behind the long bar.

Snagging a Coors from the barkeep, I used the cold can to stake my claim to a table with a view of the front door before making a recon of the place. As suspected the restrooms were located at the back with an unalarmed exit opening onto the rear parking lot. Anyone could easily leave the place without being observed, but the door locked in place as soon as it shut. Gaining access would be impossible unless a confederate opened it for him later.

I was seated and halfway through my beer by the time Spence showed up, dressed in work dungarees and a form-hugging T-shirt covered by a windbreaker against the mid-November climate. Did he know how sexy he looked? Of course, he did.

He claimed the chair opposite and favored me with a smile. "Came straight from work. Hope I'm not too ripe to be pleasant company." The strawberry birthmark on his left cheek played as he spoke. It put me in mind of the way Pedro…. No time for that now.

"It's a working-man's bar, and I'm guessing you'll be one of the sweeter-smelling patrons before the night is over."

He laughed but sobered when I plopped my recorder on the table and asked my next question.

"Where were you seated the night Belhaven died?"

He lifted his chin and indicated the back of the big room. "Back yonder in the corner. Table 21."

I raised my eyebrows. "Surprised you know the tables are numbered."

"Aren't they always? That's not far from the kitchen, and we always hear the cook ring the bell and yell, 'Table 21.' Not hard to figure."

I turned to survey the area. "Who was sitting where?"

"I was on the bench on the south wall. Rocky was to my right. The other guys came and went."

He'd made it easy for me. "Rocky stayed the whole evening?"

"Yeah. Well, mostly. He did some coming and going like the other two. You know, Neal and Chuck."

"So your alibi wasn't here all the time?"

"One or the other of them was."

"Describe the situation for me."

Spence planted a frown on his face as he recalled the night. Rocky was already here when he arrived around eight or eight thirty. That jibed with what Rocky told me. After about half an hour, the other two showed up. It was mostly laughing and drinking and talking about women and sports. The one named Neal left for an hour or so to go meet his girl. He returned alone. Rocky stepped outside to take a phone call from some woman he later called "my squeeze." Other than pit stops, everyone pretty well stayed put until the place closed down at two the next morning.

Everything sounded normal except for Rocky's "my squeeze." So far, I'd not found a connection to a regular girlfriend. I moved on.

"Didn't you have to be at work the next day? If I recall you said you worked at the Belhaven place on Thursdays."

He gave me a crooked grin. "I'm still young enough to handle it. Besides Pierce's place was time-consuming but not hard work. I've had those grounds under control for a couple of years now. You shoulda seen them before. A mess."

"Are the four of you regulars?"

"Get together a night or two a week."

"How'd you meet?"

"Chuck and Neal go to good old CNM or did until they got their associates. Met them in one class or the other. We hit it off and started bumming around." He shrugged. "Rocky sorta just showed up one day."

I asked a few questions about Neal Chutney and Charles Mumfrey to disguise my interest in Rocky Lodeen. Doubtless Spence would fill him in on my interview, but I didn't want to set off alarm bells for these two.

"I understand you and Rocky were both with the Army in Afghanistan. You didn't meet there?"

"He was Airborne Infantry. I was Rangers. We were there at the same time in the same vicinity but never ran into one another. But that gave us a connection. Something to talk about. But like I said, I met him like the others… at CNM. He was hanging around the coffee shop one day. We got to talking and hit it off."

"He was enrolled in class?"

Spence shook his head. "Not at the time. Think he enrolled in some English course since, but if he's got plans to ever graduate, he hides it pretty good. Think he likes classes as a way to meet women."

"People," I corrected.

He glanced at me sharply before allowing his gaze to slide away.

"You ever make it with him?" I asked.

"You're sure interested in my sex life. You ever run around on your hunky newspaperman?"

I shook my head. "Never. And he's an investigative journalist, not a newspaperman. But I'm trying to get a handle on some people here. For instance… you said you took care of Pierce's needs. Did you ever put him with Rocky?"

He blinked. "What? Course not. Rocky came around a couple of times while I was working, and I introduced the two. But get together? Nah."

"Are you sure you would know?"

He snorted. "Rocky would blab. Couldn't help himself from crowing." He leaned back in the seat and signaled the waiter for another beer. "But me'n Rocky? Yeah. Made it a couple of times. It's awesome." He tilted his head and gave me a look. "You interested?"

"I'm committed," I said. "But thanks for the offer."

"Anytime."

"How well do you know these other guys? Are you a regular foursome?"

"Not dedicated, but…. Whoa, don't get the wrong idea. Neal and Chuck don't swing that way." He gave a calculating look. "Least I don't think so. We're just drinking buddies."

"So Rocky's a special friend, huh?"

"Yeah. We're close. And not because of the sex thing either. He likes cars, and I like cars. He likes—"

I interrupted and took a shot in the dark. "Speaking of cars, why did you give him ten thousand dollars to buy his Cougar?"

"Don't go making nothing of that. He needed it to buy his wheels. And thanks to Pierce, I had it. So I lent it to him."

"A day or so after you got your share of Pierce's estate."

He straightened in his seat as his eyes slid to the recorder lying nearby. "Hold on there, man. I had it. He needed it. That's all there is to it."

"Can I see a copy of the note?"

"What note? We didn't do a formal loan thing. He owes me, and he'll pay me back. Period. It's only temporary anyway. He's got an uncle back in Chicago who's going to front it for him in a month or so. I helped him buy the car before somebody else bought it out from under him."

I left the Hogshead after a few rounds of drinks with a better understanding of the dynamics between Spencer Spears and Rocky Lodeen.

Chapter 25

A FEW discreet questions established that Neal Chutney and Charles Mumfrey often played tennis on the public courts at Los Altos Park in the city's Northeast Heights. Paul volunteered to see if he could engage them and pick their brains about Spence and Rocky while I did some more checking. Rocky's tendency toward violence *plus* his stuntman training put him squarely in my sights.

It took some effort to run down the former commanding officer of the Second Battalion, 327th Infantry Regiment, 101st Airborne Division, the famous Screaming Eagles. The Second was notorious as the "No Slack Battalion." The retired colonel remembered Private First Class Rocky Lodeen well. Lodeen distinguished himself in the Battle of Barawala Kalay Valley but shortly thereafter became trigger-happy. His ex-CO reckoned the stress of the fierce battle unhinged the man. The date of the battle, late March into early April of this year, surprised me. I hadn't realized Rocky had been out of the military for such a short time.

When I figured I had all he had to offer, I asked about Rocky's rank. "I understood that Lodeen was a platoon sergeant, but you called him PFC."

"Hated to do it, but I had to bust him a couple of ranks before he went back to the States for his general discharge."

After that conversation, I drove to the Northeast Heights Auto Body Shop off San Mateo NE and talked to Rocky's boss. I'd counted on Rocky being there in order to gauge his reaction to my presence, but the manager said he was at a crash site with the wrecker. Showing only mild interest in my questions, the man painted the picture of a competent but prickly body-shop man. Rocky got along reasonably well with his coworkers, but they knew not to push his buttons. No one joshed around with the ex-paratrooper as they did with others on the work crew. Although the odd man out, so to speak, he sometimes joined the rest of them after work for a beer. He was a careful drinker. The reason became apparent when on one occasion Rocky overindulged and got so nasty the party broke up rather than deal with him.

That evening Paul and I reconnected at home, where we exchanged information. Neal and Chuck were reluctant to talk with Paul at first, but he'd unleashed his charm—and his tennis prowess—on them to loosen their tongues. What it all boiled down to was that Rocky was Spence's friend, not theirs. They were willing to put up with the guy for the pleasure of Spence's company but wanted no part of Lodeen when Spence wasn't around. They'd seen no evidence of violence in the man but suspected it lurked under the surface. They were cautiously friendly.

SATURDAY MORNING I got my revenge on the links. Paul was so impatient to see the end of our investigation into the Belhaven killing that he let it get in the way of his golf swing. I came in two under his score. On the way home from the country club, I sensed a darkening of his mood. My antennae went up.

"Vince," he said in a slow drawl. "Are we okay? I mean… are we as solid as we were?"

"I'm perfectly comfortable if you are."

He glanced at me before turning back to the road to maneuver the Charger around a big cottonwood that forced the road to jog. "We were more than comfortable."

I let that lie. He was working around to something.

"I don't know what got into me. With Jackie, I mean." He shrugged and gave a snort. "Just flattered a cute kid like that would be interested in me."

"Paul, there have been a hundred cute young men interested in you. And if you count me, it's a hundred and one. You just haven't realized it."

"I-I wouldn't have betrayed you. I was just… I don't know…."

"Let me tell you something, sport. If you ever try to betray me, Pedro will squeeze the nipple he's holding so hard you won't be capable of going through with it. Pedro and I have a special relationship, you know."

He giggled, transforming himself into a younger Paul. "I know. And I'm glad. I love you, Burleigh J. Vinson."

"Vince will do. And I love you, Paul Barton. After all these years, I've never heard your middle name. Do you even have one?"

"Nope. My folks figured I didn't need one."

"You seem to be coping fine."

"Let's go line dancing tonight."

Paul and I didn't frequent the gay bars in the Albuquerque area beyond dropping in for a drink now and then, but he loved the C&W Palace, the biggest boot-stomping joint in the state, out on East Central. It was strictly a hetero place, so he never lacked for a willing female partner to dance. He especially liked the line dances, and as I'd watch from nearby tables, his graceful, manly moves sometimes provoked an ache deep in my guts.

"It's been a while," I said.

"Yeah. It's time we hit the old barn."

WE STRODE into the huge C&W Palace that evening around eight o'clock. Despite my companion's reference to it as a barn, a cowshed this size would have held an entire herd of longhorns with room to spare.

Paul's black turtleneck and black denims perfectly complimented his coloring, but the mustard-yellow suede vest he customarily wore for dancing made him breathtaking. My western shirt and gray slacks couldn't begin to compete.

A small table at the edge of the dance floor beckoned after we got our drinks at the bar. Every place in the state still carded my companion even though he was coming up on twenty-six. Good genes.

After sitting we spent a few minutes surveying the crowd. My eyes never failed to involuntarily seek out the tables on the far side of the room where Puerco Arrullar and his Santos Morenos gang habitually sat until we took them down five years ago. But there was no evidence of anyone other than people bent on having a good time. At the first call for a line dance, Paul was off and running.

As was my custom, I admired Paul for a few minutes before glancing at the other dancers. Three places to his right, I spotted a familiar figure. Spencer Spears, looking almost as good as Paul, danced opposite a petite blonde. Both were accomplished dancers.

When the music died away, Paul signaled he was going to dance the next dance. I smiled and nodded. The band struck up a country and western tune, and the crowd of swirling dancers swept them away.

"Hullo, Mr. Vinson."

I looked up to see Spence hovering nearby. I nodded to a chair. "Join me for a few minutes."

He threw a leg over the back of the chair like he was mounting a horse and settled in his seat. "Your boy's looking good out there."

"If you're referring to Paul, I have to agree."

"Best-looking stud in the place."

I glanced at him, half expecting him to add "except for me." But he merely smiled. "Once again, I have to agree," I said.

"If I didn't know he was taken, I'd be out there rooting around. Doesn't it bother you he's rubbing thighs with women?"

"It doesn't pay to hold the leash too tightly." If Spence wanted to spar, I'd spar.

"Just tell me when you let him off the leash, will you?"

"I wouldn't wait around."

Another slow smile. "I never do."

"I'll just bet you don't. Where's your friend tonight?"

"What friend?"

"Rocky Lodeen," I said, taking in the not unpleasant alcohol and sweat aroma of the C&W.

"His shop got a rush order. He's putting in some major overtime. Said he might be here later, depending on the time."

"This one of your watering holes?"

Spence glanced around. "Couple of times a month. I like the dancing. And the band."

"Your friend's an interesting guy."

"Rocky? How's that?"

"Understand he was a standout in a battle over in Afghanistan in May and here in Albuquerque a couple of months later." I allowed my voice to rise so he could take it as a question if he wanted.

Spence shrugged. "Mustered out. Happens every day."

"Not before your enlistment's up."

His frown looked real, not studied. "You saying he had a problem with the Army? Hell, he was gung-ho from the time I met him."

"At CNM, if I remember right?"

"Yeah. In the coffee shop. Heard me talking to some dude about Afghanistan and moseyed over to put in his two cents." He laughed at the recollection. "We even figured out we were in the same place at the same time in a couple of instances. Maybe even in the same DFAC but never met up." He reacted to my confused look and explained. "Dining facility. So Rocky took an FOB taxi, did he?" That required another explanation.

"That's a vehicle leaving a forward operating base. How about that? You telling me Rocky got the bum's rush from the unit?"

I shook my head, marveling how each war develops its own jargon. "You'll have to ask him."

"I will."

"I hear he's a Los Angeles dude," I said. "Do you know what brought him here?"

"Even though he was Army, he told me he once had temp duty at the Air Force base… you know, Kirtland… for a few days and liked the town. When they turned him loose, he headed straight here."

Paul showed up fresh-faced from dancing in time to receive a long once-over. Spencer Spears lusted after my companion in a major way. I understood. After all, so did I.

I THOUGHT of Pedro as we approached our neighborhood. Paul was usually charged up after dancing, something that benefited both Pedro and me. But as we turned onto Post Oak Drive, I spotted a dark Cougar parked in front of my house.

"Uh-oh," Paul mumbled, sitting straighter in his seat. "Lodeen?"

"Looks like it." Damn, I was going to have to unlist my home number, something I'd threatened for years but never got around to doing.

"What do you want me to do?"

"Park in the driveway like usual. But keep a sharp eye out. Damn! My pistol's in the Impala's trunk. You get it while I distract him."

My back prickled as Paul pulled up behind my car in the driveway. I got out of the Charger with an eye on the dark car parked nearby. A dome light and a clanging bell warned the driver's side door of the Cougar had opened. The old wound on my thigh throbbed as Rocky exited his car.

"Hey there, Mr. Vinson. Need to talk to you a minute, okay?"

"Sure. Come on in." I headed for the front of the house. Rocky met me at the steps. He didn't offer a hand but didn't appear to be holding a weapon. I felt exposed as he trailed me onto the porch. Perhaps perceiving my anxiety, he stood where I could see him as I keyed the lock, stepped aside, and motioned him inside. Paul came through the door and pressed the Ruger into my hand. I stuffed it into the belt at my back as I closed the door.

Rocky paused, and I motioned him to the left into the den. "Drink?"

"Beer if you have it."

"Coors okay?"

"Sure."

Paul went for drinks at the small wet bar while I settled in my recliner across from Rocky on the sofa. Paul handed around the drinks and sat in the other recliner.

Rocky popped the tab and took a sip before speaking. "Hear you talked to my boss yesterday."

"That's right."

"How come?"

"I'm an investigator. Got a license from the state and all that. That's what licensed investigators do… talk to people."

"Cut the bullshit. Why're you asking questions about *me*?"

"Simple. I'm investigating anyone who spent any time at the Belhaven house."

"I was only there a couple of times," Rocky said.

"But you *were* there a couple of times. And you have a relationship with one of the regulars at the house." I paused, recalling how Rocky spoke to Sarah at the police station. "Maybe two."

"Relationship? Hell. Me'n Spence are friends." He arched an eyebrow. "Well… relationship if that's what you call screwing around a couple of times." He frowned. "Two? Who else? I didn't know the old man. Only met him once."

"Sarah Thackerson."

"Sarah? I never said more'n half a dozen words to the woman."

"You said more than six words to her at the police station the other day."

"Just asking if she'd seen Spence. You can ask her yourself. So what did my boss say about me?"

I fed him his own line. "You can ask him yourself. Why did the Army boot you so fast, Rocky?"

He flushed, his gray eyes sparkling. "We decided we wasn't right for one another."

"Takes a lot for the military to decide that. I know. I was a Marine. Didn't matter how much I screwed up, they held on to me."

Rocky gave an exaggerated sigh. "Claimed I was harming relations with the hajis."

"Hajis?" I asked.

"You know, the LNs, local nationals. The Afghanis."

"How did you do that?"

He pursed his lips and lowered his head. "Had trouble telling the friendlies from the Ali Babas."

"You shot at them all?"

"Wasn't about to let nobody make an angel outta me. After a couple of days, they all gave me a wide berth."

A silence grew while I considered that. Then Paul gave my thoughts voice.

"The Army could have handled the problem by shipping you stateside. But they discharged you."

Rocky finished his beer and put the can on the coffee table. His movements seemed studied… controlled. He leaned back on the sofa. "Called me a fucking hero at Barawala Kalay. Then I shoot a couple of hajis, and the next thing I know I'm at BIAP being hustled on a troop transport back home. Hardly get my boots on the ground before I'm discharged." He glanced at both of us in turn. "Not no dishonorable. A general."

His facial expression told me he considered them about the same thing. Here was a man who yearned to be back among his comrades. As a silence built, he returned from wherever he'd been. "Anyway stop poking around in my business. I ain't bothering nobody, and I don't want nobody bothering me."

"I heard you were a stunt driver," Paul said.

"Stunt*man*."

"Same thing. When was the last time you stunt *drove*?"

"That was over before my Army days."

"But it's like riding a bicycle, isn't it? You don't ever forget how to do it."

"What you getting at?"

"Two months ago somebody deliberately T-boned me at Copper and San Mateo in a stolen car. The driver disappeared before my head cleared."

"How come you say it was deliberate? Hell, you know Albuquerque drivers. They bang into one another all the time."

"It was deliberate. Car shot right out on San Mateo in time to hit me broadside."

Rocky's stare gave me a look into his psyche. His voice dropped in pitch. "If it'd been me, you wouldn't be here right now."

Conviction or braggadocio?

SUNDAY SHOULD have been a pleasant day, but it wasn't. Paul and I couldn't agree on the purpose behind Rocky's late-night visit Saturday. I couldn't even agree with myself. At first I considered it an angry confrontation—absent the anger—about our prying into his life. The next moment it appeared an effort to show himself an open book… no harm done. Or perhaps a recon of hostile territory to plan retribution. Had the signals been *that* mixed? Was he just a complicated human being? Of course, being a simple human being was complex enough. What made him so hard to read?

I'd expected resentful anger from Rocky but encountered none. More like a halfhearted warning coupled with acceptance that we'd piddle in his life to our hearts' content. But when challenged about a staged wreck, his dander rose. I hadn't liked what I saw in his eyes when that happened. I believe I glimpsed his soul then, a tormented thing dark with hate and fiery with wrath. He killed the enemy in battle and killed in the peace of the moment without distinction between the two. This was why the Army discharged him instead of simply shipping him home.

At this point I had no idea if Rocky Lodeen was involved in Belhaven's killing or not. Even so I vowed my weapon would no longer be locked away in the trunk of my car. His perception of the danger I represented to him counted more than the reality.

Paul and I managed to salvage some of the day on the country club's tennis courts where both of us went above and beyond our usual efforts. We quit at two sets each, unable to muster the energy to play the tie breaker.

Chapter 26

MONDAY MORNING I sent Paul to APD to check the fingerprints on the beer can Rocky Lodeen drank from Saturday night. There was no reason to doubt his identity, but an investigation is an investigation. Cover all the points. He returned to confirm that Rocky Lodeen was, indeed, the former Sergeant Rockwell B. Lodeen of the famous Screaming Eagles.

Charlie arranged for Alan Mendoza and Tim Fuller, two retired cops we sometimes used for overflow work, to keep a discreet eye on Rocky. I toyed with the idea of assigning one of them to surveil Spencer Spears, but Rocky was of more interest at the moment.

"Who's going to pay for this?" Hazel asked.

"If our client won't, we will," I said.

Apparently my tone was enough to keep her from coming back at me with anything more than "*Humph.*"

Even so she got her pound of flesh when she put a file on my desk and asked me to handle it. It was the type of case I dislike the most and only take from really good clients who give me repeat business. A bail skip.

Chowderhead Jones fled Charleston, South Carolina, ahead of his trial for manslaughter. He was almost apprehended in Memphis, Tennessee, at the home of a cousin, and again in Texarkana, Texas, where he was staying with an ex-girlfriend. Chowderhead slipped away both times but was known to have another cousin in Albuquerque, and he seemed to be heading west.

One reason I don't like bail-jumper cases is that usually the individuals involved are the dregs of the criminal caste, the lees of humanity. Not always, of course, but it pretty well sums up my experience with such cases. More often than not, they involve violence. Not only because of the quality—or lack thereof—of the jumper, but also because bounty hunters have reputations—whether earned or not—of employing muscle and dirty tricks in the pursuit of their own brand of justice. Learning the Albuquerque cousin was named Muley Jones, made me question the mettle of this whole branch of the larger Jones family. I've known some likable Joneses, bright Joneses, even brilliant Joneses, but apparently this branch shouldn't be hard to keep up with.

Muley Jones lived on a difficult-to-find street in the Barelas area. Bad news, because the people in such a neighborhood watched out for one another. Jones would know I was searching him out minutes after I hit the neighborhood. That was my reasoning for walking straight up to the door and knocking on the frame. A short man with salt-and-pepper hair opened the door and glared at me… mulishly.

"Mr. Jones?" I ventured.

"Who's asking?"

I went through the ID procedure, hauling out my extremely unimposing private investigator's license, and as I suspected, he wasn't impressed.

"If you're here about Chowderhead, forget it. If he shows up, I'll haul him to the cops myself."

"You're not on good terms with your cousin?"

"Bastard's owed me six hundred dollars for six hundred years."

I handed him a card. "In that case if he shows up, don't call the cops. Call my office, and you might recover some of what's owed you."

Sometimes skip cases aren't difficult at all. Fewer than twenty-four hours later, Muley phoned and said his cousin was lashed to a kitchen chair awaiting my arrival. What would have happened if Chowderhead brought his cousin the six hundred he owed? Probably the same thing. Muley would consider anything I gave him as interest.

THANKSGIVING DAY was almost upon us, and neither Alan nor Tim had much to report on Rocky Lodeen. The man apparently made the circuit from work to the Hogshead and back home a daily routine. His circle of friends seemed to be Spencer Spears, period. He hadn't been seen in the company of a woman other than barflies hitting him and his buddy up for drinks. But none of the women ever went home with either man. I mentally shook my head. My gaydar was pretty well honed, and while it was no surprise Spence and Rocky occasionally got it on, I couldn't see either one of them being satisfied with that as a permanent arrangement.

The fact I'd noted the other day that Spence's and Sarah's apartments were literally around the corner from one another prompted me to haul out an Albuquerque street map and plot the position of

Rocky's apartment. In so doing, I discovered something interesting. All three apartments were at different street addresses *on the same block.* Furthermore, the rear entrances to the buildings were merely feet away from each other. Pulling up Google Earth on my computer, I zoomed in on the block and found what appeared to be a small neighborhood park in the space behind the buildings. Either man could have left by the rear of his apartment building and made his way to the others' abode without being observed by anyone from the street. This complicated things.

Rocky Lodeen had no motive for killing John Pierce Belhaven unless the writer hit on him and Rocky found it offensive. Doubtful. But possible. Belhaven was genteel; Rocky was rough trade… but attractive bait. So it could have happened, but my impression of Rocky was he wouldn't be offended. He'd probably get a kick out of romping with Spence's sugar daddy. He certainly wouldn't be offended enough to bash Belhaven's head in and set the body afire.

If Rocky did the killing, there had to be something in it for him. Like money. Like a $10,000 payment on his new car. Which pointed me right back to Spence Spears.

But here I ran into a problem. Why would Spence need Rocky to handle Belhaven? He could do the deed and avoid exposing himself to possible blackmail from a partner in crime. Physically Spence was capable of killing Belhaven, but did he have the mental makeup? He'd undoubtedly killed in Afghanistan, but a different set of morals applied there. On the other hand, his buddy Rocky Lodeen got booted from the Army for being unable to differentiate between the two ethical premises.

Sarah, however, would probably need someone like Rocky to handle Belhaven. But why should she—or Spence, for that matter—want to kill the golden goose. Both prospered from their relationship with the author. Each lived a comfortable existence with a steady income by doing work he or she enjoyed. And they both willingly serviced the carnal needs of their employer. Had jealousy or envy gained the upper hand with one of them?

By their own admission, both had prior knowledge of their $250,000 bequest in Belhaven's will, but each denied knowing of a life insurance policy. Despite her claim, Sarah almost certainly knew because she paid Belhaven's bills. Or at least prepared them for payment. But this didn't necessarily hold water. I owned a policy paid each month by an automatic charge to my bank account. She might know of the payment, but not what it represented. Still she filed his paperwork, and a folder marked insurance was likely to provoke curiosity. The chances were good that she knew of the policies. Would she tell Spencer of his? The interplay between the two of them—or lack thereof—was becoming of more interest.

PAUL AND I customarily ate Thanksgiving dinner with Charlie and Hazel, and this year was no exception. Paul typically took a pineapple salad he whipped up from his mother's recipe. All I contributed were pumpkin and pecan pies from a local restaurant specializing in "home-cooked" pies. In my defense, the Village Inn made excellent pies. I'd had to preorder to be assured I would have the privilege of paying for them.

The Weeks' modest, redbrick pitched-roof home collected the rich aromas of Hazel's cooking and released them to us slowly. Turkey and old-fashioned cornbread stuffing dominated, and soon hints of cinnamon and sweet potatoes and the yeasty aroma of rolls came through. I hadn't really been hungry… until then. Paul headed for the kitchen to help Hazel, while I settled in the living room with Charlie.

This was traditionally a time for strengthening personal ties and feeding appetites, not for discussing business. Until after dinner, that is, which was around 3:00 p.m. By that time no one knew how much conversation anyone else absorbed as we all sat around in a gastronomic stupor. Drunk on food, as it were.

But one tidbit in Charlie's monologue plucked me from my dreamworld. I straightened in a chair that suffered from my own affliction—overstuffed. "Say that again."

"Given your insight into the proximity of the three apartments, Tim and Alan double-teamed Lodeen last night. Alan stayed in his car on the street to watch the front door to the apartment building. Tim drew the short stick and hunkered down in the cold park behind the buildings to watch the rear. Lodeen came out around two."

"Hadn't he had enough of Spence by then?" Paul asked in an ennui-laden voice.

"Apparently so, because he went to the other apartment house. To Thackerson's."

"Why am I just finding this out?" I asked.

"Tim called me here at the house when he headed home after keeping watch all night. Said Lodeen hadn't returned to his place by the time he left."

"Rocky spent the night with Sarah?" Paul wasn't so sluggish now.

"That puts a new light on things," I said.

"Smart of you to sit down and plot the position of their apartments," Hazel said. "What caused you to do it?"

"Frustration," I said.

"Oh what a twisted web we weave…." Paul misquoted Sir Walter Scott. "Damnation. Sarah and Spence were both screwing Pierce. Now it looks like Rocky's screwing both Spence and Sarah."

I SUSPECTED Sarah was the weaker link between the two, but this might not be true. Rocky's nature was to crow about his exploits, so he might more readily admit a relationship between them. Judging it a toss-up, I learned neither CNM nor UNM held classes on the day after Thanksgiving and sent Paul to discuss the merits of Chargers vs Cougars with Rocky while I braced Sarah in her apartment. I hit her with it as soon as she allowed me through the door.

"You told me you had no relationship with Rocky Lodeen."

She halted midstride on the way to the sitting area. "Who says we do?"

"I do. He spent Wednesday night with you."

Sarah dropped into a recliner and pulled a pack of cigarettes from the table beside it. Lighting the tube of tobacco gave her time to think. "When you first asked me, there wasn't one. This is something recent. And I saw no reason to share it with anyone."

"Not even Spence?"

She shrugged. "Why should I? I don't think it's a secret I loathe the man."

"Why?"

"He preyed on Pierce. Took advantage of him."

"That's his assessment of you."

Her color heightened, but she remained in control. "Yes. He would, wouldn't he? But then he can't see beyond the end of his nose." She left the rest unsaid.

"They are best friends, you know. Spence and Rocky, I mean."

She leveled attractive brown eyes at me. "For the moment."

Oh-ho. She genuinely resented that Spence received the same consideration from Pierce as she had. "Burns a little, does it?"

Her cheeks reddened. "I don't know what you mean."

My approach worked enough to get what I wanted from her, but it shut down all other avenues of conversation. She was finished with me for the moment, so I took my leave and waited five minutes before dialing Paul's cell.

"Did you find Rocky?"

"Yep."

"Still with him?"

"Yep."

"Did she call him after I left her?"

"Yep." His voice dropped. "On the line now."

"His apartment?"

"Uh-huh."

"Tell him I'm on the way over."

"OKAY. SO I like to bang a chick. Understand that's not on your menu." Rocky's eyes flickered to Paul sitting beside me on a cheap yellow settee.

The man, looking like the paratrooper he once was with camos tucked into military boots and an olive undershirt showing off his pecs, had admitted me to his apartment on the first ring of the doorbell. The big smile on his face wasn't intended as a welcome but rather to show his appreciation of the forthcoming battle of wits. His apartment looked like Sarah's without the feminine touches. The place was furnished for comfort, not show.

"How does Spence feel about that?"

He squinted momentarily as he considered my question. "Why the hell would he care? There's no love lost between those two. She'd like to scratch his eyes out, and he'd like to chuck her over a waterfall… any waterfall."

"You didn't get enough from Spence, so you're planning on nursing on the Thackerson nipple too?"

Out of the corner of my eye, I saw Paul eyeing me, probably confused by my confrontational approach. But I wanted to poke this rattlesnake to see if he had fangs or just rattles. If it was the former, he was a good candidate for broadsiding Paul's car and tossing shots at us from the back alley.

"How much is too much? I'm in my prime. I can go at it all day."

"Don't play games, Lodeen. I'm talking about money, not your stamina. You hit Spence up for $10,000. How much are you going for with Sarah? Maybe marry her and get the whole quarter of a mil plus the two mil in insurance?"

Something happened to Rocky Lodeen's face for a fraction of a second, but it was enough. He hadn't known about the $2,000,000 life payout to Sarah. But he did now. I could almost follow his thought process. *Did Spence have a payoff like that coming too?*

He fell back on my prior comment. "I got nothing from Spence except a ten-grand loan on my car. I'd rather pay him interest than some loan company."

"How much interest?" Paul asked.

Rocky shrugged. "The going rate."

"What's that?" Paul pressed.

"That's between Spence and me. Our business. Not yours."

"Do you own a gun?" I asked.

He blinked. "Course I do. Couple of them."

"A .38?"

"What the hell does that matter?"

"Somebody took a shot at us."

"No shit! When?

"October 20," Paul said without hesitation.

"Hell that was over a month ago. Did I even know you guys then?"

"That's immaterial," I said.

"Man, if I was the shooter, wouldn't neither one of you be around now. I was Second Battalion, 327th Regiment. We don't miss."

"Maybe it was just a warning," Paul said. "Like T-boning my car. Just so you know it, I'm tired of warnings."

"I'll remember that."

Paul was taking things down another road. I stepped in again. "Do you mind if we take your sidearm to the police for testing. They recovered a slug from our kitchen wall to compare it with."

"I ain't gonna turn it over to you two. Have the cops come and get it if they want it!"

I noticed the lapse into the vernacular where he was probably more comfortable. "They'll be happy to. You can expect a Detective Guerra to come calling."

"Be waiting for him. This is all about that old queer, ain't it? Belhaven. You can tell your Detective Whatever-His-Name-Is I didn't shoot him or light him up with gasoline. Why would I?"

"Money is the most likely answer."

"We're back to that? I didn't get none of his money. Spencer lent me ten grand for my car, but he'll get his dough. Uncle of mine in Chicago's gonna send me the dough to pay off Spence. So I get a car, and Spence gets his money back with some vig. Now get outta my apartment."

After we were settled in my Impala and heading back downtown to the office, Paul turned to me.

"He didn't know about the life insurance, did he?"

"He covered it pretty well, but my guess is that he didn't."

"Gives him more to go after, doesn't it?"

"Wonder where he'll expend most of his effort? Spence or Sarah?"

Chapter 27

SATURDAY MORNING I sat in my home office reviewing the Belhaven file online. When I reached the transcription of our talk with Rocky Lodeen a week earlier, something he'd said yesterday jumped out at me. "*If I'd been the shooter, neither one of you'd be around now.*" I closed my eyes and envisioned the ambush in our backyard. It appeared my drawing a weapon panicked the shooter. Both Paul and I agreed he wasn't a professional. If it was Rocky, he wouldn't have been seen, much less missed his targets.

How about Spence? I opened my eyes and shook my head. Same thing. He was a Ranger. Our shooter wasn't either of the two ex-military men. Who, then? Two people popped into my head: Harris Belhaven and Sarah Thackerson. Why the two of them? Because they both had a significant financial gain to protect. The insurance payout. Five mil for Harris and two for Sarah. I had no idea of their skill with firearms, but they weren't trained killers.

Why did I so readily dismiss the Harpers? Distance was one factor. A second was the nature of the two. They seemed to be genuine nose-to-the-grindstone people who worked hard to take care of their own problems. Still… an investigation's an investigation, so I needed to tie down their movements on the afternoon and evening of Wednesday, October 12.

MONDAY MORNING Paul and I settled onto a bench in a New Mexico district courtroom to witness Wick's sentencing. He'd pled guilty to his part in the VPMR scam, including the killings of four people: Barron Voxlightner, Dr. Walther Stabler, Thelma Rider, and Dr. Damon Herrera. No mention of John Pierce Belhaven or Everett Kent, the attorney who first blew the whistle on the scam. No doubt he'd struck a deal with the district attorney to avoid the death penalty, although the state hadn't put anyone to death since the 2001 execution of a man named Terry Clark.

During Wick's allocution to his crimes, as was required by the court, he spoke in a monotone, although firmly enough to reach every part of the courtroom. He seemed to have recovered from the stabbing in the shower at the detention center, but he'd lost weight, and his normally erect carriage was slightly stooped. Once he finished, the judge asked if all parties were satisfied before sentencing Wick to life imprisonment.

We stood as the judge adjourned the proceedings. The crowd began to clear. "He didn't mention Pierce Belhaven," Paul said in a whisper as they led Wick out a side door.

"Nor Everett Kent. I think Stabler killed Kent. Can't prove it, of course."

"Does this really mean Wick'll die in prison?"

"The New Mexico statutes offer the possibility of parole after thirty years, although it's seldom granted to murderers. Wick's in his midfifties, so chances are good he'll die behind bars." I looked around at the departing crowd. "I didn't see any of his family."

"Word down at the *Journal* is Wick asked his wife to divorce him and move back east to be with her family."

"Did she?"

He shrugged. "I thought Dorothy Voxlightner wouldn't want to miss this."

"I talked to her. She had no interest in coming. Resolving the issue of her son was enough for her. And of course, identifying Belhaven's killer."

Paul scratched an ear. "That's not coming along too well, is it?"

"Maybe better than you think."

"Huh? What?"

I smiled at him. "Give it some thought."

He spent the rest of the day at his desk in our home office going over the files. Toward evening I checked to see how he was doing. He lifted his head and stared at me.

"Harris or Sarah or Spence or Rocky."

I smiled. "Or a combination thereof."

I WAS convinced Rocky Lodeen was involved in Belhaven's death—at least to some extent—for two reasons: he was a trained stuntman and he got booted from the Army for being an indiscriminate killer. No one can know for certain he'll walk away from a car wreck, but a stunt driver has more chances of doing so than most people. And a man who has trouble telling the difference between a combat and a noncombat death deserves special consideration.

Hazel and Charlie had also taken a deeper look into the service record of the other ex-military man in our cast of characters. Spencer Spears also learned to kill in the Army. Perhaps that was like a gateway drug and led to easier killings. Unlike Rocky, Spencer probably made a distinction between sanctioned and unsanctioned killing. But was a quarter-of-a-million-dollar inheritance enough to get him to suspend his morals and kill another man? Particularly one he'd been intimate with? Could the intimacy have been a negative factor? Young guy tired of catering to the needs of an old guy. Paul's brief flirtation flashed through my mind like a hammer blow, but I put it aside. A $2,000,000 insurance payoff would provide an even more powerful temptation. But did Spence know of his policy? Even if—as I believed—Sarah possessed such knowledge, her frosty relationship with her rival argued against her alerting him.

I sighed aloud. Every time I traveled a mental road, detours appeared all up and down the line. Nothing unusual in that. That was part of the confidential investigator's game. If I'd done nothing else, I'd convinced myself Rocky was the most dangerous player on the field.

The place to start was with the tenants in those three apartment buildings situated so conveniently close together. Believing I was about to seriously piss off Rocky Lodeen—not to mention Sarah Thackerson and Spencer Spears—I didn't want Paul involved, so Tuesday morning Charlie went along with me to begin the survey. I pacified Paul by asking him to look up Guerra's report on the T-bone incident and interview anyone the cops spoke to about the "accident."

Charlie and I spent two full days making sure we spoke to all thirty-eight tenants of those small apartment buildings. Neighbors like to think they respect one anothers' privacy, but once you get them talking, strange things come out. Not so with these neighbors. The only thing they could come up with was that the two men sometimes snuck off in the middle of the night. That fact excited some idle speculation, but little else.

We heard nothing from any of the three individuals we were investigating. I figured Sarah was cool enough to take it in stride, Spence was cocky enough to let it slide, but Rocky was incapable of ignoring the intrusion. I was right. The day after we finished our survey, Rocky was on the phone raising hell. He'd only waited that long because we tackled his building last. The ex-paratrooper called me to vent and then went silent. I wasn't sure what to make of that.

According to Tim and Alan, Rocky continued to spend a couple of nights a week at Sarah's place and a couple at Spence's. No wonder those two never brought women home from the bar. They didn't have the energy for it. I was mildly curious over how a macho ex-Ranger and a tough former paratrooper managed things between them, but it was a fleeting thought.

"Do we keep Tim and Alan on Lodeen?" Charlie asked.

"Maybe it's time to have them look at Spears."

He rubbed his balding head. "Seems to me Lodeen is the volcano waiting to erupt. Spears would just invite them to coffee."

"You know, when you think about it, there's no reason a tail should shake up Rocky. The fact it does confirms for me that he's involved somehow. But unless he starts throwing around money he shouldn't have, I'm not sure how to prove he's Belhaven's killer… providing he is."

Charlie shrugged. "Maybe we can make him nervous enough to do something rash."

"Even if we rode his ass every day for a month, there's no reason for him to do anything stupid," I said.

"When does reason enter into it?" Charlie asked. "Treat a guy like he's guilty, and sometimes he'll admit it."

I mulled over my partner's suggestion. "Do it. Have them stop double-teaming him and put them in shifts around the clock. And tell them to be obvious about it. They might talk to his boss at the auto body shop and to the bartender at the Hogshead."

"While he's watching?"

"Make sure he's watching. Get him tensed up good and tight, and then there's something we can try."

"What's that?"

"You remember the beer can Paul took to APD."

"The one Lodeen drank out of?"

"That's the one. It gave us his fingerprints—"

"*And* his DNA," Charlie finished my sentence. "So what? We haven't found his DNA anywhere."

"He doesn't know that. And where's the most likely place we'd find it?"

"In the Caravan that plowed into Paul. Shock like that shoulda left some stray hair or skin or something."

"Maybe we better remind Guerra to check on that."

"Hell, the minivan's probably gone to the scrap yard by now."

"Once again, Rocky doesn't know that." I paused. "Come to think of it, neither do we."

"I'll get ahold of Guerra," Charlie said.

Chapter 28

WE WERE all surprised the Caravan involved in Paul's crash was still in the APD impound lot. Gene wasn't convinced the incident was an accident and held the vehicle as evidence in a possible crime. Guerra was embarrassed he hadn't run Rocky Lodeen's DNA to match against hair samples and skin cells found in the disabled van.

As he set about correcting that oversight, Tim and Alan made themselves a more obvious and irritating factor in Rocky's life. He reacted as anticipated. I arrived home one evening to find him on my front porch arguing with Paul through a latched screen door. I spotted Alan's car half a block down the street. Rocky turned his ire on me as soon as I got out of the Impala.

"Why are you hassling me, man?" he demanded as he stomped down the front steps.

"Not hassling anyone," I said. Damn. Despite my pledge, my weapon was in the car trunk again. I hoped Alan would react if things went wrong. "I'm investigating a murder."

"How come you think I done it?"

"You needed money. Belhaven died. You got money."

"Yeah. What's the connection?"

"Spencer Spears."

"I knew Spence before I ever heard of Belhaven."

"So what's your point? Spence inherits, and you get your car."

"How many times I gotta tell you, that's a loan!" He snorted like a quarter horse blowing after a race. "You got no proof, man. Lay off. Hear me. Lay off. I don't wanna see those two cops again, including that bozo down the street in his car. And nobody talks to my boss. Shit they even got the bartender at the Hogshead looking at me sideways. Call 'em off."

"Those two men are conducting an investigation. When it's finished they'll go away."

His shoulders rippled with frustration. His voice grew hoarse. "I'm gonna get me a lawyer and sue your ass. You hear me?"

"When the investigation's over, Rocky. They'll go away when it's over."

He seemed to grow larger each time his fists clenched and unclenched, as if he were pumping himself up. I wished for my Ruger.

"You got no proof!" He spit the words out with a rush of air like a miniature sonic boom.

I decided on a ploy. "Rocky, do you remember the last time you were here? I offered you a beer. You accepted and drank it. Paul took the can to APD. You have any idea what's on a can like that… besides your fingerprints, that is?"

"Wh-what?"

"Your DNA. Marvelous stuff, DNA. It can trace a single hair back to the head it grew on. It can identify skin cells. In other words, it can put a stunt driver right into the seat of a Caravan used to deliberately try to kill Paul."

The light went out in his eyes. And then it fired up again, brighter than ever. "You don't know who you're fucking with. Watch your six!"

He stomped to the curb, got into his Cougar, and squealed his way down the street.

Paul joined me as I watched the black car, followed by Alan's Honda, lurch around a corner. "So you found DNA in the Caravan?"

"I might have been a bit premature in my declaration."

"But he doesn't know that, does he?"

I shook my head. "Nope."

"Then you better do what he said. Watch your six."

"No. *We* better watch our six."

WINTER DECIDED to strike a blow the first weekend of December, meaning a cold, blustery couple of days with a little sleet keeping the roads wet. It was enough to discourage golf or tennis, so we hit the indoor pool at the country club, Paul for the love of swimming, me for therapy… and the pleasure of admiring his grace in the water.

Monday morning Charlie let me know Tim and Alan had noticed a change in Lodeen's pattern of behavior. He'd spent the last three nights with Spence. Sarah didn't rate a single visit, and Friday nights were usually devoted to her.

"Anything else change?" I asked.

"Nope. Work, Hogshead, home, and then slip out the back door in the night hours."

"He knows we're watching him, including at night," I mused aloud. "Why the change?" Then I told Charlie about Rocky's visit to Paul and me the previous Friday.

"Looks like they're plotting their strategy. Calming one another's nerves," Charlie said.

"They could do that at the Hogshead in plain sight. This calls attention to Rocky's change in pattern."

"Deliberate?"

I nodded. "Deliberate. Like Rocky's trying to lead us somewhere."

"To Spears. But we know about the ten grand Spears gave him. There's already a strong connection. If it was me in that situation, I'd cool it, not intensify things."

I looked at my tall, thin business partner. The overhead lights reflected off his glasses. "Exactly. He's pointing a finger right at Spence Spears. Why?"

"Misdirection?"

"That would be my guess."

"So what do we do now?" Charlie asked.

"Any sign Rocky's getting ready to bolt?"

"Not according to Tim and Alan."

"Then keep doing what we're doing. In the meantime, I want to talk to Spence again."

BEFORE I could arrange to meet with Spence, Paul showed up in my office with Guerra in tow.

"Great news." Paul's beaming smile lent emphasis to his words. "Roy found Rocky Lodeen's DNA in the van."

"Correction," the detective said. "The lab found it. Got confirmation this morning."

I nodded. "That connects him to Paul's car wreck but doesn't prove he had anything to do with Belhaven's death."

"But it moves us closer," Paul said.

"Possibly," I acknowledged. "It throws light on his change in behavior. He knew the odds were that we're gonna be able to tie him to the deliberate attempt on Paul."

"What change in behavior?" Paul and Roy asked in unison.

I thought about the DNA evidence while Charlie explained.

"Might not be proof," Roy said, "but there was no reason to stage an accident with Paul if it didn't tie back to the Belhaven murder somehow. And if Lodeen was rattled after you told him about the DNA, Spears is probably calming him down."

"I didn't even know Lodeen existed until Spence let us know about him," Paul said. "Has to be the Belhaven connection."

"Agreed. And your explanation for why he's paying more attention to Spence now may be correct. But what if it's Rocky's attempt to throw us off target? I asked. "Any sign of panic on Spence's part?"

"Tim and Alan are spending their time watching Lodeen. The only time they see Spears is when they're together at the Hogshead. They haven't reported anything like that."

"Ask them about it," I said.

While Rocky might be trying to shield someone else by paying more attention to Spence, I couldn't afford to ignore the obvious.

"In the meantime," Roy said, "I'm picking Lodeen up for questioning in the staged car wreck."

IT WASN'T that simple. It did not take long to discover Rocky had disappeared. Apparently while Tim or Alan watched the comings and goings through the back door, their target simply went out the front sometime Tuesday night and took off for parts unknown. He'd planned well, telling his employer he needed the next week off to handle some family business… an obvious attempt to avoid raising an alarm. And if I was right, he'd want to clean up a couple of details before he vanished… namely, Paul and me. Possibly Tim and Alan. I told Charlie to alert them to any possibility.

I contacted Spence by cell phone while he was at work in the Belhaven's backyard. He invited me over, although he looked to be sucking on persimmons when I showed up. I didn't give him time to vent.

"Where's Rocky Lodeen?"

"How the hell would I know. At his apartment, I guess. Why?"

"Because we can't find him. He's not at the apartment or at work. He and his Cougar have disappeared. Apparently right after he snuck over to your apartment for the third night in a row. And don't try to tell me you didn't know he's on the run. He hasn't met you at the Hogshead as usual the last couple of days."

"Yeah, well… you guys riding his tail kinda set him off."

"And you had to calm him down before he blew everything sky high, right?" I said.

"I tried to take the wind outta his sails as a friend. That's all."

"Come on, Spence, he's involved in Belhaven's killing, and you know it."

"How do you know that?"

"We found his DNA in the Caravan that T-boned Paul."

"Yeah, he told me."

"And Paul was here not thirty minutes before the incident asking you questions about Belhaven's death."

Spence snatched off his sunglasses and glared at me. "You think I put him on Paul?"

"Somebody did. He didn't even know who Paul was." Spence stood stock-still with a slight frown on his face, so I hit him with another question. "Was the ten thousand a payoff for killing Belhaven for you?"

"For me! Why would I want Pierce dead? He was my meal ticket."

"Still is. A quarter of a million dollars' worth." I paused before throwing out some bait. "And that's nothing compared to the insurance… if you ever get it."

"Why shouldn't I?"

"Life insurance companies don't pay beneficiaries who kill their insureds. It's called profiting off murder."

"I didn't kill anybody."

Bingo! Spence did know about the policy. "Maybe not. But it's beginning to look like Rocky Lodeen might have. And who introduced him into the Belhaven circle? Who paid him $10,000 right after he received his inheritance?"

"That's a loan!"

"Show me the paperwork."

"Handshake."

"Not many people do a handshake deal for ten grand."

"Not many people go through the hell of Afghanistan together, either."

"I thought you didn't know him over there."

"He was there. I was there. That's what counts."

"From the way things are looking, I wouldn't bet on getting your money back. But it must have felt pretty good."

"What felt pretty good?"

"You apparently won out over Sarah. Rocky was visiting you every night. She seems to have been cut out."

"Yeah, I heard how you put a cop in the alleyway to spy…." He stopped midsentence as I saw something in his eyes. "You wanna talk to me again, talk to my attorney."

"Okay, give me his name and number."

He flushed. "I don't have one yet, but I will."

"One last question before you get one. You have any idea where Rocky would run to if he wanted to disappear?"

Spence was slow to answer. "Comes from some little berg in Southern California called Deer Lick. But he's independent. Don't think he'd go near there again."

"So no idea?"

Spence's sexy strawberry birthmark on his left cheek fairly glowed. "Not a one. Remember… lawyer."

"Okay, guy, but if you're telling the truth about having nothing to do with Belhaven's death, you have two million reasons for helping me prove who did."

HARRIS BELHAVEN had cooled off a bit and agreed to talk to me again. I met him at his office after the stock markets closed late in the afternoon. This time I was less interested in Harris than in learning what he knew about the relationships swirling around his late father. I learned little new—other than there had been a second partial payout of Belhaven's estate—but came away convinced he didn't know Rocky Lodeen beyond saying hello whenever Spence brought the ex-paratrooper around.

I wasn't able to run Sarah Thackerson down until that evening at her apartment. I thought for a moment she was going to slam the door in my face, but she relented and allowed me to come in. Books scattered across the kitchenette table let me know she'd been studying.

"Physics," she said when she saw I'd noticed. "It'll be the death of me yet."

"Required?" I asked.

"Shoulda opted for chemistry. What do you want this time?"

"Have you seen Rocky Lodeen lately?"

"You tell me. I understand you have two ex-cops keeping a close eye on him."

"Including his nighttime trips out the back door of the apartment house. Looks like you lost out to Spence."

Other than a tinge of color to the cheeks, she didn't react. "He'll come back. And if not, it's not much of a loss."

"It's a double loss, I'd say. Spence too."

She got red in the face and bit her lip. "I don't know what to say to convince you I have nothing to do with that shit."

"Back to the issue. Where's Rocky?"

She shrugged and sat down at the table. "How should I know?"

"You spent more time with him than most people. I suspect you know a little bit about the man."

"We didn't spend a whole lot of time talking. I have studying to do, and you're wasting my time."

Chapter 29

REASONING THAT Rocky wouldn't abandon the field without claiming more from his coconspirator than the $10,000 used to buy his car, I asked Gene whether or not he could get warrants to access the financial and banking records of Harris Belhaven, Sarah Thackerson, and Spencer Spears. We already knew Rocky's account at the local bank was still open with a few dollars in it.

After Gene agreed to give it a try, we turned to other matters.

"Any sighting of Lodeen?" I asked.

"BOLO hasn't turned up anything. Checked with Deer Tail—"

"Deer Lick."

"—Deer Lick, California, and they haven't seen hide nor hair of him in almost a year. But we'll get lucky sooner or later."

GENE WAS able to get the required warrants but came up with nothing. No one had tapped the checking or investment accounts of any of the suspects beyond what was explainable. He saw fit to include the Harpers over in Grants in his warrants and found they raided their inheritance more than the others, but most of it went to attorney's fees for their son's trial. Nothing unusual for any of the suspects. This puzzled me. I couldn't see Rocky leaving without his fair share of the loot. That meant he was still in the vicinity.

I marshaled all the forces at hand and concentrated on finding the missing man. Charlie, Paul, and I joined Alan and Tim in the field while Hazel hit the computer to sniff out a trace of Rocky. Guerra went to work trying to find his phone. Gene's cops were on the alert for Rocky's car.

We continued the search even through the weekend. Sunday night we got our break. Paul and I had just arrived home when my cell phone went off.

"Found him," Gene said in my ear.

"Where?"

"In his Cougar. Bullet hole behind his right temple."

"Dead?" I asked, wasting my words.

"You might say that."

"Can I have a look at the scene?"

"Come on out."

Following Gene's instructions, Paul and I headed for Nine Mile Hill. At Ninety-eighth I turned south in a semirural area. The lights of multiple cop cars guided me the rest of the way to a fall-down shed that obviously hadn't seen regular use in a long time.

I parked, and Roy Guerra led us to where Gene stood talking to another cop about thirty yards short of the shed.

"What brings the commander of CID out on a call like this?" I asked.

"Personal interest," Gene answered. "He's in the front seat. Pretty ripe. Probably been there ever since he disappeared last week."

"Can I take a look?"

"Forensics won't even let me inside. Medical Inspector's on the way. We'll get a peek at the corpse when the doc arrives to cart him off."

I glanced around in the darkness. We'd driven over a fallow field to reach the shed. Lights and the muted growl of moving automobiles reached us from Central Avenue. The traffic on Ninety-eighth was spottier. "How'd you find him?"

"Couple of kids out rabbit shooting spotted the car. Took a closer look and boogied. One of the kids' mothers called the station."

"What time was that?" I asked.

"Around four. Patrolmen recognized the car from our BOLO, and the call finally gravitated up to Roy."

"It took a pro to take down someone like Rocky Lodeen," Paul observed.

"Not necessarily," Gene said. "Not if it was someone he trusted. Not that hard to get the drop on a guy who's dropped his guard."

"That pretty well narrows the field down to one," Paul said. "Spencer Spears."

"Not sure that's true," I said.

"You mean the Thackerson woman?" Gene asked.

"Or Harris Belhaven. Any of the three could have been in on the plot."

"Why not the Belhaven daughter and her husband… and their delinquent kid? He's already been involved in one shootout, I understand," Gene said.

"I'll have to check, but I'll bet we find the delinquent kid's in Virginia."

"I'll have Grants PD check out the rest of the Harpers."

After that, we stood around in the cold and stomped our feet to keep warm. I'm not certain if it was a macho thing or not, but no one took advantage of a car with a heater. After half an hour, an ambulance turned off Ninety-eighth and rocked its way down the rough dirt track to deliver the OMI medic. Fifteen minutes later Rocky Lodeen was laid out on a gurney. While half a dozen cops held flashlights to illuminate the scene, the doctor gave us a preliminary.

"Dead several days." He pointed to a discolored hole behind Rocky's right ear. "Probably small-caliber gunshot wound. Autopsy will tell us more." With that he whisked the body into the ambulance and made off back down the road.

"Right ear. That's consistent with the shooter being in the passenger's seat," Gene said.

"But why would Rocky drive out here in the middle of nowhere with his killer? It could be suicide," Paul suggested.

I turned to Gene. "Any sign of a weapon?"

"Forensic leader showed me a .25-caliber semi. He sent it for testing."

"Does suicide make sense to you?" I asked Gene.

"You knew him better than I did. But if his general discharge is any clue, he had a flaky character. Maybe he just liked pulling the trigger, even if it was on himself."

"You'll have to convince me he shot himself," I said. "He was too much in control for suicide."

"Those wound tightest eat the gun fastest," Gene came back at me.

I looked around again. "Did the arriving patrol officers locate any other tire prints?"

Roy answered in the negative.

"Footprints?"

A shake of his head. "It was already getting dark. They spotted the kids' footprints before they lost the light. Have to recheck in the morning."

I glanced around at the boots trampling the area and wished him luck before concentrating on the Central Avenue traffic. "What's the closest bus line?"

"That would be Westgate Heights. It turns south off West Central onto Ninety-eighth," Roy said.

"Let's see, we lost touch with Rocky last Tuesday. Any idea of the operating hours for weekdays?"

Roy didn't, but he got on his cell and minutes later answered my question. "Last run on weekdays starts at 11:00 p.m. Reaches the end of the run at midnight."

"And then returns."

"You're thinking he wasn't killed here?" Gene asked.

"Someone drove his body here and caught a bus back to town."

Guerra frowned. "Lodeen wasn't a big man, but it would still take strength to move him from behind the driver's seat and back again. That points to Spears."

"When can we see photos?" I asked.

"Forensics will have them for us tomorrow."

"Paul, let's go. There's nothing more for us here tonight."

I don't know about my companion, but my fanny felt a little safer with Rockwell B. Lodeen out of the picture.

BY NOON Monday we knew several significant things about Rocky Lodeen's death. Although neither OMI nor Forensics was finished with its report, they were able to tell us the little nickel-finish Phoenix Arms .25 found in the Cougar was the murder weapon. We also knew it belonged to Rocky Lodeen. He'd been killed by his own gun. No fingerprints on the weapon, not even his. And OMI confirmed there was no GSR, gunshot residue, on the victim's hands.

Rocky didn't commit suicide. He was murdered. The angle of the bullet was consistent with someone sitting in the back seat and putting the pistol to the side of his head. Crime scene photos showed his body slumped against the driver's door and forward against the steering wheel.

This caused me to reconsider the way I envisioned the murder taking place. It wasn't someone in the passenger's seat. Someone got the drop on Rocky from the back seat and forced him to drive to the remote area where the pop of a .25 wouldn't be noticeable. But would Rocky have handed his murderer his handgun? And why the .25? Records show he also owned a Colt Competition 1911 .45-caliber handgun, and a couple of long guns, including an AK-47. He legally bought the .25 just over a month ago. It was possible he used the small gun as a backup, but we found no ankle harness. Of course, it was small enough to fit in a pocket.

Paul tended to agree with my conclusion but was hung up over logistics. “How did the killer manage it? We kept a close eye on Rocky virtually around the clock.”

“We took the double team off him,” I said.

“Meaning?”

“When we put an around-the-clock watch on him, that meant there was only one man watching Rocky at a time.”

Paul nodded. “So when we’re watching the back door, he goes out the front. But if his killer was in the car with him, like you figured, he didn’t have a vehicle to get away in. That’s why you asked about the city bus route.”

“Right.”

He frowned. “But buses don’t run after midnight.”

Paul’s point sent me to the computer. A check of the bus schedules showed the first run came at 5:30 a.m. with the trip taking about an hour. That would put the bus in Westgate Heights at 6:30 and back on Ninety-eighth maybe twenty minutes later.

“Possible,” I said. If Rocky left by the front door around two or three in the morning, the timetable fits.”

“But where could they be going that time of night without raising Rocky’s suspicions?” Paul pressed. “And how did Spence get Rocky’s gun away from him?”

“You’re assuming Spence was his killer? Could be. Maybe the killer jerked it out of Rocky’s waistband.”

Paul shot me a sideways look. “Or maybe Spence suggested some hanky-panky.”

“In a car in a remote field on a cold December night? Not when they had at least two comfortable beds available.”

Paul shrugged. “Maybe they needed to add some spice. We’ve had a go at it in the mountains when there was a whole house to chase one another around in.” He waved a hand in the air. “Maybe Rocky simply picked up the wrong mark and got killed for his efforts.”

"You really think Rocky went around picking up strange guys for sex?"

Paul looked sheepish. "No."

ALTHOUGH THE police didn't release the identity of the victim, the *Journal* carried the story of the shooting on the Westside. The article indicated the authorities had not determined if the death was a suicide or murder. I wanted to get to the three most likely suspects before Rocky's name slipped out.

I ran Spence down at a grand old house in the Huning Highlands neighborhood. If the lawn clinging to a bit of green this late in the year was typical of his work, Spencer Spears was good at what he did. The winter flowers in beds flanking the stone steps to the minimansion added a welcome bit of color, although I could detect no perfume.

Spence straightened from his cart full of clippings, holding shears in his gloved hand. He frowned before smiling a halfhearted greeting.

"You don't look happy to see me," I said.

"Other circumstances, you'd be a pleasure to look at."

"What circumstances?"

"You know. Asking nosy questions. Lawyer, remember."

"I'm not here to ask questions. Today I'm the bearer of bad news."

The frown returned.

"Rocky Lodeen is dead. Murdered."

"R-Rocky? You must be wrong. Who could take down a guy like that?"

I held my hands palm up, as if weighing something in each. "Paratrooper… Ranger."

"*Me*? Why would I do that? He was my friend. He… he was more than that."

"You've been spending more nights together than before, but maybe he told you he'd decided to go back to Sarah. Maybe that was more than you could take."

Spence's laugh held tragedy. "Sarah? She couldn't hold his interest for long. He always came back to me."

I shook my head. "I don't get the picture. I've got you pegged as somebody who moves on after a short stay. I figure it doesn't matter if it's a man or a woman, it just has to be somebody who attracts you."

"That's the way it's always been." His eyes clouded. "Until…."

"Until Rocky."

His nod was almost invisible.

"But surely you knew he wasn't a stable lover. The man-on-man thing was just a diversion for him."

He shrugged, his face long. He'd aged a couple of years in the few minutes since I'd arrived. "Maybe a diversion was enough." He straightened his spine. "At any rate I wouldn't kill him, jealousy or not. He is… he was what I needed right now."

A small silence grew until he looked at me sharply, his eyes wide. "The story in the *Journal*? That was Rocky?"

I nodded. "Do you own a .25 semiautomatic?"

"No. I have a .38." He gave me his patent stare again. "But Sarah does."

"Sarah Thackerson? There's no record of her buying a gun."

"Rocky bought it for her. She asked him to. They met at an indoor firing range over on the Westside every once in a while."

"She tell you this?"

"Rocky did."

"I've had him under surveillance, and we never saw evidence of any firing ranges."

I saw the rebuke forming in his mind, but he never uttered it. *Then how did he get away from you and get himself killed?* Instead, Spence shrugged. "Before you started watching, I guess. Sometime after you had the cops haul us down to talk to the detectives."

I thought that one over. That fit with when Rocky bought the pistol, which meant Sarah lied to me about when their relationship began. Why was I surprised? I engaged Spence's attention again. "I want to deliver the news about Rocky's death to her myself. Keep it zipped."

"You got it."

After I got in the Impala, I glanced in Spence's direction and saw him standing with his back to me, his shoulders shaking. Now that there was no witness, was he surrendering to grief?

Maybe I owe you an apology, Spencer Spears.

RATHER THAN racing to confront Sarah, I dialed Paul at home and asked him to meet me at Gene's office. A call to Gene got us an appointment.

Then I parked on a side street and located the telephone number for the Super 8 Motel on West Bataan Memorial in Las Cruces to reconfirm Sarah Thackerson registered there the night Belhaven died. It took some time for them to pull up their records, but eventually a bored-sounding clerk made the confirmation. The record also showed she prepaid in order to leave whenever she wanted. By the time they phoned the next day to ask about an extended stay, Sarah had already vacated the room.

When I arrived at APD both Paul and Roy Guerra were waiting. Gene finished a phone call and invited us inside. Everyone listened carefully while I brought them up to date.

"Sarah Thackerson?" Gene asked when I finished.

"Makes sense. She needed muscle to help with Belhaven's murder."

"But she was in Las Cruces. You checked the motel," Roy said. "So did I," he added.

"Right. We knew she checked in at four thirty on the afternoon of Belhaven's death and prepaid for one night's stay. But we don't know when she left. She could have started for home at any time. But as Paul noted when she gave us her alibi, it was only a three-hour drive to Albuquerque. She probably ate dinner at the motel's café to be seen and maybe even took a short nap. She had plenty of time to arrive back in Albuquerque, meet Rocky, and enter the house through the garage. Rocky probably killed the writer while she cleaned out the office and smashed the computer hard drives to throw us off track."

"Why?" Gene asked.

"Both she and Spence knew about the $250,000 bequest in Belhaven's will. And she almost certainly knew about a $1,000,000 life policy in her favor. Maybe the double-indemnity clause on the policy was too tempting. Perhaps she was tired of servicing Belhaven. Or she'd just met a new man who she knew would be high maintenance. Whatever the reason, she decided to collect for her work."

"Why kill Rocky Lodeen?" Paul asked.

"He was probably safe until we discovered a connection between them. Smart work on Tim's and Alan's part. When we started putting the screws to him, he tried to hide his connection to Sarah by shifting his attention to Spence."

"Why bother?" Roy asked.

"To lead us away from his girlfriend. Spence was physically capable of doing away with Belhaven on his own, but Sarah needed

Rocky's help. If we concentrated on Spence, they thought they might get away with it, especially since Spence had already given Rocky $10,000 for his car."

"What? Rocky thought we'd ignore DNA evidence in the Caravan that ran into me?" Paul asked. "That already connected him."

"It's one thing to stage a car wreck to try to warn someone off for a buddy. It's another to murder for him… or her."

Roy shook his head. "Something doesn't make sense. We don't think she could take down an old man in his sixties, so how could she handle a trained killer in the prime of life?"

"The Belhaven killing required physical strength. He was bludgeoned to death, remember? Killing Rocky merely meant putting a pistol to his head and pulling the trigger. Besides, the first killing was avarice, the second was self-preservation."

"Rocky wanted to bail, huh?" Paul asked.

"And take his share of the loot with him. Probably half the bequest since the insurance hasn't paid yet."

"Why didn't she just give it to him and let him go?" Paul asked.

"She knew we were keeping an eye on everyone's finances. She couldn't afford to yank half her assets and give them to him. That would alert us."

"Okay," Roy said. "Tell me how she got this ex-paratrooper to drive out on the Westside in the middle of the night without alerting him she was up to something?"

"You'll have to ask Sarah that question."

Chapter 30

THE SARAH Thackerson who opened her door to Roy, Paul, and me appeared to be another woman. The severe look was gone. Her brown hair now sported chestnut highlights and flowed generously around her cheeks. Her big doe eyes, no longer framed by black-rimmed glasses, widened briefly at the sight of us. She recovered quickly and invited us inside her small apartment. The books I had come to expect were open on the kitchen table. She had been studying.

"Ms. Thackerson—" Roy began.

"Miss. Miss Thackerson," she interrupted.

"Miss Thackerson, we need to discuss your relationship with a man named Rocky Lodeen."

She waved a hand in my direction. "Ask Mr. Vinson. He set some people to watching us. He knows Rocky visits me occasionally at night."

"Not so much anymore," I said. "He seems to have switched his attention to Spencer Spears lately."

"Mutual decision. Things were getting too intense. Getting in the way of finishing my education." She gave an obligatory glance toward the table in the kitchen area. "But I remained fond of him." Her words seemed to be a mere formality.

"You make a habit of sharing all your partners with Spence Spears?" Paul asked.

Sarah looked down her nose at him. "I should probably broaden my horizons."

"I'd say so," Roy put in. "Since your horizon has been cut in half."

"What do you mean?"

"Rocky Lodeen was found dead Sunday night."

Her legs seemed to go limp, dumping her on a settee. "Rocky? H-how?"

"Shot to death in his car out on the Westside."

"Th-that was Rocky?"

"What do you mean?" Roy asked.

"The murder in the paper. That was Rocky?"

"How do you know it was murder?" Paul asked.

"That's what the paper said."

"The article made it clear it wasn't known if the death was suicide or murder," Roy said. "How did you know it was murder?"

She didn't hesitate. "I knew Rocky. He wouldn't kill himself. And don't try to tell me he would. Who killed him?"

"That's why we're here," Roy said.

Her voice went shrill. "You think *I* killed him? Why on earth would I do that? *How* would I do that?"

"Do you own a handgun, Miss Thackerson?" Roy asked in his most official voice.

"No."

"We understand Mr. Lodeen bought a .25 semiautomatic for you at your request."

"Then you understand wrong." She faltered. "That's not exactly true. He owned a small gun he loaned me when we went shooting at the range. But it was his, not mine."

"You never brought it home with you?"

"He took it with him."

"So the gun was never in this apartment?"

"Well… I can't say it was never here. He brought it over to show me after he purchased it."

"When was that?"

Sarah shrugged. "A few weeks ago."

Roy questioned her about the gun range they visited. He finished by asking when they last went shooting.

"We only went three times, and the last time was a month ago. A Thursday. My light day at school."

"Why did you stop going?"

"I found I don't like being around guns," she answered.

"Do we have your permission to test you for GSR?"

"For what?"

"Gunshot residue," he answered.

She nodded. "Of course. If it will help."

His bluff called, Roy turned gruff. "Can you explain why they found your DNA in Rocky Lodeen's Cougar?"

"I don't know much about that, but I was in his car several times over the past few weeks."

I saw her realize her mistake.

"Besides, how do you know it was my DNA? I've never given any samples, unless you took it without my permission."

"We can argue over that in court," I said. "Answer Detective Guerra's question."

"Were you ever in the back seat of his car?" Roy asked.

"Once. When Rocky gave a ride to two of his friends from CNM. But just once. Would that account for it?"

"Miss Thackerson, you need to come to the station with me. They'll do the GSR test, and you can give a formal statement about your relationship with the victim."

"Victim? So it was murder."

As she went for her coat, Paul whispered. "Nice try, Roy."

Paul went with Roy to witness the gunshot residue test and sit in on her interview while I headed straight for Gene's office. His digs as head of CID were a bit grander than that of a mere lieutenant, but he was the same old boy I rode with as a detective all those years ago… merely a bit more grizzled and a smidgeon wiser. I explained how the interview with Sarah Thackerson went.

He thumbed his nose. "So she didn't balk at the GSR test, huh?"

"Perhaps she knows it doesn't linger long on a living person. She's a computer person, and research on such subjects would be second nature." I paused. "She might know it only hangs around for six hours or so, but maybe she doesn't know it transfers easily. It might still be on clothing or handkerchiefs if they haven't been laundered. Can you get a search warrant for her place?"

"Why? She's probably done laundry multiple times since then. Besides, if we found some, she'd claim it was from one of the range sessions."

"Let's see what we find anyway. I'll visit the shooting range they used to see if anyone remembers them."

"And what they wore? You're reaching, my man."

"I'm open to better ideas," I said as I paused in the doorway. "I know there were no fingerprints on the gun used to murder Rocky, but how about the bullets?"

"Only his fingerprints."

"Damn."

THE PEOPLE at the Westside Indoor Shooting Range remembered the couple vividly, even though they'd only used the facilities three times.

Rocky, with his brash military demeanor, tended to show off, and everyone remembered the intimate lessons he gave the woman, standing behind her and cupping her arms in his as she pulled off shots. He was a marksman; she was an amateur. The rangemaster, as he called himself, said one thing that caught my attention.

"You could tell she was a beginner. She wasn't comfortable with a weapon. She handled a little .25 like it might bite her. I noticed one thing. Her first shot was usually reasonably accurate, but after that, they went all over hell and gone. Like she steeled herself for the first one but then became unhinged. You see that sometimes in new shooters."

A sudden anger heated the back of my neck as I thought of our ambusher in the backyard. The first shot drilled the windowpane where Paul was standing before I pushed him out of the way. We couldn't even find where the other two shots ended up. And if this was her pattern with a peashooter, it would probably be even more so with the heavier .38. I tamped down my emotions. This required professional work, not personal reactions. But I now viewed her through different eyes.

MY MISSION became making life as miserable as possible for Sarah Thackerson. Tim and Alan double-teamed her. I wanted Sarah to know she was under the microscope, but one watcher was always within easy eyesight, the other less obvious. We recruited two more retired cops to watch the front and back doors to her apartment house during the night. I occasionally appeared on her horizon as an added irritant.

This went on for seven straight days as she did her holiday shopping and met with a few friends. Any confidential investigator must have three characteristics. He must be at least slightly paranoid—that's how he remained healthy—and he must be persistent and patient. I prided myself on having all three, but this wasn't moving fast enough to satisfy me, so I went to see Spence. I found him at the Belhaven place. He did not look happy to see me.

"Hell of a Christmas present, having you show up on my doorstep." He couldn't quite hide the irritation lacing the quip. "Lawyer, remember?"

"Do you have one yet?"

"Not yet, but I can get one in a hurry."

I switched on him. "Only two more shopping days left. Are you ready?"

"Doesn't take much for me to be ready."

Now came my shot in the dark. "Spence, something's bothering me. So I wanted to check it with you. Okay?"

"Shoot… figuratively speaking, that is."

"Both you and Sarah claim you despise one another, but our surveillance showed you paid her a few visits in the middle of the night. What gives?"

A frown tried to blot his features, but he retained control. "Don't know what you mean."

"My operatives said you visited her at least once."

"Then they're scamming you. Maybe you need to pay the help better and get reliable information."

"They're two of the best," I said. My fabrication wasn't producing much of a reaction. Then I had a thought. "Ah, I see the source of our problem. You didn't know I set them on you before I put them on Rocky. They'd been watching you for a few weeks before that."

He thought for a minute, giving the pruning shears he held a click or two. "Love-hate thing, I guess."

"Unless you were lying to us about your feelings."

"Nah, she's a bitch. But Rocky arranged it."

"How?"

He shrugged and tossed the shears on top of the cuttings in the barrow. "Said I oughta give it a try. She was pretty good in bed."

"But—"

"But how do you climb in bed with someone you won't even talk to? Rocky again. He told me to show up one night, and she'd open the door to me. I did, and she did. End of story." He sniffed. "She wasn't as great as he claimed. But okay, I guess."

"Why would Rocky do that?"

"You have to ask him—" His breath caught in his throat. "I still can't believe he's gone. But I guess he is. So I don't have an answer except he shared damned near everything with me."

I studied the handsome man in front of me for a moment. "You tell a nice story, Spence. But there's one problem. The time I'm talking about was before Rocky was on the scene."

His face fell. He pivoted on his heel and muttered, "Lawyer," as he walked behind the house.

I left the conversation mentally shaking my head. Two macho ex-military men sharing drinks and friends and stories, I got. Sharing a woman while they got it on with one another? No way, unless they did it together in the same bed. But maybe I shouldn't have clued Spence I knew he'd lied to me.

When I told Roy and Paul about my interview, Roy was all for picking up the two of them for a session down at APD. I discouraged it.

"I'd rather keep up the pressure," I said.

"Hauling them down to the station is pretty good pressure."

"I want them free to do whatever they're going to do. Make a break for it, walk into the station and confess… whatever."

THAT AFTERNOON Sarah cracked. As I later read in my operatives' report, she was shopping in Macy's with Tim hard on her heels when she suddenly whirled, sprayed him with Mace, and yelled "pickpocket." It took Tim a good ten minutes to wash out his eyes and convince the security personnel he was a private investigator on the job. By that time Sarah had disappeared.

But Sarah didn't know Alan was watching from a distance and followed her out of the store. Remaining as invisible as possible, he trailed her from Coronado Center straight to a house in the North Valley where Spencer Spears was working. According to the report, they didn't greet as foes. She collapsed into his arms.

Maybe I didn't owe Spencer Spears an apology after all.

Chapter 31

ARMED WITH the report from Tim and Alan detailing their surveillance of Sarah Thackerson, Gene agreed to haul both her and Rocky down to APD for a grilling. Paul and I watched the monitors in the communications room with Gene as Roy Guerra went at first the one and then the other. Spence handled himself well, although before the interview was over, he grew a bit sullen.

Sarah was tough, but she had been under the microscope for over a week and was showing the effects. She probably realized by now the ploy in Macy's with Tim was a mistake as it effectively tied her to Spencer Spears. Nonetheless she managed to hold her own. Neither of them asked for an attorney.

After several hours they were released and departed separately. I caught Spence as he was leaving the building.

"Thanks for wasting my day," he said, not bothering to hide his anger.

"Spence, this was only a prelude. We're going to waste a lot more of your time before long. Your girlfriend made a bad mistake leading us to you. You know she's going to fold, don't you?"

He mustered what passed for a grin. "Don't bet on it."

"I can interpret that a couple of ways. Let me just say she better remain in good health. At least for the foreseeable future."

He merely looked at me for a long moment before turning and tripping down the steps. I watched him out of sight before joining Paul and Roy in Gene's office.

"I got bupkus, boss," Roy said, looking like he had been through the wringer. Being a bad-ass interviewer wasn't always easy.

Before Gene could respond, the phone on his desk rang. He answered and handed the receiver to Roy. Most of the conversation occurred on the other end of the line. He grunted a couple of times before handing the receiver back to Gene, who cradled it.

"That was Tibedeau of Tri State Insurance giving us a heads-up. They're paying the Belhaven insurance policies."

"Really?" Paul asked. "Aren't beneficiaries considered suspects?"

"Yes," I acknowledged, "but there are four policies in this case. That means there are four attorneys threatening to sue the insurance company because of an unjustified delay. It's not surprising the company folded." I slapped my forehead with a palm. "*That's* what they're waiting for. Once they get their hands on the insurance money, they'll take a powder."

"Someplace that's got no extradition," Roy added. "We need to arrest them."

Gene shook his head. "For what? We've got no proof they killed Belhaven. Or Lodeen, for that matter."

"We've got to push them. Sarah's already weakening," Paul said.

BY FRIDAY I could no longer delay my Christmas shopping. I have no idea why I procrastinated each year, but I did, even though my gift-exchanging circle was small. I was actually ahead of schedule by a few hours. For the last two years, Christmas Eve had found me in the stores, and that wasn't until tomorrow night. I picked out a silver tea set and delicate porcelain cups I knew Hazel was hoping to catch on sale. A new fishing rod for Charlie, gift certificates for the other guys on staff and Gene's clan, and potted African violets for my neighbor, Mrs. Wardlow, to transplant into her backyard flower garden.

For Paul—and me—I got matching friendship rings, simple golden circlets with the Zia sun symbol engraved on them and filled with white gold. They could easily have been mistaken for wedding rings, and that's the way I would treat them, although I was old-fashioned enough to remain uncertain about formal vows. I was up-front with the world, never denying my homosexuality but never volunteering it either. And here I was hung up on an outdated attitude toward marrying the man I considered my natural mate. Why are we humans so damned complicated?

Between Vinson and Weeks, Confidential Investigations and the Albuquerque Police Department, we ruined Christmas for Spencer Spears and Sarah Thackerson. Roy made a point of hauling them down to APD separately on Christmas Day, despite the fact it was both a major holiday *and* a Sunday. By then both Spence and Sarah were yelling "lawyer" and threatening to sue for harassment. Even so we intended to ruin their New Year's celebration as well. But time was getting short. Roy confirmed with Tri State the insurance checks were already cut and mailed.

Monday morning I fielded a call from Dorothy Voxlightner and reassured her we were making progress in identifying Belhaven's killer. I didn't go into details. Thereafter the day turned slow, and then insufferable, when Hazel decided it was time to do administrative things like go over the ledger books, sign a couple of contracts, and la-di-da. My eyes crossed before I escaped the office and ran for home. By then it was my usual quitting time… if such a thing even existed.

The weather had turned over the holiday and dumped a couple of inches of snow on the Albuquerque landscape. By now most of the white stuff had disappeared, leaving muddy places and icy patches. Black ice was sometimes a problem, so as I approached a spot where a gigantic cottonwood forced the road to jiggle right and shielded the asphalt from sunlight, I slowed the car and pulled the wheel to the left to avoid a sheet of ice covering the right side of the road.

My windshield starred and cracked, clouding my view. It took a second to realize someone was shooting at me. But when I did, I hit my seat-belt release, flopped over into the passenger's seat, and took my foot off the brake. As the car idled forward out of control, more shots rang out. Two more holes appeared in the shattered safety glass. The Impala bumped into something solid and stopped.

Hardly daring to breathe, I pulled the Ruger .57 Magnum from my belt and twisted over on my back. Those had been rifle shots. The shooter was Spence, a marksman, not Sarah, an amateur. Would he retreat or press his advantage? He likely didn't know if he'd hit me or not, but from the way the car meandered into the tree, he might suspect so. Sunlight dancing through the big cottonwood's leaves was distracting, almost stupefying. But that same sunlight saved me. I caught a shadow. He was approaching from the driver's side. A moment later he stood framed in the window, his rifle at the ready. He was obviously having trouble seeing through the window because of the dancing sunbeams, but I had no trouble seeing at all. I lifted the Ruger and pulled the trigger.

I wiggled out of the passenger's side door and slid out of the car onto all fours in the icy mud. Spence had disappeared when my shot shattered the window, but I had no idea if I'd hit him or if he'd ducked. I lowered myself to the cold ground and looked under the car and found my answer. Spence lay sprawled on his back. Before I could move, footsteps raced toward the Impala, and Sarah dropped to her knees to embrace her lover, crying his name over and over again. Her tone morphed from grief to rage. She snatched a little pistol from her coat pocket and got to her feet. Her footsteps brought her to the side of the car.

"Where are you, you murderer!" she screeched. Her voice died away leaving only the silence of this semirural stretch of land. A crow cawed from the tree umbrellaing us.

The woman was clearly enraged because their effort at murder resulted in Spence's death. She wasn't accurate with the pistol she held in her hand, except—as the rangemaster said—with her first shot. There was a hard way and an easy way to handle this. I took the easy way and shot her in the left foot.

Epilogue

AS WE drove to Voxlightner Castle to report to our client, I asked Paul if he'd found a market for the piece he was writing on the case.

"Three of them, actually," he said. Gonna hit *Alfred Hitchcock Mystery Magazine* with one approach, *Suspense* with another, and the *London Mystery Magazine* with a third. I've got feelers out already. But there's one thing I've gotta clear up."

"What's that?"

"Why did Spencer Spears confide to you that Rocky bought a handgun for Sarah? That pointed a finger right at his girlfriend."

"We'll never know for sure, but this is the way I have it figured. Spence knew we thought Rocky might be Belhaven's killer. But Rocky had no motive except for money. Who was the only person to give Rocky money? *Spence* was. I think it was deliberately done to confuse the issue and take our focus off him."

"Confuse matters until the insurance company paid, you mean," Paul said.

"Exactly. And perhaps to give himself an out if things went wrong."

"At the expense of his girlfriend. What's that they say? There's no honor among thieves… or killers either, I guess."

DOROTHY VOXLIGHTNER answered the door herself. I'd called earlier to let her know Paul and I would be over with our final report. Gracious—as usual—she invited us into the parlor where her daughter, Lucinda Caulkins, stood beside a coffee table holding a splendid sterling tea set, the demitasse cups beside it on the tray very similar to my mother's bone china.

After polite acknowledgments were made and cups poured, we took a moment to savor Dorothy's excellent brew. I did not recognize the leaf, but I strongly suspected it was terribly expensive.

As requested during the phone call making the appointment, I handed over both the final report and the final bill to my client.

I cleared my throat. "To summarize, Dorothy, John Pierce Belhaven was murdered by Spencer Spears and Sarah Thackerson."

"His two lovers," she murmured in a distant voice. Then she spoke in a stronger tone. "I understood there was a third man involved."

"You're referring to Rocky Lodeen. He wasn't involved in the murder but was recruited later to do some things."

"Like wreck my car and nearly kill me," Paul added.

"But he wasn't in on the scheme. I believe he figured it out later and was trying to deal himself in for a full share of what the others expected to collect. A total of $4,500,000 if Sarah's and Spence's insurance policies paid double indemnity."

"Was that why Spencer killed this Rocky person?"

"It wasn't Spence. Sarah did it. Our investigation panicked Rocky to the point where he wanted to bolt, but he wasn't about to leave without some serious money."

Sarah Thackerson had confessed all from her hospital bed. The loss of Spence, whom she apparently loved deeply, drained her spirit and prompted her to bring everything out in the open. She and Spence truly detested one another at first, each considering the other a rival. But over time, they grew closer. Probably as a result of this, Belhaven's attentions grew oppressive. Spence's apartment's proximity to hers wasn't an accident. They'd used the back entrances to their apartment buildings for quite some time.

After it became clear our investigation into Belhaven's death was serious, Spence drew Rocky into the conspiracy because he wasn't under suspicion or surveillance. Rocky engineered the car wreck with Paul. Sarah attempted the ambush on Paul and me on her own without consulting either man. Spence, a complicated young man, was willing to share his lover with his buddy in order to lure Rocky into the scheme. Sarah suffered Rocky's attentions at her lover's insistence.

But when Rocky made monetary demands before leaving for parts unknown, Sarah bowed her back. To disturb her inheritance money in a serious way would compromise her in the investigation. She lied and told Rocky she had converted some of her assets into gold and coins stashed in a 24-hour storage facility on the Westside. This was how she induced Rocky to drive up West Central in the middle of the night while she lay prone on the back seat to avoid being seen by passersby.

Once they were close to Ninety-eighth, she put her pistol to his head and forced him to drive to the abandoned shed where she killed him. Then, as we surmised, she walked back to Central and caught an early morning bus. Spence picked her up in the downtown area and drove her home. All this while Alan Mendoza kept watch on their back doors.

I observed Dorothy as I explained a few remaining details, noting her drawn, sallow features. Perhaps I'd done her no favor in undertaking her quest. But there was also a peacefulness about the eyes that wasn't there when I first met her. Cause and effect. She'd wanted the truth… and now she had it. Justice had been rendered to two of the three conspirators and would be dealt to the third. Sarah Thackerson would likely spend the rest of her days in a prison hobbling around on a crutch.

"Thank you, BJ. And you too, Paul. You've lived up to your reputations." She sighed. "That was quite a crooked path, wasn't it? The place you started had nothing to do with the place you ended up. But that's all right. My sweet Barron is resting now as he should be, not lying in a mine shaft. That gives me a measure of peace…."

She blinked as if coming out of a reverie. "And Pierce can rest easier knowing his murderers have been brought to account."

I approved of her word "account." Justice did not quite fit the situation.

DON TRAVIS is a man totally captivated by his adopted state of New Mexico. Each of his B. J. Vinson mystery novels features some region of the state as prominently as it does his protagonist, a gay former Marine, ex-cop turned confidential investigator. Don never made it to the Marines (three years in the Army was all he managed) and certainly didn't join the Albuquerque Police Department. He thought he was a paint artist for a while, but ditched that for writing a few years back. A loner, he fulfills his social needs by attending SouthWest Writers meetings and teaching a weekly writing class at an Albuquerque community center.

Facebook: Don Travis
Twitter: @dontravis3
Website: dontravis.com

THE ZOZOBRA INCIDENT

A BJ VINSON MYSTERY

DON TRAVIS

A BJ Vinson Mystery

BJ Vinson is a former Marine and ex-Albuquerque PD detective turned confidential investigator. Against his better judgment, BJ agrees to find the gay gigolo who was responsible for his breakup with prominent Albuquerque lawyer Del Dahlman and recover some racy photographs from the handsome bastard. The assignment should be fast and simple.

But it quickly becomes clear the hustler isn't the one making the anonymous demands, and things turn deadly with a high-profile murder at the burning of Zozobra on the first night of the Santa Fe Fiesta. BJ's search takes him through virtually every stratum of Albuquerque and Santa Fe society, both straight and gay. Before it is over, BJ is uncertain whether Paul Barton, the young man quickly insinuating himself in BJ's life, is friend or foe. But he knows he's stepped into something much more serious than a modest blackmail scheme. With Paul and BJ next on the killer's list, BJ must find a way to put a stop to the death threats once and for all.

www.dsppublications.com

THE BISTI BUSINESS

A BJ VINSON MYSTERY

DON TRAVIS

A BJ Vinson Mystery

Although repulsed by his client, an overbearing, homophobic California wine mogul, confidential investigator BJ Vinson agrees to search for Anthony Alfano's missing son, Lando, and his traveling companion—strictly for the benefit of the young men. As BJ chases an orange Porsche Boxster all over New Mexico, he soon becomes aware he is not the only one looking for the distinctive car. Every time BJ finds a clue, someone has been there before him. He arrives in Taos just in time to see the car plunge into the 650-foot-deep Rio Grande Gorge. Has he failed in his mission?

Lando's brother, Aggie, arrives to help with BJ's investigation, but BJ isn't sure he trusts Aggie's motives. He seems to hold power in his father's business and has a personal stake in his brother's fate that goes beyond familial bonds. Together they follow the clues scattered across the Bisti/De-Na-Zin Wilderness area and learn the bloodshed didn't end with the car crash. As they get closer to solving the mystery, BJ must decide whether finding Lando will rescue the young man or place him directly in the path of those who want to harm him.

THE
CITY OF
ROCKS

A BJ VINSON MYSTERY

DON TRAVIS

A BJ Vinson Mystery

Confidential investigator BJ Vinson thinks it's a bad joke when Del Dahlman asks him to look into the theft of a duck… a duck named Quacky Quack the Second and insured for $250,000. It ceases to be funny when the young thief dies in a suspicious truck wreck. The search leads BJ and his lover, Paul Barton, to the sprawling Lazy M Ranch in the Bootheel country of southwestern New Mexico bordering the Mexican state of Chihuahua.

A deadly game unfolds when BJ and Paul are trapped in a weird rock formation known as the City of Rocks, an eerie array of frozen magma that is somehow at the center of the entire scheme. But does the theft of Quacky involve a quarter-million-dollar duck-racing bet between the ranch's owner and a Miami real estate developer, or someone attempting to force the sale of the Lazy M because of its proximity to an unfenced portion of the Mexican border? BJ and Paul go from the City of Rocks to the neon lights of Miami and back again in pursuit of the answer… death and danger tracking their every step.

www.dsppublications.com

THE LOVELY PINES

A BJ VINSON MYSTERY

DON TRAVIS

A BJ Vinson Mystery

When Ariel Gonda's winery, the Lovely Pines, suffers a break-in, the police write the incident off as a prank since nothing was taken. But Ariel knows something is wrong—small clues are beginning to add up—and he turns to private investigator BJ Vinson for help.

BJ soon discovers the incident is anything but harmless. When a vineyard worker—who is also more than he seems—is killed, there are plenty of suspects to go around. But are the two crimes even related? As BJ and his significant other, Paul Barton, follow the trail from the central New Mexico wine country south to Las Cruces and Carlsbad, they discover a tangled web involving members of the US military, a mistaken identity, a family fortune in dispute, and even a secret baby. The body count is rising, and a child may be in danger. BJ will need all his skills to survive because, between a deadly sniper and sabotage, someone is determined to make sure this case goes unsolved.

ABADDON'S LOCUSTS

A BJ VINSON MYSTERY

DON TRAVIS

A BJ Vinson Mystery

When BJ Vinson, confidential investigator, learns his young friend, Jazz Penrod, has disappeared and has not been heard from in a month, he discovers some ominous emails. Jazz has been corresponding with a "Juan" through a dating site, and that single clue draws BJ and his significant other, Paul Barton, into the brutal but lucrative world of human trafficking.

Their trail leads to a mysterious Albuquerquean known only as Silver Wings, who protects the Bulgarian cartel that moves people—mostly the young and vulnerable—around the state to be sold into modern-day slavery, sexual and otherwise. Can BJ and Paul locate and expose Silver Wings without putting Jazz's life in jeopardy? Hell, can they do so without putting themselves at risk? People start dying as BJ, Paul, and Henry Secatero, Jazz's Navajo half-brother, get too close. To find the answer, bring down the ring, and save Jazz, they'll need to locate the place where human trafficking ties into the Navajo Nation and the gay underground.

www.dsppublications.com

CPSIA information can be obtained
at www.ICGtesting.com
Printed in the USA
BVHW040945171219
566921BV00013B/240/P

9 781641 082082